PRAISE FOR

HARVESTING ROSEWATER

"My heart broke and then healed as I read this powerful novel, swept up in Farah's courageous journey from Iran to America. Her transformation from a guilt-ridden teenager carrying a devastating secret to a brave woman who saves and cherishes lives consumed me. Paria Hassouri captures the beauty of Iran alongside the brutal erosion of its citizens' rights under religious autocracy, while also celebrating Farah's deepening awe of the immense diversity around her: the magic of love in all its forms, the spectrum of gender, the dedication of healers, and the wonder of friendship. Through it all, the novel explores the struggle to balance this complex world with the demands of marriage and motherhood. I loved this book."

—RANDY SUSAN MEYERS,
internationally bestselling novelist and author of
The Many Mothers of Ivy Puddingstone

"*Harvesting Rosewater* is a deeply human, beautifully layered story that explores what it means to live between cultures, between truths, and between the past and present. Farah's journey is heartbreaking, fierce, and ultimately redemptive. This novel isn't just about one woman's reckoning—it's a testament to the power of truth, memory, and the courage it takes to finally stop running."

—DIANNE C. BRALEY, multi-award-winning author
of *The Summer Before* and *The Silence in the Sound*

"A moving exploration of being caught at a cultural and professional crossroads in midlife and of the transformative power of finally facing the stories we've buried to survive."

—MARJAN KAMALI, best-selling author of *The Lion Women of Tehran* and *The Stationery Shop*

"This haunting and hopeful novel presents the journey of Farah, a devoted doctor and mother whose American life begins to fracture under the weight of secrets from her Iranian childhood. *Harvesting Rosewater* is an engaging, deeply felt story that shimmers with themes of identity, resilience, the struggles of the immigrant experience, and the long arc of healing."

—LIESE O'HALLORAN SCHWARZ, author of *What Could Be Saved*

"In *Harvesting Rosewater*, Paria Hassouri deftly and compassionately explores identity through the lens of Farah—newly divorced and trying to reset her life in California wine country on an extended leave from her job as the chief of OBGYN at a New York City hospital—as she learns what it takes to see, understand, and accept who we (and others) are. Along the way, Hassouri captivates readers with a beautiful window into Persian culture juxtaposed against the authoritarian regime that drove Farah's family to flee to America when Farah was a child. The detours into wine education and tantalizing food are icing on the cake."

—KRISTIN KOVAL, author of *Penitence*

"A powerful, eye-opening narrative that transports readers from the rich, traditional life of a young girl growing up in Iran to her complex, modern identity as a doctor in the United States. This beautifully written story offers an intimate lens into Persian customs, family dynamics, and the quiet strength of women who came of age under a tyrannical regime. The author tackles several tough issues including cultural repression and gender transitioning, with remarkable sensitivity and deep respect. An unforgettable read that is a compelling blend of resilience, identity, and hope."

—MUFFY WALKER, award-winning novelist and author of *Memory Weavers*

"In this impressive debut, Paria Hassouri evokes the painful divide felt by her protagonist, Farah, who comes with her family to America in pursuit of education and professional achievement only to discover in middle age that she has lost a true sense of herself. Hassouri writes with depth and emotion of Farah's escape to a rural haven where she sheds the denial and distance that have been her survival mode. The rosewater of the title is the healing balm of memory, tears, family, childhood, and culture."

—ANNE MATLACK EVANS, author of *The Light Through the Branches*

Harvesting Rosewater

by Paria Hassouri

© Copyright 2025 Paria Hassouri

ISBN 979-8-88824-798-3

All rights reserved. No part of this publication may be reproduced, stored in a retrieval system, or transmitted in any form or by any means—electronic, mechanical, photocopy, recording, or any other—except for brief quotations in printed reviews, without the prior written permission of the author.

This is a work of fiction. All the characters in this book are fictitious, and any resemblance to actual persons, living or dead, is purely coincidental. The names, incidents, dialogue, and opinions expressed are products of the author's imagination and are not to be construed as real.

Cover art and design by Lauren Sheldon

Published by

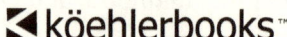

3705 Shore Drive
Virginia Beach, VA 23455
800-435-4811
www.koehlerbooks.com

HARVESTING

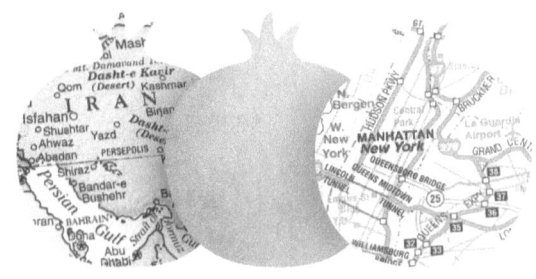

ROSEWATER

A NOVEL

PARIA HASSOURI

VIRGINIA BEACH
CAPE CHARLES

For Armon, Ava, and Shayda—
May you be inspired to pivot at any point and as many times as you need.

PROLOGUE

JULY 1984: TEHRAN, IRAN

"Add this to the list of things I won't miss about Iran." Farah was practically shouting so her cousin Zareen could hear her as they were walking. The siren from the ambulance stuck in the chaotic traffic jam of cars around Maydan Vanak blared in Farah's ears, the hijab covering them barely muffling it. A cacophony of honks and shouts came from the hundreds of cars that were in five-to-six crooked lanes around Vanak Circle like a jigsaw puzzle, none of them in the designated three lane lines painted on the asphalt. "Baba says in America people drive like normal human beings and stay in their lanes, so an ambulance can actually get through."

Zareen laughed. "Yeah, but you're definitely going to miss this," she said as she licked her *akbar mashti*, a saffron rosewater pistachio ice cream with chunks of frozen cream that she had gotten in a sandwich style between two thin wafter. Farah had gotten her ice cream in a bowl, with *faloodeh* added, a sugar and rosewater sorbet-type dessert mixed with frozen pieces of rice noodles and topped with lemon juice to counter the sweetness.

"Maybe," Farah replied, "but I'm going to have Kit Kat bars and Hubba Bubba gum and cornflakes with sugar on top every day." Farah tried to recall when the last time she'd had a Kit Kat bar was and realized it had been six months prior when their family had hosted a visitor from the US. She missed being able to regularly purchase

American goodies at the convenience store that was a short walk from their home—another casualty of revolution and war. "I can just close my eyes and taste that creamy chocolate and feel the wafer dissolving in my mouth now."

As they turned the corner onto a side street off the main circle, the noise finally died down a little, and they could speak in a normal voice. "I'm not jealous of the Kit Kat bars you'll be eating. I still can't believe you're going to start high school in America. You'll go to a US college. I'm sure you'll get into medical school there. I'll never get to be a doctor here. There's no future for me in Iran," Zareen said.

This wasn't the first time they were having this conversation. "That's not true. And, like I've said, hopefully you'll move to America one day too. Maybe once we're settled, my parents can figure out a way to get a visa for you. You can come live with us, and we'll both be going to school with boys again." Farah threw her bowl in a nearby trash can and put an arm around her cousin. They were only four months apart in age and had grown up together, seeing each other almost every day. Farah was closer to Zareen than she was to her younger sisters. As children, they had fantasized about marrying two brothers when they grew up and living next door to each other. But after the Islamic Revolution and the start of the Iran-Iraq war, which made it nearly impossible for women to get accepted into professional university tracks, their fantasies had gone away from marriage and toward being able to leave Iran and one day being college roommates. When they'd spoken of their dreams, they had always pictured moving together, not one of them getting left behind.

Zareen removed Farah's arm. "I'm too hot as it is. You're going to have to save your hugs for when we're inside with air conditioning." She reached for her neck and slightly loosened the knot of her headscarf. "I'm dripping in sweat under my manteau. You're so lucky to only have two more weeks of wearing all this."

"I know. I am looking forward to feeling the wind in my hair every day," Farah said, before realizing she should probably stop gloating. "But hopefully you will get out of Iran soon, too, and who knows, maybe when the war is over, things in Iran will gradually change too. Go back to how they used to be."

"Okay, now all this excitement about your move has made you deevoneh. Nothing is getting better in this country. Every day it gets worse." Zareen was quiet for a minute before saying, "Sometimes I'm so tempted to just take my hijab off for a minute. Spin in a circle on the street with my manteau unbuttoned so it can twirl around me."

"You would never do that! And you're calling *me* deevoneh? Sounds like you're the one who's lost it," Farah said.

"I would do it. What do I have to lose? They've already taken everything away from us."

"Oh come on. Fine. Forget about unbuttoning your manteau. I dare you to take off your headscarf for just thirty seconds. There is no way you'll do it."

"Oh yeah," Zareen said, raising an eyebrow, "watch me." She slipped her finger into the knot around her neck and loosened it completely. Then she took off her headscarf, unclipped her ponytail holder, and started twirling, laughing as her long thick chestnut waves flared out around her.

Farah watched in disbelief, her hand over her mouth, and then heard the rev of an engine. She turned her head and saw the classic white patrol car of the *komiteh* speeding toward them. "ZAREEN!" Farah screamed. Zareen stopped spinning exactly as two morality guards in olive-green fatigues jumped out of the back of the car.

"Bah, bah," one guard said with his arms crossed over his chest, an amused look on his face, while the other took out a truncheon and began tapping his palm with it. "What have we here?"

Zareen frantically started trying to put her headscarf back on, her hands shaking so hard that her scarf slipped through her fingers onto the sidewalk. Farah lunged to pick it up and help her, but the second officer held Farah back. "It's okay. This jendeh doesn't want to wear her hijab; well then, she can show off her hair on the drive all the way to Evin Prison."

In what seemed like a blur to Farah, Zareen was handcuffed and shoved into their car. A screeching wail filled the air. Farah fell to her knees, clutching Zareen's headscarf. As she watched the car drive away and buried her head in Zareen's scarf, she noticed the wail did not fade away.

It bellowed from her own mouth.

CHAPTER ONE

SEPTEMBER 2022: UPPER EAST SIDE, NEW YORK CITY

The glare from the sun on Farah's computer screen had grown stronger over the last hour, worsening her headache, so despite only having to reply to one more patient email before being done for the day, she decided to get up and lower the blind. The headache had started at their departmental meeting at seven that morning, then progressively worsened throughout the day. As she stood up, the silver photo frame in the middle of her bookshelf caught her eye. She stared at it. It was the only family photo left in the office with Mark in it. She'd taken down all the other family pictures over a year ago, but this one of them on vacation in Barcelona—from before everything started to change—was one of her favorites. The kids were caught in a fit of laughter, and Mark's smile radiated true joy, away from the stresses of everyday life. Seeing the picture now, a sense of melancholy overtook her, and she was glad she had texted Julia after her morning meeting to ask if they could meet for dinner tonight. She turned to the window, taking in the Manhattan skyline before closing the blinds. She sat back in her desk chair and began robotically typing:

Hi Rebecca. Sorry for the delayed response. I'm just getting your email now. What you're describing sounds like Braxton Hicks contractions, which are quite common. You will want to give us a call if you experience more than eight contractions in an hour, notice decreased fetal movement, have any leaking of amniotic fluid, or notice any vaginal bleeding. Please remember that email messages are for nonurgent questions only. I will not be checking any emails over the weekend. If you have any urgent questions, please call and speak to the doctor on call. Have a good weekend. Best, Dr. Afshar.

Farah moved the mouse over the "Send patient reply now" button and clicked. She looked at the time on the bottom right of her computer screen, shook her head, and logged off. She had spent the last forty-five minutes replying to patient emails. It seemed like every day she was spending more time answering messages. She slid off the nude pumps she had put on for her afternoon clinic, storing them in her desk drawer and switching them out with the New Balance sneakers she used for her walk to and from the subway. Farah pushed back her office chair and stood up. She removed her stethoscope from around her neck and put it in the pocket of her white coat before slipping it off to hang on the hook of her office door. She grabbed her handbag and turned around to take one last look at her office, glancing over at Mark in the family picture again. She sighed, switched off the light, and closed her office door.

Farah walked out of the subway and headed south on Houston toward Vernetti's to meet Julia. Vernetti's was just a few blocks from Julia's apartment. Julia and Farah had met on the first day of preschool for their daughters and, as rarely happens when people meet after their college years, formed an instant friendship. Even more rare, once their husbands had met, they had hit it off as well. They had gone on many couples' dinners and family activities together—at least until the separation. In the last year, Farah and Julia had gone back to only solo dates with each other.

When Farah walked into Vernetti's, Julia was already sitting at a table, replying to emails as her fingers flew over the keys on her phone.

Farah still texted with one finger, something her kids made fun of. As Farah approached the table, Julia put her phone down and jumped up to give her a big hug. "Let me just finish this last sentence and hit send, and then the phone goes in the bag and I'm all yours," Julia said.

Julia was the master of giving everyone she talked to her full attention as if they were the most important and fascinating people in the world and no one else existed. It was what drew everyone to her, and Farah always felt lucky to be among Julia's closest friends, able to call on that attention at a moment's notice.

They decided to order a glass of orange wine first. A few years prior, they had taken a wine-tasting class on orange wines. The sommelier teaching the class had explained that an orange is to a white as a rosé is to a red. "Red wine gets its dark color from prolonged contact with the skin of red grapes. A rosé is made by sometimes just a few hours of fermenting time with the skin on. For example, a rosé of pinot noir is made by using pinot noir grapes that you usually associate with red wine and leaving the skin on for just a few hours to a few days before making the wine." Farah and Julia looked at each other quizzically.

"I've been drinking for all these years, and I never questioned how a rosé is made or what's a rosé of pinot noir versus a rosé of Syrah. I love getting an education," Farah had whispered to Julia, fascinated.

"Yes," Julia whispered back. "I'm not the doctor, but I've heard learning new things in our old age can help us fight Alzheimer's." Farah had snickered and the somm gave them a dirty look.

"An orange wine, also called a skin-contact wine," the somm continued, "is when you leave the skin on a white grape so that when the crushed grapes are fermenting, they take on a more tannic quality from the skin. The wine can look anywhere from an amber gold to a light orange to an orange-brown. You'll see the array of colors in the orange wines we'll be tasting tonight." The somm started pouring the first orange in each of the "students'" glasses. "Hold it up and look at the color, give it a swirl, give it a nice deep sniff, then take your first taste."

As Julia had taken her first sip, she puckered her lips, "Wow!" She turned to Farah. "I think orange is our new white."

Ever since that class, if there was an orange on the menu, they would order a glass of that first before moving on to red. As they quickly browsed the menu at Vernetti's, they decided to order a cheese and charcuterie board and a white pizza with truffle oil, rosemary, and fingerling potatoes to share. Even ordering food with Julia was easy. They would scan the menu for two seconds and agree on something right away.

Julia closed her menu and placed it on the table. "Okay, Farah, what's going on? Your eyes, they've got that heavy tired look again."

"You mean the look they've had for the last twenty-five years?" Farah sighed. "I don't know. Things are great. They really are." She paused. When she saw Julia still looking at her, waiting for more, she added, "I love my apartment. It's really come together. It feels comfortable and unpretentious, and I love walking into it at the end of the day. I love not worrying about what anyone else is going to eat. I love watching whatever show I want to stream rather than trying to find something that would interest Mark too. Sometimes I just sit on my couch with the TV off and stare ahead, listening to the street noise. I've got more street noise here than in Brooklyn, and I love street noise. It reminds me that there's a whole world of people out there going about their lives. I've missed that."

Julia leaned in, not saying anything again, nodding and waiting for Farah to say more.

"I don't miss being married. That's not the issue. I love this alone time. I need it! When have I ever lived my life just for myself? Never. It feels like I've always been living for other people and trying to accommodate and please them. But I guess every woman I know could make that same statement."

"Okay," Julia said, nodding, "what made you text me today exactly when you did? What happened that made you say you needed girl-chat time?"

Damn, Julia was good. Why pay a therapist when you had Julia? This was part of the reason why, over the years, Farah had only made the time to see a couples' therapist with Mark when the situation was dire and never sought out an individual therapist for herself.

"Ugh," Farah sighed, put a piece of Manchego in her mouth and chewed, and then resumed. "I had just come out of our departmental meeting. I had to present all these stats about length of stay and C-section rates and readmission rates and patient satisfaction scores. I hate going over patient satisfaction scores. We're not Macy's, for God's sake, sending patients customer satisfaction surveys after their visit. The customer isn't always fucking right. The 'customer' is a patient," she said, making air quotes. "Anyway, all these numbers just give me a headache. Being the department head used to be about actually improving patient care and mentoring and teaching younger OBs. Now it's all just about numbers and what hospital administration wants and what insurance companies want. It's like they stripped away every part of the position that gives job satisfaction and replaced it with bureaucratic bullshit. And then of course Brian is always sitting there so smug," Farah sighed, putting her head in her hands, her long dark hair covering her face.

"Ah, Brian. Dr. Handsome but Irritating as Fuck . . . Dr. McNightmare!" Julia's eyes widened as she said the new nickname she had come up with, and Farah burst out laughing. "But seriously, Farah, look at me," Julia continued. "Why are you holding onto this extra responsibility if it just brings you stress and you don't enjoy it?"

"Now you sound like Mark!" Farah looked at Julia with irritation, but Julia sat cross-armed, wine glass on the table, waiting for an answer.

The waitress approached their table. "Ladies, I have your white truffle pizza. Enjoy. Is there anything else I can get you now?"

"We'll do two glasses of this Oregon Pinot, and she'll take a Xanax if you have it," Julia said as Farah grabbed a slice of pizza and took a big bite. The waitress smirked and turned from the table.

"Oh no you don't," Julia said to Farah. "Don't shove pizza in your mouth. You still have to answer the question. Why are you holding on to this position?"

"Because . . " Farah replied, still chewing. She swallowed and took a swig of wine before continuing. "Because you know how hard I had to work to get it. And I don't want to give this up and then it goes to who? To Brian? When most of our new hires are women, we're going to go back to having a man be our chief again?"

"It's not about who the next chief will be. It's about whether continuing to be chief is the right decision for *you* right now," Julia answered.

Farah shook her head. "These young OBs, they need me. They need me to fight for their ability to not have to take calls for all their patients and have to do all their own deliveries, to take their maternity leaves, to maintain some semblance of work-life balance."

"And how well did *you* maintain work-life balance?" Julia raised an eyebrow.

"Listen, 'Mark', that's not the point. And I couldn't maintain work-life balance while I was fighting to become chief so I could make things better for the rest of the department. And I do enjoy it. I do! I enjoy it," Farah defended.

"Okay, okay. I believe you," Julia held up a hand. "You enjoy it. You don't need to call me Mark. I'm just trying to help you figure this out, not upset you. You've been through a lot the last five years. Just having your kids go to college is stressful enough, but you guided one kid through a transition, you worked in New York City during the pandemic—while I stayed home safely behind my computer, by the way—you sold your house, got a divorce, moved. I'm out of breath just talking about it!"

"Yeah. I guess. I mean I know I did all that. But now, it's just me. I'm pretty much only responsible for me and my job and still . . ." Farah sighed.

"You are still working like crazy. Maybe you are just really fucking tired. It's all caught up with you. Maybe living alone isn't enough.

Maybe you just need to take a couple of weeks off, a vacation, by yourself. Imagine that. And then maybe you'll come back rested, and the work thing will work itself out. No one goes through what you've gone through without taking just a little time off to regroup."

The waitress arrived with their two glasses of Pinot. "Here we are. We're out of Xanax I'm afraid. Table three ordered the last one," she smiled as she set down their glasses.

Maybe Julia was right. The only time she had traveled without Mark and the kids was for short getaways with her friends, a few days in wine country or a weekend yoga retreat. She had never traveled alone.

"Remember what you said after your trip to London with Mark and the kids?" Julia prodded.

"That I wish I'd had just a couple days alone there to do what I wanted on my own schedule?"

"Yes. You came back complaining about all the things you wanted to do in London that you didn't get to do because of Mark's agenda."

Julia really was a good listener. How did she remember conversations from a few years back? Farah could barely remember their conversation from their last girls' night.

"So, why don't you take a week or two to be in London by yourself?" Julia continued. "No excuses. What's the point of being department head if you can't take a vacation without getting approval from others? Make it happen."

The thought of time in London by herself with no agenda put a little smile on Farah's face, picturing herself running through Hyde Park while it drizzled. Why was rain so ugly and dirty in Manhattan and so beautiful and peaceful in London? Maybe she would visit Bath, see Jane Austen's home. People at work would be pissed if she took a couple weeks off with less than three months' notice. Pregnant moms whose deliveries she would miss would be disappointed, to say the least. But what was the worst that could happen? "I guess I could try to do it," Farah said tentatively.

"Of course you can," Julia raised her wine glass. "To the chief spending time in London by herself!"

Farah raised her glass, but just before they could clink glasses, her phone went off with the shrill tone she had assigned to her daughter's texts. Farah picked up her phone.

Mom, did you hear about the news in Iran? Do you know who Mahsa Amini is?

Farah took a sip of her wine and clicked on the video link Darya had sent with her text. As she watched the video, Farah choked on her wine and coughed, the pinot burning her throat.

CHAPTER TWO

SEPTEMBER 1981: TEHRAN, IRAN

Sitting in the front seat of the parked car, Farah stared at the school gate, willing herself to open the door and get out. This was the first time in several years that Farah hadn't spent days planning her first-day-of-school outfit. She looked at the sea of other middle-schoolers in their identical navy manteaus, long trousers, and headscarves. She reached and pulled her own hijab forward, tucking in a loose strand of hair. It was the first year that she was attending her local public school. Since preschool, her parents had put her in private coed dual-language schools, making sure she would be fluent in English from childhood. But in the last year, the government had shut down all coed and dual-language schools.

"Go on. It's going to be okay. You're going to make new friends. I'm not allowed to walk you in anymore—you're too old for that. But I promise you'll be okay," her mother Soraya said.

"How am I going to make friends with them?" Farah gestured toward the sea of identical girls.

"They are no different from you. They went to school without hijab last year. They came from other places too. You'll see. You'll get to know each other. You have everything in common with them. And a lot of them probably live in our neighborhood, so you'll be making more friends that are walking distance from home," Soraya said.

Farah grabbed her school bag and lunchbox and stepped out.

She walked through the gates into the courtyard of the school. There were groups of girls already huddled together, talking and laughing. She guessed that they probably knew each other from going to public school the previous year. But there were also plenty of girls standing by themselves, looking at their feet or around—these must be the other private-school girls who had gotten displaced like she had. Farah heard a series of shrill whistles and everyone in the courtyard instantly quieted down and faced the building.

An adult in the same drab navy ensemble the kids were wearing stood at the top of the short set of steps leading to the school building, the whistle still in her mouth. She gave one final blow and removed it from her mouth. From where Farah was standing, she couldn't make any guess at the woman's age, just seeing a make-up-free face surrounded by a hijab with no stray hairs showing. The woman put a megaphone to her mouth.

"Be Esme Allah Rahmon o Rahim,"—in the name of Allah, the most gracious, the most compassionate. She introduced herself as the principal, Khanoom Adibi, and welcomed the students who were new to the school this year. She reviewed the rules of the school and informed them that during the midday break they would all gather to do the noon prayer in the courtyard before having lunch and recess. And then she said, "And before we go inside, we will spend two minutes every morning chanting 'Marg bar Amrika.'" Repeat after me. She raised a fist in the air as she chanted "Death to America," then waited for the students to repeat it.

Farah's breath caught. She couldn't believe her ears. Her heart felt like it stopped. She tried to open her mouth but couldn't, as she heard the principal say, "Louder. I can't hear you. Marg bar Amrika."

She willed herself to open her mouth, move it as if she were saying the words.

Again, the principal addressed the courtyard. "Louder! I still can't hear you. And let me see your fists in the air. Marg bar Amrika!"

Farah heard the voices around her getting louder, more hesitant voices joining the crowd with each repetition of the chant. She caught the girls standing next to her looking at her lips, studying her. Fear seized her as she raised her fist, swallowed the bile in her throat, and heard her own voice shout, "Marg bar Amrika!"

CHAPTER THREE

SEPTEMBER 2022: WEST VILLAGE, NEW YORK

The blare of her alarm startled Farah. Although she set it for five o'clock every morning, she woke on her own before it went off most of the time. But in the last week, all the texts, TikTok video links, and calls from her kids, her sisters, her parents, and every Iranian she knew had made her go down a rabbit hole every night. She would spend at least an hour going through all the links that were sent to her once she crawled into bed, then have nonsensical disturbing dreams that woke her throughout the night. Although Farah had hoped that some new topic would intrigue Soraya and that she would finally stop leaving voicemails about how she didn't understand why Farah had gotten a divorce, this was not the distraction she'd had in mind.

Her children, Darya and Rumi, had rarely wanted to embrace their Iranian roots as kids, always identifying more with their Italian-Irish-American dad. They'd shown more interest in learning about Iran's history and culture as adults, and for whatever reason, Mahsa Amini's death had sparked a flame in both of them. Even Mark, who never reached out to her for anything other than logistical reasons since the divorce, had sent her a text the day before:

Hey. All this going on in Iran is crazy and with Zareen, I can only imagine how close to home this hits for you. Let me know if there is anything you need from me.

Except he couldn't imagine. No one could. Not Mark. Certainly not her kids, who didn't even know about Zareen. Not her parents. Not her sisters. No one knew she was the one responsible for what had happened to Zareen. And one particular viral TikTok video of a girl in Iran with the same long wavy chestnut hair twirling with her hijab off while the song "Royaye Ma" played in the background had been haunting Farah's mind ever since Darya had sent the video to her.

Farah knew that skipping her run today would only make things worse, compounding her anxiety without a way to release it, but she just couldn't get herself to put on her running clothes. She had a departmental meeting again, and it was all just too much. She decided she would just go to work early instead.

The elevator doors opened, and Farah was relieved to find it empty. She pressed the button for the eighth floor, hoping there wouldn't be too many stops in between. Since she had gotten to the hospital early, she might as well try to see a few of her patients before the departmental meeting. If she could put a couple of discharge orders in before eight, then those patients could be out by eleven, and that would save another day of hospital charges. She scanned room 8703's chart: vaginal delivery, first child, twenty-six hours since birth, uncomplicated pregnancy; no reason to keep her another day. She tapped on the door and opened it. "Good morning, Jenna, how are you feeling today, mama?"

Jenna stirred and opened her eyes while Farah flicked on the overhead lights and then sanitized her hands. "Hi. I'm okay, I guess. I'm not really sure how I'm supposed to feel at this point, but I feel okay."

Farah ran her hands over Jenna's abdomen. "Your uterus feels nice and firm. Your blood pressure has been great. Looks like you've been nursing. What do you think about going home today?"

"Today?" Jenna said tentatively. "I mean, I guess I could, if you think that's all right. I'm not sure the baby is latching right. The nurses seem to think she is, but I haven't been seen by a lactation consultant. So, I mean, I know that Chad would probably like us to sleep at home tonight." Chad was passed out on the cot in the room.

He hadn't stirred at all since Farah walked into the room, although Farah had made no attempt to keep her voice down. To Chad's credit, Farah had noticed that he'd made it to the majority of Jenna's prenatal appointments, and during Jenna's thirty-six hours of labor, every time Farah had walked in to check on Jenna's progress, Chad was right by her side—feeding Jenna ice chips, wiping her forehead, counting and breathing with her through every contraction.

"Jenna, if you want to stay another day, you can. It's your first baby. If another day of getting help with getting the baby to latch is what you need and you're not sure you want to go home, you stay." Farah squeezed Jenna's hand. "I'll be back to check on you later."

Farah left the room and shook her head. If it had been her colleague Brian checking on Jenna this morning, he would have just walked in and announced that she was all set to go home, even though her insurance would cover the second night in the hospital. He would have made it seem like she and the baby would be better off at home. This was why his "Days of Hospital Stay" numbers were better than Farah's. But Farah was tired of practicing medicine that was about numbers and costs and insurance companies and not patients. When she had first started as an OBGYN, every vaginal delivery stayed at least two days, every C-section at least four. Now, women having C-sections, major abdominal surgery in addition to getting handed a newborn baby, were often being rushed out after two days.

She remembered how she had felt when she gave birth to Darya and the postpartum nurse, Patty, helped her go to the bathroom for the first time. Her vulva was swollen to the point of not being a recognizable body part. She was shocked to feel something that felt like a cluster of grapes when she'd tried to pat herself dry after the nurse cleaned her with a spray bottle of water. Farah had been so embarrassed and yet so grateful for Patty, who'd gently explained how hemorrhoids were common for mothers, then patiently helped her latch Darya—the first of many nursing sessions over the next two days. And she could still distinctly remember how painful that first week of nursing was. Every time Darya had latched, it felt like her nipple was being repeatedly shot with a laser gun for the first thirty seconds, as Farah counted and breathed through both the nipple pain and the abdominal cramping that came with those early feedings.

Farah shook her head and decided to check on the rest of her patients later rather than trying to rush in a couple more before her meeting. She walked into the conference room, and of course, Brian was already there.

Brian wasn't just "hospital cute," a term used to describe male physicians who, without their scrubs and titles, were just average at best. Brian was objectively handsome. He would definitely fit in on *Grey's Anatomy*. He was six foot two and slim without being too skinny. His gray hairs blended with his overall thick dirty blond hair, making him look younger than his forty-five years, and his crow's feet made him look distinguished rather than old or tired. Unlike many other male surgeons, he always wore his wedding ring, even on operating days when he would have to take it off and tie it to the waistband of his scrubs for most of the day, and perhaps that made him even more attractive. But to Farah, his good looks were not enough to charm her into not noticing his arrogance.

"Hey. Good morning." Farah smiled at Brian as she poured herself a cup of coffee and turned on her laptop to pull up the meeting agenda.

"Good morning. I noticed you have quite a few Day Twos on the census today," Brian said.

So predictable. Farah felt her shoulders tense. Who the hell was he to watch her numbers and keep track of how many days her patients were staying in the hospital when it ought to be the other way around? She was the department chief, not him. Then she remembered Julia's new nickname for Brian, Dr. McNightmare, and chuckled to herself. She wasn't going to let him intimidate her. "I've had a lot of first-time moms deliver the last couple of days. They'll go home when it's appropriate. I keep saying I'm not going to accept any more new patients, but then my other patients keep referring me their friends, begging me to take them on." She took a sip of her coffee and gave him an icy smile. She felt a sense of satisfaction as she heard Brian give a half chortle.

The door opened and Aniyah walked in, followed by two of the younger OBs, Mei and Erin. Farah turned to them, smiling genuinely now, and changed the subject. "Good morning. Mei, I saw Kimberly Hanson for her six-week postpartum visit yesterday. You covered her delivery for me on call. She raved about you."

After the meeting, Farah's day was a whirlwind of seeing patients, interspersed with two deliveries. She sat at her desk at the end of the day and put her head in her hands. She heard a knock on her door and said, "Come in." When Aniyah walked in and sat in front of her, Farah smiled. Aniyah was her favorite colleague, a real friend.

Aniyah crossed her arms and leaned back in her chair, an amused smile on her face. "You saw the email we just got from Oppenheim?"

Alan Oppenheim was the chief medical officer of Mount Sinai. "I did," Farah said.

The email said that in light of the recent tragedy, the hospital was giving all the physicians a free one-year membership to the Headspace app. "The tragedy" referred to the suicide of one of the internal medicine doctors who'd been in practice for twenty years. He had closed his office door after seeing his last patient and hanged himself from the drawer handle of a tall filing cabinet. His medical assistant had found him later, screaming when she opened the door. He left behind three kids, ages fifteen, twelve, and eight. He hadn't left a note, so no one knew for sure why he'd ended his life. Some guessed that where he'd chosen to hang himself probably meant it was work-stress related. Others said that maybe he'd just wanted to make sure his wife or kids would not be the ones to find him. And now this free meditation app membership was the hospital's attempt at continuing to work on physician wellness and stress, a goal they had set for themselves during the pandemic when the number of physician suicides and physicians leaving medicine had skyrocketed.

In 2021, the hospital had arranged for a weekly meditation session at noon in one of the hospital's largest conference rooms. The weekly attendance ranged from three to ten people at best. A weekly wellness email went out, urging all staff to reach out if they needed help and listing numbers and resources they could call if in crisis.

Aniyah rolled her eyes and said, "Yeah, sure, add 'make sure you meditate' to our to-do list rather than doing something that may help alleviate our stress, like, oh, I don't know, taking away a responsibility from us or giving us an extra personal day or two—and then don't count it against our productivity. Meditate? No thanks."

"I know, believe me, I know," Farah said. Aniyah was the only person at work she felt she could be fully honest with, drop the cheery attitude she was supposed to have regarding all the administration's actions. "Anyway, are you done for the day too? I'm just getting ready to log off and leave."

"Yeah. Let me grab my bag."

"Oh, shoot. Never mind. I forgot I'm supposed to check back in on a patient from the morning. I'll see you tomorrow," Farah said.

She had almost forgotten about checking on Jenna, and she prided herself on being a doctor who always followed up with patients when she told them she would. She had her own system of elaborate electronic sticky notes attached to every patient's chart and sent herself electronic messages, which helped her keep track of everything she promised patients she would follow up on. Over the years, there were many times when she told herself that if she relaxed just a little bit in the way she practiced, her quality of life could be better—she could have more time for her family. But every time she tried to "relax" the way she practiced medicine, she couldn't commit to it for more than a few hours. If she was going to be a doctor, she could only do it the way she had always done it, emphasizing the care and compassion part as much, if not more than, the science part of it.

This time, when Farah knocked and opened the door to Jenna's room, the baby was not in her bassinet, but in Jenna's arms, latched and nursing. Jenna looked both exhausted and radiant. "Look at how well she is doing," Farah said. "You can see her jaw moving up and down rather than her cheeks puckering with each suck, so you know she is latched on correctly. Keep this up and your milk will be in within a couple of days."

"Yeah," Jenna said. "The lactation consultant finally came by around four. She showed me a couple of different hold positions and was really helpful." Then Jenna caught Farah looking toward Chad's empty cot and added, "He went home to take a shower there. He said he can't take one in the hospital room. And he's going to pick up some dinner for us. He had cafeteria food for breakfast and lunch and . . . you know."

Farah smiled. "I know. I'm glad the lactation consultant helped, and I'm glad you decided to spend another night here. Tonight, you just nurse and sleep. Let Chad or the nurses take Stella to burp and change and put her to sleep in between feeds. Take every minute of rest and help you can while you're here. I hope Chad is picking up your favorite food. I'll see you in the morning again before you leave."

As Farah headed out of the hospital and walked toward the subway, anxiety crept in again. She thought that maybe she should download the Headspace app. Maybe she should give meditation another try and see if she could clear the images from Iran out of her head. Then she remembered that Neesha and Bridget would get a kick out of hearing about the hospital's latest wellness plan. She opened her group text with them and typed:

Guess what the hospital gifted me?

She followed it with the emoji of a brown-skinned woman sitting in the lotus position, followed by a laughing emoji.

CHAPTER FOUR

SEPTEMBER 1992: DURHAM, NORTH CAROLINA

Three copies of Netter's *Atlas of Human Anatomy* lay in the center of the coffee shop's small circular table, all open to the same page. Farah sat across from Bridget and Neesha, twisting and untwisting a lock of hair around her finger while thinking, a study habit she had acquired at some point in high school. The three of them had spent the day dissecting their cadaver's abdomen, identifying and separating the superior mesenteric artery from the inferior mesenteric artery, and now they were studying it all again. Farah's gloved hands had been deep in peritoneum and intestines all day, her hair in a ponytail so it wouldn't spill over onto the cadaver's body. They all wore scrubs for anatomy and reeked of formaldehyde after. At this point, three weeks into their anatomy rotation, they were used to the aroma and the bodies. On the first day of anatomy, they had walked into the lab and the smell had been overwhelming. Each group unzipped their bag and saw the cadaver they would be dissecting. Holding their breath, their hands shaking as they took the scalpel to cut skin, they'd first sliced open the bodies to reveal the yellow subcutaneous fat. Now they dissected through body parts without any hesitation and had to remind themselves that this was someone's body they had the privilege of learning from whenever a classmate cracked an inappropriate joke.

Farah, Bridget, and Neesha had met on the first day of orientation for Duke's medical school class of 1996 and subsequently all been assigned to the same PBL group, problem-based learning. Rather than sitting in lectures all day, their medical school had jumped on the train of a new method of teaching, alternating lectures with small groups of ten meeting to discuss individual cases and applying what they'd learned in lectures to real-life medicine.

Bridget was from Southern California, just outside San Diego. She had shoulder-length strawberry-blond hair, a smattering of freckles over the bridge of her nose and cheekbones, and an overall easy style about her. Neesha had thick, dark honey-blond hair that almost matched her light caramel skin, and her dark charcoal eyes stood out against her honey-colored eyebrows. When Farah had first met her, she found herself trying to guess what her ethnicity might be and had finally just asked her.

Neesha laughed. "I could see you studying my face and trying to figure it out. It happens to me all the time. My mother is Indian, and my dad is Swedish. I know, a Swede marrying an Indian is not the most common pairing, but I still had to follow all the rules that good little Indian girls do."

The three of them had become fast friends. Farah had noticed that medical school seemed to have this effect on all of her classmates. Once the first day of classes started, Farah felt as if the outside world no longer existed. Medical school was such a shared intense, all-consuming experience of forced time together. Farah observed classmates dating each other and dividing into little cliques and subgroups. It was almost like being back in high school. Farah often wondered why there were so many medical TV show dramas, but no reality shows. *The Real World—Medical Students of Duke* edition might be popular on MTV.

As Farah, Bridget, and Neesha quizzed each other on the vasculature of the internal organs they had dissected that day, a man interrupted them from the next table. "I'm going to get myself a refill. Can I get any of you ladies one? I see you're very busy studying." He was staring right at Farah the entire time.

"I think we are okay. Besides, we'll need to get up and stretch our legs when it's time for a refill," Farah responded, barely looking up at him.

"How about something to eat? A muffin, a scone? I'm Mark by the way." He still had his eyes fixed on Farah, even though the question was supposed to be directed at all three of them.

Right when Farah started to shake her head no, Neesha piped in, "I'm Neesha. This is Bridget and—"

Farah cut her off. "We're grabbing dinner in a little bit, but thank you." She turned back to Neesha and Bridget. "So, tell me the three major branches off the celiac trunk," she said, ignoring Neesha's death stare.

Twenty minutes later, Mark packed his backpack and left, nodding a goodbye to their table. "Oh my god," Neesha said, "Farah, that guy was totally into you. Bridget and I were basically invisible to the poor guy. I would have taken a free scone. And he was really cute!"

"Was he cute? Or are there just no cute guys in our med school class other than Chris Kapetan, who we all know is a stuck-up asshole." Farah rolled her eyes.

"I mean, there are no cute guys in med school, but that guy was genuinely cute," Bridget agreed with Neesha.

"This is a small place. So maybe I'll see him again somewhere at some point, and if I don't, then I don't." Farah shrugged. She had barely gone on any dates since her procedure the year before, and she was determined not to get into a relationship or do anything that could ever come close to potentially derailing her from becoming a doctor again.

CHAPTER FIVE

SEPTEMBER 2022: WEST VILLAGE, NEW YORK

At the sight of her phone screen lighting up with Darya's face, Farah's chest tightened. For a moment, she considered letting the call go to voicemail. What was wrong with her? When had she ever not immediately answered a phone call from one of her children when she was available? She picked up the phone just before it went to voicemail and said, "Hi, Little Bunny." Farah's occasional nickname for both kids came from having read *Pat the Bunny* to each of them an infinite number of times. After Rumi had legally changed his name from Delara, Farah had asked if she could at least still call him Little Bunny sometimes. He'd rolled his eyes and agreed.

"Mom, you've seen all the posts about the Global Day of Marches for Mahsa this Saturday, right?" Darya had an urgency to her voice.

"Of course I have! I'm not living under a rock. And even if I missed one of them, your aunts and grandmother have been doing a fine job of forwarding them all to me. I don't know when your Maman Soraya got so tech-savvy," Farah said.

"Okay. I know this is short notice and not super convenient, but I'd be happy to fly home for the weekend to go to the Manhattan march with you."

Farah paused to steady her voice before responding, trying not to sound flustered. "Why would you do that? There's a march in San Francisco. You don't need to fly across the country."

"I know, Mom. But this one is really important. And I thought you'd be happy if I was there with you . . . Wait, Mom, you were planning to go, right?"

"Well, I may have to cover the hospital some on Saturday, so it's not definite that I'll go." It wasn't a complete lie. One of her colleagues could always need backup.

"Mom! You *have* to go! Have that Brian guy you don't like cover for you. I can't believe you'd consider not going."

"I do not dislike Brian. I don't know what gives you the idea that I do. He's a very responsible and hardworking colleague."

"Okay, Mom, whatever. But how could you seriously consider not going? We went to DC as a family for the Women's March."

Farah smiled, remembering all of them there with their pink pussy hats. "That was different. We had a lot more notice. It directly affected us."

"It directly affected us? Are you serious right now? What about when we marched for George Floyd in the middle of a freakin' pandemic? Did that directly affect you more than this?"

Farah knew Darya was right. She had marched with her kids for everything from gun control to reproductive rights. How could she not go to a march for freedom for Iranian women? "You're right. I've just been a little overwhelmed and stressed lately, but I will find coverage and I will definitely go. But I don't need you to fly here. That's really so thoughtful and wonderful for you to offer and want to do this with me, but you can march with your Aunt Azita in San Francisco. She would love that." If Farah was going to go to this march, she had to do it alone. Who knew how she would feel once she was there.

"Okay. If you're sure, I can go with Aunt Azita, but why don't you take a day to think about it and let me know," Darya suggested.

"Okay, I'll do that," Farah said.

"You know Rumi is driving from Oberlin to Columbus with a group of his friends to march there, right?"

"I didn't know that," Farah said. Rumi didn't keep in touch with

Farah nearly as much as Darya did. He had always been closer to Mark, although, since Mahsa's death, he had been bombarding her with links to posts and videos as well. "I'm surprised he hasn't told me. He's been texting more recently." This wasn't exactly the event that she wanted her son to finally bond with her over. Farah was quiet.

"Mom, can I ask you something?"

"Sure. Anything," Farah said, dreading whatever Darya's question was.

"You sound so down lately. And I don't mean just since Mahsa, which is understandable. I mean in the last year. I thought the divorce was what you wanted; not what Dad wanted. But you haven't seemed any happier since you moved from Brooklyn into your new place. What's going on?"

Farah got teary-eyed. How had she raised such a perceptive daughter? "It's nothing, honey. I'm fine. Like I said, work has just been a little overwhelming, but I'm fine. I promise to go to the march. And I want to see pictures of you and Azita in San Francisco. I love you. Thanks for calling."

Farah hung up and sat on her couch, thinking about what Darya had said about her not being any happier since her move. A 650-square-foot two-bedroom was the most her rent budget had been able to get her in the West Village, but it was more than enough for Farah at this point in her life. And she loved this apartment. She'd started over from scratch with what she truly wanted. She'd furnished the main room with a comfy shabby ivory couch covered with throw pillows in various shades of blue. A worn walnut chest filled with books and albums acted as her coffee table. A mix of mismatched antique plates from the Brooklyn farmers' market had replaced her wedding china. She'd kept some of her old coffee cups like the "Best Mom" mug Darya gave her when she was ten and the "Shhh . . . it's wine in here" one from Julia. All her Wedgewood teacups were packed into boxes and in storage, just in case one of her children wanted them one day.

They hadn't planned to register for fine china. When Farah had dragged Mark to Macy's during their engagement to register for wedding gifts, the saleswoman had convinced them that they needed it. "And what do the two of you do?" she'd asked, smiling from ear to ear in an exaggerated way.

"I'm in my last year of medical school, and Mark is getting his doctorate in political science."

"Oh my, how impressive. You will definitely want to register for the perfect formal dinnerware and glassware. We can pick the place settings first, and that will help us pick silverware, water goblets, wine glasses, and champagne flutes to go with it," the woman had said, walking away from the everyday section to the formal ware displayed in cases against the wall without turning back to see if Farah and Mark were following her.

Mark had looked at Farah and pointed an imaginary gun to his forehead. Farah had laughed and grabbed his hand and dragged him toward the display cases. She'd picked up a Wedgewood plate with an intricate blue and gold pattern and turned it over. "A hundred twenty-five for a plate?" she'd asked in disbelief.

"No," the saleswoman had laughed. "One hundred twenty-five is for the whole place setting. That includes a salad plate, bread plate, coffee cup, and its saucer."

"I don't think we need this. We'll never use it," Farah had said. Iranians never had sit-down dinner parties with place settings for each person. Every party was a big buffet-style event with a stack of plates on the corner of the buffet table. They didn't dirty a separate plate for bread. They also only drank tea from clear glasses. If you couldn't see the color of the tea, how could you tell if it was brewed to the strength you liked?

"Of course you'll use it," the saleswoman had pushed. "As a future doctor and professor, you're going to be invited to dinner parties with other doctors and professors, and when it's your turn to entertain them in your home, you'll thank me for having your wedding guests pay for all this. Oh, and you absolutely must register for one picture frame."

"A picture frame? I have so many of those," Farah had said.

"If you don't register for a picture frame, all the people who look at your registry and can't find something in their budget will say to themselves, 'Oh, they didn't register for a picture frame. I'll get that.' But if you register for one, they'll see that you've already chosen what you want, and someone has bought it. So, they'll just get a gift card or decide about something else on the registry. You'll probably still end up with more frames than you need, but less than you would otherwise. Trust me on this—and trust me on the china."

Farah had tried to picture their future selves in a home with a formal dining room, the Wedgewood china set up on the table along with crystal water goblets and wine glasses, a folded napkin on each plate, the silverware flanking either side of the plate. Would they ever host a fancy sit-down dinner party like that? She didn't think that would ever be who she was, but what did she know? She hadn't been to any adult American dinner parties. She had grabbed the registry gun and scanned the Wedgewood onto their list, entering twelve as the quantity requested. Then Mark had groaned as she took his hand and said, "Help me pick champagne flutes."

Now Farah shook her head at the memory. The china had remained in boxes for years until they had moved to the Brooklyn home, then moved to the hutch for display but was never used. And then it had gone into boxes again. She had known when they were registering for it that she would probably never use it. She should have spoken up for herself and who she knew herself to be and what she wanted then. She was speaking up for herself now. That saleswoman had been right about the picture frame. But picture frames were what Farah couldn't have enough of, not fine china.

In her new apartment, framed photos of her kids and inspirational sayings covered the little bit of wall space she had. Mark had refused to let her hang any inspirational signs when they lived together. "Are we really going to be those people? If I'd wanted to marry my mother,

I would have," he'd said once when he came home to find a framed quote over the stove.

Kitchen [kitch-en] noun: A gathering place for friends and family to make memories and create deliciousness.

Farah had hung the quote next to a framed print of pomegranates. "But I want our apartment to have warmth. To be a home," she had protested.

"And what about this sign says *home*?"

"You wouldn't understand." Farah had shaken her head.

"Try me," Mark had replied.

Farah had then told Mark about Jessica, her honors chemistry classmate in tenth grade. Her teacher had randomly paired up students to work on a project. Farah had only been in the homes of a few people from school, and each time, she would notice the difference between American homes and their own.

"I walked into Jessica's house, and it was like I'd stepped onto the set for *Family Ties*. The walls were covered with family photos and sayings like this. There were these huge comfortable sectionals with throw pillows and blankets all over them. Jessica's mom came out of the kitchen with an apron around her waist and oven mitts on, holding a loaf pan with freshly baked banana bread. I can still smell the bread." Every time Farah had gone to Jessica's, her mom had been home, baking something in the kitchen.

Farah had come up with some excuse for why they couldn't alternate and sometimes work on their project at her house. She had said her parents were having most of the walls repainted, and that there were workers and fumes in the house. She had been too embarrassed to have Jessica over. Farah's home was beautiful and ethnic, filled with Persian rugs, classic miniature paintings, and antique furniture. The only family photos on the walls were formal portraits taken at Olan Mills and no random messy candid family moments captured with natural laughter. Her parents' house was the opposite of warm and homey. It usually smelled like frying onions, and on the rare occasion her mom had time to make a dessert, it was usually *sholeh zard* or *halv*a, with the scent of rosewater filling the air.

"That was Cincinnati in the eighties. Rosewater wasn't exactly in. My mom never just made a simple chocolate chip cookie and let me eat some of the dough."

"I understand what you're saying. I really do. But no cliché words on the walls. Are we going to hang a *Live, Laugh, Pomegranate* sign next? The quotes have to go. The pomegranates can stay," Mark had said.

The pomegranates were a hint of Iran. Next to the kitchen quote, they reflected their blended home. By themselves, they were just fruit.

Now, Farah looked at the sign she had put by her kitchen sink window that she saw every time she washed a dish:

Create your own happiness; Follow your heart; Enjoy the little things; Laugh out loud; Cherish Every Moment; Embrace every possibility; Remember to breathe.

Maybe it was cheesy, but it still made her happy. Maybe she should have a *Live, Laugh, Pomegranate* sign made for her place. She looked around and the space felt like a home, yet she sighed, frustrated with herself. It still felt like something was missing, but maybe that something was nothing at all. Maybe that something was just that she needed time to settle into all the changes. She tried to dismiss the thought that there would be no perfect Brooklyn flea-market find, and even more worrisome, no amount of time that would fill that corner of empty space in her heart.

Why had she been able to tell Mark about so much, but never told him the full truth about Zareen? He was right, she never fully opened herself up to him. And he wasn't the only person she'd held back from. There was so much more that she had kept from her sisters, from everyone. Farah glanced back at the time on her phone and dreaded the insomnia that would await her again that night.

CHAPTER SIX

OCTOBER 1981: TEHRAN, IRAN

The cool water cascaded over Farah's body and her new budding breasts. She stood still and raised her head, taking a few extra minutes to enjoy the tingling sensation in her nipples before the water became unbearably cold. She missed being able to bathe whenever she wanted to, rather than having to shower on Mondays and Thursdays. Those were now the only days their building had hot water, ever since the Iran-Iraq war had started. Although since everyone in the quadplex they were living in bathed on those days, the water was never hot by the time she showered after school, just lukewarm at best.

"You need to hurry up and finish." Her mother, Soraya, poked her head into the bathroom. Farah immediately covered her chest. It had been six months since she had started refusing to bathe with her sisters, both proud of and very private about her changing body.

"Okay, okay. Keep the door closed," Farah said, annoyed. There was no school the next day, Friday being the start of the weekend in Iran and school days being Saturdays to Thursdays, so why couldn't her mom just let her be for a few more minutes?

A minute later, Soraya opened the bathroom door again. "Just rinse off all the soap and get out. Now!"

There must be an air raid siren, Farah thought. They had been happening more frequently, at least a couple times a week. The radio would start blasting sirens, warning that an air raid was likely about to happen in their area. Everyone in the quadplex would run down to the basement and stay there until the all-clear signal was sounded. At first, the sirens scared Farah and everyone in the building. During the first one, Farah had sat huddled with her parents and sisters in the corner of the basement, all of them trembling. Farah had looked around to see the other three families in the building huddled together as well, each in their corner, and all of them quiet. It was as if they feared that if they made any noise, they would make their building a target, the Iraqi army zeroing in on them. By the time they heard the all-clear signal, everyone was exhausted, slowly leaving the basement to go back to their respective units.

But after about five air raid sirens when nothing happened, no damage to their street or anything close by, they started to become immune to them, and eventually, they became fun. It was an adventure to be awakened at 2 a.m., rushed to the communal basement, and see the other kids in the building. They would chase each other and play games. The kids started leaving some board games and toys in the basement. The adults left playing cards, a chess table, a samovar, and bulk bags of loose-leaf Darjeeling tea.

Now, despite Soraya's urgency, Farah was unfazed. She wrapped herself in a towel and went into her bedroom. "Get out. I need to get dressed," she said to Azita.

"I'm just grabbing my markers and pad and then I'll leave. Mitra and I decided we'd draw for the next air raid. We're tired of playing with the same board games," Azita said.

Farah stared out the window as her sister grabbed her things. Farah no longer saw the thick blue antishatter tape crisscrossing all the windows of their home. Everyone's eyes had adjusted to looking right through them. Farah gazed past the tape, thinking about seeing Alireza in the basement. She was starting to have a little crush on him after all these years. She hoped he'd soon see her as something more than just a playmate.

CHAPTER SEVEN

OCTOBER 2022: MANHATTAN, NEW YORK

Throngs of people were walking from Midtown toward Washington Square Park carrying an array of signs, many of them with pictures of Mahsa Amini and the words *Zan, Zendegi, Azadi*—"Women, Life, Freedom." Farah's heart started beating faster as she got closer to the crowd and joined in. She looked around, realizing that she had not been surrounded by this many Iranians in one place in thirty-eight years. She felt a wave of mixed emotions—grief, love, pride, sorrow, guilt, belonging—travel up her body, enveloping her chest, spreading to her neck. She put her right palm on her neck, feeling the flush, her carotid pulse thumping against her hand.

Everyone in her immediate family had gone back to visit Iran except her. Her parents had generally gone every other year until Trump imposed the first Muslim Travel Ban in 2017. Despite being US citizens, they were worried about going and not being able to return to the States. All of their Iranian friends had also paused international travel for a while. In 2021, Farah's parents had gone back to Iran again, feeling reassured that they would be able to return to the States. Azita had gone to Iran three times since moving to the US, and even the youngest of the trio, Parisa, had gone once before having kids.

Farah had seen so many videos of families reuniting in Tehran's airport, and she just couldn't picture herself there. She couldn't imagine passing customs, getting to the area where extended families wait with flowers, and then seeing her family without Zareen. The thought of it made her feel like her throat would close up. And although Soraya used to push her about going back home, seeing her aunts and uncles and whatever cousins were still in Iran one more time, eventually she had stopped asking, realizing that Farah seemed to have closed herself off from that part of her life. It wasn't like there was just one reason for Farah not to want to go back. There were multiple, none of which they ever talked about, none of which anyone ever saw a therapist for. Iranians didn't do therapy. The first time Soraya heard that Farah and Mark were in couples' therapy she was shocked, asking Farah why they would share their private lives with a total stranger.

"We're going to therapy because maybe the therapist can help us work out our differences—not get that dreaded divorce you're so against," Farah had said. She had started to let her mother know about some of their marital problems, so she wouldn't be completely shocked if they did separate. But in the end, she hadn't been able to make her mother understand. Although Soraya and Behnam had left Iran to give their daughters every opportunity America had to offer and independence, divorce "for no reason" was not Soraya's definition of exercising a woman's independence. Reasons for divorce included infidelity, abuse, and addiction. "Irreconcilable differences" were just part of marriage, and you learned to live with them.

When Farah and Mark had first separated, Soraya had been devastated that one of her daughters was getting a divorce. She kept pleading with Farah to try to work things out. "You know, Maman, even in Iran now, the divorce rate is fifty percent. Things haven't stood still there the way it was when we left," Farah had said. It was true. As a matter of fact, Farah had three first cousins in Iran, out of twenty-seven first cousins—so not exactly consistent with the 50 percent rate—that had gotten divorced. She hadn't been sure if mentioning them would strengthen or weaken her argument with Soraya, so she'd held back.

"I know what is going on in Iran. Unlike you, I visit regularly. When did I say anything about Iran? I don't care about Iran. I don't care about America. I care about my daughter! Mark is a good person."

"Since when are you such a big fan of Mark's? You've always been so critical of him. You never wanted me to marry him in the first place," Farah had reminded Soraya.

"No, I always said he is a good person. Anyway, why are you bringing up how I felt twenty-five years ago? We're talking about now. Divorce is not good for anyone." Farah had sighed and found an excuse to end the phone call. Much like discussing therapy with her mother, she knew this was a conversation that would go nowhere.

Now, as Farah fell in step with the other marchers, she tried to breathe through the mix of emotions that were overtaking her. She took out her phone, taking a selfie so she could send it to her kids, showing that she had kept her promise of going. She looked at the picture she'd taken and was again surprised to see herself surrounded by Iranians. Then she surveyed the crowd once more and realized there were hardly any Americans there. She would guess that, at best, non-Iranians represented five percent of the crowd. Where was the support for one of the most courageous feminist movements? Women in Iran were being killed fighting for freedom. This was a cause every single person could and should get behind. Even Julia hadn't asked Farah if she was going or if she wanted her to go with her. And although Farah no longer posted anything on social media, Julia and many of Farah's close friends followed Darya and Rumi, so they knew about the Global Day of Marches. Farah had stopped posting on social media once her divorce was approaching. The thought of changing her Facebook relationship status from married to single or divorced had made her feel like she was back in high school again, so instead, she decided that she would stop posting on Facebook altogether and therefore avoid the relationship status change as well.

As the chanting got louder, Farah couldn't contain her emotions anymore. Tears trickled down her face, as she raised her fist and joined the chanting, "Zan, Zendegi, Azadi!" When the chant switched to "Marg bar Diktator," death to the dictator, she had a flashback to her years of being forced to chant "Death to America," surrounded by girls in identical dark navy hijab. Around her now, there were men and women in what appeared to be about equal numbers, in an array of clothing and colors, although many were in green, with hair of different lengths flowing around them. Farah realized that all the green could not be a coincidence and must be to honor the Iranian Green Movement, also known as the Persian Spring or the Persian Awakening, a political movement in which protesters were demanding the removal of Ahmadinejad. Farah didn't recall any of the posts she had seen about this Global Day of Marches asking people to wear green, but she guessed that people more in tune with Iranian politics had chosen to wear the color on their own. She felt a tinge of shame for distancing herself from certain aspects of Iranian news.

When the march ended at Washington Square Park, the song "Baraye" by Shervin Hajipour started blaring out of a speaker, and the crowd started singing along.

The song talked of girls wanting education. A normal life. To dance. It was too much. Farah sat on the curb, put her face in her hands with Zareen in her thoughts, and said, "I'm sorry. I'm sorry. I'm sorry."

When Farah got home that afternoon, she went straight to her kitchen, grabbing a bottle of Shiraz, a corkscrew, and a glass. She sat on her couch and began drinking, her tears starting again. She looked through the barrage of texts from her sisters, her parents, her kids—pictures of them at marches in their respective cities, holding signs and posters. Even her mother was holding a sign with a photo of Mahsa. In Rumi's pictures, he was with three college friends, all American-looking. Farah was proud that he had gotten friends to go with him. He looked so different in the pictures than when she had last FaceTimed with him. He was growing out his facial hair, and it seemed like the testosterone injections combined with his Middle Eastern half were giving him a fairly full beard. Hints of who she'd considered her daughter Delara were barely visible in his face now. She felt a brief pang of nostalgia that she forced herself to push away by looking at the glow in his eyes. In the pictures of Darya and Azita, she noticed how much Darya resembled her aunt, with the same big chocolate brown eyes that were framed by full, arched eyebrows that are classically portrayed in all Persian miniature paintings. It made her smile for the first time that day. Her daughter may have gotten Mark's coloring and square jaw, but she had unmistakably Middle Eastern eyes.

Farah rose up, taking her wineglass with her, and went to look at herself in the bathroom mirror. Darya was right. She looked older—unhappy—and it wasn't just about that day. She opened the drawer by the sink and pulled out a pair of scissors. Then she took a sip of her wine, set the glass down, and started cutting her long dark brown hair. "This is for you, Mahsa and Zareen," she said to her reflection in the mirror.

◆

On Monday morning, Farah sat at her office desk, going through patient labs and emails before the day started. After a weekend, she always gave herself at least an hour to go through everything and catch up before her first patient. Brian popped his head in her office. "Hey, good morning. Nice haircut. Kind of a choppy shag look. I like it," he said.

What an idiot, Farah thought. Hadn't he seen any of the videos of women across the world, from Australia to Israel to Brazil, including actresses like Juliette Binoche, cutting their hair in solidarity with the women of Iran? Even if he was off social media, CNN was showing it too. She smiled and said, "Thanks. How was your weekend?"

"Great. Nothing too exciting. How about yours?"

"Same," Farah said and then slipped her reading glasses back down from on top of her head, turning back to her screen and typing.

"See you later, then," Brian singsonged and then walked away.

Twenty minutes later, Aniyah poked her head in. "Oh, hi there. Nice haircut. Women, Life, Freedom," Aniyah said, raising a fist. "You went to the march, I take it?"

"Yes. I did," Farah said.

"We were there too. Left the kids at a friend's. What a march! Let me show you a picture of us," Aniyah said, looking down at her phone. She pulled up a picture of herself and her wife and held it out to Farah. Then Aniyah's eyebrows furrowed with concern when she saw Farah's eyes had filled with tears. "Hey, you okay? This must be a lot for you. I'm sorry I haven't asked you about it." She went over and put her arms around Farah.

Farah sniffled and nodded, squeezing Aniyah's hand. "It's okay. Thank you for going. That means a lot. Now get out of here before I get too emotional and can't do my work."

"Okay, but anytime you want to talk, I got you," Aniyah said. "But I'm sorry—I'm not going to cut this," she said, pointing to her hair in its box-braid bun. "Too many years and way too much money has been invested here."

Farah laughed through her tears. "Understood."

Once Farah started seeing patients, she was able to quiet her mind a little and focus on her patients. She didn't have time for anything else. Before she knew it, it was 2 p.m. She sat at her desk and took the chicken tarragon sandwich that she had picked up from Pret a Manger out of the mini fridge in her office. As she took a bite, she refreshed her work email and saw a new message from Gregory Silverman, the hospital's risk management attorney, with the subject line "Update." She put her sandwich down, forcing herself to swallow the bite that was already in her mouth. She just couldn't do this anymore.

CHAPTER EIGHT

JULY 1984: TEHRAN, IRAN

Farah was still clutching Zareen's headscarf when she felt a hand on her left shoulder.

"Are you okay? What happened?"

Farah looked up to see a woman who seemed to be about her mom's age peering at her with concern. "I'm . . . I'm fine. I just. The komiteh . . . *my cousin.*" Then she stopped speaking.

"Something happened to your cousin? Did the komiteh arrest your cousin?" the woman asked, her voice rising with alarm. "Do you need me to call someone? Let's call your mother."

"NO!" Farah shouted and then softened her voice, wiping her tears. "No. I don't need my mother. Nothing happened. The komiteh just scared my cousin but then they let her go and she ran off. I'm just shaken up, but I'll be okay in a minute. Thank you. I don't need anything." She hurriedly stood up, trying to convince the woman she was fine.

"Are you sure?"

"Yes. Absolutely. Thank you so much. I'm going to walk home now and call my cousin. I'm sure she's back at her house by now and fine too," Farah said.

"Inshallah," the woman said. "Movazebe khodet bash"—Watch out for yourself. And then she walked off.

Farah tried to stop her hands from shaking. She had to get a hold of herself. She couldn't risk someone else trying to help her, insisting on calling her family. She couldn't let her parents know it was her fault that Zareen was taken away. No one would ever forgive her. When the komiteh eventually released Zareen, everyone would find out that she had been with her, but by then they would be so happy to get Zareen back, her lie wouldn't seem as important.

She looked at the headscarf still clutched tightly in her hands. She had to get rid of it. She looked around and remembered the trash can where she had just disposed of her ice cream bowl. She walked back to the trash can, the bowl still on top with a small amount of melted *akbar mashti* in it. She lifted the bowl, buried the headscarf deep in the trash, then put the bowl back in and ran.

When she reached her front door, Farah could hear Googoosh's voice through the door. Her mother was always listening to music. Maybe if she went in quietly, she could sneak into the hall bathroom and wash her face before seeing her mother. She quietly turned the key in the lock, slowly opening the door. Her youngest sister Parisa ran to her, hugging her and exclaiming, "You're home!" Parisa was six years younger than Farah, so at eight years old, she was just below the cutoff of when girls had to start wearing a hijab. Parisa looked behind Farah and asked, "Where's Zareen? She didn't come with you."

"No. We had ice cream and then she decided to go home. Maybe she'll come over later with Khaleh Nasreen," Farah said.

Then Soraya came out of the kitchen, stretching the phone as long as the cord allowed. "Oh, I'm on the phone with Nasreen. Nasreen, Farah says Zareen headed home. Is she there yet?"

Farah couldn't do this anymore. Tears started gushing down her cheeks.

Soraya looked over at Farah. "What's wrong? Why are you crying? Nasreen, let me call you back. Or just come over with Zareen when she gets there. See you soon." She hung up the phone and ran toward Farah. "What happened? What's wrong?"

"Nothing. It's just that after Zareen walked toward home, I

realized just how much I'm going to miss her. I've been so excited about moving to America, that I haven't thought too much about how much I'll miss her, and all my cousins, and Khaleh Nasreen and Khaleh Maryam, and Maman Bozorg." Farah felt terrible for lying, but she was afraid of what Soraya would do to her if she found out she was why Zareen had taken off her scarf, why she had been arrested. She looked up at Soraya's face and saw her mother's lips quiver, eyes filled with tears, a look of pure anguish on her face.

"I'm going to miss everyone too. But we'll visit. They'll come to visit us. It will be okay. We'll see them all again," Soraya said, squeezing Farah tight in her arms. It was the first time Farah had seen her mother be emotional about the move. So far, Soraya had seemed so matter-of-fact, businesslike, about it. But Soraya was leaving her own mother, and given Maman Bozorg was almost seventy, maybe she was worried that she may not ever see her again.

Half an hour later, Khaleh Nasreen called. Farah had gone to her room, saying she just wanted to rest a little. When she had gotten to her room, Azita was sprawled on the floor, reading a book. Farah wanted to yell at her to get out, to give her privacy, but she didn't want to do anything that may seem suspicious, so she just went to her bed and lay on it facedown.

Parisa came to their room and opened the door. "Farah, Maman wants you to come to the living room."

Farah placed a hand over her chest as she approached her mother, afraid Soraya would be able to see it thumping rapidly.

"Farah," Soraya went as close to Farah as the telephone cord allowed. "Come closer. I'm on the phone with Khaleh Nasreen. Zareen isn't home yet. Did she say she was going straight home?"

"She didn't say she was going anywhere else." Farah worried that her voice shaking would give her away, but maybe her mother would just assume that she was concerned about Zareen not getting home yet too. Farah could hear Khaleh Nasreen panicking on the other side of the line.

"Negaran nabash. Paydash meesheh," Soraya said—Don't worry. She'll show up. "If she's not home in another hour, call me and we'll all look for her. Everything is okay."

Despite her reassurances to her sister, as soon as Soraya hung up the phone, Farah saw her start dialing another number. When a male voice on the other line answered and Soraya started speaking, Farah could tell her mother was on the phone with the police. She walked back to her room, climbing into bed again.

The next morning when Farah went out to the main living area, she saw that her father Behnam was still home, sitting at the dining table drinking a tea, shaking his head. He was never at home when Farah woke up in the mornings. He always left for work by 7 a.m. Soraya was on the phone again, pacing back and forth in the same twenty-meter area that the cord extended to, repeating things to Behnam as information was relayed to her. They knew that Zareen had been arrested by the morality guards for not wearing a hijab and dancing in the street. Farah wondered how many lashes and how much bribe money it would take to get Zareen out from this double crime.

By that evening, they knew Zareen was in Evin Prison, and the komiteh had no intention of releasing her anytime soon. Every so often, the komiteh would decide to make an example of someone, giving them a harsher punishment, scaring people into a stricter following of their so-called moral code. It seemed like they thought Zareen was the perfect candidate for them to make an example of and use for their scare tactics. They didn't allow anyone to speak to Zareen, not even her parents, not even for a minute.

As the next few days went by, Soraya was barely at home. She spent most of her time at Khaleh Nasreen's house, trying to comfort her. Farah gathered as much information as she could from her parents' conversations. It seemed that so far, the komiteh had turned down all the money they had been offered, still refusing to let Zareen speak with anyone, let alone release her. Farah wondered how long this would go on. They were due to leave for America in less than ten days. Would this result in her family delaying or canceling their move? Farah felt guilty, but she couldn't bear the thought of their move getting delayed. She was sure Zareen would be released eventually, and it would be even better if that happened once Farah was away in America. And she just couldn't stand the idea of not leaving for the US. She had been waiting for this for so long. Zareen was right—there was nothing left for them in Iran. Other than her family and Alireza, who had recently been putting his arms around her when they were alone, there was nothing Farah would miss about Tehran. She was sure she would see her family again someday, and Alireza, well, there would be plenty of boys in America. She just couldn't stay in Iran. She couldn't.

CHAPTER NINE

JULY 2019: UPPER EAST SIDE, NEW YORK

Hovering over the delete button, Farah's hand shook. What was she thinking? It wasn't like deleting the email would just make everything go away. She kept staring at the words typed out on her screen from the hospital's risk management attorney:

Dr. Afshar. Please call my office as soon as possible to discuss an urgent matter.

She knew what this was. She had been waiting for this email for ten months, three weeks, and five days. It had been such a long day at work. It was already 6 p.m. on a Friday, and this was the last thing she wanted to deal with. Farah picked up her office phone and dialed Gregory Silverman's number.

"Dr. Afshar. Thank you for getting back to me. I trust you're familiar with the name Hannah Raye?" Silverman asked.

"Yes," Farah said, putting her left elbow on her desk, her forehead in her hand, and closing her eyes.

Eleven months earlier, she had been on call and in a patient's room when a nurse had rushed in. "Dr. Afshar, we need you in L-D-R-Five right away."

Farah ran out of the room and into labor and delivery room five to find two nurses on either side of the patient, who was semireclined in the bed, pale and sweat-soaked. She glanced over at the fetal heart monitor. No signal. Then she looked between the patient's legs and felt immediate panic at the copious amount of blood gushing out. "O-R," she shouted. "Right away! And call the Code Pink!"

What happened next was a blur. She remembered running down the hallway with the nurses as they wheeled who she would later learn was Hannah Raye into the nearest clean and ready operating room where somehow the anesthesiologist was already waiting. Although she didn't remember it exactly, Farah knew she must have told Hannah that she was bleeding, that she had to have an emergency cesarean section.

She remembered a man's voice asking, "Is our baby going to be okay?" and looking at a nurse and saying, "Get dad out of the O-R."

She could still see the anesthesiologist putting the mask over Hannah's mouth and nose while Farah said, "I'm ready to make my incision" and then seeing Hannah's arms flail before they were suddenly still.

She made eye contact with the anesthesiologist who nodded her head.

From the time Farah had gotten to LDR-5 to her first incision could not have been more than five minutes. That first incision was at 11:24 pm, the baby was out at 11:25 pm.

But none of that mattered. There was no cry. No breath. No heartbeat.

The baby was handed to the neonatologists who had rushed into the operating room at some point when they heard the Code Pink. What efforts they made to revive the baby, Farah didn't notice. She was trying to stop the bleeding from the uterine rupture, aware that she still had not heard a cry but focused on the mother now that the baby was out.

When the surgery was complete, Farah had finally asked the nurses what the sequence of events had been before she was called in. She had to go speak to the father, and she needed to be armed with as much knowledge as she could before facing him.

Hannah had come into labor just one hour prior. The fetal heart rate was perfect, in the 140s, when she had initially been hooked up to the monitor. She was already five centimeters dilated and having contractions every eight minutes. The nurses called Hannah's private obstetrician, Dr. Alex Klein, who was not in the hospital but said he would be there in about an hour. Hannah was a primigravida, and a first labor usually does not progress very quickly. All was stable.

Hannah's contractions were severe, so the nurses had called the anesthesiologist to see if she could get an epidural. As Hannah was hunched over squeezing a pillow while the anesthesiologist was inserting the epidural, she noticed blood trickling down her leg. "Why am I bleeding? Is that normal?" she asked.

The labor and delivery nurse had looked at the blood and reassured her that minor bleeding was normal. After the epidural, Hannah lay back down, and the fetal heart rate was erratic and kept dipping low. The nurses tried to adjust the position of the monitor on her abdomen, but the heart rate was still erratic. "The monitor must not be picking up for some reason. I'm going to see if we can put a fetal scalp electrode, which is a much more accurate way to monitor the baby's heart rate," the nurse reassured again. When the nurse came back with the electrode and went to place it, she saw that the trickle of blood was now a steady stream. She made eye contact with another nurse and said, "We need a doctor in here. Right away."

Farah walked out of the operating room and went back to LDR-5, where the father had been taken to wait. He was pacing the room. As soon as he saw Farah he said, "Is my baby okay? Can I see him? My wife?"

"I'm Dr. Afshar. Let's have a seat." She gestured to the chairs in the room and sat down. As she told him that Hannah had a uterine rupture and the baby died in utero, she saw his face contort with anguish and reached out to put a hand on his shaking shoulder. She waited for him to absorb some of what she'd just said before continuing.

"Hannah lost a lot of blood, and she is getting a blood transfusion. She has not woken up from anesthesia yet. Unfortunately, I was not able to repair the uterus. I had to do a complete hysterectomy to stop her bleeding."

"Wait. What does that mean? We can't have kids at all?"

"We saved her ovaries. That means her eggs can be used but she will not be able to carry a baby. You would have to use a surrogate."

It didn't matter that Farah had no fault in what happened. It didn't matter that Hannah's private obstetrician had later explained to Hannah and her husband that about one in every 8,500 patients experience uterine rupture during labor and delivery, a rare and unpredictable occurrence. It didn't matter that he told them they were fortunate Farah had been there, that she had potentially saved Hannah's life. Hannah had been the first to notice the trickle of blood, then be reassured by the nurse. Everyone knew the hospital would be sued—and when you sue the hospital, every person who had any patient contact is named in the suit, especially the surgeon who didn't save the baby or the uterus.

Farah now got off the phone with Silverman, who'd confirmed what she knew was coming from the moment she had walked out of that operating room. She felt overwhelmed. Should she agree to a settlement and just move on? She knew she hadn't done anything wrong, but did she have the energy to go through multiple depositions and sit in a courtroom for two weeks and be interrogated on the stand by Hannah's attorneys to have the judgment most likely be against her anyway?

"I'm sure I don't need to remind you of this, but I'll say it anyway. You can't talk to anyone about the case. No one," Silverman said.

"But—" Farah started.

"I'm sure you'll probably share this with your spouse, but please do not talk to anyone else about the case. Absolutely no one," Silverman said again.

"Understood," Farah said before hanging up the phone. She put her head down on her desk. Ten minutes later, her phone buzzed with a text from Mark:

Are you coming home first or are we meeting at the theater?

They had tickets to see *To Kill a Mockingbird* on Broadway. They'd decided that now that Rumi would be leaving for college, making them empty nesters, they should start planning dates that would re-anchor them as a couple.

I can't go tonight. I just can't. She hit send.

CHAPTER TEN

OCTOBER 2022: WEST VILLAGE, NEW YORK

The next J train would arrive in three minutes. Farah was rushing to the subway to catch it when her phone rang with Julia's ringtone. She'd texted Julia asking if she could meet her for dinner that night. She had made a life decision, and she needed to talk it out with Julia. After reading Silverman's "update" email on Hannah Raye, stating that the trial would most likely be in August of 2023 after dragging out for more than four years, Farah knew that she needed a break. She'd slept on her decision overnight, and in the morning, she was surer than she had ever been. Farah answered her phone.

"Of course I can do dinner tonight. You see, this empty-nesting thing is not so bad. And I have some of my own news to share with you anyway," Julia said.

"I'm about to jump on the J train, so I may lose connection. Just text me where and when to meet you, but make it after seven," Farah said, out of breath.

At work, Farah was surprisingly calm, despite her overflowing inbox. Having made her decision, she had a sense of inner peace. She didn't have to address every single email today. They were supposed to have three days to reply to emails and this was made clear to patients, even if their expectations were otherwise. She would give her full attention to each scheduled patient for the day, then only address the most urgent issues in her inbox and leave the rest for another day. Her inbox didn't have to be cleared at the end of every single day. Julia texted to meet at Buddakan at 8 p.m. Farah got there at 7:45, took the liberty of ordering them a bottle of Shiraz, and waited for Julia to arrive.

The hostess ushered Julia to their table. This time, Julia was the one still in her work attire, wearing a fitted pantsuit over a silk blouse and simple pointed black Christian Louboutin heels, her auburn hair pulled back tightly into a low ponytail. In contrast, Farah had gone home and quickly changed, throwing on worn, relaxed jeans, a floral-patterned billowy top from Anthropologie, and studded cowboy booties. Her dark brown choppy hair was loose and just grazing her shoulders.

"Woah! Love the hair! Okay, you're here before me for once with my wine ready. Now I'm nervous. I hope this isn't really bad news. Just tell me that no one has cancer, and no one is dying," Julia said as she gave Farah a hug.

"No one has cancer, and no one is dying."

"Okay. Fine. I think I can handle anything else you have to tell me, so let's toast first to your freestyle haircut. I'm guessing it has a little something to do with women, life, freedom," Julia said, raising her glass. "I'm starving. Let's order and then you can tell me all about whatever decision it is you've made."

They scanned the menu and easily settled on the crispy cauliflower lollipops, the pea shoot salad, and the ginger scallion chicken. "I want to hear about you and your news first. I'm guessing you made a decision about that project," Farah said.

Julia animatedly told Farah how she'd accepted the offer to be the lead designer on a new project her firm had acquired. This was the biggest project she had ever taken on—it could be a game changer for her career. "There will be lots of evening meetings and some travel, but with Violet out of the house, I can finally focus and give a hundred percent to these types of opportunities that I've had to pass up before."

Farah noticed that Julia was glowing with excitement, rather than looking exhausted from a long day at work. "I'm so happy for you, Julia.

You've always wanted to be able to travel for work. This is your time. And you look... you're glowing. You look at least five years younger."

"Until all the travel and time-zone changes age me ten years, but yeah, I'm excited." Julia took a bite of her cauliflower and said, "Wow. How do they make cauliflower taste so mouth-watering? Okay. What about your news? You've finally decided to join Tinder and start having lots of sex with random hot men?"

Farah finished chewing her bite of salad and said, "I hate to disappoint you, but that's not it. I've made a major life decision that does not revolve around men. Sex and dating are the last things on my mind right now. I need to figure everything else out first," Farah admitted, seeing Julia feign a look of disappointment.

"Okay, so what have you figured out so far? What's the big noncancerous news?" Julia raised an eyebrow.

"Yeah, so the good news is that you're right. I need a break. I have gone through too much these last few years, and the protests in Iran combined with all the work stuff have put me over the edge. And I don't think it's as simple as taking two weeks to go to London by myself or giving up being chief. I know it's not as simple as that."

"Go on," Julia nodded.

Farah took a sip of her Shiraz and then took a big breath. "I've decided to take a leave of absence from work, a long one. At least six months—more if I end up needing it. And if that means I risk losing my position as chief, or losing my job altogether, then I'm willing to take that risk." There. She had actually said it out loud to another person.

"Okay, so you'll have time for lunch dates for the first time in our friendship. What's the bad news part?" Julia leaned forward.

"I don't just need a leave from work. I need a bigger change than that. I want to take a leave from New York too. I want to just go away for a little while and figure out who I am. That's the bad news part. I need to leave. I just have to figure out where to go and how to do it."

"Okay, that's not so bad," Julia said. "It's fine. I can do this. We can do this. It's a good thing I'm going to be too busy to breathe with this project over the next year. So, where are you going to go? Forget that question. What's your happiest memory from the last five years? Not something related to your kids or their accomplishments. I'm talking about in the last five years, when did you laugh most freely—without it having to do with your kids?"

Farah leaned back in her chair and thought. "You really should have been a therapist. Okay. I've got it. When we went to the Opolo October harvest festival in Paso Robles and stomped grapes." Stomping grapes had been on Farah's bucket list, and as she and Julia had their own Lucy and Ethel moment, it had been one of those experiences that was even better than what she had pictured. The squish of grapes under her feet had been so satisfying. The grapes were so slippery, and they had dodged falling over multiple times. Farah hadn't laughed that hard in a long time. "Honestly, every single time I'm in wine country, I'm more relaxed and happier than ever. And it's not just the wine."

Julia tapped her forehead with her right index finger and suddenly got excited. "Okay, so you remember my friend Amanda who met us in Paso? She has a friend who owns this gorgeous vineyard called Braxton Vineyards. The friend has a guest house on her vineyard that she rents out for short periods. What you could get for rent for your place on Bank Street would probably cover your rent AND living expenses in Paso. I'll find out when her guesthouse will be available, and we can get you a longer-term rate. You'll just need to figure out how you're going to take a leave from work."

"Okay, so when are you going to start charging for being a life coach to your friends?" Farah asked.

"Don't worry. You're paying the tab tonight. And, I get to visit and stay with you for free whenever I want while you're there," Julia smiled and winked at her.

"I don't deserve a friend like you," Farah said, dabbing a tear from the corner of her eye.

"Okay, stop it now," Julia said. "It's not like you haven't been there for me when I've needed you. Save your tears for when you're missing me like crazy."

CHAPTER ELEVEN

NOVEMBER 2002: EAST VILLAGE, NEW YORK

The vibration of Farah's flip phone in the back pocket of her scrubs woke her up. She had gotten home minutes before and started reading *Pat the Bunny* with Delara on the couch. Darya pretended to cook in her play kitchen alongside Leticia, who was finishing up the dishes before leaving. Feeling the buzz, Farah opened her eyes to see Delara still in her arms but the book on the floor. She realized that she must have dozed off. She pulled out her phone.

Farah. I need your help. Like right away. R u home yet?

Seeing the text from Julia, Farah immediately called her. "Hey, what's going on?"

"So, you know, my egg retrieval is supposed to be in exactly thirty-six hours. And I've been doing all my own subcutaneous injections just fine, but this one is supposed to be intramuscular in my derriere, and I'm afraid I won't get the angle right. I tried to have Ethan do it. He saw the size of the needle and turned green and he says he just can't." Julia sounded desperate.

"The trigger shot. Yup. I'll be right there," Farah said.

"Thank you! You're a godsend," Julia said.

Farah went into their bedroom, which was also Mark's makeshift home office. "Julia is having a little sort of emergency. I'm going to run over and help her with something and be right back. Leticia is leaving in a few minutes. Can you watch the kids? I'll be back in an hour." She kissed him on the forehead and headed back out of the bedroom.

"Hold on. What's this sort of emergency? Didn't you just meet this Julia person? You're going to drop everything and go there during the kids' dinner and bedtime?" Mark asked.

"Yes, but . . . I'll explain when I'm back." Farah ignored the irritation in Mark's voice and left the apartment, hailing the first cab she saw.

Farah hadn't exactly just met Julia. She had met Julia two months prior when she'd taken the day off work so she could both drop off and pick up Darya herself for her first day of preschool. She had left Delara home with Leticia. After drop-off, a group of moms decided to grab coffee together. Farah found herself sitting next to Julia in the bright sun. She couldn't help noticing Julia's dark fiery auburn hair, or that she'd tried to cover her freckles with foundation. Farah had always loved freckles and been drawn to people with them. Julia reminded Farah a little bit of her friend Bridget, with the same distribution of freckles over the bridge of her nose and cheekbones. Farah had hoped that at least one of her kids would have red hair or at least freckles, given their quarter Irish ancestry, even though Mark had dark brown hair. But of course, both kids were born with medium brown hair and skin tone that was surprisingly fairly light, and not a single freckle anywhere.

Over breakfast, Farah learned that Julia, an architect, had also taken the day off work to drop off her daughter Violet for her first day of preschool. Most of the other moms at breakfast were not working outside the home, at least for the moment. Farah and Julia had immediately hit it off, exchanging numbers and planning a playdate for their daughters a few days later. At that first playdate, they'd decided to plan a couple's night out with their husbands, but many text exchanges later, they still hadn't coordinated a date for that.

When Farah rang the doorbell at Julia's apartment, a teddy-bear-looking but distressed man answered the door, Violet clinging to his leg. "You must be Farah. I've heard so much about you. I'm Ethan. I can't thank you enough for coming. I'm sorry that Julia married such a wuss."

Farah laughed. "No worries. I've seen my share of queasy partners over the years."

"Farah, is that you?" Julia called from the bathroom. "Thank you for getting here so quickly. We're only half an hour off from when I was supposed to get my trigger shot."

In the bathroom, Julia handed Farah the syringe and an alcohol swab.

"Okay, drop your pants, show me that ass. Let's do this," Farah said. Once it was done, they both sat on the bathroom floor and laughed.

"Why doesn't anyone talk about secondary infertility?" Julia asked. "I wasn't even really trying with Violet. I had just come off the pill. Now it's been a year of ovulation prediction kits and regular calculated sex and nothing. I can't drink during this process, these shots are making me crazy—and I swear I've gained a hundred pounds from them!" Julia said, starting to sob.

"I'm sorry," Farah said. "There's a lot that women don't talk about. And secondary infertility is definitely one of them. It's more common than you think. But if that shot worked, you better name this baby after me, regardless of the sex."

That made Julia laugh through her tears. "Okay. If it works, this will be baby Farah, penis or not. And if it doesn't work, we're going out for drinks and getting drunk before I have to stop drinking again in preparation for the next cycle."

"It's a deal," Farah said, squeezing Julia's hand.

CHAPTER TWELVE

NOVEMBER 2022: WEST VILLAGE, NEW YORK

A sliver of the Manhattan skyline was visible between other buildings from Farah's obstructed office view. Phone still in hand, Farah pushed back from her desk, pausing to take in the earlier sunset resulting from daylight savings time. She would miss her little peek-a-boo view, but she felt proud of herself. She put the phone back on its receiver, in disbelief of what Oppenheim had just agreed to. One week before, she'd met with the chief executive officer and chief medical officer of the hospital and without getting into a detailed explanation or overly apologizing, said that she needed to take a leave of absence.

"Farah, this is a highly unusual request. I don't think we've ever had a physician request a leave for such a long length of time without a medical necessity for it," Ferguson, the CEO, said.

"I know. I'm sure I don't need to enumerate all that I have done for the OBGYN department over the last ten years, the sacrifices I have made in my own life to enhance and ensure the success of the department—not because I had to, but because I wanted to. And now it's time for you to trust that I need to take this leave without losing my position permanently."

"And what if we say we can't do that? Brian has done a fine job covering your duties any time you're on vacation. What if we say we can't hold your position as chief?" Oppenheim, the CMO, asked, his frustration evident in his tone.

"Well, I'd say that I think you should strongly consider my ask. We all know that there has been way too much physician turnover at the hospital, especially in OBGYN. I don't think you'd want to lose me altogether, and if my position as chief isn't held for me, then I'd have to explore other positions outside of Mount Sinai when I get back. But I'm taking the time off. I've made my mind up about that." Farah was not about to let them know that she feared losing her job. But she knew she was well-known in the OBGYN community in Manhattan and could get another job, if not necessarily another chief position.

Now, despite the confidence she'd portrayed at that meeting, she couldn't believe that they had actually agreed to her request. She would have to hold a departmental meeting soon—inform the staff. But for tonight, she was going to go home. She was going to open a bottle of wine and find a mindless binge watch. She was not going to click on any social media or video links sent to her for one night.

◆

Farah jumped out of bed before her alarm rang at 5 a.m. Despite what had probably been one too many glasses of wine the night before, she felt rested, energized, excited. As she ran along Hudson River Park, she felt like she was flying. Had she completely lost it? Was this a midlife crisis that had spun out of control? Had the pharmacist accidentally mixed up the Lexapro she had started six months ago with something else the last time she refilled it, and she was just delusional to think that she could do this? She didn't know. Certainly, the Lexapro, which seemed to be what all women her age were taking now, as if it's just a multivitamin for your fifties, had never given her a sense of euphoria or even just joy. It had at best eased the sense of hopelessness she was feeling when she finally decided to give in and start taking it. After all, she prescribed antidepressants to mothers with postpartum depression all the time, reassuring them that starting a medication didn't say anything negative about who they were as new moms. She was always trying to destigmatize mental health issues in women, yet she had resisted taking an antidepressant herself for so long, as if it said anything about her autonomy over her life.

But now, for the first time, Farah didn't feel like she had to know everything that would happen—she didn't feel the need to be in control. She just knew that she could not go on this way, and for once in her life, she wasn't afraid to fail. If there was anything the last five years had taught her, it was that she could come out the other side of whatever life threw at her. But maybe if she had started the Lexapro a few years earlier, she would have handled the last few years better, rather than bottling in her emotions all day and then letting the tears quietly flow at night when she finally pulled the covers over her head. Somewhere buried deep inside, she had known this day was coming. Years ago she'd even known something was off. Maybe that explained the anxiety she'd had walking into her twenty-year medical school reunion.

CHAPTER THIRTEEN

JUNE 2016: DURHAM, NORTH CAROLINA

Walking into her medical school reunion holding Mark's hand, Farah felt an unexplainable heaviness in her chest, despite having met Neesha and Bridget at their hotel bar for a drink beforehand. She didn't know what was holding her back from being fully relaxed. Maybe it was because it was the first time she had left Darya and Rumi alone together in Brooklyn since Rumi's coming out. Or maybe it was because she wasn't in the headspace to make small talk and catch up with people she hadn't seen in twenty years. Other than Neesha and Bridget, her relationship with her other classmates was mostly giving each other Facebook status likes and wishing them happy birthday when prompted.

Immediately, she ran into Ted and Michelle. Farah had not thought about them since graduation. She remembered when Ted and Michelle started dating their first year of medical school. Farah reached out and gave Michelle a hug, pulling back to study her face. She looked the same, other than some fine lines around her eyes and mouth. She had always liked Michelle and wondered why they had not been better friends. They started making small talk, catching up on the intervening years. Farah felt her shoulders start to relax. She was enjoying herself. Within a few minutes, Michelle said, "I literally just left my job. I'm taking some time off medicine, at least a year."

"Oh, you are? Is everything okay?" Farah asked, thinking that maybe Michelle or someone in her family was having a health problem.

"Everything is fine. I want to take a year to myself to write. I've been thinking about my past a lot. I have all these stories about my childhood and my mother, who I now realize had undiagnosed bipolar disorder. I spent so much of my childhood moving with my mom from one city to another, taking care of her. I want to write it all down." Farah looked at Michelle with disbelief and Michelle laughed. "You look like you're in shock."

"Sorry. I think it's great you're taking time for you, but it's just so hard to leave medicine and then come back to it," Farah said. How was leaving medicine for a year to write an option? Farah had always been intrigued when physicians became authors. Khaled Hosseini's *The Kite Runner* and Abraham Verghese's *Cutting for Stone* were among her favorite novels. She knew Hosseini had woken up at 4 a.m. every day to write his first novel while still practicing medicine, but she had recalled reading that Verghese had taken a leave to get an MFA from the Iowa Writers Workshop and then gone back to medicine, so she supposed it was possible. Farah thought about how in medicine, you build a practice and a reputation over time. She had heard so many stories of physicians who took off more than a few months and could not get a job or hospital privileges unless they were willing to move to the middle of nowhere. Farah was not willing to do that. She had spent enough years in Cincinnati, which wasn't even the middle of nowhere. Cincinnati could be great if you were White, but she was not, and growing up there had not been easy. Moving to a diverse city had been a very deliberate decision for her. She had also heard of physicians who took more than a couple of years off and had to go back and do an additional year of residency.

"I'm not going to worry about what will happen after the year. Maybe I'll take longer. Maybe less. I just know this is what I need to do right now," Michelle said, breaking Farah's train of thought.

"That's great. Let's keep in touch. I'm not just saying that. I'd love to know how this year goes for you," Farah said genuinely, suddenly happy that she had come to the reunion after all.

"Kobe beef slider?" a server came up to them with a tray.

"I'm going to grab a drink at the bar first," Farah said and walked toward the bar. She made it only a few steps before running into Alessandra, both of them shrieking like teenagers and going in for a hug. Alessandra and her husband Gabe had come into medical school already a couple and gotten married around the same time as Farah and Mark, but they had waited a few years longer to have children. Now they had two highschoolers and a tween, and Farah had seen their kids grow up on Facebook, feeling like she knew them despite never having met them.

As Farah and Alessandra started catching up, Farah said, "I just saw Michelle for the first time since graduation. You know she's taking some time off medicine?"

Alessandra gave a little laugh and said, "Yeah. I just gave notice to my practice too."

Farah looked stunned. What was happening? Alessandra explained some of what she had been going through working full-time and having three teenagers. Just then Mark walked toward Farah with a glass of red wine and handed it to her. Farah mouthed a "thank you" as Mark kissed her cheek and walked back toward Neesha's husband. Farah took a sip.

"Having to send Kara to a therapeutic boarding school for a year was the final straw for me. I just can't keep at this anymore. I need to take a few years to get them through the teen years. I can figure out the rest of my life later," Alessandra shrugged. Farah thought about how she would have loved to take a family leave of absence for part of the last year. Taking Rumi to various therapists and appointments to start medical transition had been both time consuming and emotionally exhausting, and she had constantly made herself checklists and set calendar alerts, afraid that she would drop the ball on something, anticipating a catastrophe. But Farah just hadn't felt like taking time off was a viable option.

At dinner, Farah and Mark sat at a table of eight next to Neesha and her husband. Bridget also sat at their table, but her wife had not come with her. Their table was made complete by three other classmates, all of whom had come solo as well. Farah had been peripherally keeping up with Rhonda on Facebook, noticing when her status went from married to single. Farah hadn't updated her home page in quite some time. It had likely been at least six months since she had posted anything, but she still couldn't quit her habit of going through her daily scroll. "Didn't I see you standing at a podium or accepting something on your latest profile pic?" Farah asked Rhonda in between bites of her heirloom tomato crostini.

"Yeah," Rhonda smiled. "It was from the night I officially became chief of staff at my hospital." Rhonda had not left medicine. She recounted for Farah how she had gone from practicing internal medicine part-time at various practices while following her pediatric neurosurgeon husband from one institution to the next, to now working full-time and eventually becoming chief of staff. "I just couldn't follow Alan to his last job," Rhonda explained. "For years, I justified putting my own career on the backburner with the fact that as a pediatric neurosurgeon, he couldn't just get a job anywhere, while as an internist, I could. But following him around from one academic position to another, I could never develop continuity for my own patients or get a better position myself. And he didn't even appreciate or see the sacrifices I was making for him. Just because I didn't go into a super specialized field doesn't mean I don't have my own ambitions. Now I finally feel like I have a career in medicine rather than just a job."

"That's great, Rhonda. Hope you don't mind me saying this, but Alan was kind of always a self-centered, arrogant ass in med school. He's not here, is he? I haven't seen him," Bridget asked.

"No, he isn't. And yes, he was—"

"Hey now," Chris interrupted Rhonda. "I'm still good friends with Alan, remember?"

"Yes, I know." Rhonda rolled her eyes. "Anyway, no regrets about our time together because otherwise I wouldn't have my three beautiful kids."

"When did you get married, Chris? I see you're finally sporting a wedding band," Neesha said. Chris Kapetan was the Dr. McDreamy of their class, rumored to have had one-night stands with many of their classmates.

"Two years ago. Still kind of a newlywed, I guess. My wife Jess is eight months pregnant with our first, which is part of why she didn't come."

"Congrats!" Farah said, while thinking that there was no way she would want to be a new parent at her age.

"Yeah, thanks. And my schedule is a lot more flexible now, so I'll be able to spend time with the baby and Jess. I'm a medical expert consultant for lawsuits now."

"Seriously?" Farah asked in disbelief.

"Yeah, fuck being told how many patients I need to see an hour or that my referral rate to an orthopedist is eight percent of patient visits while the average internist's referral rate is seven point two. Two can play this game." Chris downed the rest of his scotch. "I'm making more money doing this than I ever did seeing patients, and I don't have all the calls or the stress and liability of missing someone's cancer."

"But don't you miss seeing patients?" Farah asked.

"I did at first, but nah, you get over it." Chris shrugged as he put a piece of steak in his mouth and chewed. "Lots of doctors aren't providing direct patient care anymore. So many people are moving into the admin and business side of medicine—opening med spas, becoming medical reviewers, starting their own skincare lines. More money, less stress."

"I guess," Farah said. She had no interest in starting her own skincare line, and she couldn't imagine herself going from complaining about how rising malpractice insurance rates were putting so many of her OBGYN colleagues out of business to working for malpractice litigation lawyers. "It's just, I'm sure you've heard that particularly in OB, rising malpractice rates have caused a real crisis. So many of my colleagues have stopped delivering babies and are just practicing gynecology because with how low insurance reimbursements are, they can't afford to pay their OB malpractice rates. And of course, that affects the patients. Some of them have a really hard time finding an OB in their network that will take on new patients."

"Yup, exactly. The system is a mess and instead of it taking advantage of me, I'm now making it work for me," Chris said.

Farah didn't know what to say to that. She didn't think it would be good reunion form to tell Kapetan that he was now part of the problem. She made eye contact with Bridget, who just raised an eyebrow.

Back in their hotel room that night, Farah couldn't stop ruminating about the classmates who had just quit medicine.

Two days later, Farah sent a text to Bridget and Neesha: **Did you notice how many of our classmates have just left medicine?**

Bridget wrote: **Well, Kapetan claims he hasn't even though he's working for the enemy now.**

Neesha wrote: **Yeah. McDreamy suddenly looks a lot more sleezy than dreamy.**

Farah responded: **I'm not talking about Kapetan. Michelle and Alessandra both did. Do you guys ever think about leaving?**

Bridget responded with: **I get tired and fed up, but I don't ever seriously consider it. What would I do? Go from being an oncologist to sitting at home? Doctors aren't qualified or have the skill set to do anything else. I'm not working at Starbucks.**

Farah wrote: **Don't knock Starbucks. They provide great insurance, which apparently covers medical transition now!**

Neesha wrote: **I'd love to leave medicine and just rest. But who are we kidding? That would give my mother a heart attack and then she would tell everyone about how her cardiologist daughter literally broke her heart.**

Farah responded with three laughing emojis and then changed the subject on the thread, feeling a little bit of shame at even suggesting leaving medicine.

CHAPTER FOURTEEN

NOVEMBER 2022: UPPER EAST SIDE, NEW YORK

Farah took a few deep breaths. She was about to go to her departmental meeting and make her announcement. She knew her colleagues would be surprised, since physicians usually only took extended leaves for a major health problem, a family crisis, or a mental breakdown. But while she was not exactly having a mental breakdown, she felt like she might be on the verge of one. As she shared her news, she noticed that Brian immediately looked intrigued, smirking and unable to hide his excitement while all her other colleagues looked not just disappointed but concerned.

"I want to assure you that I am healthy, and everything is okay. This is just something I need to do right now. I know that Brian has always done a great job taking care of my responsibilities as chief when I have been away on vacation, but since this is a longer leave, I want to be fair to all of you. So, anyone else who is interested in being acting chief during my absence, please send me an email about why you would like this opportunity and position, and we can vote at our meeting next week," Farah said, knowing full well that it was unlikely any of her other junior colleagues were interested. Everyone knew the thankless administrative headache that this position had become was not worth the extra pay.

On her walk from the hospital to the subway, Farah thought about how everything was falling into place. She had just found a young couple to sublease her apartment, and Julia was right, the rent she could get for her West Village unit was enough to cover renting Amanda's friends' guesthouse and basic living expenses. The last thing she had left to do was to tell her mom. Telling her kids had been easy. They had been unfazed. It didn't matter to them whether she was in the West Village or in wine country. Rumi, who was more bitter about the divorce, had surprised Farah, saying that he was happy she was taking some time for herself after years of working so hard. It seemed that the very thing that was pushing Farah's mental state over the edge, the uprising in Iran over Mahsa Amini, was what had suddenly garnered her children's interests, bringing them closer to her and helping them move past blaming Farah for the divorce. She had called Mark to let him know that she was leaving medicine and New York for a while, but that everything was okay. He hadn't picked up his phone, so she had left him a voicemail. A few hours later, he had sent her a text:

Got your voicemail. Do what you need to do.

She had been both relieved and disappointed about not having to talk to him. Relief and disappointment were the same feelings she'd had when her lawyer had called her about signing the divorce papers. It turned out that getting a divorce wasn't always the way it was pictured on television. They didn't have to sign them together, sitting across from each other in a conference room. They hadn't had a chance to look at each other one final time, with one of them possibly changing their mind at the last minute and standing up and suddenly saying, "No. This is all wrong. You're the only one for me. Always and forever."

Looking at his text now, she realized that despite being happy that she could make decisions about her life on her own now, she did miss talking through certain things with him.

She had put off telling her mom until she was sure it was unequivocally happening. Why was it that at fifty-two years old, it was still harder to disappoint her mom than anyone else? She knew that her mom had given up a lot in her life and was vicariously living through her daughters. Soraya had married their father and gotten pregnant in college. She had completed her bachelor's in economics but didn't get her master's as planned. Once they had moved to the US, her bachelor's from the University of Tehran, combined with her thick accent and broken English, impeded her ability to get anything more than a secretarial position. In Tehran, Soraya had been a high school calculus teacher until she had gotten fired shortly after the Islamic Revolution. She had refused to wear a headscarf while teaching in her classroom to all girls. The administration had countered her arguments, saying that men on the street passing the window of her classroom could look in and see her. Soraya had conceded and kept on her headscarf in the class, but when word leaked out that she was discussing politics with teens, she'd been fired.

Shortly after their move to Cincinnati, Soraya had swallowed her pride and become the front desk girl in a beauty salon, but eventually, she was able to make a new career for herself. She started bookkeeping at night for the salon. She was smart, efficient, reliable, and trustworthy. Eventually, she got more bookkeeping clients and quit the front desk position. After being forced to leave everything in Iran and start from scratch, she'd had to make money to help put a down payment on a home and save to send her daughters to college. That was why they had come to America. Within five years, she had her own business, with three employees. But she still missed teaching calculus and using her degree. She still lamented not getting a master's and eventual PhD. Soraya took so much pride in having three working daughters, and the most pride in Farah, the one who had followed in her father's footsteps.

"What are you talking about? Deevooneh shody? Why are you throwing away your life?" Soraya demanded.

"No, I haven't gone crazy, and I'm not throwing anything away, Maman. I'm just taking a leave. I know this may be hard for you to understand, but this is something I need to do for myself. I'm not giving up anything—just hitting a pause button for a little bit."

"Farah, don't be ridiculous. You know it's not that simple. You worked so hard to become chief. You could lose your job. You're acting like a teenager."

"Maman, in the worst case that I lose my job—which is not going to happen—I would get another."

"You haven't experienced or seen financial hardship in your life the way I have. You don't know what you're giving up," Soraya pleaded.

"Maman, you experienced hardship and then you started from scratch and now have a business with employees under you!"

"I'm not talking just about myself, and I'm not talking about when we left everything to come here." Soraya sighed. "You think you know everything, but you don't."

"Then who are you talking about? What is it that I don't know?"

Throughout Soraya's life, she'd witnessed the consequences of women trapped in bad relationships due to limited rights and lack of financial independence. Soraya's father, who had passed away when Soraya was fifteen, had been an alcoholic and physically abusive to her mother. "Of course, back then, we didn't call it being an alcoholic. He just came home drunk at the end of every night, which is what a lot of the other businessmen in town did," Soraya explained. Some nights, he would come home, eat dinner first, and then go out, only to come home drunk after midnight. Other nights, he would miss dinner altogether. Whenever he got home, the kids would be awakened by his yelling and often heard dishes being thrown and broken.

"Your grandmother tried to arrange marriages for your aunts as soon as she could, hoping she could protect them. That's why Maryam was married by sixteen, Nasreen by seventeen. Neither of them went to college. When my father died, we followed all the rituals. We had the third day ceremony, the seventh day ceremony, and the most elaborate fortieth day ceremony you've ever seen. At each one, your Maman Bozorg acted like she would kill herself from grief, bawling and beating her chest. She wore all black and no makeup for two years. But I think, secretly, she was happy and relieved."

"Maman Bozorg always talked about Baba Bozorg like she loved him and missed him when we were in Iran," Farah protested.

"Of course she did. What choice did she have? She couldn't tell anyone her true feelings. You don't do that in Iran. She never exactly told me either, but I just knew. About ten months after he died, I remember getting home and walking into the kitchen one day and she was sitting with Nafiseh Khanoom on the floor, a big sofreh in front of them with piles of herbs laid out that they were destemming. My mother was singing. I had never heard her sing before. I watched her for a few seconds, never having seen her look so beautiful, never having known that she had this melodious voice. Then she noticed me and immediately stopped singing. 'Soraya, either sit down and help or go start your homework,' she said. I sat in front of a big heap of parsley and started helping, hoping my mother would start singing again, but she didn't. I wondered to myself if the maid knew her better than I did; if the maid was getting to hear her sing regularly and I never had. Two months later at the one-year ceremony for my dad, I saw her crying and beating her chest again for the first time since his fortieth day ceremony."

Soraya's father had been wealthy enough that the money left was enough for Soraya to not follow in her older sister's footsteps and go to university first instead. The rest of the money was enough for Soraya's mother to live a modest life in peace and to leave a sufficient inheritance to Soraya's two brothers, who took over the family business. Maryam and Nasreen got nothing since they were already married. Unfortunately, they had both married sons of businessmen their father went out with. Those sons followed in their father's footsteps. "As far as I'm concerned, both my brothers-in-law are alcoholics. They drink every night. They come home late. Who knows how much infidelity and abuse there has been. Maryam and Nasreen, they don't talk about the details."

Farah didn't have too many memories of her uncles from when they lived in Tehran, but the ones she had were all good ones. Rarely were they home. When she would go to her khalehs' homes, the only times she would see them was on an occasional Friday, Fridays in Iran being the only day off of the week. Any other time, they were not there. When they were home, they would tease the kids and tell jokes. "I can believe that my uncles may have been functioning alcoholics, but it's hard to imagine either of them being abusive. Khaleh Maryam and Khaleh Nasreen always seemed happy," Farah said.

"Sure, they seemed that way on the outside. Why do you think Khaleh Maryam would stay at our house with her kids for days at a time when we lived fifteen minutes apart?"

"Because it was so fun for us cousins? Those were some of the best days of my childhood," Farah said as she recalled memories of her mom and Khaleh Maryam having their own hushed conversations while she played hide and seek with her cousins.

"If it was just for the cousins to have fun, then we would have gone to their house for a few days sometimes," Soraya said.

"Maman, why didn't you ever tell me this before? My uncles always seemed fun . . . lively . . ." Farah trailed off.

"Yes, they seemed that way to other people. You were never up late enough to see them truly drunk. What seemed fun and lively was because you were always seeing them earlier in the day, when they had only had a few drinks."

Farah thought it was no wonder that Soraya was not a fan of how much she liked wine, always feeling like her mom judged her for having a glass of wine most nights. "But why didn't you tell me this before?"

"I guess I tried to protect you. When you were a kid, it wasn't appropriate to tell you. Once you were an adult, I didn't want to give you a negative impression of Iranian men. But obviously, Iran has good men and bad men, just like America or any other country. Your father is a good man. My sisters' husbands were not. The difference is in Iran, when men are bad, women don't always have choices."

"I don't think women in America always have choices, either. Why do you think people in marriages with domestic violence take so long to leave, if they do at all? You could have trusted me with an adult conversation," Farah said.

"Well, I also tried to protect your cousins, their father, my sisters. You know how our culture is. We don't talk about these things. I wanted to protect myself too. I don't want you to have a negative impression of my family, your khalehs, your Maman Bozorg. Not everyone has options, but I made sure that my kids would. My sisters, they could never leave their husbands. They would have no way to support themselves, and you know, in Iran, custody automatically goes to the father. I got a degree. My degree gave me a certain amount of independence. Allowed me to meet your dad and not have an arranged marriage to a businessman's son. Your position . . . you could support your kids on your own if you had to. That gives you power and something no one can take away from you. You don't realize what you're giving up."

"I appreciate you sharing all this with me, and of course I appreciate everything you and Baba sacrificed for us, but I will always be able to be independent. If I lose my job, I'll start over. You and Baba were immigrants with three little kids and look at you now. You don't think I can support just myself? The kids are adults with enough in their 529 plans to get through at least part of graduate school, and Mark would always take care of them anyway if I couldn't for some reason."

"So, you would start all over? Not making as much money and not being chief? You start a new job, it doesn't matter your experience, you are the newest person. You would be okay with giving up what you worked so hard for?"

"Yes, maybe I would. Financial security and status are not the only things that make a person happy. And I'm *not* happy. I know that you and I are different, and maybe I can't make you understand. But I don't need to make you understand. It's happening. It's already done."

"Protesters in Iran are being killed every day now fighting for what you have, Farah!"

"I know that, Maman! I don't need any reminders!" Farah hung up the phone.

CHAPTER FIFTEEN

MAY 1982: TEHRAN, IRAN

As she turned the key in the front door, Farah simultaneously loosened the knot from the headscarf around her neck. It had become a habit to instantly remove her headscarf while opening the door, feeling like her head could finally breathe. She was surprised by the relative silence. On most days when she got home from school, she either heard her mother and the downstairs neighbor laughing in the kitchen, or she heard Googoosh's voice coming from the cassette player and filling the house, or both. The smell of fried eggplants filled the air. She took off her manteau, the oversized navy cloak she was required to wear to school that covered her from neck to mid-shin, and hung it on the coatrack in the entryway. Then she checked in on the two goldfish who were indeed still swimming around their crystal bowl on the living room table. This was the longest their goldfish from Nowruz had stayed alive, and Farah took pride in how meticulously she was making sure to change their water and not overfeed them. After sprinkling a little bit of fish food into their bowl, she walked into the kitchen to find her mother quietly working at the stove. Soraya turned to look at Farah, then turned back to flipping eggplants in the pan.

"Maman, is everything okay?" Farah asked.

"Yes. Why do you ask?" her mother responded, without turning around again.

"There's no music playing."

"I just have a headache today. Everything is fine. Change and start your homework. Your sisters are at the neighbors', but they'll be home soon."

Farah wasn't used to studying or doing homework without any noise in the background. She sat at her desk, pulled out her notebooks, and got to work. She opened her Arabic textbook and started copying the phrases they had learned that day in her notebook. In the last year, Arabic had become the mandated second language for all students to learn. A few minutes later, Soraya walked into the bedroom, looked over Farah's shoulder, and shouted, "What are you doing? Why are you doing your Arabic first?"

Farah suddenly felt scared of her mom, unsure of how to answer her question. "I have a test in Arabic tomorrow."

"I don't care," Soraya yelled and then saw the alarm on Farah's face. She lowered her voice to a normal volume. "Arabic is useless. Useless! You do your science and math first ALWAYS, while your mind is fresh. You leave your Arabic for last."

Farah nodded and Soraya left the room.

Later that night, Farah snuck into the hallway to hear her parents' conversation. Often, her father Behnam got home from work after the girls were already in bed. It wasn't uncommon for there to be a week when Farah only saw him on Friday. She heard Soraya telling Behnam that her cousin Roshanak had not been accepted into the University of Tehran's medical, dental, pharmacy, or engineering program. Her cousin had been *shagherde aval*, the number one student, from first through twelfth grade. She had taken an entire year after high school to do nothing but trap herself in her bedroom and study for the *konkoor*, the university placement exam, and gotten a near-perfect score. But none of that mattered anymore. Since the Islamic revolution and the start of the Iran-Iraq war, Farah kept hearing how it was almost impossible for women to place into professional programs at top universities.

"I'm not staying here, Behnam," Farah overheard Soraya say.

"I'm not going to have my daughters working so hard and then get accepted into a teaching program at best."

"You loved being a teacher," Behnam said.

"Yes, I did. Until the Islamic Republic took that away from me too. And I want them to have choices and to be able to be independent. I'm certainly not going to have them end up in a marriage with no rights and no way to leave and support themselves if they need to—there has been enough of that with the women in my family."

Who was Soraya referring to? Farah didn't know anyone stuck in a bad marriage in her mother's family.

"This war is temporary, and hopefully the Islamic revolution is too," Behnam said.

"Things are getting worse every day. I'm not gambling our daughters' futures. They are going to be doctors one day, no matter where we have to go or what we have to do to escape this country and make that happen."

CHAPTER SIXTEEN

SEPTEMBER 2015: UPPER EAST SIDE, NEW YORK

"Did you hear the news?" Aniyah walked into Farah's office, beaming. Aniyah had been Farah's colleague for five years now, their offices adjacent to each other's. Farah had been the one to take Aniyah for lunch during her interview process, convincing her to join their group instead of the small private practice that was also recruiting her.

"What news?" Farah was in the middle of finishing up her charting for the day.

"Check your email," Aniyah smirked, pulling out a chair in front of Farah's desk and sitting down.

Farah opened her inbox and saw an email from Alan Oppenheim, the chief medical officer, with the headline "notice of departure." She read the email in disbelief. Tim Klapper, the chief of their OBGYN department, was leaving Mount Sinai and starting his own private concierge practice. Farah gave out a whoop. "Serves them right. That ass only lasted three years."

When Tim had been offered the chief position, he'd only been five years out of residency—Farah's junior that she'd trained. He was now the third male chief to be leaving in the fifteen years since Farah had been an attending at Mount Sinai. When Farah was first hired, the chief was Dr. Aaron Schneider, a man in his late sixties who had dropped the obstetrics part of his practice ten years prior and was only practicing gynecology. When Schneider was finally retiring at seventy-two, Farah was thirty-five. She'd only been at Mount Sinai for five years, but she had worked extremely hard during that time and had served on multiple committees. She threw her name in the pool of applicants interested in being chief next. But Schneider was replaced by Dr. Michael Bronffman, a sixty-three-year-old who'd been on staff at Mount Sinai for thirty years. Farah wondered why she'd even bothered applying if they were going to replace one old White man with another old White man who would retire within ten years.

When as predicted, Bronffman retired seven years later, Farah had thought that maybe the chief medical officer and the voting board would have evolved by now, realizing that they should pick someone who was younger and would be there longer—someone like her who taught residents, mentored younger OBs, and looked for ways to improve patient experiences, going above and beyond for every one of them. She applied for the position again, outlining everything she had already done for the department and her vision for what else she could accomplish as the next chief. Farah received the announcement that Tim Klapper would be the new chief via email along with everyone else. No one had even had the decency to pull her aside separately first to notify her that they'd chosen someone else again. They'd gone with someone younger alright. Her eyes had filled with tears when she read that email from Oppenheim with the heading "Announcement of New Chief of OBGYN Department." Not only was Klapper her junior, but he wasn't on as many committees as she was. He did, however, make sure to attend any meeting or event that Oppenheim was at, even if it meant rescheduling patients. Farah had called Mark and cried, then pulled herself together to finish seeing patients for the day. That night, she'd almost finished a full bottle of Cab Franc by herself, and the next morning, she'd woken up at 5 a.m. like any other day.

Reading the announcement about Klapper leaving now, she couldn't help but laugh out loud. "These assholes will never learn their lesson," she said to Aniyah.

"It's your time, Farah," Aniyah said.

"No way. No way am I applying again. Fuck them. I'm just going to keep being the doctor I am, the colleague I am. Fuck them if they can't appreciate just how much I've done for this department. You appreciate it, the patients appreciate it, the nurses know it." Aniyah was ten years younger than Farah, so she hadn't been there to see all the changes in chiefs that Farah had, but she'd been there when Tim Klapper was chosen over Farah, and she'd heard about the history of the department before that. There was a push to hire more diverse doctors, but it seemed like there wasn't a push to put those diverse doctors in head positions.

"You're seriously not going to apply? You've been in the department longer than anyone else at this point," Aniyah pointed out.

"Yeah. No. I'm good. I'm just glad Tim is leaving. Concierge practice. So predictable. I swear I saw that coming," Farah gloated. She was so tired of having to work harder than any of her male colleagues ever would to prove herself worthy. On weekend rounds, sometimes male colleagues would bring their kids to the hospital, leaving them at the nurse's station for an hour or two to be loosely supervised while they checked on their patients. These male colleagues would be praised for being great fathers, being responsible for watching the kids on the weekends while still working. The unit secretary and the nurses would dote on the kids. A female physician never dared to do the same. If you couldn't find childcare for a couple of hours on the weekend, then that was your problem. You shouldn't have become a physician if you couldn't handle being a doctor and a mother.

A male colleague leaving early for a family matter was a great doctor and a family man. A female physician leaving work early for a family matter hadn't figured out what it means to dedicate yourself to being a physician.

Farah had taken away from her kids, missed so many of their activities, given her best years to this department. She was not going to offer yet again to give them more and be passed over for a third time.

"Is there anything I can say to convince you to apply? Come on, Farah, we need you," Aniyah said.

"Nope. If you want to apply, you go for it. I just hope all of Tim's concierge patients in his concierge practice are the ones who want to take their placentas home and make placenta pills."

"Right!" Aniyah laughed. "Maybe we should buy him one of those placenta cookbooks as a parting gift. He can display it in his office."

"We definitely should!" Farah clapped her hands.

The next day, Farah got a phone call from Alan Oppenheim, asking to meet in his office. She sat across his desk facing him, scanning the framed photos of his family, noticing the addition of pictures of new grandchildren.

Oppenheim clasped his hands together on his desk, leaned forward, and smiled. "Farah, you have put your heart and soul into your work. You are an excellent physician and mentor and advocate. I know that you must have been disappointed when Tim got the chief position, given all you've done for this department."

Oppenheim paused to take a sip of his coffee, and Farah wondered where he was going with this.

"We've decided not to have an open call for nominations for the next chief. Instead, we would like to ask you to be the next chief."

Farah was in shock. They had finally learned their lesson. She tried to not let her disbelief show, to maintain her professional demeanor. "Wow. I wasn't expecting this. It's an honor to be asked," she said.

"So, you'll do it?" Oppenheim was grinning from ear to ear.

"Thank you for this opportunity, but I'm going to need a few days to make a decision. I need to think about the extra time commitment, how it will impact my family—make sure that this is a responsibility that I can take on right now." Farah couldn't believe this was coming at this time. She had two teenagers who seemed to need her more than when they were babies. She had a child who was possibly in the middle of transitioning. It was too much all at once. But as soon as she left Oppenheim's office and closed the door behind her, she knew she would say yes.

CHAPTER SEVENTEEN

DECEMBER 2022: UPPER EAST SIDE, NEW YORK

Twenty-eight patients—Farah reviewed her schedule. It was her last day in the office before leaving for Paso Robles. The front desk hadn't gone easy on her. Her schedule was packed with a patient every fifteen minutes, and several slots were double-booked. She took a deep breath and thought, *It's okay. It's your last time doing this for a while.*

Every single name was a patient she knew well, all women she had built relationships with, and one man, James Hollinger-Ward, as well, pregnant and expecting with his husband. She was perhaps most sad to be missing that delivery, her first time delivering a baby carried by a trans man.

Her first patient was Celia Vogel. She was twenty-two weeks pregnant with her fourth child. Farah had delivered her first three—all boys. *Who has four kids in New York these days?* Farah thought as she walked in with a big smile, rolled the stool up to the exam table, and sat on it. "How are you doing Celia? I reviewed your ultrasound report from this morning. It looks like you're having another perfect, healthy baby."

"Yes," Celia sounded a little defeated to Farah, or maybe resigned. "A fourth perfect, healthy *boy*. There will be no fifth. I guess I was not meant to have a daughter." Farah had heard statements like this from mothers having all same-sex kids at least a hundred times since she had been in practice, but since Rumi's coming out, she winced internally when she heard it. She would think *you never know what you're having or what's in store for you*, or *you don't know how much the sex of your child doesn't genuinely matter one bit*, but of course, she would not say this out loud. She understood both when mothers celebrated the sex of their unborn child, and when they were disappointed by it. But this new trend of gender reveal parties, which she considered to be genitalia reveal parties, she just could not understand. At a time when people seemed to be learning more about the spectrum of gender and the harm imposed by gender roles, Farah thought these parties were taking several backward steps in imposing stereotypical gender expectations on an unborn child.

"So, then you're sure you want to have a tubal ligation after this? It's marked in your chart that it's what you want, but you know, at any point you can change your mind," Farah said.

"Dr. Afshar, Dean didn't even want to have this one. If I'm having a fifth child, it's with my next husband. And who are we kidding—after four kids, I have neither the body nor the time to find a new one."

Farah smiled. "I'm going to miss you. And again, I'm sorry I can't be here for these last few months, but you will be in excellent hands with Dr. Robinson."

"I'm just grateful I've had you as my doctor for all this time. I've noticed you haven't been wearing your wedding ring for a long while. No need to say anything. Just take care of yourself after all these years of taking care of us." Farah blinked back her tears and squeezed Celia's hand.

When they'd first separated, Farah had replaced her wedding rings with an old antique chunky ring that had a wide band and a turquoise stone, just to feel the weight of something on her hand. But once she had moved into her own apartment, she'd taken the turquoise ring off, too, allowing her ring tan line of twenty-five years to slowly start to fade.

When Farah opened the door to Phyllis Rossi's room, she

immediately got a whiff of fresh oregano and roasted garlic. Phyllis had been bringing her a tray of her eggplant parmesan at every annual visit for years now, except it had been a few years since she'd last seen Phyllis this time. "Phyllis, where have you been?"

"I know, I know. But at my age, do I really need pap smears and mammograms? I mean, if my breast cancer comes back, it comes back. I don't have it in me to go through all that chemo again. And also, the pandemic—I tried to minimize doctor appointments for a while. But I got the letter that you were taking some time off and I thought who knows if you'll come back or how long I'll be alive, and so I made an appointment." Farah could still remember chatting with Phyllis thirteen years prior while doing her breast exam. She had finished the left breast and axilla and the right breast. All had felt normal. Then as she was examining Phyllis's right axilla, she felt a one-centimeter lump that was unmistakably hard and fixed, and she'd known exactly what it was.

"Phyllis, you are still young and full of energy. You have grandkids who want their nana at their weddings. You're still making the best eggplant parm I've ever had, which you really didn't have to do again—but I'm still glad you did. My kids aren't home anymore, so I get it all to myself."

When the kids were still home, that big tray had fed her family for a week every time. Whenever Farah would see Phyllis on her schedule, she knew she wouldn't have to worry about dinner that week. Fortunately, thanks to all the Persian foods her kids had eaten as soon as they could eat solids, they loved eggplant. When Farah was growing up in Cincinnati and her father was in practice, she remembered him coming home with gifts from patients on a daily basis. Now, everyone was too busy and patients' relationships with their doctors had changed. Fifteen-minute visits didn't provide enough time to get to know each other. Gifts from patients were not as common. She appreciated those rare gifts and treasured the birth announcements and holiday cards she still received from former patients. She just wanted the thank you, the appreciation, the evidence of actual relationships. But Phyllis taking the time to roast eggplants and make this dish from scratch for her every time was better than any other gift she ever got from a patient.

"You can cut it up and place squares in individual Ziplocs and it freezes very well. How are those daughters of yours anyway? They must both be in college now. How far from home did they go?" Phyllis asked.

Farah paused. This was a scenario in which she found herself often. Someone she hadn't seen in a while and who was off the social media grid asking about her daughters. As tempted as Farah always was to just give a simple answer and move on, she could never do it. She wanted to honor her son. Just a month ago, a patient had asked her how her two daughters were doing, and Farah had simply said, "I have a daughter and a son. They're both doing great and are in college now." Her patient had said, "You do? I could've sworn you have two daughters. I must be losing my mind or getting Alzheimer's." And then Farah had felt bad and explained that she wasn't losing her mind and that one child had transitioned. Now while Farah's hands moved over Phyllis's breast in circles, feeling for any hard lumps or irregularity, she found herself saying, "My older one went all the way to Stanford and graduated. She's working now and applying to master's programs. She's doing great. The younger one is at Oberlin in Ohio, which still feels pretty far. He's my son now, or I guess he always was. And he's doing great too. Thank you for asking."

Phyllis didn't really show any reaction. Maybe that's what came with age and all Phyllis had been through. "Wonderful. Life is full of ups and downs. As long as they're happy." It was hard to say goodbye to Phyllis. They both knew that there was a possibility that this was their last visit together, not because Phyllis would have a recurrence of her cancer or wasn't doing well, but because they both knew there was a possibility that Farah was not coming back. They hugged like they knew it, but didn't say a word.

Her last patient of the day was James. She'd purposely scheduled him last so that she could spend a little extra time with him and then have Dr. Robinson come in and introduce herself, transfer James's care as smoothly as possible, and assure him that he was in good hands. She had specifically chosen Aniyah to be his new OB since Aniyah was married to a woman who had birthed their two kids. It was certainly nowhere close to being a trans man giving birth, but at least there was a little bit of the shared experience of a nontraditional family and doing whatever it takes to have one. Farah moved the probe over James's abdomen and the familiar rapid whoosh-whoosh of the baby's heartbeat filled the room. Farah, James, and James's husband Craig all broke into beaming smiles and got teary-eyed every time it happened.

"I'm not going to insist on FaceTiming during your delivery, but I'm going to need pictures of this baby and this happy family as soon as the baby is out," Farah said. James and Craig knew that Farah had a trans son. That was how they had ended up with her as their chosen OB. They knew how sorry she was to be missing the delivery of their baby. Following James's pregnancy so far had given her such hope, although she knew it was very unlikely that Rumi would ever carry his own child, particularly given his attraction to women. Rumi would likely end up in a long-term relationship with a cisgender woman who would carry their babies, but you never knew. Anything was possible. James and Craig were a testament to that. Farah left the exam room and smiled to herself. She was officially done with her day and moving to wine country soon.

CHAPTER EIGHTEEN

NOVEMBER 2016: GREENWICH VILLAGE, NEW YORK

"Welcome back." Dr. Jeffers smiled at Rumi first before directing his gaze at Farah and Mark. "I trust that you've reviewed the informed consent for masculinizing hormone therapy in detail, so let's go over any other questions or concerns you may have about starting testosterone."

When they'd met with Dr. Jeffers for the first time three months prior, Farah had grilled him with questions. She'd done her research on him and knew where he had attended medical school and residency, and that he'd only been in practice for three years. "I don't know why Dr. Shah would refer us to a pediatrician who has only been treating trans kids for a few years," she'd told Mark the night before the first appointment.

"He's working at NYU's Children's Hospital. I'm sure he has seen plenty of trans kids in those three years," Mark tried to reassure her.

At that first appointment, Dr. Jeffers had extensively gone over all the permanent effects of starting testosterone. "The four permanent and irreversible effects are one—growth of facial and body hair. If you ever change your mind, you'll have to do electrolysis or laser hair removal to get rid of it. The second permanent effect is a deepening of the voice. That's permanent. The only way to reverse that is possibly through vocal cord surgery and vocal therapy may help a little. The third is the bottom growth or enlargement of the clitoris. That's irreversible.

And lastly, depending on family history, you can over time have scalp hair thinning or male-pattern baldness. If that happens, we can use the same medications that cisgender men use to decrease male-pattern baldness or slow it down. These are the four permanent effects."

"Yup, I know all of this. And I know what's reversible and what the risks are. I've already told my parents all of this," Rumi had said.

"Usually, I find that people your age have done their research and know all of this," Dr. Jeffers said, "but I still need to go over everything with you and your parents, even if your mom is a doctor."

Farah had looked over at Rumi. When it came to her children, she did not feel like a doctor. She was a mother—a mother who still hadn't gotten used to a buzz cut on her fifteen-year-old, so how long would it take her to get used to the other changes? A few months before coming out to his parents, Rumi had taken Mark's clippers and shaved his hair off, and then casually walked into the kitchen to grab a snack. At first glance, Farah had screamed, her initial thought at seeing the back of a shaved head being that there was an intruder in the home. She hadn't thought that it makes no sense for an intruder to walk into the kitchen and grab a snack in front of everyone. Then Rumi turned around and Farah said, "Oh . . . Delara . . . what . . . why did you do that to yourself?"

"I just you know, I was tired of it. I wanted a new look for our trip. Something easy," he'd answered. They were going on a trip to London the next day. Standing there with a shaved head, wearing a baggy sweatshirt and basketball shorts, Farah's eyes had filled with tears as she realized that she didn't recognize her child anymore.

"It's just hair, Mom. You don't have to cry about it. And remember that I asked you to call me Del. Why is that so hard for you? Everyone else calls me that. Even Dad," Rumi looked angry and frustrated.

"But what's wrong with the name Delara?"

"It's just so . . . so flowery. I've never been flowery."

"But the word Del means stomach in Farsi. You want me to call you stomach?" Farah had asked, all the while thinking that their family London pictures would now be ruined due to Delara's shaved head.

"Just. Never mind." Rumi had gone back to his bedroom, leaving the bread and cold cuts he'd taken out of the fridge on the counter.

As Farah tried to picture the permanent changes on her child that Dr. Jeffers had listed, she was glad that at least she wasn't calling him Del anymore. Then Dr. Jeffers had gone over the reversible effects of testosterone, the risks, the benefits, the side effects, before moving on to discuss fertility. "For most people, within six months of starting T, they stop getting a period and are not ovulating. That being said, you can't 100% rely on testosterone as contraception. And of course, testosterone does not protect from sexually transmitted infections. For Rumi, since he has already been regularly menstruating, if he chose to have a biological child in the future, he should be able to come off of testosterone and would likely start to ovulate after three to six months and be able to have a biological child and then go back on testosterone. We can't guarantee this, but based on what we see in other trans men being able to do this, it's most likely possible—"

"Nope. Not gonna happen. Never gonna be pregnant," Rumi had cut him off.

"Rumi, we need to hear all of this," Farah had said, and then seeing Rumi shake his head and roll his eyes, she added, "I want to hear all of this."

"Another theoretical option is to retrieve eggs and preserve them prior to starting testosterone, but it's too tedious, distressing for the youth, and cost-prohibitive for most, so it's rare for someone to choose this. I've actually never had someone choose this option," Dr. Jeffers added, while in her head Farah muttered, *Yeah, in all your three whopping years of experience no one has chosen this.*

Now, as they sat in Dr. Jeffers's office three months after that first visit, Dr. Jeffers turned to Rumi first, a warm smile on his face, leaning forward in his chair, "Rumi, let's start with you. What questions do you have?"

"I don't have any. Am I starting T today?"

"Maybe in a few days. If we all sign the consent form today, I'll have my nurse do injection training with you when we're done, and then order your testosterone, syringes, and needles. On average it takes three to five days to get everything authorized through your insurance so you can pick it up at the pharmacy."

Then Farah spoke up. "I still have a lot of concerns, particularly about future fertility. I wish Rumi would consider freezing some eggs—"

Rumi interrupted her. "Mom, stop! I already said I don't want to freeze eggs first. Let's just sign the forms." His face was turning red. Farah looked at Mark with tears in her eyes. Mark remained silent.

Dr. Jeffers looked between them and said, "I understand your concerns as his mother, but it is very rare for a teenager to decide to retrieve and freeze eggs. You know how difficult a process it is for an adult woman struggling with infertility, so I'm sure you can understand how distressing it can be for a teen boy with gender dysphoria. And there are trans men who come off testosterone as adults for a time to have a baby. As we talked about last time, we can't guarantee future fertility if he comes off testosterone, but it most likely is an option, should he choose that."

"I won't. I'm not ever going to be pregnant. Let's move on," Rumi said through clenched teeth.

Mark finally spoke up. "We're here to support our son. These are his choices to make, even if he isn't an adult. Thank you, Dr. Jeffers. You've addressed all our concerns repeatedly. I'm ready to sign." Mark held Farah's gaze with a look that said *no more questions, enough is enough*, and reached over and patted Rumi's back.

CHAPTER NINETEEN

DECEMBER 2022: WEST VILLAGE, NEW YORK

Looking at the colored string lights that framed her window, Farah thought that maybe she should have gotten a small Christmas tree for her apartment, even if she was moving to Paso Robles before the New Year. She'd always loved Christmas—the lights, the music, the cookies, the parties. As a teenager in Cincinnati, her family had always celebrated a very simple Christmas, putting up the same small fake tree every year and getting each child just a few presents. When Farah became a parent herself, she'd finally had an excuse to go all out for this holiday, although Mark was not religious either.

This was the first year since becoming a mother that she wasn't spending Christmas with the kids. It seemed only fair that if she was going to claim Thanksgiving, her favorite American holiday, he should get Christmas with them. Mark and the kids were in Charlotte, celebrating with his parents. Soraya had pleaded for Farah to go home to Cincinnati for Christmas this year and spend it with them and Parisa and her kids, but Farah had declined, saying that she needed to get ready for her move, reassuring Soraya that she would be okay. And hopefully, she would get to spend Nowruz with at least one of her kids this year.

Nowruz, the Iranian New Year, correlates with the spring equinox. When the kids were growing up, Farah had made a big deal out of Nowruz, trying to impart as much of her culture as she could onto her half-Iranian, half-American kids, feeling the need to compete with the Irish and Italian ancestry they'd gotten from Mark. Growing up in Tehran, Nowruz had been Farah's favorite holiday. It was the only holiday her family celebrated until they moved to the US. Some of her favorite memories were going shopping for her Nowruz outfit, particularly her Nowruz shoes, with her mom. She could still remember peering through the storefront of every shoe store as a kid, her palms on the glass and almost pressing her face to it, excited by shiny patent leather and grosgrain ribbons. Her love of shoes had begun decades before Sarah Jessica Parker, or rather Carrie Bradshaw, had introduced her to Manolo Blahniks in *Sex and the City*. Every Nowruz, she got to buy one pair of new dress-up shoes that lasted her the whole year. They would buy a pair that was half a size too big, so that her feet slipped a little bit in them through the spring and early summer, then fit just right in the fall, and were tight and smooshed her toes by the winter. Farah's kids had never appreciated Nowruz shopping, always having multiples of everything.

Farah would try to make decorating the *haft-seen* table a big event with them each year. When she was pregnant with their first, Mark had bought a pair of cushiony soft, baby-pink shoes and placed them right in the middle of the haft-seen table, in between the goldfish and the hyacinth. Farah had gasped when she'd first seen the shoes, with Darya simultaneously kicking her from the inside, causing Farah to move her hand from covering her mouth to pressing on her right side, where a distinct foot was creating a bulge. She was so emotional in that moment, the shoes being proof that Mark had listened to her childhood stories—remembered them. When the kids were at home, she would let them skip school on Nowruz if they wanted to, which they always did, but once Darya left for college, Nowruz wasn't quite the same either, even if their family was still intact.

The ringtone of her cellphone pulled Farah out of her thoughts, Rumi's face on her screen. Everyone had been calling her more recently, worried about her being alone. Normally, Farah would be sad to be without her family at this time, but she was so relieved to be taking some time off from medicine and going away, that she felt okay. "Hi, honey. How are you enjoying Grandma's?" Farah asked in a chipper voice.

"It's nice being here," Rumi said. "Almost every house in the neighborhood is decorated with Christmas lights, so you would actually love it, Mom. Sorry . . . just, we do miss you."

"Don't be sorry. I'm glad you're enjoying it and I'm sure Grandma Janet is thrilled to have you there. And I am doing just fine. I will probably take up Julia on her offer and go spend part of Christmas Day with her family, so don't worry. I won't be drinking a bottle of wine on my own on my couch."

"That's good, Mom. Definitely go to Julia's. You know, I talked to Baba Behnam the other day," Rumi said.

"You did?" Farah was surprised.

"Yeah. We've been sending each other video links to the protests in Iran. It looks like they are still going strong. Baba Behnam seemed optimistic that things may really change in Iran this time. He said the only thing he wants to see happen before he dies is for there to be another revolution in Iran and the Islamic government to be replaced."

"I'm afraid that I doubt he's going to see that. These uprisings happen every few years in Iran, although this is lasting longer than the other ones. It seems like for once the whole world is watching," Farah said.

"Yeah. I've never seen so many US celebrities talking about Iran. Did you see the YouTube of Jamie Lee Curtis wearing a Mahsa Amini shirt?" Rumi asked.

"Yes. Darya sent it to me."

"Mom, you had to wear a hijab in school before you guys moved here, didn't you?"

"Yes, for a few years."

"How come I've never seen pictures of you in a hijab? You never talk about those years."

Farah was glad this wasn't a FaceTime call. She didn't want Rumi to see how much anxiety this topic gave her. "I'm sure Maman Soraya has pictures of me in a hijab in old albums in Cincinnati. It just wasn't an easy time, so I try to not think about those years too much."

"Can I tell you something, Mom?"

"Sure," Farah said, feeling her heart rate pick up.

"This massive feminist movement is happening in Iran. And I think—actually, I know—that part of why it took me longer to come out was because I've always been a feminist. I felt like saying that I am a guy rather than just trying to be a butch lesbian was somehow anti-feminist or would be perceived that way. I tried to make peace with being a lesbian, but I just couldn't do it. That's not who I am. I'm a straight guy."

"Rumi, thank you for sharing that with me, but we need more straight-guy feminists. We need you to be exactly who you are and be the fierce feminist you are. I'm so proud of you."

"Thanks, Mom. I needed to hear that."

When Farah hung up, she thought about how much we keep from the people we are closest to. She wondered if she would ever be able to share Zareen's story, or Alireza's, or everything else her kids and so many people didn't know about with them. She didn't know, but she was glad she had these next six months to figure it all out.

And she had to figure it all out.

She had put all of it off for too long.

CHAPTER TWENTY

DECEMBER 2012: BROOKLYN, NEW YORK

Crumpled wrapping paper covered the floor. "I'll Be Home for Christmas" was playing in the background, and Farah had just presented Darya and Delara with their last gifts—two identical small rectangular boxes. If it had only snowed, it would have made a picture-perfect morning, but Farah still felt grateful to be home with her family rather than visiting her in-laws in Charlotte for the holidays.

"Okay, open them together," Farah said to her daughters.

They both tore through the shiny gold paper to find a jewelry box. Inside were custom-made necklaces—their names in gold script centered on a pearl chain. "I love it," Darya gasped, but Delara looked disappointed. Farah looked over at Mark, who raised his eyebrows in that *I told you so* manner. Three days before when Farah had been wrapping their presents, she'd shown the necklaces to Mark, telling him she would save those presents for last.

"I don't know about that. You hype the last present every year as the best one, and I don't think Delara is going to like hers," Mark said.

"Why wouldn't she? I would have loved a personalized name necklace at her age."

"Because she's always been a tomboy. She's not the same girl as Darya, you know. Delara has been obsessed with basketball for the last few years. If you wanted to get her a personalized present, you should have ordered a number seven Knicks jersey with her name on it," Mark said.

Farah had put her hands on her hips and looked at Mark. "No one is stopping you from thinking ahead and buying them Christmas presents. This is *your* holiday, but I'm always the one getting them all the presents and putting both of our names on them."

Mark had held up his hands in surrender. "Don't get mad at me because I said I don't think Delara will like it. And don't even pretend that you don't love celebrating '*my holiday*' and buying presents. You've hijacked this holiday just like you have with Thanksgiving."

Farah couldn't believe her ears. "Did you just use the word hijack with me?"

Mark put his hands up again. "Sorry. Poor choice of words. *Very* poor choice of words, but you know what I mean."

"No, I don't. Why don't you spell it out for me?"

"Come on, Farah. Your family has turned Thanksgiving into a Persian holiday. All the *addass polo* and *loobia polo* and *sheereen polo*. Just because you put a turkey in the middle of the table, it doesn't make it Thanksgiving."

"Funny, the way you scarf it all down, I never realized you didn't appreciate us hijacking Thanksgiving," Farah had turned and left the room before Mark could say anything else.

Now, as Delara half-heartedly hugged Farah and thanked her for the presents, Farah wished she had gotten something else for her. "Who's ready for Christmas pancakes?" she singsonged, more in an attempt to cheer herself up.

Later in the day, Farah noticed that only Darya was wearing her necklace. She stroked Delara's cheek and kissed the top of her head. "Do you want me to help you put the necklace on? Did you not like it?" Farah asked.

"No. It's fine, I guess. You know I don't really like jewelry," Delara said.

"I know. I just thought that since this is custom-made with your name, and you have such a beautiful unique name, that you may like it. I can keep it for you for now. You'll probably appreciate it when you're older."

"Mom," Delara seemed hesitant. She looked down at her hands and asked, "What would you have named me if I'd been a boy?"

"Rumi," Farah answered instantly. "That's the name I'd always wanted if I had a son. I don't think it has a meaning in Farsi, but it is the name of one of the greatest Iranian poets. But I didn't have a boy. I had you, my perfect strong sporty girl." She rubbed Delara's head and gave her a hug.

Delara was quiet, so Farah continued. "Delara was not a name I was familiar with. I started looking at girl names that start with a D. I first wanted to go with Donya, which means 'world.' But I just loved the ring of Delara once I came across it. And I can't think of a more perfect name for you now."

Delara squirmed out of the hug. "Do you know any of his poetry by heart?"

"Rumi's poetry? I remember some famous lines . . . 'The wound is the place the light enters you' is one of my favorites. Another is 'We're all just walking each other home.' There are so many. I have a book of his poetry somewhere on one of the bookshelves. I can find it for you if you're interested in Iranian poetry. I also have a couple of books by Hafez. Iran is known for its poets."

"You could have named me Rumi. It would have worked for a girl too," Delara said.

"I could have, but why are you asking all this? Do you suddenly not like your name?" Farah asked.

"No, it's fine. I was just wondering."

Two days later, Farah was cleaning Delara's room, and she found her book of Rumi's poetry under her covers. She sat on Delara's bed, flipped through some of the pages, then put the book back under the covers. She walked to their study and went to the bookshelf. There was a small gap where the book had been removed. The two poetry books by Hafez were still in their place on the shelf.

CHAPTER TWENTY-ONE

JANUARY 2023: PASO ROBLES, CALIFORNIA

Before settling on her new couch, Farah fiddled with the dial on the radio, trying to find the music stations in Paso. She thought, *You know you're officially old if you have to find the oldies station to listen to your favorite eighties music.* Suddenly, she heard a familiar voice singing "Cheeseburger in Paradise" and stopped turning the dial. She hadn't heard Jimmy Buffet in years, and she loved this song. She was clearly not in the city anymore.

Farah felt her body sink into the middle of the maroon velvet couch. She put her feet up on the coffee table, crossed her arms, and surveyed her home for the next six months. She felt like Elizabeth Gilbert on her own version of an *Eat, Pray, Love* adventure—although despite doing the leaving the perfectly good husband part, she had no interest in replicating the "Love" part of Elizabeth's journey. Maybe she was on more of a "Drink, Rest, Be Selfish" journey. Was she being selfish, or would a younger woman consider this self-care?

The Bennet family's guest house was a little larger than her West Village apartment and on twenty-five acres of land. It was surrounded by windows, and other than seeing the main house two acres away, the rest of Farah's view was rows upon rows of grapevines over rolling hills. Farah hadn't ever visited wine country in the winter before, usually coming in the fall or late spring. She hadn't seen the grapevines so bare before, but the bare vines had their own ghostly beauty, with the lanes between the vines fully green at this time of the year.

The tasting room and cellar for the Bennet's vineyard were close to the main road off Highway 46 and could not be seen from Farah's window. The Bennets were a couple in their early sixties who had moved from Seattle to Paso Robles twenty years ago and taken over a small-batch winery, Braxton Vineyards. Their wines could only be purchased through their tasting room or through club membership since they made limited bottles of each varietal and under three thousand cases of wine per year. After taking a few days to settle in, Sarah and Josh Bennet had given Farah a tour of the vineyard, introducing her to everyone who worked for them, other than Miguel, their head winemaker, who was away for a few days. Farah had read *Wine Folly* and *Wine for Normal People* cover to cover in the preceding month in anticipation of her move.

Farah wanted to go to bed early that night. The next day, she would be meeting Miguel, who was back and supposed to give her an overview of their wine-making process. As she lay in bed, her mind started to wander to the first time she had come to Paso Robles with Mark. The kids were ten and eight years old, and her parents had stayed with them. They'd had an incredible three days together. That was the trip when she'd fallen in love with Paso, realizing that going forward, her future California wine-country trips would all be to Paso instead of Napa. Paso had many wineries making biodynamic wines, without all the pretension of Napa. The people were so nice, the tastings were half the price of Napa tastings, and at least prepandemic, you could walk into the best tasting rooms without a prior reservation. The winding roads and views took her breath away.

Farah and Mark had made a pact to make time for getting away together without the kids more often. Yet the minute they'd stepped back into their Brooklyn home, Mark had walked into his office to catch up on work, leaving Farah to figure out dinner for the family. A fight started again. There were so many years when Farah was ready to pounce on Mark for every little thing he did wrong. Farah called these the miniheartbreaks and microdisappointments, a term she thought she should patent, that gradually added up to her leaving for "no reason," as Soraya called it.

One time, she'd been in the shower, listening to a podcast with Cheryl Strayed. It had probably been an episode of *Dear Sugar*. She'd heard Cheryl say, "Just wanting to leave is enough reason to leave. Go because you want to go. Because wanting to leave is enough." It was something like that. She hadn't written down the exact words, since she was in the shower, but she'd hit the thirty seconds back button three times, relistening to the same line, water dripping all over her phone. When she was finally ready to tell Mark she wanted out, she tried her best to summon her inner Cheryl and not let the fact that it was just microdisappointments—not alcoholism, infidelity, or abuse that had gotten her there—make her feel she had to stay. She'd imagined herself writing a letter to Cheryl and saying, "Dear Sugar, for once in my life, I don't want to give a fuck about anyone else but myself. Is that a good reason to leave?" She had pictured Cheryl writing back, "Yes. Leave and live your life like a motherfucker. Love, Sugar."

Now, flashbacks of pointless fights paraded through her mind. How many times had they fought over the division of labor in their home? How many times had she tried to make him understand the concept of emotional labor and how she felt like she took on over 99 percent of it in their marriage? How many times had she taken her exhaustion out on him? But why was she dredging up these old memories? Why was it that every time she got into bed, no matter how tired she was, she couldn't shut down her mind and fall asleep? She finally got up, took a hot shower, and then fell asleep in her bathrobe.

◆

"Miguel," Sarah Bennet called toward the direction of the man walking between the large barrels. The man turned around to face Sarah, holding a small glass in his hand, and smiled from ear to ear. "Sarah, good timing. I was just about to taste the 2021 zin and see if it's ready to start being bottled," Miguel said as Farah took in his accent.

"Great, but I'd like you to meet someone first," Sarah said as they caught up to him. "This is Farah. She's staying in the guest house for a little bit, and she'll be here through the spring."

Miguel extended his hand. "Pleasure to meet you, Farah." He had wavy jet-black hair that fell over his forehead, a dark tan, and his slightly crooked teeth somehow added to his sex appeal. Farah had already heard from one of the tasting room attendants that Miguel was hot, thirty-seven, and single. He was the head winemaker at Braxton now, having been recruited by the Bennets after a trip to Rioja five years earlier. As Farah shook his hand, she was surprised at how rough it felt. She broke his gaze to look down and see all the calluses and cracks on his hand.

"Farah is very eager to learn about the wine-making process and our wines from the master himself, so if today's still a good day, maybe you can show her around," Sarah said. "But first, let me go grab a couple of other tasting glasses so we can all try the zin."

"So, how long have you been working at Braxton?" Farah asked Miguel, pretending that she hadn't already gotten the low-down on him.

"Five years now. I hadn't ever heard of Paso when I was in Rioja, and here I am. What brings you here?"

"Um . . ." Farah paused awkwardly, and Sarah arrived with the extra glasses just in time, handing one to Farah.

"You want to do the honors, Miguel?" Sarah asked.

"Sure. Before we taste, what do you already know about zinfandel, Farah?"

Damn, that accent and those eyes, Farah thought, and then blinked and turned to Sarah. "I know it's also called Primitivo. It's usually very fruity, and thick or jammy. I guess that's all I know. It's generally not one of my favorite varietals, if I'm being honest. It's too thick for me."

"Ah," Miguel said, as he turned the spout on a large barrel and poured half an ounce into a glass that he handed to Farah. "Try this and tell me what you think." He then poured a taste for Sarah and himself.

Farah swirled her wine, took a sniff, and then tasted it as Sarah and Miguel did the same. "Wow, I get the fruit—blackberry—and some spice . . . maybe clove. But I like it. It's definitely not thick or overly jammy."

Miguel smiled broadly and Farah felt a rush of excitement, like she had just passed some test and her handsome teacher was giving her a gold star, except she was fifteen years older than her teacher and not in fifth grade anymore. "Exactly. Not too thick or jammy. You've been drinking the wrong zinfandel. Zin in Paso is something else."

"I'm going to leave you two to it," Sarah said and walked back toward the tasting room.

"Now this has been in neutral French oak for a year. We'll start bottling it soon, and it will be ready to hit our tasting room in the fall of 2023. It's still too young, but another few months will make a big difference, although you could also lay it down for five to ten years before drinking it," Miguel continued.

"I'll be back in New York by then, so I guess I'll have to make a trip back for it," Farah said, getting lost in her own thoughts for a few seconds, imagining herself back at the hospital next fall.

"So, you never said what brings you here?" Miguel asked again.

"Oh," Farah waved her hand. "Ah . . . long story. I fell in love with Paso years ago and I just needed a change of pace, so here I am. So anyway, do you still really stomp the grapes, or is that all done by machine these days?"

"Not everywhere does, but we do. We put on thigh-high rubber boots and do a gentle stomp before feeding the clusters through the crusher and stemmer. The boots, they're not exactly the type of thigh-highs women like to wear to seduce men, but on the right person, they don't look so bad."

Farah once again felt grateful for her inability to blush. *Is he flirting with me?* "Now, no cheating on this question. Who makes your favorite GSM in Paso?" Farah playfully asked. GSM—Grenache, Syrah, Mourvèdre—was a blend that Farah knew Paso is known for. The diurnal temperature patterns in Paso made it ideal for growing the Rhone varietals.

Miguel laughed. "I'm not going to let you get me in trouble. Of course, we have the best GSM—I'm the winemaker. But thanks to me, Braxton makes a unique wine that I'm willing to bet you have never had before." He raised an eyebrow.

I'm not imagining it. He's flirting! "Hmm, what's that?" She felt herself cocking her head to the right and brushing her hair behind her right ear.

"We make a sparkling Carignan."

"Well, if I'm going to be honest, I'm not generally a fan of sparkling wines, but maybe this will surprise me like the zin. I'll have to try it," she smiled.

◆

Farah walked into her guesthouse, carrying the half-empty bottle of sparkling Carignan they'd had together, and a loud hiccup escaped again. They had started a half hour prior, reminding her of exactly why she didn't like sparkling wines, particularly on an empty stomach. She'd been so embarrassed, each loud hiccup being so unsexy and making Miguel laugh. It was for the best. The hiccups had been like a wake-up call and a warning to stop flirting. What was she thinking? When she was ready to date or have some casual sex, it could not be with someone who worked for the Bennets. And when she was ready to get naked in front of someone again, it certainly couldn't be someone significantly younger until she had some practice and regained some confidence. She hadn't been on a first date since 1993.

CHAPTER TWENTY-TWO

DECEMBER 1992: DURHAM, NORTH CAROLINA

Walking out of the anatomy summative exam, Farah had a big smile on her face. She didn't ever have to step back into the lab or smell like a cadaver again. Farah was never a bath person, so that day, she took an extra-long shower instead, shampooing and rinsing her hair twice, replacing the smell of formaldehyde with the smell of Pantene. Two days prior, she'd splurged on name-brand shampoo over generic in anticipation of this shower, something she hadn't done since starting college. She looked through her closet to pick out an outfit for the postsummative party and settled on her black bell bottoms paired with a white blouse with bell sleeves. The seventies style was back in, and Farah wished she had access to some of Soraya's old clothes that she'd had to leave behind in Tehran along with everything else. When she was done getting ready, she looked at herself in the full-length mirror in her chunky strappy black platforms and winged eyeliner. She looked like Soraya in her twenties, just with darker skin.

Farah walked to the party arm-in-arm with Bridget and Neesha. They'd had a shot of vodka in Farah's apartment before heading out, and Farah was already feeling it. The party was at Chris Kapetan's apartment. He lived in a three-bedroom with five other guys from medical school. It was like he'd tried to create a mini frat house in medical school. Farah was talking to a group of classmates when she went to take a sip of her third screwdriver from the Solo cup she was holding and noticed she'd finished it. She headed to the bar—a table in the kitchen covered with juices, cheap vodka and tequila, and plastic cups. A keg sat in the corner.

As she poured some orange juice into her cup, she heard an unfamiliar voice. "Hey, congrats on your exam being over. I'm guessing your other anatomy test went okay too," Mark said.

Farah looked up at him, "Do I know . . . oh . . . coffee shop guy. What are you doing here?"

"My friend Alok knows one of the guys throwing this party. He asked if I wanted to come along. And, I don't know if I should say this, but I hoped that I'd run into you."

"Oh, great. Well, I'm glad you did. What was your name again?" She was surprised to be asking him, but maybe Bridget and Neesha were right. Maybe he was cute. Or more likely she'd just had too much to drink. And if this guy still remembered her—that was a little creepy . . . or was that cute, too? The room started spinning around her. "Um, I think I need to sit down." She flopped on the floor, spilling her full cup all over herself. "Oh, fuck!" She yanked her shirt off and lay down on the floor in just her bra and pants, half asleep.

"Um." Mark looked around and then took off his sweater and covered her with it. He gently shook her shoulder. "Hey, let's try to get my sweater on you and get you home. Who did you come here with?"

Farah groaned, "I'm fine. I don't want to go home. I just need a little nap. Or food. Fries. I need fries."

"Okay, well, did you come with your friends from the coffee shop? I saw them on the balcony earlier."

"Yes. My friends. I love Neesha. And Bridget. I love Bridget too. I love all my friends."

"Great. Don't move. Don't go anywhere. Take your nap. I'll go find them," Mark said. When Farah didn't respond, Mark looked around and tapped another girl on the shoulder. "Hey, can you watch my friend for a second? Make sure she doesn't move. I'm going to find her friends and get her home."

"Farah!" the girl looked down at the floor. "Yeah, okay."

Mark ran out of the kitchen and went to the balcony. Bridget and Neesha were there, each with a Solo cup in hand, talking to a big group. Mark walked up to Neesha. "Hey, not sure if you remember me. I'm Mark—"

"Coffee shop guy? I do remember you," Neesha smiled.

"Your friend, she's not doing great. She's lying down in the kitchen. If you give me your address, I can walk her home safely, maybe get some food in her stomach."

Neesha opened her mouth to respond, and Bridget immediately jumped in. "Wait. You seem like a nice guy, but we are not giving you her address and letting you walk our girlfriend home." Bridget glared at Neesha, who just shrugged her shoulders. "The two of us will leave and walk her home."

Mark led them to the kitchen, where Farah was sitting on the floor now, holding her head in her hands, his sweater draped over her shoulders.

"Farah!" Bridget said. "What happened to your shirt?"

"She spilled her drink. That's my sweater," Mark said.

"Oh boy!" Neesha said. "Tell you what, Mark. Give me your phone number. I'll make sure she calls you when she's sober and get your sweater back to you."

The next morning, Neesha insisted that Farah call Mark. Farah picked up the phone receiver and dialed the number. An answering machine message came on: "You've reached Doug, Mark, and Alok. We're not here. Leave a message."

"Hi. This is Farah calling for Mark. Just wanted to thank you for helping me last night, giving me your sweater . . . and getting my friends. So, thanks." She hung up. She was not going to apologize for being a drunken mess.

"Farah!" Neesha groaned. "You didn't leave your callback number. Call him back and leave it."

"If he really wants to find me, he can. How many Farahs are at Duke med school? And he knows I know Kapetan." She turned away from the phone and walked to the fridge.

CHAPTER TWENTY-THREE

JANUARY 2023: PASO ROBLES, CALIFORNIA

Just as Farah was about to leave the guesthouse, her phone rang with Darya's ringtone. "Hi Mom, how's it going in wine country?"

"Great. I'm just about to leave to go to the tasting room. I'm learning how to be an attendant today. How have you been? Wait, why are you calling me at five thirty in the morning your time?"

"That sounds fun, and I'm not calling you at five thirty. We're in the same time zone now, remember? I was calling to ask you about Kurds in Iran. I'm sure you know that Mahsa was a Kurdish Iranian?"

"Yes, I saw that."

"I've been reading about the treatment of Kurds in Iran, and how even though all ethnic minorities are supposed to have equal rights, that's not really the case. Do you remember anything about their treatment when you lived there, both before and after the revolution?"

Farah had to stop herself from sighing. Although she had come to Paso to be able to figure everything out, this wasn't what she wanted to think about today. "I don't remember much, bunny. I do remember that it seemed people generally looked down on Kurds, but these would be better questions for your grandparents. Why don't you call Baba Behnam? I'm sure he would love to talk to you about this." Farah was relieved to have come up with an answer that was both the truth and got her out of this conversation so she could head out.

When Farah arrived at the tasting room at nine, Stephanie

was already there, sleeves rolled up and showing her yoga-toned, tattooed forearms, wiping any water spots off each wineglass as she took it out of the dishwasher rack. "Good morning," Farah said to Stephanie with a big smile on her face.

"Someone looks excited," Stephanie said.

"I am excited. I've always thought that being a tasting room attendant seems like fun."

"It certainly can be. Let's get started. As you know, we have the classic and the deluxe tasting. We're going to go through everything you need to know about both today, and some of the bonus pours we are doing this month. I've already opened one of every bottle to allow it to breathe before that first ten o'clock tasting. I figured I'd wait for you to see if any of the bottles are corked."

"Great. Did you already smell the corks?" Farah had noticed how the sommelier at a restaurant always smelled the cork of a bottle they opened before setting the cork down on the table. In her reading on wine, she had learned that this is to detect TCA taint, which would give a funky damp basement or wet cardboard smell, indicating a possible corked bottle.

"Yes, I did smell the corks. They were all fine. Today we'll go through the tasting together, and then you'll shadow me for the morning and see what questions come up both from you and what people ask me. I'll have you shadow Jake and Andrea after that, so you get a sense of how each of our styles differs while talking about the same wines. I'll send you home with some reading material, and tomorrow, you'll try it yourself—with me by your side for your first few. What do you think?" Stephanie asked.

"I'm a little nervous about getting it right, but if I mess up, what's the worst that can happen? No baby ends up in the NICU. No mother bleeds out." Farah shrugged her shoulders.

"Right," Stephanie responded with a raised eyebrow. "Let's start with the first white on our classic flight, a Clairette Blanche. Why don't you pour us each a little taste and tell me what you think."

Farah picked up the bottle and poured a splash in each of their glasses. First, she raised her glass to look at the color. It was very light, a pale hay she thought. Next, she swirled the wine and buried her nose in it, taking a deep sniff. "Hmmm. I get a little apricot, and a light floral scent too." Then she took a small sip, swirling it on the tip of her tongue before moving it to the back of her tongue and letting it sit there a few seconds before swallowing. "It's dry, crisp, a smooth finish, the taste is a little more golden apple with maybe a hint of honey?" Farah asked.

"Okay, now look at what the description on the tasting sheet is," Stephanie said with an amused look on her face.

Farah looked at the sheet and read. "Ninety-two percent Clairette Blanche. Eight percent Picpoul. Stone fruit and magnolia." She had gotten the apricot right. It was a stone fruit.

"Some attendants will basically read the description for people, but I don't like to do that. I like to give them a chance to smell and taste without influencing them by telling them what they should smell and taste. Hold on," Stephanie walked over to the end of the bar and grabbed a map of Paso. "We're here, in the Adelaida district. For this wine, we grow all the grapes right here on our own property. We only have a couple of wines for which we source grapes from other districts, and I'll get to those and show you where they are on the map. Some people won't have any questions for you. Other people will want to show off their wine knowledge to you and ask you a hundred questions, so you'll want to be able to answer them as confidently as you can while flattering them on their wine knowledge and boosting their ego."

"I guess there's no escaping having to boost certain people's ego in any job," Farah said.

"Unfortunately not. Of course, there are some people who will ask you a lot of questions because they genuinely do want to learn more about wine. You'll learn to tell them apart from the others in no time. They tend to be the best tippers too."

Farah thought about how she had never had a job where she made tips or was even what might be called fun, for that matter.

During her undergraduate years, she had done research in science labs, hoping it would enhance her chances of getting into a good medical school. In high school, she had done some babysitting to make extra pocket money. Soraya didn't believe in giving them an allowance and didn't want them to have a part-time job at the mall. Thinking back, she realized that residency had likely been the most fun job she'd had, despite the grueling hours.

Farah had been a resident before the "eighty-hour rule" was instituted, a regulation that said residents should work no more than eighty hours in a week and no more than thirty hours in a row. Doctors who trained before the eighty-hour rule often distinguished themselves from those who trained after it was instituted, wearing it as a badge of honor. Despite the inhumane hours she'd worked during residency, she loved that time in her life. There was an immediate sisterhood among her and her female coresidents, all strong and determined young women in a field dedicated to taking care of other women. There were a couple of men in her program, but over the years, OBGYN had become the most female-dominated specialty. She thought about how someone should make a TV drama about a group of OBGYN residents.

Once they had gone through both the classic and deluxe flight wines, Stephanie walked Farah through some of the reserve wines they used as bonus pours for people who seemed to be really enjoying their experience and may be convinced to sign up for a membership. "Getting people to buy two bottles to waive their tasting fee is great, but membership signups are what ultimately keeps us afloat," Stephanie said. "So, let's go through all the perks that come with your Braxton membership." As Stephanie enumerated the perks—the free tastings, the 20 percent discount, the exclusive members-only bottles, the pick-up parties, the free entries to the summer concert series, and the discounted winemaker's dinners—Farah realized that she and Mark hadn't discussed their wine club memberships. He had probably either canceled them or changed the delivery address to his new apartment, since he was the one who got the emails about the shipments. She wondered if there may be other little things he took care of that she hadn't noticed.

"Farah?" Stephanie broke Farah's train of thought. "You ready to shadow me on a couple of tastings now, or do you need a break?"

"No, no break needed. I'm ready." She smiled.

That evening, Farah got herself a glass of water and sat on her couch, the Braxton binder with all the information on their wines, the history of the winery, and some general information about Paso Robles wine country on her lap. Despite spitting most of the wine she'd tried into the spittoon, she had no desire to taste another sip of wine that night. Observing Jake and Andrea as attendants after she'd followed Stephanie on a few tastings, Farah took note of each of their styles—how they described the wines, how they handled questions, and how effective they were at making their membership pitches. She was glad that she was just there to be extra help on busy weekends. As she studied her binder, she realized that she hadn't studied since she took her first OBGYN board exam. The person who had cried tears of joy when she had passed her boards would never have guessed that one day she would voluntarily put it aside and study wine.

The next day, after Stephanie observed Farah on a tasting, she said, "That was pretty good for your first try. I think maybe you were born to do this! You're ready to go and do the next one on your own."

Farah had just poured the third wine in the deluxe tasting, the Shadow—a Petite Syrah, cab franc, and zinfandel blend—when she got the first comment that surprised her. "I get a hint of dead ant taste in this. But in a good way. Dead ant on asphalt," a middle-aged man remarked.

"Interesting. This is the first I've heard of that tasting note, but I can see how the mix of blackberry and gravel could create that same profile," Farah said. If this guy was trying to throw her off, she was not going to let him win.

"So how did your winemaker decide what percentage of each varietal to use in this blend, and does it change from vintage to vintage?"

he asked, removing his sunglasses to make direct eye contact.

"I'm not sure. I'm new here, and to Paso, so let me ask and get back to you," Farah said, smiling sweetly.

"How long have you been here? Where did you come from?"

"Just a couple of months. From the Midwest . . . Ohio," Farah replied. It wasn't exactly a lie.

"Ohio? And what did you do there—"

"Carl, what's with all the questions? Let her get to her other tables," the woman sitting next to him said, gently slapping his arm. Farah presumed she was his wife, or maybe his girlfriend.

"That's okay. I was an accountant. An accountant in Ohio. All those years of numbers. My kids went to college and here I am. I'll be back shortly with your answer and your next wine." Farah excused herself. *Why did you lie?* she asked herself.

Because if you tell anyone you were a doctor in New York who left for this, they'd think you're crazy. Farah heard Soraya's voice in her head.

She shook her head and Soraya's voice out of it. No one knew her here and they were all passing through. She could be whoever she wanted to be. Maybe she would try a different identity each day until she figured out which one she would truly like to explore.

CHAPTER TWENTY-FOUR

JULY 1984: TEHRAN, IRAN

Sitting next to Alireza, Farah was deep in her own thoughts, not really listening to what he was saying. It was the night before she was to fly to Turkey and then on to America, and although Zareen was still in Evin Prison, Farah was glad that her family's leaving had not been delayed. In America, she could be a completely new person. She could distract herself with everything America had to offer, until Zareen was released.

Surely, she would be.

Alireza faced Farah, looking directly into her eyes and swiping away a lock of hair from her forehead, forcing Farah out of her thoughts. They had snuck to the basement of the building for some privacy to say goodbye. They sat on an old Persian rug, one of the items that had been brought down to make the damp space more comfortable since the air raids started. Alireza had brought a tape recorder, and Googoosh's haunting lyrics from her song "Do Panjereh" spoke to them, whispering about what might be, if only they lived in another world.

Alireza sang along with the lyrics to "Two Windows" and said, "I hope you don't forget about me. This will be our song. Every time you hear it, try to remember me trapped on this side of the world."

"I am not going to forget about you! And I don't need a song to remember you. We'll see each other again. You know, I think this is the first time we've been down here not because of an air raid," Farah said, looking around at the space and changing the subject.

"Yeah. No more air raids for you, unless there is one tonight. And I'm not so sure we'll see each other again. This could very well be the last time," Alireza said. He put his arm around Farah, and she leaned into him. This was as intimate as they had dared to get with each other. The first time Farah had felt him slowly sneak an arm around and felt his hand on her shoulder, her heart had beaten so hard that she was afraid he would be able to hear it. She still felt shivers down her spine every time he reached for her hand, rubbing the back of her hand with his thumb as he held it.

Farah turned to him, initiated reaching for his hand for the first time, and looked directly into his eyes, which were so dark she could barely make out his pupils. "I'm sure your family will leave Iran too. So many people are finding ways to leave. Hopefully we'll see each other in America next. Maybe we'll even go to the same school together again someday, the way we used to. In America, we can walk in the school hallways holding hands."

Alireza snickered and withdrew his hand. "These are crazy pipe dreams you have. It's different for men. I'm never going to be able to leave this place. The only way I can ever leave is if I try to smuggle through the border to Turkey, and I don't know that I'll ever be brave enough to do that."

Farah knew what he said was probably true. Her family was fortunate that her father had obtained a green card years ago, before the revolution, while he was doing his medical residency training in the US. She felt guilty that she was so excited to be moving to America while Alireza's future in Iran was so uncertain. Would he get accepted to a good program at the University of Tehran one day, or would he have to enlist? Hopefully the war would be over before he was old enough to have to enlist. She wanted to cheer him up. She leaned into him, resting her head on his shoulder, inhaling his scent to commit it to her memory—a mix of sweat and musky cologne. "I promise we'll see each other again. Your parents will find a way for you to leave, and if they don't, it's not like I'm never coming back. I'm sure that even if my family doesn't move back when the war is done, we'll visit. All our family is here."

"Move back?" Alireza laughed again, shaking his head. "No one who manages to get out of this country is going to move back. War or no war. Not as long as Khomeini and all the stupid mullahs are in power. And you're kidding yourself if you think they're going anywhere."

"Okay," Farah conceded, reaching for his hand again and forcing him to look in her eyes. "You're right. Maybe the Islamic Revolution isn't going anywhere anytime soon. But I will promise you that I will still visit. This is where I was born. Iran is in my blood, in my soul. It will always be a part of me."

Alireza let go of her hand and cupped her face with both of his hands instead, leaning close to her, placing his lips gently on hers.

CHAPTER TWENTY-FIVE

FEBRUARY 2023: PASO ROBLES, CALIFORNIA

The morning fog was so dense and low that it hovered just above the grapevines, making them barely visible. Farah opened her front door and stepped outside. She'd made a promise to herself to try meditating for just ten minutes per day. She was in Paso to face her past and find a way forward, but she hadn't done anything toward that goal yet. Maybe meditation would help. How many times over the years had she heard about the benefits of meditation? And yet she'd never truly tried to make it a regular practice. She always considered running her meditation and therapy, but she knew running was not a real substitution for either. There was something to be said for just trying to be still for ten minutes a day. Three minutes in savasana was as much stillness as she had ever been able to achieve, and that was because she was usually a sweaty, exhausted mess by the end of a sixty-minute power-yoga flow, the only type of yoga practice she ever did.

A couple of times Farah had tried to do the Oprah and Deepak Chopra free twenty-one-day meditation challenge. She'd listened to Oprah's soothing voice followed by Deepak's, and sat and tried to clear her head, repeatedly saying the mantra Deepak had presented for that day. Both times that she'd attempted this challenge, by day four, she'd come to feel stressed about having to get her session in, growing irritated by the same voices that soothed her on day one.

And then there was the time she'd gone to this one-hour sound bath event with Julia. They found themselves on the apartment terrace of a woman in the city. The three-hundred-square-foot terrace was covered with rugs and patterned cushions. Two shirtless young men with hairless chiseled chests wearing harem pants and turbans sat with giant sound bowls in front of them. About twenty people piled onto the terrace, finding a spot where they could lie down or sit. Julia and Farah decided to go to opposite sides of the terrace, so they wouldn't make each other laugh. Farah had to admit that she'd enjoyed that hour, the sounds making her body feel like it was vibrating out of her head. But the whole time as she lay there, she couldn't stop asking herself how in God's name this woman could afford an apartment with this size terrace in the city? What did her husband or partner do? How did anyone in New York City afford their apartments? Why had she become a doctor, when clearly people in New York were crazy enough to pay a hundred dollars to lie on someone's balcony for an hour and hear two guys bang some bowls. I mean, sure, the guys were hot despite their ridiculous outfits, but your eyes were closed the entire time anyway. She never went back. Although she had enjoyed the vibration in her body, she'd felt mad at herself for her random thoughts and felt that much like goat yoga, this was a gimmicky activity you only needed to experience once.

Now in Paso, she rolled out her yoga mat facing the vineyard and sat in lotus position. She set a timer on her phone for ten minutes. When she was ready, she hit the start button and closed her eyes.

Just breathe, she told herself. *Big breath in, big breath out. Inhale, exhale. There, that's not so bad. You're doing it. Look at you. Who needs Chopra or Oprah? And you know they get something for this "free" service they provide. They probably get sponsors and sell more things and it's not so altruistic, is it? Wait, stop. Stop thinking. Breathe only.*

She inhaled and exhaled for about twenty seconds before she found herself thinking about what she would do as soon as the ten minutes were up. She caught herself again. Damn it. *Okay, maybe I'll keep saying oms. Maybe that will work. Om… Om… Om…. I wonder how many minutes it has been. No, you can't open your eyes and check your phone. It doesn't matter. Om ... inhale ... Om ... exhale.* She stilled her mind for less than thirty seconds before she suddenly remembered a guy in her yoga class. His mat would always make these distracting fart-type sounds when he got super sweaty and the mat got wet. It was really quite annoying. She was glad there were no farting sounds now. It was noticeably very quiet out. Very peaceful. She tried to focus on if she could hear anything at all. Nothing. And then before she knew it, her phone dinged. She opened her eyes. She had achieved stillness, even if just for a little bit. She was proud of herself. "I'll be back tomorrow," she said to the mat, to the outdoors, to the grapevines, to herself.

She walked back inside and placed her rolled-up yoga mat in the corner. She turned on the shower to allow the water to warm up a little while she undressed. As she waited, she examined her naked body in the full-length mirror on the bathroom door. Her body was looking stronger already in the short time she had been in Paso. At five foot four and about one hundred twenty-five pounds, she was thin and toned thanks to all her running and yoga, but her brown skin lacked the elasticity of youth. No matter how religious she had always been with sunscreen, not so much because she worried about skin cancer, but because she didn't want her skin to get any darker than it already was, it still wasn't the same. Despite the muscles underneath, her thighs were dimpled and full of nooks and crannies.

I have English muffin thighs, she thought.

She ran her hand over her C-section scar and cupped her breasts. They sagged but not terribly. Every time she saw her breasts, she couldn't help but think of how Rumi had removed his just before going to college. She remembered sitting in the plastic surgeon's office with whom she still saw as her baby girl Delara in her mind sometimes, despite calling him Rumi for over two years at that point—despite sitting in court and hearing a judge declare his new legal name. Dr. Cohen had taken the last of Rumi's dressings off and then turned him around to face the mirrors. Rumi's face beamed in a way Farah hadn't seen since childhood when he saw his chest masculinized for the first time after the dressings came off. In that moment, Farah truly saw her son. She knew that they had made the right decision.

Farah stepped into the shower and took a few deep inhales and exhales, still feeling grateful about her morning and the few seconds she had managed to clear her head. She tilted her head back and let the warm water run over her body. She opened her eyes and ran her fingers over the white subway tiles of the shower. When she and Mark had renovated their Brooklyn home, they had wanted to save money where they could, so they had chosen a simple gray subway tile, but then had it installed in a herringbone pattern rather than in horizontal rows to make it look more interesting. She thought about all the decisions she and Mark had made together, from simply picking out a tile to consenting to their teen's top surgery. She was happy to feel like she was in charge of making decisions on her own for the first time in her life, but she did miss having someone to hold her hand through the ones she was unsure of.

When she stepped out of the shower, Farah saw that she had missed a group text between her sisters and mother, initiated by Azita, with a link to a video and three sobbing emojis attached. She sat on her couch and clicked on the link.

Jill Biden walked out onto the stage at the Grammy Awards in a floor-length fitted gold-sequin dress, everything covered other than her shoulders, which glistened. She was holding an envelope and started to speak. "A song can unite, inspire, and ultimately change the world . . ." After speaking some more, she went on to announce that she was honored to be announcing the first-ever "Best Song for Social Change Award" to Shervin Hajipour for the song "Baraye." As Dr. Biden said the song's name, the camera panned out to Harry Styles clapping. Then she went on to say how the song had become the anthem for the Mahsa Amini protests, a call for freedom and women's rights. The song played as Shervin's face came up on the screen behind Biden. Farah realized that millions of viewers across America were hearing Farsi lyrics, likely for the first time in their lives. She broke down in tears, which turned into heaving sobs.

CHAPTER TWENTY-SIX

SEPTEMBER 1984: CINCINNATI, OHIO

A voice came over the speaker. "Please stand up for the pledge of allegiance."

Farah noticed all her classmates get up, placing a hand over their hearts. She did the same as she listened to them recite the words. Then everyone sat down, and a series of announcements followed. When they were done, Mrs. Stevens walked to the front of the room. "Welcome to your first day of high school, class. As you probably know based on your schedules, we'll have homeroom here every morning for fifteen minutes before moving on to your first class." Then she looked around and spotted Farah.

"Why don't you come on up here to the front of the class." Mrs. Stevens changed her pace, enunciating every word slowly as she pointed to Farah and then pointed to a spot by herself, as if Farah needed both her slow speaking and her hand gestures to understand her.

Farah pushed back her chair and stood up, feeling like every eye was on her as she walked toward the front of the class and stood beside Mrs. Stevens.

"Class, we have a new student in our district this year from another country. This is Farah Afshar. She is from Iraq."

"No," Farah said in her English, which had a moderate accent. "I'm from Iran."

"Oh, that's right," Mrs. Stevens corrected. "She is from Iran.

Iran. Iraq. The Middle East. But I believe Iran is the one where that hostage crisis was a few years ago. Why don't you tell the class a little bit about yourself."

It was the first time that Farah wished she could just disappear, be invisible—the first time she had felt shame at who she was. "My family moved here two months ago from Tehran. I have two younger sisters, and my father is an endocrinologist. I love listening to music and reading." She heard a snicker from the back of the class.

"Wow, your English is very good," Mrs. Stevens said while she continued to enunciate each word. "I'm going to have Jennifer show you how your locker works and walk you to your first class. I know our high school may be overwhelming to you." Mrs. Stevens gestured toward Jennifer, who rolled her eyes.

"That won't be necessary. I got a school tour yesterday," Farah said and walked back to her seat. She kept her eyes on the schedule in front of her until the bell rang and she could walk to her next class.

Her first period was Algebra I. As Farah flipped through the textbook the teacher handed her, she realized she had learned all of this in seventh grade in Iran. At least she would ace the tests. Then she felt the person behind her tapping on her shoulder. She turned around and faced a pimple-faced, skinny brown-haired boy with braces.

"Nice outfit. You're at school, not a dinner party," the boy said, laughing.

Farah's face burned. She had taken so much care choosing her pencil skirt, blouse, and kitten heels. She turned away from the boy, looked down at her desk, and untucked her hair from behind her ears in an attempt to hide her face in case her eyes welled with tears.

"Hey. Shut up, doofus," Farah heard a voice say.

"Fuck you, Jared," the pimple-faced boy said to the voice.

Then the voice turned to Farah and said, "Just ignore him. He's an idiot." Farah looked up to see a boy with a chiseled jaw and thick straw-colored hair that waved over his forehead. His hazel eyes were piercing. He was better looking than John Travolta as Danny Zuko in *Grease*, her favorite movie. She gave him a half smile and turned back to her textbook. Maybe this wouldn't be terrible.

When she walked into her second-period class, US History, she looked at the American flag hanging by the chalkboard and the posters of all the presidents around the room. Just as the bell for the start of class rang, Jared walked in with two beautiful girls who truly did look like Barbies and took a seat a few rows behind her. The teacher, Mr. Mead, introduced himself and started going over the course syllabus. It seemed that he had no intention of wasting any time on the first day, so he began with his first lesson. Within a few minutes, he said, "To be the president of the US, you have to be born a US citizen. So, for example, our new student Farah over here, could never be president."

Farah couldn't believe her ears. He had singled her out in front of everyone, in front of Jared, who was turned around in his chair and looking at her. Why had she looked forward to moving to America? She didn't belong here. She wondered if she ever would.

CHAPTER TWENTY-SEVEN

FEBRUARY 2023: PASO ROBLES, CALIFORNIA

When Farah opened her eyes, she was surprised to see that it was getting dark outside. She'd laid on the couch to take a twenty-minute afternoon nap and then get ready for a potluck she was invited to, but if it was getting dark, it had probably been at least an hour since she'd fallen asleep. She sat up on the couch, stretched her arms out, and picked up her phone from the coffee table.

Seeing a missed call from Rumi, her heart started racing. Had he called to talk about Iran again or was something else wrong? Rumi hardly ever called just to catch up. Every once in a while, he would initiate a "love you" Bitmoji text to Farah instead of the other way around, and that was enough for Farah to know that he had thought of her and was happy and well.

She went to call him back and noticed her hands shaking. She forced herself to take a moment, steady her breath and her hands, and then pressed the call button. "Hi honey, I had a missed call from you. Is everything all right?" She tried to sound relaxed.

"Yeah, Mom. Everything is fine. I was just calling to talk. Catch up. How's it going out in wine country?"

"It's been great." Farah's shoulders relaxed. "The days go by surprisingly fast. I've been working in the tasting rooms some, and it's been fun. I miss you. I know that if I was in New York, I wouldn't be seeing you anyway, but somehow being more miles away makes me miss you more. It feels different. How are things going with you?"

"Pretty great. Classes are going well. I did go on a couple of dates with a new girl, so we'll see," Rumi said.

"Oh great. What's her name? Where is she from?"

"Jackie. She's sort of from your new side of town. She's from Portland."

Farah felt a sense of relief when she heard "Portland." To her knowledge, people from Portland were fairly liberal and open-minded. Certainly, a young adult would be. "And..." Farah questioned.

"And... I know what you really want to know, Mom. She doesn't know. At least I don't think she does. I'm going to give it one more date and then I'll tell her. It will be fine," Rumi reassured.

Farah knew that the question of when to disclose that he was transgender to people he met was Rumi's decision and his alone, but Farah still always worried about how people would react to him when they found out. Thanks to his Middle Eastern half, the testosterone injections had given him fairly full facial hair, so he always passed, despite his small stature. When putting in his dorm requests for Oberlin, Rumi had purposely asked not to be in the LGBTQ dorm, wanting to just room with other guys and experience what that would be like. It had made Farah very nervous. When one month into his freshman year, he had informed his three suitemates at Oberlin, they'd all been surprised, but much to Farah's relief, none of them cared. Farah knew that at some point, she had to stop projecting all her own fears onto Rumi and trust his judgment on if and when to disclose the trans part of his identity to others.

"Anyway, Mom. There is another reason why I called you. Don't worry, it's not bad," Rumi continued. "I just came from visiting Dad for a couple of days."

What? Farah had been so busy the last few days that she hadn't checked her friend finder, completely missing Rumi's location being in New York instead of Oberlin. "Oh, that must have been nice. I'm sure he loved getting to see you. How was he? Did you guys have a good time?" Farah tried to sound nonchalant.

"Yeah. It was nice. He . . . well . . . I wanted to tell you . . . He is dating someone. He has a new girlfriend. I met her." Rumi waited for Farah to respond, but she was quiet. "Anyway, I just wanted you to hear it from me. She seemed nice and Dad looked good. And I don't know how serious it is, but he did ask if I'd like to meet her and I said yes . . . because, you know, you should both be happy, Mom. You both deserve to be happy."

"Okay," Farah realized she had been holding her breath and took a deep one. "I'm a little surprised, I guess. It feels early, but obviously, I knew this would happen at some point. And I guess it's not really so early. And I'm glad you told me. Thank you. And you know your father is a great person and he does deserve to be happy . . . and I'm glad that you are having a good time in college and meeting people. And I don't know if I say this enough, but I'm really proud of you and I know it doesn't always seem like it, but I do trust you to make decisions about yourself and who should know what . . . and I'm just your mom, so I guess my job is just to find something to worry about, but I'm going to keep trying to get better at that. And I miss you and I love it when I hear from you . . . but when I don't hear from you, that's okay too. It means you are busy and doing well and that's all I want for you." Now she was just trying to blurt out what she needed to say without crying on the phone to Rumi.

The truth was that she was stunned, and she was hurt. She had hoped that Mark would have told her if he was going to introduce people he was dating to the kids. And it did feel like he was moving on fast if he was in a serious enough relationship to introduce someone to the kids. She resisted the urge to ask Rumi how old Mark's new girlfriend seemed to be and what she did. Farah hoped that Mark wasn't dating some thirty-five-year-old who would want to have kids. He wouldn't be stupid enough to do that, would he?

When the call was done, she got off the couch and went to look out the window, looking at the view to calm her mind. Who was the person he was dating? And who else knew about it? Did Julia's husband Ethan know? And if Ethan knew, had he told Julia? And if Ethan knew and had told Julia, was Julia keeping it from her? She grabbed her phone off the nightstand to text Julia and then stopped. A text to Julia would lead to an hour-long conversation. She had to get ready for her dinner. If this thing with the new girlfriend became serious, she would eventually hear more about it. And she couldn't bring Julia and Ethan into this. She had promised herself she would not become that person who forced friends into taking sides and put them into uncomfortable positions. Rumi had trusted and done the courtesy of forewarning her. That would have to be enough for now. She left the view and walked to the bedroom to get dressed.

◆

The long walnut dining table was covered with every type of food in mismatched serving dishes brought by each guest. Blythe, the host, had made a flatbread with pear, gorgonzola, and bacon. Farah had decided to bring her favorite Iranian dish, *albaloo polo*: sour cherry rice with toasted slivered almonds and saffron chicken. She hadn't cooked an Iranian meal since the last time both kids had been home, and surprisingly, not being in a time crunch, she had enjoyed the process.

Candles in various thicknesses and heights, hydrangeas in short vases, wine glasses, water goblets, and silverware filled the table. Farah had Julia to thank for this invitation. From across the states, Julia had contacted her friend Amanda to introduce Farah to other people she knew in Paso Robles, acting like her fairy godmother once again. Blythe hosted this potluck dinner monthly, and if Blythe was friends with Amanda who was friends with Julia, she had to be a liberal and at least a little fun. Farah was hoping that if the night went well, her sour cherry rice would secure an invitation every month.

Most of the other guests were couples. As Farah looked around, she realized that there were no same-sex couples, and everyone was

White. She was undeniably not at a dinner party in New York City. She might as well have been back in high school in Cincinnati, but it was different. Now in her fifties, she could finally be comfortable in her brown skin. She could at least temporarily live in an area where the overwhelming majority of people weren't Democrats. If Angelina Jolie was sharing pictures of Iran on her Instagram to support Women, Life, Freedom, then certainly Farah could proudly take an Iranian dish to a potluck rather than a tuna casserole, as opposed to her teen years when she refused to pack leftovers for lunch and made herself a peanut butter and jelly sandwich instead.

But what about her kids? She may have been comfortable sitting there, but how would Rumi feel at a dinner party with all cis-het couples? How would everyone in this room react if they found out that her son was trans? And if she knew for sure that anyone in this room was voting to deny her child the same rights their child had, could she ever come back and casually have dinner with them again? Farah caught herself going down this rabbit hole of thoughts and chastised herself. *Stop it. Stop making everything about identity and belonging and politics and your place in this world and make conversation with people instead.*

She turned to Cecily, who was seated to her right, and asked, "So Cecily, did you grow up in Paso, or are you a transplant as well?"

"Oh no. I grew up and spent most of my life in Austin. Can't you tell by my accent that I'm not from around here?" She laughed. Soon, she and Cecily were deep in conversation. Farah found herself starting to relax and enjoy herself. She felt glad that she'd come to the dinner, overcoming her hesitation about attending a dinner party where she didn't know anyone, not even the host. Her experience in Paso thus far had been that everyone was genuinely nice and friendly. Anytime she was running, people passing in their cars would wave hello. When she went to yoga, people would be talking to each other before class started rather than warming up or practicing handstands. Even in the Albertsons, the cashier's friendliness was on level with people who work in Trader Joe's. They asked you questions and made small talk while scanning your groceries. She knew that Paso was an area of California where most people had voted for Trump, but the people as a whole still made her feel like she belonged there.

She and Cecily moved on to talking about what each of them were reading. Then Cecily paused, looking Farah directly in the eyes, and said, "You know. I'm part of a book club and I happen to be hosting our meeting next month. We'd be happy to have you join if you're interested. For our meeting next month, we decided to choose a backlist book. We do that pretty often. We're reading *The Lowland* by Jhumpa Lahiri. It was on Obama's 2015 summer reading list."

Oh, thank God, Farah thought. *She's a Democrat.* She accepted the invitation, saying, "Perfect. I read that book when it came out and I loved it, but I would love to reread it and see if I still love it just as much and have the chance to discuss it with others. And I never had time to join a book club in New York, but now, I've got plenty of time."

CHAPTER TWENTY-EIGHT

NOVEMBER 2008: BROOKLYN, NEW YORK

"We're here!" Julia threw up her arms excitedly when Farah opened the door. Ethan was holding two bottles of wine, and their daughter Violet had a box from Magnolia Bakery.

"Oh good," Farah said. "You came prepared with my favorite cupcakes in case this night is a disaster and I need to put myself in a sugar coma and forget it all." She took the cupcakes and walked toward the big buttercup yellow kitchen island, setting the box on the butcher block counter.

"It's not going to be a disaster! Where is your 'Yes, we can' attitude?" Julia chastised.

Farah had thought about having a larger gathering for that evening, a true election party, but she was too nervous about the results. She didn't think Obama had a good chance of winning, and she didn't want her home to be the place where everyone experienced America failing by not voting for the first Black president, or her house being where Sarah Palin, of all people, became the first female vice president. Julia's family was family. They experienced everything together.

The city had been full of excitement and buzz that day, people dancing and singing in the streets with lines of people waiting at polling stations. In line to vote that day, or walking through the city, you would think that there could not be a possibility that Obama wouldn't win, but Farah had lived in Cincinnati and Durham and

Rochester. She knew that she was in a liberal bubble and that New York City was not necessarily representative of the US as a whole.

Mark walked in behind Farah, "Hey, hey. Now the party can start. Let me take your jackets. Thanks for making the trek to Brooklyn. I went out of my way today and picked up takeout from Hasiba for you, Julia."

"Yum! Thank you," Julia said, while Violet slipped past the adults to go to Darya's room. "And seriously, Brooklyn is so close."

"Right. By the way Farah was kicking and fighting about moving out here after Delara was born, you'd think we were moving to New Rochelle," Mark said.

"If you had moved there, I think that would have been the end of our friendship unless you guys were willing to be the ones to come to Manhattan to see us every time," Ethan said.

"I guess that's one perk of my job. I need to be able to get to the hospital within forty-five minutes at the most, so New Rochelle will never be an option," Farah laughed.

Mark opened a bottle of wine, and the adults settled on the couch in front of the TV. Ethan raised his glass before taking the first sip. "Let's make a toast. To our first Black president."

"Let's hope," Farah raised an eyebrow as she clinked glasses with everyone and took a sip.

Delara came down and said hi, her hair in a ponytail beneath a baseball cap. She took a seat on the floor directly in front of the TV. Julia smiled at Delara and then looked at Farah with a raised eyebrow.

"Delara insists on wearing a baseball cap all the time these days, even at home," Farah said. "She doesn't care that her mom would like to see her whole beautiful face sometimes."

"Mom," Delara groaned and got up, leaving the room.

Farah shrugged and shook her head. "Everything I say is apparently the wrong thing. Who knew second grade is when teen attitude starts now."

"These kids," Julia said empathetically. "Forty may be the new thirty, but seven is the new thirteen."

"Yeah. I guess. It's so hard to get Delara to do anything these days. When Darya and I are doing something on the weekend, most of the time I have to beg Delara to join us."

"That's because you prefer doing the things Darya wants to do," Mark interjected. "Plus, Delara's the kind of kid who needs a little breathing room. Farah wants to make up for all her time working by micromanaging them and trying to spend every free second with them on the weekends."

Farah shot daggers at Mark with her eyes, so Julia immediately changed the subject. "If Obama wins tonight, I'm going to be so happy and proud to be an American that I'm going to wrap myself in the American flag and wear that to work tomorrow," she announced.

"Cheers to that," Ethan said. "I'd like to see that. Hopefully, you'll be naked under." Ethan raised his glass, and they all toasted again.

"Do you remember the first time you voted in a presidential election?" Farah asked.

"No, I don't. And I'm pretty sure I didn't start voting until I was in my thirties," Julia said. "You remember the first time you voted?"

"Of course I do. I was only eighteen—the first year I could vote, in more than one way. It was the 1988 election, and my family had just become US citizens a year before, so my dad made sure I voted. We voted for Bush—the original."

"Wait, what?" Mark said. "Your family voted for Bush over Dukakis?"

"Yes. We were Republicans back then. I think many Iranian immigrants were at that time. Being fiscally conservative used to be the driving force behind our vote. But that was also before the Republicans were what they are today. Or at least on the surface, they weren't what they are today. I'm pretty sure I didn't switch to Democrat until the 2000 Bush vs. Gore election."

"And I thought I knew everything about you, but nope, you're still full of surprises," Mark said.

Then Delara came back into the room and Farah gasped.

"What?" Delara asked. "You said you want to see my whole face sometimes, so I cut off all my hair. Hopefully, you're happy now." She sat on the floor right in front of the TV, her back to the adults.

"It looks great," Julia said cheerily. "I love short hair on girls. So freeing. I may just cut mine too."

"Cheers to you again, Julia," Mark said. "What would we do without you here to diffuse every awkward moment." He looked over at Farah and she could sense him warning her to drop it.

Darya and Violet wandered in and out of the family room after dinner, initially not as interested in the projections and what Anderson Cooper had to say. As the night went on and the results from the various states came in, the projections looking more in favor of Obama, they all became glued to their spots in the family room, all three kids sitting in a row directly in front of the TV. As Obama started to win in so many of the battleground states, Farah finally allowed herself to believe that he may win. When North Carolina's results came in, voting Democrat for the first time since 1976, Farah screamed in disbelief. Once he was over 270 votes, they all jumped up and down cheering. Tears streamed down Farah's face. She forgot all about Delara's choppy haircut. *I hope wherever Mr. Mead is, he's watching this,* Farah thought to herself, still remembering him singling her out on the first day of US History class. Mark held her and kissed her forehead, perhaps the only person in that room who knew how important to Farah it was that someone of color, with the middle name Hussein, was now the president of the United States.

CHAPTER TWENTY-NINE

FEBRUARY 2023: PASO ROBLES, CALIFORNIA

The smell of her coffee mixed with the scent of fresh air gave Farah a high every morning. As she sat on the Adirondack chair on her little front porch, she took her first sip of coffee and let out a great sigh. She thought about the evening before and how much she had enjoyed herself at Blythe's potluck dinner. Being at a dinner party with mostly couples hadn't been uncomfortable, but she thought that maybe she should give dating a try. If Mark could move on, then maybe it was time for her to try as well.

"Don't get too excited, but I think maybe I'm ready to give dating a try," Farah said to Julia over the phone.

Julia let out a big whoop. "I think we need to make you a profile on one of those apps," Julia laughed. "Or you could also sign up for those speed-dating events. I wish I could be a fly on a wall and see how you handle one of those."

"No way. Even if I was open to it, I'm not sure they even have those things in Paso. That's how people meet in big cities. And I'm not in a rush. I don't want to turn dating into a job! I'm just saying that I'm going to let my guard down and be open to dating if it comes up."

"Honey, I love you, but we're not twenty-five. I don't think people about to celebrate the fourth anniversary of their forever forty-ninth birthday meet people easily. You're going to need to make a little bit of an effort to have this happen."

"Ummm, did Mark have to do that? I bet he didn't make an online account or speed date." Farah had pretended to casually call Darya before going to the potluck and then probed and found out that she knew about the girlfriend as well. Darya told Farah that Mark's girlfriend was in her late forties and had three kids of her own. She was a professor at Fordham. At least he'd had the sense to date someone age-appropriate who wasn't going to want to have more kids with him.

"I take it that you found out about Mark having a girlfriend. I wanted to tell you, but I didn't want to upset you. Anyway, back to online dating apps, Mark is a single professor in New York City who is fit and still has all his hair. It's different for men and you know that. And you're in Paso, which barely qualifies as a town. I'll start investigating and make you a profile." Julia had made up her mind for her.

"Well, you know I'm just here temporarily, so there also isn't a point in dating someone and then moving back to New York. Maybe I should wait until I'm back. I'm not getting into a long-distance relationship at this age," Farah said.

"Who's talking about a relationship? We are talking about going on a few dates here and there, having sex with someone new after over twenty-five years, just getting your feet wet in the dating pool. Don't get ahead of yourself and worry about how you'll break off another relationship."

"Ouch. Okay. Fine. But I am not getting a Brazilian. I don't care what style of pubic hair is in right now," Farah said.

"Fine. And I'll do all the screening and swiping for you and forward you only the best. Anyone who sends a dick pic is out." Julia laughed.

"Oh God. Don't make me throw up. You know what, seriously just forget it," Farah said.

"Too late. I'm already going through my phone and finding the best profile pic for you. Bye." Julia hung up the phone.

Farah tried to picture herself being naked for the first time in front of someone new, with her stretch marks and C-section scar, her dimpled thighs and sagging breasts. She was fit, but there was no escaping the effect of age on one's skin and body. But she realized she appreciated her body more now than she had in her twenties. She was more comfortable in her own skin now than she had ever been.

Farah's phone chimed an hour later. She had a text from Julia with a link to the dating profile Julia had set up for her. She'd chosen a picture with a profile view in which Farah's head was tilted back in laughter, a glass of red wine in her hand. Julia had taken the picture of Farah at Four Lanterns Winery on a Paso trip a few years prior. Farah would have never chosen a picture with a profile view, given that she was still a little self-conscious about her nose. Farah's nose wasn't terrible, as far as Middle Eastern noses went. It was medium-sized. It characteristically had a bump, and when she was younger, she had desperately wanted a nose job. Soraya had said that all three girls would have to wait until they were at least eighteen years old to get their nose done. A rhinoplasty was the customary high school graduation gift that it seemed all Iranian girls got. Increasingly, boys were getting the same gift, with people in Iran going out in public with their nose-splints on, wearing it like a badge of honor rather than trying to hide it.

Farah had been eagerly counting down to her summer-before-college nose job as soon as her nasal bump made its appearance during puberty, but once Soraya and Behnam had finally agreed to let Farah go to George Washington for her undergraduate, they said that she would have to wait for that nose job with the amount they would have to pay for her tuition. By the time Farah could afford to get one, it hadn't seemed so vital anymore. She was dating Mark, who couldn't understand why she would want to change her face. She had made peace with her nose, despite seeing her younger sisters each get one and noticing how much it transformed their faces, allowing their eyes to be the dominant feature on their face instead of their noses. Looking at this picture that Julia had chosen, she was glad that Mark had discouraged her from getting her nose done. The profile read:

City Girl in Wine Country:
Vivacious, big-hearted, active liberal looking to explore Paso and beyond with like-minded man. Must love wine, books, spontaneity and be fit enough to keep up with me. Not looking to be your new personal chef or refill my nest with your young kids.

Farah didn't think that she would describe herself as "vivacious" or "spontaneous." That was more Julia, and maybe who Farah aspired to be, but she had definitely gotten the "no young kids" part right. Farah was done raising kids and she had no desire to raise someone else's. It was interesting to Farah that Julia hadn't mentioned anything about Farah being a doctor or Farah being Iranian—two of the most defining aspects of her identity. Had Julia purposely left those out, thinking that being a doctor may intimidate some men, or that being Iranian would make some assume that she was too conservative and not fun? No, that didn't make sense. The profile picture she had chosen with Farah drinking wine looked like a fun person. Did Julia not realize that these were important aspects of Farah's identity? Did omitting these aspects of her make this profile a lie? Farah shook her head. She was taking this whole thing too seriously, and anyway, she was an expert at omitting certain parts of the truth by now.

CHAPTER THIRTY

OCTOBER 1981: TEHRAN, IRAN

Khanoom Rahbari stood in front of the classroom. "Girls, I'm going to show you something." She held up a deck of cards. "I'm guessing you all know what these are, and some of you may still have them in your homes." Then she was silent.

Farah knew that the next afternoon, her mother would be hosting her rummy group at their home. She could picture her mom and her friends sitting around the dining table, a sheet drawn over it to create a smooth surface, teacups and stacks of colorful poker chips by each player. Farah wondered if Khanoom Rahbari could feel the fear radiating from her, the way a dog can sniff out fear. She swallowed the acid in her throat and carefully looked around at her classmates to see if she could detect fear on any of their faces. Everyone seemed frozen.

"Now, I'm sure that you all know that playing cards are outlawed under the Islamic Republic—that gambling and fortune-telling are sinful," Khanoom Rahbari continued. "If any of your parents still have cards in your home, they need to be ripped to shreds or burned. In one week, I will ask you all if anyone still has a set of playing cards at home. You will answer honestly. Remember that Allah sees and hears everything, and liars go to jahanam. If anyone still has cards in their home, guards will be sent to their home to confiscate them, and there will of course at minimum be a fine if not a greater consequence.

Does everyone understand?" She looked around the room as all the girls nodded, their hijabed heads bobbing up and down. "Okay. Now, everyone take out your Arabic textbook and turn to page fifty-two."

When Farah got home that day, she could hear Mahasti's voice singing through the door. Her mom was already home. She went inside and stared at the empty dining table that would be filled the next day with her mom and her friends playing cards. She went into the kitchen and saw Soraya had started working on dinner. She told Soraya what happened at school, begging her to get rid of their cards and never play rummy again. Soraya's face contorted with rage. "I'm not getting rid of the cards. We'll talk about this together when your Baba gets home."

"But Maman—"

"No," Soraya interrupted. "Go to your room and start your homework. We'll discuss this later."

After dinner, once Parisa was in bed, Farah's parents called her and Azita into the living room. "Farah, tell your father and Azita about what happened in school today," Soraya said.

As Farah recounted the events again, Behnam stood up, walking back and forth across the Persian rug with his hands in fists. When Farah was done, he sat back down and looked at his two older daughters. "These criminals may be able to dictate what happens outside, but they will not police what we do in our home. Next week when your teacher holds up the cards and asks who has them at home, you do *not* raise your hand. You lie."

"I can't lie. What if she can tell I'm lying?" Farah asked.

"I lied to my teacher a few days ago," Azita said, appearing unflustered by this whole family conversation.

"What! What did you lie about?" Soraya gripped the arm of the couch.

"She asked me if my parents have any mashroob in the house or if they ever drink it. I said no. Then she asked if I knew what mashroob is, and I said, 'Yes, it's what some people drink to get drunk, but my parents don't do that. They say being mast is bad.'" Farah was flabbergasted at Azita's nonchalance as she recounted the lies she seemed to have so casually told.

Soraya and Behnam looked at each other, and then Behnam said, "You did the right thing to lie, but you should have told us about this when you came home that day. Why didn't you tell us?"

Azita shrugged, "I thought you knew that all the kids are getting asked questions in school. It's not just our school. Last Friday when Khaleh Maryam was over, Mehrak said her teacher had asked her about alcohol in school, so I wasn't surprised when my teacher brought it up."

Soraya sighed. "Okay. From now on, *anything* at school that you get asked that is not directly related to schoolwork, you tell us right away when you get home. You don't answer *anything* about your home. You can say I'm not sure or if you know it's something that goes against the Islamic Republic, you just lie and say no right away, but either way, you tell us as soon as you get home. We do not let them dictate what we do at home. I'm sure the next thing they'll be asking you about is music and dancing. If we're going to follow their fake Islamic rules, you won't be watching the ABBA videos I get you, and I won't be listening to Googoosh or Mahasti anymore. They'll take away everything. Do you understand?"

Farah nodded as she tried to imagine her home without music, or a *mehmooni* without dancing. Dancing and music were part of her soul. She had learned how to do a shoulder shimmy before she had learned to jump with two feet, a developmental milestone most kids reach by the age of three, but then she thought of her teacher's words again and said, "But Khanoom Rahbari said she can tell if we lie, and that Allah watches everything." She turned to Behnam, "Baba, I know you say religion is nonsense and there is no behesht or jahanam, but I'm still worried."

Behnam grabbed her face, kissing her forehead. "Azizam, religion is nonsense, and you've already been lying for months. Every time you cover up to go outside, that is a lie, because you know women should not have to cover. I'm sorry that this is life now, but these are not real lies. Real lies are harmful. They hurt the people you love."

Despite feeling reassured, that night as Farah slept, she wondered if the tales her Maman Bozorg told her about heaven and hell were true. Everything her father tried to instill in her did not completely combat the stories and fears her devout grandmothers had propagandized in her. She dreamt of her family, surrounded by flames and demons.

CHAPTER THIRTY-ONE

FEBRUARY 2023: PASO ROBLES, CALIFORNIA

After fluffing the pillows on her couch, Farah stood and placed her hands on her waist, surveying her space. She couldn't wait for Azita to get there. It was the first time she was having a visitor in Paso. "When are we going to be living less than two hundred miles from each other again? You need to be visiting me at least once a month," Farah had said to Azita when they last spoke a week prior. "Besides, you need this. You know you do."

Azita had texted Farah that she'd left a little over two hours ago. The middle sister of the Afshar trio, Azita was still single and the chief financial officer for a major pharmaceutical company in Palo Alto. In her senior year in high school, she'd done the impossible and gotten accepted at Wharton, although Soraya and Behnam didn't realize just how big of a deal that was at the time. Women going into business school didn't make sense to them. Why waste her intelligence on such a volatile and uncertain career path? They didn't realize the doors that were automatically opened with a degree from Wharton.

As teenagers, Farah and Azita had always been close, while Parisa seemed a little distant from them. It was probably a combination of factors. Farah and Azita were only two years apart, while Parisa was six and four years younger than them, respectively. Farah and Azita had also experienced going to coed dual-language schools in Iran and then having to move to public school and wear a hijab, while Parisa had left

Iran before she was nine years old, the age that hijab was mandated for girls, although the Quran did not specify an exact age when women should start covering. Parisa had time to lose her accent before the age when kids got mean. Although both Farah and Azita's accents were barely perceptible anymore, when they'd arrived in the US, they both had a moderate one. Farah and Azita fought over clothes, makeup, and privacy in their shared bedroom. They alternated between listening to Googoosh, Iran's Madonna, and ABBA or Bananarama. They crank-called boys from school before there was caller ID, and they woke up at 3 a.m. together to sneak into the family room and watch R-rated movies on mute. Azita had organized Farah's bachelorette party, bridal shower, and baby shower for Darya. And although she lived across the US, she would visit Farah's kids as much as she could when they were younger, taking them on little trips as teenagers, and showering them with gifts like the latest gadgets or expensive concert tickets.

At the sound of a car engine getting closer, Farah ran outside. Azita got out of her car and Farah threw her arms around her, hugging her tight and noticing how tiny she felt—how much her own arms overlapped as she wrapped them around her sister. She pulled back and studied Azita's face, noticing how gaunt it was. It aged her. Farah's eyes welled up with tears, worried about her sister. "What's wrong?" Azita asked.

"Nothing. I've missed you. I'm just happy to see you," Farah said, not wanting to alienate Azita with her concerns right away. "We haven't had time for just the two of us in so long." She squeezed Azita, planting a kiss on her head.

Azita looked around. The sun was just starting to set over the rolling hills. The sky had a pink glow. "This place is just magic. I can see what you've been raving about." She turned and looked at her sister. "And you . . . you look happy. Your face looks different . . . softer . . . that's a good thing."

"Yes. It's exactly what I need right now. Let's go in." Farah grabbed Azita's bag from her and carried it inside. "What do you want to drink? Red, white, rosé? And start eating while I get your wine," Farah said, pointing to the cheese and charcuterie board she'd set out.

"I'll start with white. But I do need to answer a couple of work emails real quick, and then I'm all yours," Azita said.

They spent that first night on the couch, catching up on each other's lives and reminiscing over childhood memories. "Remember the Cindi Lauper concert?" Azita burst out in laughter, almost choking on her Tempranillo. Behnam had taken Farah and Azita to their first concert, since Soraya did not trust sending them with other teenagers without an adult accompanying them. He had come home from work and taken them in his suit and tie. Meanwhile, Farah and Azita had begged Soraya to let them shred some of their old T-shirts to make outfits and sprayed temporary neon pink dye into their hair. Behnam had sat in his seat in his suit and slept through the entire concert, while Farah and Azita, along with everyone else around them, were jumping and screaming and singing along the entire time.

After some reminiscing, the conversation inevitably turned to the current turmoil in Iran. "Baba keeps saying that this time is different—that he thinks the people will not back down. Maman doesn't agree. She says he has always been overly optimistic and not a realist. It would be surreal to be able to visit Iran again, without wearing a hijab. Maybe even you would consider visiting?" Azita looked at Farah, arching her right eyebrow.

"I don't know. Maybe. There's just too much pain there," Farah said.

Azita reached for her hand. "I know. But we all lost Zareen. Not just you—"

"It's more than that," Farah cut her off. "There are other things, but I really don't want to talk about them yet, although I promise that eventually I will. That's part of why I'm here instead of in New York. But I'm just not ready yet. And you know, it wasn't just Zareen."

"Yeah, I know. It was Alireza too. There was something going on between you two at the end, right?"

Farah remained silent.

"I knew it. I knew it."

Then Farah got teary-eyed and Azita changed the subject. "Okay, okay. Not today, but maybe soon, or even tomorrow." Azita took a sip of her wine, wrapping a piece of Roquefort blue cheese in prosciutto and putting it in her mouth. "Why don't we talk about when you're going to finally start dating again?"

"Great," Farah rolled her eyes. "From one touchy topic to another. Julia just made me a dating profile and is prescreening men for me, you'll be happy to know."

"No way! I want to prescreen men for you too. Which app are you on, or are there multiple?"

"Why don't you worry about screening people for yourself better? Looking for someone with future potential rather than just a good time?"

"Gosh, Farah. You turn more into Maman every day. So does you finally agreeing to start dating have to do with Mark's new girlfriend?"

"Wait, you know too?" Farah asked.

"Darya told me." Azita shrugged.

As they talked, Farah kept studying Azita, watching what she ate, nudging her to eat more. She was eating, so Farah guessed that it must just be work and stress that had made her so thin. She watched the ratio of how much she drank versus how much food she put into her mouth. She decided she wasn't going to say anything on the first night. She would see how the weekend went.

"So, Jason just became a father," Azita said. Jason was Azita's ex, the only person she had been engaged to in all her past relationships. Jason and Azita had started planning their wedding a couple of months into their engagement when he'd been scouted by a new company and gotten a job opportunity in Texas that he didn't want to turn down. Azita was well on her way to climbing the corporate ladder at Pfizer at that time. She didn't think it was fair for him to ask her to quit her job and follow him to a new opportunity when he could just stay where he was. Jason had accused her of choosing herself over him, and Azita had accused him of the reverse.

"How do you feel about that?" Farah asked gently.

"It's not fucking fair." Azita shook her head. "He gets to marry someone ten years younger and become a dad. And you know his wife is going to be doing most of the raising of the kids, so it's not like his career is going to suffer from becoming a dad at his age. Meanwhile, my frozen eggs have been sitting there for ten years, and why am I even paying to keep them anymore? I'm never going to use them. I know that. It's too late. I'm too old at this point to ever use them. I'm not going to be that fifty-year-old single pregnant woman everyone talks about. I just need to donate them for research and stop paying the storage fees. To think I went through that whole process to harvest my eggs, gaining all that weight, being a moody bitch, not drinking alcohol." Farah noticed her staring ahead when talking about her eggs, avoiding eye contact, looking like she was holding in tears.

"I'm sorry. I wish you had told me about Jason sooner. You know, I know you don't like to talk about this. But you could always adopt. There are so many kids who need a home—" Azita put her hand out for Farah to stop, and so Farah did.

"It's fine. It's too late for all of that. Don't tell Maman about Jason. Don't tell Parisa, either. I don't want a pity party. I have my job, my friends. I date and have sex when I want it. I'll donate the eggs and move on and I'm fine. Let's go to bed."

Farah hugged her sister. "Okay, we can go to bed, but you know that I'm here for you anytime you want to talk about any of this. Anytime, day or night." She didn't want to push or prod any further. Once Azita was done with a conversation, she was done. There were many times when Farah had envied Azita's life: single, incredibly successful, travel, serial dating. But now, looking at how frail and tired she looked, she wasn't so sure anymore. Maybe years ago, when Azita was freezing her eggs, Farah should have pushed her to just have a child on her own then, but the truth was, as much as Farah complained about Mark not taking an active enough role in raising the kids, it would have been much harder without him. And as the kids became teenagers, she had relied on Mark more and more. Particularly with Rumi's transition, Farah had felt like it would have been so much harder to go through it on her own. Rumi's transition was the one time that Farah completely fell apart as a mother, and Mark had been the one to support her and hold their family together. And Farah had needed Mark, the only other person to fully understand the sense of loss that she felt.

Farah supposed that if Azita had a child in her forties on her own, they would have all rallied and been there for her, but anyway, there was no point thinking about possibilities that were no longer an option. She decided to go to bed, looking forward to spending the next two days getting her sister's mind off all that had been occupying it, and glad that, given all the baby news, she hadn't told Azita the truth. But she would. She must.

CHAPTER THIRTY-TWO

FEBRUARY 1991: WASHINGTON, DC

Before reaching to open the door and go inside, Farah slipped off her giant sunglasses, lowering the front of her roommate's baseball cap even further in compensation. The only baseball cap Farah owned was one that said *GW Crew*, and she didn't want to wear anything with any potential identifying agent on it, so she had snuck a baseball cap out of Melinda's closet while she was sleeping. She walked to the front desk, ignoring the sign-in clipboard, and waited for the receptionist to get off the phone.

"May I help you?" the receptionist asked.

"I have a ten o'clock appointment." Farah's voice came out barely above a whisper. "My name is Farah Afshar."

"Sign in and have a seat. We'll be with you as soon as we can." The receptionist pointed to the clipboard.

Farah hesitated, then scribbled her name on the clipboard and sat down. She looked down at her hands, then locked her fingers together to make the shaking of her hands less obvious. She didn't want to make eye contact with anyone in the waiting room or look at the posters on the wall. When this was over, she wanted to make sure that she had as little memory of this day as possible.

FUCK, FUCK, FUCK, FUCK, She'd screamed internally upon seeing the second blue line on the Clearblue Easy test she had purchased by walking to a pharmacy three miles from campus, not wanting to risk being seen by anyone she knew. She had been sitting in the bathroom stall of her dormitory, hoping no one else would walk in and wonder why she was in there that long. She wrapped the pregnancy test in a wad of toilet paper and buried it in the bottom of the tampon bin attached to the wall. She came out of the stall and scrubbed her hands with hot water and soap five times, looking at herself in the mirror and almost not recognizing herself. Her hair was frosted with blond streaks, her irises aquamarine from the colored contacts she was wearing. For a year now, she had been wearing hazel-colored contacts and had just switched to the blue ones, trying to look like Aishwarya Rai or Vanessa Williams, imagining that a child version of herself with those magical colored contacts would have looked like the Afghan girl on that famous cover of *National Geographic*. But now scrubbing her hands, she felt disgusted by the image she saw in the mirror. She couldn't believe this had happened. The one time she'd had a one-night stand—although you couldn't even call it that—the one time she hadn't insisted on a condom, and of course, this happened.

Irresponsible behavior like this was so out of character for her, but when she had seen him watching her move on the dance floor, standing against a wall and smoking a cigarette, she'd done a double take. He looked exactly like what she imagined Alireza would have looked like now, fifteen years since she had last seen him. Despite being in her junior year at George Washington where there were so many cute Iranian guys—a complete one-eighty from her high school experience—she had avoided dating any of them. She couldn't go there. It was too painful. But now on that dance floor, two screwdrivers and one sex on the beach in, she questioned why she had come up with that rule for herself. He approached her, taking her hand and leading her off the dance floor. Then he leaned down to shout his name in her ear over the music—Ali. She felt the same shiver down her spine that she had the first time Alireza had put his arm around her. Two more sex on the beaches later and suddenly they were out of the club in a side alley, and when it was done, she looked at his face and he smirked. In that smirk, she saw that he looked nothing like Alireza after all. She ran.

"Farah?" a voice called. Farah finally looked up to see a nurse holding a manila folder, scanning the waiting room. She got up and followed her.

Lynette had warm eyes and a warm smile, her braided hair pulled back into a ponytail. The beads on her braids made a jingling sound as she walked Farah down the hallway. She took Farah back into the procedure room and saw her hands shaking. She used her soft brown hands to steady Farah's. "It looks like you're here alone, but it's going to be okay. I'll be there the whole time." Farah nodded and Lynette proceeded. "First, I need to go over these consent forms with you and make sure you understand everything. We'll also go over all the after-care instructions now and then review them again before you leave." Seeing her name written below the Planned Parenthood letterhead, Farah could no longer hold in her tears.

"I'll take another," Farah had said two nights before, slamming her shot glass on the bar immediately after downing her first kamikaze shot.

"Hold on, birthday girl, let's give the first one a minute," Sahar had said. It was Farah's twenty-first birthday, and she'd spent the days leading up to it crying and figuring out what she was going to do. Farah knew that just the thought of her daughter having premarital sex would be enough to infuriate her mother, let alone getting pregnant. But she felt so guilty about the decision to have an abortion. She felt so much shame. She didn't feel like she could tell anyone. She was determined to spend her twenty-first birthday drinking as much as possible without getting alcohol intoxication, reading that sometimes even a single binge drink can lead to fetal alcohol syndrome. It was her way of ensuring that she would go through with the abortion and not chicken out—she couldn't raise a healthy baby right now, let alone a syndromic one.

Now, as Lynette went over the consent forms with her, asking her again if she was sure, she nodded, still feeling the burn of the shots down her throat, and signed. "Since you don't have someone with you to drive you home after, sedation isn't an option, but many people have this procedure without sedation. You will get local anesthesia, which helps a lot, although you'll still feel pushing and pulling. You just squeeze my hand as hard as you need to," Lynette told her.

Dr. Aberra walked into the procedure room and noticed Farah's eyes filled with tears. Farah saw Dr. Aberra look over and make eye contact with Lynette, who simply nodded her head. "I'm going to walk you through this step by step," Dr. Aberra paused and then continued, "You are making the right decision for yourself, for your body, and for your future."

Farah grimaced through all the pushing, pulling, and tugging. Her legs shook in the stirrups and Lynette squeezed her hand and stroked her forehead. She told herself she deserved to be awake for this, to never forget what choice she had made. She promised herself to always remember Dr. Aberra, kind and gentle, stern and confident, reassuring her and reminding her that at this point, the embryo was merely a cluster of cells, not a baby, not a person.

CHAPTER THIRTY-THREE

FEBRUARY 2023: PASO ROBLES, CALIFORNIA

A few minutes before sunrise, Farah woke on her own. Instead of the complete morning silence that usually greeted her, she heard clicking in the main room. She tiptoed out of the bedroom to find Azita already up. She sat at the small dining table, hunched over her laptop, black coffee next to her. Her perfectly manicured fingers were typing away furiously. Farah went over and kissed the top of her head, the way she would her kids. "Hey. You're up working awfully early. Why don't you look up from that screen and take a break for a couple of minutes? The sunrise is magical right now."

"Give me two minutes. I can't lose my train of thought right now," Azita replied. Farah sighed and got her own mug of coffee. As she watched Azita's fingers flying over the laptop keyboard, Farah wondered if Azita was surviving on coffee and wine. There were so many moms who joked about that. Farah had joked about it as a reference to herself. But where Azita was concerned, it didn't seem like a joking matter. Azita worked through the sunrise and missed it, Farah watching her.

"I've made tasting appointments at my favorite wineries, and our first one is at eleven, so if you want to go for a run or do yoga or whatever beforehand, you need to be showered and ready to head out the door by ten forty-five," Farah said.

"Yes, *Mom*. I'll be ready on time. You gave me the rundown last night, remember?"

At 10:45 sharp, Azita walked out of the bathroom, her makeup fully done, wearing skinny jeans, a cinnamon-colored sweater, and oversized gold hoop earrings. First, they went to Farah's favorite of the wineries she had tried so far, Loma Seca. "We're going there first because I want you to taste their wines while your palate is fresh. They are a completely dry-farmed vineyard. When you use drip irrigation, which is what most places do, the vine roots remain close to the surface waiting for the next watering. Dry-farmed grapes send roots deep searching for residual moisture and nutrients in the soil, so you really get a sense of the terroir in their wines." Farah had learned all about terroir on prior trips to wine country, the characteristic taste imparted to a wine by the environment in which it is produced, affected by factors such as soil, topography, and climate. But she had really developed a true appreciation for terroir after the owner of Loma Seca had spent an hour walking her through tasting their wines.

"Wow, listen to you," Azita said. "Next you're going to start your own dry-farmed wine label."

"Not a chance. The more time I learn about this process, the more I realize just how complicated it is. And you're completely at the mercy of the weather. Having rainfall determine my livelihood is a different kind of stress I don't need in my life."

When they arrived at Loma Seca, Azita took in the view of the rolling hills around her and turned to Farah. "I think even a corked wine would taste amazing with this view around me."

When they tried the Primitivo, Farah said, "This one is my favorite. The tart plum taste—it's as if you married lavashak and wine." *Lavashak* was one of Farah's favorite Iranian treats—a very sour natural fruit roll-up made of plums and prunes. Just thinking about it made her mouth pucker and salivate.

"Now that is the terroir in you," Azita said. "You can take the girl out of Iran, but you can't take Iran out of the girl, even if she refuses to go back for a visit. Of course this is your favorite."

"Hmmm," Farah mused, ignoring Azita's comment about her

refusal to visit. "My terroir. I love that. I've been thinking so much about my identity and who I am now, but you're right, my terroir will always be a part of me, no matter how many times I've tried to deny it." She smiled.

"Wow!" Azita said. "That's the first time someone brings up you visiting Iran once and you don't snap their head off. Wine country really is mellowing you out."

"I've just been thinking a lot lately while I'm here. And everything going on in Iran. The videos. There are things you don't know and I'm not sure how much longer I can push them down. But let's not talk about that today. Let's just have a good time. You need that. We both need it," Farah said.

After Loma Seca, they went back to Braxton. Farah introduced Azita to the Bennets and to everyone she had been working with. As they took a seat to taste some of Braxton's wines, Azita's cell phone started periodically pinging, causing her to answer an email or a text that just couldn't wait.

"Why don't I hold on to your cell phone for just one day so that you're forced to unplug? Nothing is going to happen in a few hours," Farah suggested.

"That will just make me more stressed, not more relaxed. Don't worry. I'm so used to this. Taking a minute to address things as they come up does not take away from my enjoyment."

"Hmm . . . I don't see how that's possible, but okay." Farah knew well what it was like to be on call versus off, but once again, she didn't want to push anything.

"I heard you brought a very special guest in today," Miguel said, approaching their table, "so I brought out a reserve 2016 Syrah for you to taste."

"Miguel, this is my sister Azita. Azita, Miguel is the winemaker here. I've learned so much from him already," Farah said.

Miguel took a seat at their table and asked one of the attendants to bring them three fresh glasses for the reserve. As he walked Azita through the tasting, he managed to turn on his charm and flirt, as he did with all women. When he left the table, Azita raised an eyebrow at Farah and whispered, "Does hot winemaker man know that he doesn't make your favorite wine in Paso?"

Before Farah could answer, Azita's phone chimed again, and she was answering another text that just couldn't wait.

On Azita's last afternoon in Paso, as they sat next to each other on the couch, Farah studied her sister's face, unable to hide its stress despite the smooth Botoxed forehead. Farah couldn't help herself anymore. She had to say something. She reached over and grabbed Azita's hand, squeezing it. "Listen, I'm worried about you. You're constantly working. You've lost weight. I've never seen you this thin. And you look . . . you look beautiful as always, but you look tired. Maybe you need to slow down for a little bit too."

Azita's eyes filled with tears as she rolled them. "Not everyone can just slow down, Farah. I don't have the same options you do. I don't have the same life. This job is my baby. What else do I have?"

"Listen. I know what it's like to work really hard for a position, and I'm not saying that my situation is the same as yours. And I'm obviously not comparing being chief of one department in a hospital to being CFO of a major company. What you have done is a huge accomplishment, but you don't have to show or prove anything to anyone. If you're happy, then great. But if you're not . . . if it's too much . . . you do have options."

"I don't, Farah. I don't. And I love what I do. I love how it makes me feel . . . You're one to criticize me. I'm not the one running away from my life. No one really knows why you got a divorce. Or why exactly you took a leave."

Farah's lips began to tremble. Azita was right. "I'm here trying to figure that all out. I haven't been honest with anyone about a few things. But if I tell you, you can't tell Maman. I'm not ready."

"Okay," Azita said, reaching and grabbing Farah's hand. "You can tell me anything. You know that."

Farrah lifted her eyes to Azita's. "I was there when Zareen was arrested. I saw the *komiteh* take her away for taking off her hijab, but I was too scared to tell Maman and Baba . . . and then it was too late." Farah's entire body was shaking now.

Azita closed the distance between them on the couch and enveloped Farah in her arms. "Okay. That's horrible that you had to witness that. But it wasn't your fault. You shouldn't have kept that in all these years."

Farah shook her head. It *was* her fault, but she wasn't ready to share more.

"Farah, listen to me. You witnessed something terrifying when you were what, thirteen or fourteen? And you've held it in all these years? Did Mark know?"

Farah shook her head, her "No" barely audible.

Azita pulled away and grabbed Farah by her upper arms. "Farah, there was nothing you could have done. Nothing. Maybe you could have told the truth that you were there, but they would still have taken her to Evin. Nothing would be different. You have to know that. You have to."

Azita held Farah again until she stopped crying. "There's other things, but I need more time to figure things out first."

"Okay, I understand," Azita said. "I hate leaving after all of that, and I want you to promise me that you'll gradually tell me more."

"Okay, I will. But then I want you to promise me something. I want you to take care of yourself. I just want you to know you do have options and make sure you're happy. And I want you to try to find a little more balance in your life. I want you to promise that you are going to come see me at least one weekend a month for this short time that we are living close to each other. I mean, I can visit you, too, of course, but I think getting away to Paso will do you good. Promise me that and I promise to tell you more over time."

"I'll try. I really will," Azita said. "And on that note, I do need to hit the road and get back." She gave Farah a hug and stood up.

As Farah watched Azita drive off, she had a sense of unease. It was a little like dropping off each of her kids at college, except in those cases, her emotions were mixed—she felt sadness and anxiety along with pride and hope. Now, the emotion that was missing for Azita was hope.

As Azita's car drove off, Farah stayed outside, taking a seat on the Adirondack chair and looking out at the view. She thought about what Azita had said about no one really knowing why she and Mark had divorced. How had they started so strong and then grown apart?

CHAPTER THIRTY-FOUR

JANUARY 1995: DURHAM, NORTH CAROLINA

Neesha and Bridget were halfway through a bottle of white zinfandel as they watched Farah try on and discard multiple outfits. "Just go with the black dress. You can't go wrong with that," Bridget said. She always seemed to have the least patience when anyone was having a wardrobe crisis.

"No. That's so boring. Wear the pink slip dress and the plaid blazer on top. Trust me, it won't be too much," Neesha suggested.

"It would help if I knew where we were going or what we were doing. I'm going to freeze in the slipdress. It won't look stupid with tights?"

"No!" Neesha and Bridget said simultaneously.

"Jesus, okay, okay." Farah laughed. It was the two-year anniversary of her first date with Mark. He was picking her up in the midafternoon, saying he had something planned before they went to dinner. She got dressed and did a little twirl in front of Bridget and Neesha.

"Gorgeous!" Neesha clapped her hands together. "You look like Yasmeen Ghauri."

"Ha! Poor Yasmeen. Not with this nose, I don't," Farah said.

"Who's Yasmeen Ghauri?" Bridget asked.

"She was, like, one of the first if not *the* first Brown model to be on the cover of *Elle*," Neesha said.

"Yup. January 1991. I probably still have my issue somewhere in a desk drawer in my parents' house," Farah said. When Farah had first seen that cover, she'd placed her hand over her heart, the thumping palpable. The only dark-skinned models she'd been exposed to growing up were Iman and Naomi Campbell, and they were black. She hadn't seen any Middle Eastern or Indian or any Brown people on the covers of magazines. When she learned later that Ghauri had a Pakistani-Indian father and was raised Muslim, she looked at the mirror and saw herself as beautiful in a way she hadn't in a long time.

"Well, I don't know what Yasmeen looks like, but you do look beautiful, and anyway, Mark always looks at you like he has never seen anyone more beautiful in his life," Bridget said.

When the apartment buzzer rang, Farah went outside and found Mark holding a small gift bag. "Happy two years, babe."

Farah hugged Mark before opening the bag. Inside was a small silver antique mirror on a stand. "It's beautiful," Farah said, tracing her hand over the details. "You know I have a thing for mirrors." She had a mini collection from all the places she had traveled. Her favorite, featuring an intricate border of alternating lapis blue and turquoise tiles, hung in the little entryway of the apartment she shared with Neesha and Bridget now. Soraya had brought it back for her from a trip to Istanbul.

"Let's take a walk through the gardens, and then we'll go to dinner," Mark said. It was a beautiful sunny day, so it felt warmer than the fifty-three-degree reported high. When they arrived at the entrance of the Sarah P. Duke Gardens, Mark gave her a map. "I planned a little anniversary scavenger hunt for you," he said.

"You know," Farah said as she studied the map, "I'm pretty sure this is my first-ever scavenger hunt."

"Really?"

"Yes, really. They're not a thing in Iran, so, yeah, my first one."

The first clue led her to find a small box with a jar of artisanal honey inside. Farah looked at Mark quizzically.

"I know how you like to put honey in your tea sometimes. I figure this would make you think of me when you're having your tea." Mark shrugged.

The next treasure she found was a little mauve velvet sack. Inside were almonds in their shell painted silver, and some decorated porcelain eggs. Farah suddenly realized what Mark was doing. He was giving her the items used to make a *sofreh aghd*, the traditional wedding ceremony spread for Iranians. "Mark, what are you trying to say with these gifts?" she asked, knowing the answer.

"I thought this year you could set up your own little haft-seen in your apartment for Nowruz," Mark said.

"The haft-seen has the mirror and eggs, but not the almonds and honey," Farah said with a raised eyebrow.

"Oh, maybe I got a couple of the items mixed up between the two sofrehs," Mark said. Farah was trying hard to control her emotions, not wanting to seem too excited or emotional just in case this wasn't what she thought it was. She looked down at the map. There were three items left to find before this was done and they could stop pretending. When Farah found a little jewelry box under a bush at the base of a fountain, her heart raced, but when she opened the lid, inside were some foreign coins from several different countries. Coins belonged on both a *haft-seen* and the *sofreh aghd*, representing prosperity and wealth for either the coming year or for your marriage, depending on the spread. The next item was a *termeh*, an embroidered cloth that is handed down from generation to generation. It symbolized family and tradition and is used as the base for the haft-seen or placed on the side of the sofreh aghd. Farah recognized the termeh as one of her mom's, given to her by her mother. She looked at Mark with tears in her eyes. He had asked her parents.

She stood up and went over to Mark and hugged him. "What?" Mark asked. "Why are you getting so emotional? Just because I told your mom I think you should have a termeh for your own apartment haft-seen?"

Farah shook her head, wiping tears from her cheeks. "Mark,

you're a terrible actor." And then she was laughing through tears.

"Come on. You have to find the last treasure," Mark grabbed her hand as they followed the map. The last item was not a small box but a big heavy bag. When Farah opened it, there was no longer any question that this was part of a proposal and had nothing to do with Nowruz. Farah lifted one of the two *kaleh ghand*, giant sugar cones wrapped in cloth that are rubbed together by happily married women over the couple's head during the ceremony to shower their marriage with sugar and sweetness. Farah turned around to see Mark on one knee, ring box in hand. He was talking, but she couldn't hear or understand what he was saying at this point. She just kept saying "Yes, yes, yes, yes," as he slipped the ring on her finger.

Four months prior, Farah had taken Mark to the wedding of an Iranian family friend in Washington, DC. The ceremony had been in the living room of the bride's parents' home. "Traditionally, the bride goes directly from her mother's home to live with the groom—no stops of independent living," Farah explained to Mark, "I know it is very antifeminism, but I still love a home ceremony." In that wedding, the groom was American as well. They had printed a card for all the American guests, explaining the significance of each item on the sofreh aghd and what took place during the ceremony.

As Mark read through the card, Farah had pointed out all the items to him. A large elaborate silver mirror and candelabras brought over by a family member from Esfahan, the mirror representing bringing light and a bright future for the couple, the candles symbolizing energy and clarity. The bride and groom sat on two stools in front of the sofreh looking at each other in the mirror during the ceremony. In the era of Farah's grandparents, the groom would be seeing the bride's face for the first time at the ceremony in the mirror, everything being arranged by families with the couple having no say and not even seeing each other until the wedding day.

Friends and family gathered and stood all around the sofreh. The bride's close single friends and family held a white cloth over the couple's head, the first roof over their heads, while the happily married women took turns rubbing the kaleh ghand as sugar rained over that first roof. Meanwhile, the bride's maternal aunt was using the *soozan nakh*, a needle and thread, to sew and create some stitches in the overhead cloth. The card explained that while this is supposed to symbolize two families becoming one, rumor is that it also represents sewing shut the interfering mouth of the mother-in-law, the groom's mother.

The officiant asked the bride if she agreed to marry the groom. The bride stayed silent the first time, while a family member shouted, "The bride is out picking flowers." The officiant recited some more verses and asked the bride again. She continued to remain silent while another family member made another excuse for her. Tradition dictates that the bride should not seem too eager to say yes. On the third ask, the bride finally said "*Baleh*,"—Yes, and all the guests erupted in cheers. The groom was not asked if he wished to marry the bride. Everyone's presence assumed this. He was the one who asked for her hand in marriage.

Another aunt presented the new couple with a dish of honey. The bride and groom simultaneously dipped their index finger in the honey and fed it to each other, their first taste as a married couple, bringing more sweetness in their life. Modern tradition says that whoever bites the other's finger first will have the upper hand in the marriage, and the bride had made sure to bite first and bite hard, with everyone laughing when they heard the groom say, "Ouch." After the honey, the bride's mother was the first to start adorning the bride with jewelry. "Do you see yourself having such a traditional ceremony one day?" Mark had asked.

"I think so. I know it's not exactly in line with feminism, but this is what I know of weddings. I grew up watching all my older cousins get married this way."

Mark had put the card explaining the ceremony in his suit pocket and squeezed Farah's hand.

CHAPTER THIRTY-FIVE

JUNE 1984: TEHRAN, IRAN

On the last day of eighth grade, Farah and Marjan walked home together for one last time. Farah would be leaving for the US in less than a month. They'd met almost three years earlier, on the first day of sixth grade at Razi Middle School, only to discover that they had lived within blocks of each other for over five years. On that first day, during their lunch period, after their mandatory noon prayer was over, a discussion of American movie stars had revealed that they both claimed to be Rock Hudson's number one fan. They became fast friends and were inseparable for the remainder of middle school, both being new to the school.

While Farah had spent the previous years at Rostam Abadian, a dual Farsi and English private school, where she had her science and math classes in Farsi in the morning, and her afternoon classes—writing and history—in English in the afternoon, Marjan had been in a dual Farsi and French private school. They would often say that their friendship was the one good thing that had come of the Islamic Revolution because the closure of all private dual-language and coed schools had brought them to their default local public school.

On the way home from school, they stopped at a street vendor selling fresh-squeezed pomegranate juice. Whenever they got the tart juice, they liked to dip their lips in it, the maroon staining their lips like lipstick. Farah pursed her lips and said, "I'm going to wear real lipstick every day in America."

Marjan laughed, "Sure you are, but you'd still have to hide it from your mother. I'd be more scared of her than the komiteh."

"Maybe," Farah said. "Or maybe she will relax about these rules in America. Adopt some of their culture."

When they got to Farah's home and closed the front door, Zareen was already there, waiting for them. Zareen and Marjan were supposed to help Farah sort through her clothes and pack for the US. Farah and Marjan immediately reached for their necks, loosening the knot of the headscarf, taking off their hijab, and shaking out their hair. Then they took off their shoes, followed by their manteau. After hanging their clothing on the coat rack in the entryway, the three girls went into the bedroom Farah shared with Azita, kicking her out for privacy, and pulling out the single large suitcase Farah's mom had provided for Farah and Azita to pack their belongings for the move to America.

"How am I supposed to pack all my things in half a suitcase?" Farah had asked Soraya a week earlier.

"You just need underwear, socks, and a little bit of clothes. You don't need anything else. What about me? I'm leaving everything I have behind," Soraya had said, dismissing her. Their home was filled with antique furniture and Persian rugs, and Soraya's most prized possession, a cabinet filled with Lalique and Baccarat crystal pieces she had collected over years of travel to European countries. The one good thing was that there was no need to pack any headscarves or manteau sets with their matching trousers. "You'll just need the one we wear to the airport and Iran Air, and once we land in Istanbul and get off the plane, you'll never need them again," Soraya had told her daughters.

"But won't you need them when we visit home sometimes?" Parisa had asked.

"We probably can't visit for a little while, and when we do, we'll wear the same ones for the plane ride back and have the rest waiting for us here," Soraya answered.

Now, as the girls went through Farah's pile of clothes to pack, Farah couldn't believe how much of her wardrobe had been taken over by drab-colored manteau sets that had covered her entire body. "It's fine if I can't take much. I'm going to buy so many new miniskirts as soon as I get to America, and when Rock Hudson sees me in them, he's going to ask me to marry him," Farah boasted, giggling with excitement.

"Doesn't Rock Hudson live in Hollywood? What's the city you're moving to again?" Marjan asked.

Farah rolled her eyes. She had told all her friends and cousins multiple times that they were moving to Cincinnati, but none of them seemed to remember any US city names other than New York and Los Angeles. "Cincinnati. I'm sure flying from there to Hollywood is as easy as going from Tehran to Shiraz. And I'll be in school with boys again, American ones, so I'll meet plenty of Rock Hudson types there," she gloated.

Zareen sighed, shaking her head. "I don't know when you became so boy crazy. Do not let the boys there distract you from getting into a good college so you can go to medical school."

"Zareen, you sound more and more like Maman every day. You've become so boring lately. I can be boy crazy *and* go to medical school. I'm not worried about school right now. I just can't wait to get out of here. Now, anything I'm not taking you guys can divide among yourselves. Maybe to make it fair, you take turns picking things."

"Okay. Who gets to go first? Should we flip a coin?" Marjan asked.

"I don't care," Zareen said. "What does it matter? You can pick first. You can have all of it. There are no Rock Hudson types or anything in my future."

CHAPTER THIRTY-SIX

MARCH 2023: PASO ROBLES, CALIFORNIA

Snuggled in her pink terry cloth robe, her feet warm in her L. L. Bean shearling slippers, Farah looked out the window. She loved the temperature fluctuation in Paso, the chill of the mornings compared to the heat of midday, the diurnal weather pattern that was optimal for the grapes. She held her mug in both hands, took a sip of the steaming black coffee, and took in the view. The sun was just starting to rise, hitting the rows of grapevines at an angle that made them look like they sparkled. New bright green leaves were sprouting on the vines, the sign of new beginnings bringing a smile to her face.

The previous day, she had tried to talk her sister Parisa into taking a break from her three young children and coming out for a visit. The youngest of the Afshar trio, Parisa was the most well-adjusted of the sisters. She had pursued her passion, majoring in English literature. She was now an English teacher at a public high school in Cincinnati. She never left Ohio and married her college boyfriend. She seemed quite content with her family and her home just a few miles from her parents. Parisa's three kids all had American names: Hunter, Sawyer, and Penelope. In contrast to Farah, Parisa hadn't felt the need to hold on to her Iranian identity by insisting on Iranian names for her kids. She also hadn't held on to her last name, happy to be Parisa Hoffman.

Parisa turned down Farah's invitation for a visit, saying she would just wait to see Farah when she visited Cincinnati next, or wait until

Farah was back in New York and take her kids for a trip there. "I love you, but coming to wine country for a break by myself is just not doable right now. And I'm perfectly happy here. I always have been." Farah thought about how Parisa seemed the most assimilated into a "normal American life," whatever that was, among the three of them. She was happy for her.

"Okay. Well, maybe I will make a trip out to see you soon. I miss your little kiddos. I just don't necessarily want to come out there for a few days and get grilled by Maman on what I'm doing with my life for three days straight, but it will be worth seeing your kids. Have you spoken to Azita lately? When she just visited me, she looked so thin and so stressed," Farah said.

"That's how Azita has always been. Undereating and overworking are what fuel her," Parisa argued. "Besides, how tired and stressed can someone who doesn't have kids be? How she chooses to spend it, even if it is a hundred hours a week of work, is her choice. And any nonworking time she has is her own."

"Yeah, I get it. I had young kids once, too, but something was different this time. Can you call her? Try to convince her to take a break or come home for a little while, or maybe the three of us can plan something. Just promise me you'll call her more often," Farah said.

"Okay," Parisa said. "You worry too much. But I will call her."

Farah hung up the phone, only a little disappointed that she hadn't convinced Parisa to visit. The truth was that she really was enjoying being there by herself, and as it turned out, she wasn't having much alone time. The days and weeks seemed to be going so fast. She was working her way through visiting as many of the Paso wineries as she could, meeting many of the head winemakers. She had become friends with all the tasting room attendants at Braxton and was helping when someone was unable to make their shift, or they just needed an extra pair of hands. She helped in the vineyard, pruning and cutting off dead branches. She loved the manual labor. It exhausted her body in a different way than a long run did, allowing her to sleep better at night. Farah finished her coffee and sat on the yoga mat outside for her morning meditation.

Three minutes into her attempted ten-minute meditation, Farah opened her eyes, ready to give up. Clearing her mind from random thoughts for more than ten seconds at a time seemed impossible. *Maybe I should actually focus on thinking rather than not thinking,* she thought. *Maybe I need dedicated thinking time each day to help me figure out my life.* She closed her eyes again and took another deep inhale, followed by a slow exhale. She knew why her mind was back to racing recently. Ever since that small admission to Azita, she couldn't help but think about how so many things might have been different if she had been honest with everyone, including herself, from the start. And Azita's questions about her divorce and leaving her job also burned through her mind.

It was true that she had been unhappy with the changes in her job for quite a while, and that the lawsuit had likely pushed her over the edge, but it was more than that. She wasn't sure that she had ever actually chosen to go into medicine. Once they had moved to the US, and particularly after Zareen's ultimate fate, she felt like she had to be a doctor. She never considered any other option. She would have felt guilty not taking advantage of an opportunity that so many young people in Iran would do anything for—the opportunity that Zareen would have given anything for. Had becoming a doctor been her dream or Zareen's dream or her mother's dream?

Once she went to medical school and started her rotations, she genuinely enjoyed her OBGYN rotation. She loved the relationships with the patients, the privilege of helping bring children into the world, the camaraderie among the residents. If she had never actively chosen to become a doctor, she had actively chosen to become an ob-gyn. But over the years, once the stress became too much and the job was causing her more distress than joy, it was that same guilt that had kept her paralyzed and staying in the position she should have left sooner. If she went back to New York, and in addition to no longer being a wife she was no longer a practicing doctor, then who would she be?

Suddenly, she missed home. She had an urge to visit it. Home meaning the house she had lived in during her middle and high school years. When Farah was in medical school, her parents had moved to a new home outside of their old neighborhood. All her visits to Cincinnati in her adulthood were spent either in her parents' new home, or at Parisa's, going to spend time with her each time she gave birth. She never visited the streets of her formative years, or went downtown to see how the city had changed or went to Skyline Chili. She hadn't had Skyline Chili since high school, and suddenly she had a desperate craving for it.

She went inside and called Soraya. "Maman, I'm going to come home to Cincinnati for a few days, but before you get too excited, I want to really see Cincinnati this time. I don't want you to invite all your friends over to see me, or to have me go with you to their homes. I want to walk around the city, visit our old neighborhood. And one night I want to go out to dinner with just Parisa."

"Why even come if you don't want to spend any time with us?" Soraya started her guilt trip.

"I'm staying at your house. I could easily stay with Parisa or in a hotel if you want," Farah threatened. Soraya would be mortified if her friends found out that her daughter came into town and stayed at a hotel. So American.

"Okay fine. You stay here and do what you want. You don't listen to anything I say anyway," Soraya said.

Farah decided to let Soraya have her last jab and ignore it. "It will be nice to be home, to see you and Baba. We'll have breakfast together. We'll see the kids together. And I promise to make another trip sometime when you can invite everyone. But I just need a few days of seeing the city where I grew up again." She didn't expect Soraya to understand. Soraya would never fully understand what Farah's experience in Cincinnati had been like, immigrating from

Tehran at the age of fourteen. Sure, Soraya had immigrated too. But the challenges an adult faces and the strength and perspective they have to face them are completely different from the challenges of a teen. The high school years are the most difficult as it is for young girls, without adding being a brown girl from Iran with an accent and none of the latest fashion on top of that.

Farah then called Parisa. "Wow. You're calling me two days in a row," Parisa said. "If you're calling to check to see if I called Azita, I have not yet, but I will by tomorrow at the latest. I promise."

"Good. Call her. But that's not why I'm calling you. I'm going to visit home for a few days, and I'd like to go to a girls' dinner one night with you and some of your closer friends when I'm there. Try one of Cincinnati's new *trendy* restaurants—and I mean whatever is all the rage and you never get to go to. Maybe Doug can watch the kids while we do that?"

"Sure," Parisa said. "That sounds fun, but have you cleared these plans of yours with Maman?"

Farah laughed. "Yes, I have." Farah wanted to see what Parisa's life in Cincinnati was like. She wanted to compare the Cincinnati she had grown up in with the one Parisa lived in now. She didn't really know why she suddenly had the urge to do that. Maybe because she was in Paso Robles now, making friends and finding a community. But she knew that if she had moved to Paso in 1984 as a teen instead of to Cincinnati, her formative years would have been just as difficult, if not more so. As she sat at her laptop looking at flights and thinking about the places she would want to revisit, she couldn't help but remember Mark's first time in Cincinnati.

CHAPTER THIRTY-SEVEN

MAY 1994: CINCINNATI, OHIO

Soraya leaned against the kitchen sink, wearing her yellow Rubbermaid gloves as she hand-washed the dinner dishes, humming to herself. Farah figured it was as good a time as any to tell her mom that she was dating someone, that it was getting serious . . . that he's an American. Farah had offered to wash the dishes minutes before, but Soraya had shooed her away, always criticizing her for wasting too much water and using too much dish soap, and of course, loading the dishwasher was out of the question—it used too much electricity. "Maman, I wanted to talk to you and Baba about something," Farah said. Her dad was sitting at the kitchen table, reading a book of Hafez's poetry, his teacup half empty.

"Okay, we're both here. Talk," Soraya said, continuing to wash the dishes. Her dad put his book down on the table.

"I've had a serious boyfriend for a while now. His name is Mark. He's a graduate student at Duke and comes from a great family . . ." Farah paused and studied Soraya's face, which had no expression. "I'd like you and Baba to meet him and then eventually meet his parents."

Soraya put the platter she was washing down, turned the faucet off, took off her yellow gloves, and rested them over the sink. Then she turned around and went upstairs into her bedroom, closing the door behind her.

Farah was not surprised. She turned to her father, Behnam, and feigned disbelief. "What was that, Baba? Why does she always react like this to things she doesn't want to hear?" she asked, hoping that this would be one of the instances her father would stand up to her mom, try to reason with her.

Behnam shrugged. "Give her a little time. Then bring up the subject again." He turned back to his book.

Farah looked at her father incredulously. "I don't know why I expected you to stand up to her." She marched upstairs, flinging open the door to her mother's bedroom. She found Soraya sitting on her bed, staring straight ahead. "What the hell, Maman? I tell you I'm dating someone important to me, that I want you to meet his parents, and you just walk off?"

"I don't need to meet anyone you date or his parents unless it is someone you're going to marry. We're not Americans. Everyone meeting everyone for no reason. No need to meet Mike," Soraya responded.

"Mark! Not Mike! And we may get married, which is why I want you to meet his parents too. It's pretty serious. We've been together over a year now."

"Americans cheat on their wives and get divorces. You're not going to marry an American," Soraya said it like a statement of fact.

Farah burst out laughing. "Seriously? What did you expect when you moved to America? That we'd all just go to college and do what you want and none of us would end up with an American?"

"I know that Parisa might end up with an American. She was only eight years old when we moved here, and she has been impossible since we got here. But you and Azita . . . You! You! You are Iranian," Soraya declared.

"Maman, I'm sorry. I'm already going to medical school, but I can't be the daughter who gives you everything you want. And Parisa has not been 'impossible' since we got here. You don't know what impossible is." Farah left the room, slamming the door behind her. She marched back down to the family room, finding Behnam still on the couch. "Baba, you have to talk to her. She can't have a tantrum and refuse to meet Mark. There is a good chance I will marry him. And if I do, he will not cheat on me, and we will not get a divorce."

◆

Two weeks later, despite all her protests, Soraya gave in. She would meet Mark, but she would not invite him to her house for dinner. They could all meet at a restaurant. "Really, Maman, he's going to fly to Cincinnati for a weekend to meet you and you're not going to let him in our house? If this was some guy named Kamran, you'd roll out the red carpet for him. You'd make Ghormeh Sabzi and Gheymeh and Tahchin for just one extra person!" Farah exclaimed, frustrated with Soraya's attempt at maintaining a distance from Mark and keeping the upper hand.

"I would do no such thing. I don't need to impress anyone, Iranian or not. My daughters are all impressive on their own," Soraya said. Farah huffed air out of her nostrils and rolled her eyes. She didn't have a comeback for that, even though she knew her mother would treat an Iranian differently.

When Farah, Soraya, and Behnam walked into Angelini, Mark was already waiting at their table. He stood up immediately upon seeing them, walking over with a bouquet of flowers for Soraya. "Mrs. Afshar, Dr. Afshar, so nice to meet you." He shook their hands nervously. He was wearing navy slacks, a pinstripe gray shirt, and a navy and gray tie. Farah had only seen him wear a tie a handful of times.

Farah's parents returned his handshake, her father more warmly than her mother, but neither said, "Call me Soraya," or "Call me Behnam," the way American parents probably would. Farah made a mental note to herself to later explain to Mark that this was nothing against him—that they would have maintained that formality even if they had been meeting a Kamran instead of a Mark.

When the waiter took the drink orders and Farah's parents said they were fine with just water, Mark ordered the same. "I'll take a glass of Sauvignon Blanc," Farah said, returning her mother's glare.

"Great. Three waters. A Sav Blanc. I'll be back with those and then take your food order," the waitress smiled.

"So, what was Farah like as a child?" Mark asked.

"Very smart," Soraya said, making minimal eye contact.

Farah turned her head and glared at her dad. Behnam cleared his throat and elaborated, "Well, yes. She was always at the top of her class. You know in Iran, there is class rank even in grade school. Farah was always what we call '*shagerde aval*' which means first top student. Even as a kid, she worked very hard." Behnam went on to add that even before the revolution, before coed schools closed and Farah was mandatorily placed in an all-girls Islamic public school, she was still shagerde aval. "She was in the best, most prestigious, dual Farsi-English private school in Tehran, and she was smarter than all the boys too."

"I think he got it, Baba. And I think since we have been together for over a year now, Mark is very aware of how smart I am," Farah interjected, fuming inside. "Let me remind you that Mark went to Yale for undergrad. Maybe you guys would like to ask him some questions about himself?"

Mark gave a fake laugh. "No. I'd much rather spend our time learning more about you and your family's experiences. Dr. Afshar, how has practicing endocrinology been here compared to in Iran?"

When the check came, Behnam immediately reached for it and said, "I'll take care of this."

"Thank you. That's very kind of you," Mark said, without any offer to pay the bill. Farah internally winced and knew her mother would make note of this. Of course, her parents would never have let Mark pay anyway, but they would expect at least one fake attempt from Mark to offer to pay. The art of *taarof* was a custom all Iranians had mastered. It was a type of social etiquette in which cultural pleasantries and back-and-forth polite gestures were made when anyone was either giving or receiving any type of gift, food, or money.

Even a grocer would initially say your produce is on the house or a cab driver would say your fare was being waived at least once before accepting money. Farah made a note to teach Mark this custom for the next time he met with her parents.

The next morning, Farah found her parents having breakfast at the kitchen table. She poured herself a tea and sat down, crossing her arms. "I can't believe how rude you were to Mark last night, Maman. At least Baba asked him a few questions about himself."

"I was nice. What did you want me to do? Anyway, he's nice, for a temporary relationship. But in Iran, you don't introduce your parents to temporary boyfriends. You introduce them to the person worthy of marrying you."

"He is worthy of that! And you should start getting used to the idea that he most likely is not my temporary boyfriend." She grabbed her tea and went up to her bedroom.

Later, Farah overheard her parents talking about Mark. "Well, at least his parents are still married to each other, not divorced like other Americans," Soraya conceded. So, her mom had been listening to everything Mark said at dinner.

CHAPTER THIRTY-EIGHT

MARCH 1977: TEHRAN, IRAN

Normally Farah would be upset about having to watch Parisa while her cousins played, but on this day, it gave her an excuse to stay in the living room with adults and eavesdrop on the fortune teller's reading of their fortunes in their coffee cups. Every year, just before Nowruz, Khaleh Maryam had a different fortune teller come to predict their prospects for the coming year, and although Soraya claimed that it was all nonsense, she went every year and drank her cup of thick Turkish coffee, leaving just a little at the bottom and then turning the cup upside down on its saucer while the sludge and grinds mapped out her future.

Parisa was holding onto Farah's pinky fingers, taking excited steps with her chubby feet, babbling and periodically falling down on her diapered bottom onto the Persian rug. As Farah pointed to various colors in the rug, telling Parisa what they were, she listened to Sekineh Khanoom sigh before reading Khaleh Maryam's fortune.

"This river with each fork coming off it being narrower and longer shows what a difficult life you've had. And here is a heart with a crack in it . . ."

What is she talking about, Farah thought. Khaleh Maryam was always laughing, dancing, vibrant. No wonder her mom thought this was nonsense. Khaleh Nasreen may have been the prettiest among them, but Khaleh Maryam always seemed to be the happiest.

In Soraya's cup, she saw two continents separated by a vast ocean. "You will leave Iran. You'll lose everything and start over again. You want a fourth child, but you won't have it because you'll be focused on starting over. But in the end, you will prosper."

"Why would I ever leave Iran? That doesn't make sense," Soraya said. "Maybe you mean I'll take a vacation? We're going to Europe again this summer. We travel all the time."

"Not Europe, that's too close. And not a vacation. A move. And you'll start a business. I see success in your future. This is a good fortune," Sekineh Khanoom said, while Soraya shook her head. "Now time for your thumbprint." Soraya took her right thumb and pressed it into the bottom of the coffee cup. This was the last step in reading everyone's fortune. "You have a long life ahead of you. Some ups and downs but mostly prosperous." Soraya shrugged.

"Maman, can I please have my fortune read?" Farah asked.

"You're only seven years old. This coffee is too strong for you to drink, and anyway, you're too young for this," Soraya said.

"You can drink the coffee for her and then have her take just the last sip. That will work," Sekineh Khanoom said.

Farah started jumping up and down, pleading with Soraya. "Please, please, please. I want my fortune read. And I've been watching Parisa this whole time while everyone else has been playing."

"Fine," Soraya said. "But remember, this is just for fun."

Soraya drank a second cup of the thick coffee, leaving just enough for Farah to take one sip before turning the remnants over. Farah grabbed the cup and closed her eyes, as if she were making a wish before blowing out a birthday candle. *I want four kids, two sets of twin girls, and a white puppy, and to live in a white house*, she thought. *And I hope I look like Khaleh Nasreen when I grow up.* Then she took a sip, and her tongue puckered at the bitter taste. She forced herself to swallow it and then coughed before carefully turning her cup over and placing it in the saucer.

Sekineh Khanoom turned over Farah's cup and it seemed to

Farah like she examined it for an eternity before she started speaking. "You see this face here? The hair thick but the face so white. You'll marry a very fair, handsome man. And here, under him these two shapes, one more square. You'll have two kids. First a daughter, then a son." Farah felt disappointed. Only two kids? And only one daughter? No sisters for her daughter. Then she saw Sekineh Khanoom's face cloud over. "You see this branch breaking off this tree? You won't be happy. You'll leave your husband."

"Baste!"—Enough, Soraya said, grabbing the cup out of Sekineh Khanoom's hand. "Just like I said. Mozakhraf!"—Nonsense.

CHAPTER THIRTY-NINE

MARCH 2023: CINCINNATI, OHIO

As the plane was landing, the city came into view. Farah spotted the Great American Tower at Queen City Square and the Scripps Center. She was glad she had booked herself the window seat, paying the extra fee to choose it. As she stared out the window, cupping her face with her left hand, she felt a moistness hit her hand and realized it was a teardrop. *Why are you getting all teary-eyed?* she asked herself. She blinked and wiped the few tears that had streamed down her cheek. *Stop being ridiculous. Get ahold of yourself.*

At the passenger pickup area, she spotted her parents. Her father was still sitting behind the wheel, her mother standing outside the car waiting for her. Soraya gave Farah a hug and then stepped back and studied her face. "You are darker than usual. Are you using sunscreen every day?"

"Yes, Maman. I am. But I'm outside a lot more now than I was in New York, so even with sunscreen, I'm going to tan. Even in the winter. It's good to see you too." There's an old Iranian limerick that says women should be beautiful and white, while men should be bald and slightly plump but rich.

Then Soraya stroked and smoothed out Farah's eyebrows. "I'll clean them up for you when we get home. Don't worry." And then she kissed Farah on each cheek and opened the car door for her. Maintaining your eyebrows in a perfect clean arch was as important as brushing your teeth twice a day to Soraya. These little things were what Farah and her sisters loved and simultaneously made fun of about their mom. Farah would never forget when Soraya had met Bridget in her first year of medical school. Within half an hour of meeting her, Soraya had said, "Bridget, your eyes would stand out much more if you shaped your eyebrows the right way."

Later Farah had reprimanded Soraya. "You can't just comment on people's looks and give them unsolicited advice the first time you meet them!"

"What?" Soraya shrugged. "You said she is one of your best friends. Your best friend is like my own daughter. I say what I want."

"No, Maman, she is not like your daughter. She is an adult woman you just met. And anyway, you shouldn't feed into this cycle of women being judged by the shape of their eyebrows or how fluffy they cook their basmati rice."

"Chinese rice is not edible," Soraya had countered. "Even a five-year-old can make a big clump of rice that sticks together."

"Okay, Maman. You're missing the point altogether." Farah had sighed. The memory still made Farah laugh and cringe at the same time. Later, she'd apologized to Bridget, trying to explain that her mom had her own set of social rules.

When they arrived home, Farah walked in to the aroma of rosewater and cardamom filling the air. Farah knew what foods would be awaiting her in the kitchen before walking into it. Sure enough, her mom had made *albaloo polo*, the same sour cherry rice Farah had taken to Blythe's potluck, *fesenjoon*, a stew made from pomegranate paste, ground walnuts, and little meatballs served over saffron rice, and *halva* for dessert. All her favorites. "Maman, you know I'm one person. How much do you think I can eat?"

Soraya was already busy filling the samovar with water to brew tea. "You need to eat real food. I know when you're on your own, you never cook. Go wash your hands and change and then tea will be ready. I'll fix your eyebrows after tea." *Tea before eyebrows, got it*, Farah thought.

Farah took her bag and went upstairs to her designated bedroom. Other than missing posters on the walls, you wouldn't know that this wasn't the bedroom of her teenage years. When her parents had moved, they'd transported everything from her old bedroom and set it up in the new house. The white canopy twin bed they had bought from Sears in the '80s was in the middle of the room. She'd loved that bedroom set when they'd bought it for her in ninth grade. The desk with its hutch was against the right wall, the shelves still filled with Sweet Valley High and V. C. Andrews books. She opened the desk drawers, and her diaries were there. Maybe she would take a couple back to Paso and read them.

The few stuffed animals she had were on the bed. Her collage picture frames had been transported to these walls, but otherwise, the walls looked pretty bare compared to her teenage years. Of course, Soraya had not thrown away all her Duran Duran and Madonna posters. Soraya did not throw anything away. She had carefully taken them off the walls, rolled them up, and put them in the closet the last time Farah had looked. Farah opened the closet door now. Along with the posters being rolled up in the corner, hanging in the middle of the closet, was the giant white bag that housed her Cinderella-style white wedding dress. Farah sighed. *You're not going to unzip the bag,* she told herself, while she unpacked and hung the few clothes she had brought with her. She walked into her bathroom to splash her face with water and wash her hands again before going downstairs. She opened the drawer next to the sink and an old tube of Revlon lipstick rolled to the front. She picked it up and knew it would say "Cherries in the Snow" without even reading the label. It was her favorite color during her senior year of high school. She had felt a certain transformation, a certain power, every time she put it on. For the first time it occurred to her that maybe "Cherries in the Snow" referred to dark cherry lips against snow-white skin. How many messages about what was considered beautiful had she been bombarded with as a teenager without even realizing it? She tossed the old tube in the trash and left the bathroom.

Despite the jetlag, her body woke up early the next morning. She put on her running clothes and went downstairs. The smell of rosewater still lingered in the kitchen from the halva the night before, and Farah made a mental note to take some rosewater back to Paso with her. Behnam was already up. He had always been an early riser, leaving for work before they got up when she was a child, and coming home just before they went to bed. He had already started brewing the tea and was setting up the breakfast table. Feta cheese, sliced tomatoes and cucumbers, fresh mint, walnuts soaked in water, watermelon cubes, and sour cherry jam were all on the table already. "This looks great, Baba. I'm just going for a quick short run, and I'll be back in time to eat with you guys."

After breakfast, she borrowed her parents' car and headed out. She drove to the first neighborhood they had moved to when they immigrated from Iran. She parked in front of the apartment complex they lived in and got out of the car and leaned against it, just looking at the building. Before she knew it, tears were streaming down her face again. She allowed herself to cry for the girl who had left her home in Tehran, not able to bring any of her belongings with her—forced to start over in a city and a school that didn't seem to want or welcome her.

She'd come to the US so full of dreams of what it would be like to go to high school wearing normal clothes and being in classes with boys. It had been such a rude awakening from that first day of school when Mr. Meade had singled her out as not being able to ever be president. She'd gotten to wear regular clothes instead of the manteau and hijab to school, but her family couldn't afford the brand names other girls wore or a different outfit for every single day. She'd found herself wishing that she was back in a manteau, nothing to differentiate her from the other girls and tell her she didn't belong. And as for boys, there had been no dates, not that Soraya would have allowed her to date anyway. Most people were not outwardly mean to her, but the ones who were, she could still remember their faces, their voices still fresh in her brain. Recalling these memories, she allowed herself to cry for the person who had been told that she was "other" from the moment she had arrived in the US—the person who had never been allowed to forget it.

CHAPTER FORTY

SEPTEMBER 2001: UPPER EAST SIDE, NEW YORK

As she walked out of the delivery room, Farah tore off her protective gown and threw it in the trash bin. She walked toward the nurses' station to find it empty. Where was everybody? She thought that maybe they had a staff meeting, but when she opened the conference room door, it was empty as well. Finally, she opened the doors to the breakroom to see all the floor nurses crammed in there, some staring at the TV, others on the phone and crying. She looked at the TV and saw what looked like smoke coming out of the twin towers. She couldn't hear what the news anchor was saying, so she read the underlying news banner. "Planes crash into Twin Towers. Terrorist attack on New York City suspected."

She read the banner over and over without registering what it said. Once she understood, her first thought was, *Please don't let them be Muslim,* before realizing that the city she was in right now was under attack. Her next thought was relief that they'd moved to Brooklyn, that her kids were not in Manhattan at that very minute.

Farah ran out of the nurses' station to make her way to her office. Her flip phone was in her bag in her desk drawer. She crossed the bridge connecting the hospital to the outpatient office and stepped into a packed elevator before the doors shut. Everyone in the elevator was talking about it. Some people knew, others were hearing about it for the first time, not seeming to comprehend what they were hearing. She ran to her office and grabbed her cell phone just as her pager started beeping at her waist. Three missed calls and then a voicemail from Mark. "Hey, I'm trying to get home to pick up the kids from school. It's pandemonium here. I tried calling Leticia and can't get a hold of her. I also couldn't get through to their schools. The phone lines are busy. I'm on my way to them. I love you."

Farah's pager beeped at her waist again. She hadn't checked it yet. She looked down and saw the extension for operating room number three. She dialed the number, and the operating room nurse answered. "Dr. Afshar, we need you in O-R 3. The house staff brought back a patient whose baby keeps having decels."

"I'm across the bridge in my office. I'll run over now," Farah said, but she wasn't particularly concerned about the baby. Decelerations in heart rate were very common in late stages of labor.

The next two days were chaos. Mark had gotten to Brooklyn and picked up the kids from school, and so Farah had stayed in the hospital late to allow other doctors to get home. Some nurses went home in fear, others called off their shifts and never came in, and some doctors were having trouble getting into the hospital. Farah's plan to stay late and help on September 11 turned into staying there for fifty-six hours, much longer than any shift she'd done during her residency. In those two days, she was nurse and doctor and resident and did whatever she could. Everyone who was already at the hospital or could make it in was doing whatever they could. Mark had taken care of the kids. Leticia had been too scared to leave her home and asked for a few days off. When Farah got to the point that she couldn't think straight from exhaustion anymore and was afraid that she wouldn't be able to follow the Hippocratic Oath, "First, do no harm," she finally went home. She held Mark and her kids and crumpled on the floor, finally breaking into sobs.

She cried for the people that she'd watched jump out of buildings on TV. She cried for her city. She cried because she was grateful that her kids were only half-Iranian and looked White, only their first names giving away any possible Muslim or Middle Eastern connection. She cried for herself, because she hadn't been safe in Iran, and now she wasn't safe in New York. She wasn't safe anywhere. And she cried because she was still trying to prove her worth and who she was—still stuck between two worlds and still worried that she would never quite belong.

CHAPTER FORTY-ONE

MARCH 2023: CINCINNATI, OHIO

After leaving the street with their first apartment, Farah drove to the house they had moved to just before junior year. She parked and surveyed the street from inside her car. It looked the same and yet different. The trees were more mature. Some of the homes had been renovated. Her house was the same, other than now having better landscaping. It was a traditional Tudor, a real American home. She'd had better memories in this house, from these years. In this home, she had at least had her own bedroom, where she could escape behind its closed doors and make plans for her future. Farah got out of the car and walked up the block and past a curve in the road until she got to Jared's home. Jared Anderson, her crush from the moment she'd laid eyes on him in ninth grade. The basketball hoop was still in the driveway. In high school, there had been so many days she would go on a walk and pass his driveway, hoping he would be out there shooting baskets. Anytime he was there, he would acknowledge her, just saying, "Hey, Farah," or simply giving a wave. Even in the hallways at school, or if he was on the sidelines of a football game and sighted her, he would nod or smile. Maybe that was why her crush on him, almost an obsession, had grown stronger and stronger—just his simple acknowledgment of her existence, it never went beyond that, was more than any other cute boy in high school ever gave her.

Every year on Valentine's Day, her high school had a fundraiser.

Students could buy a carnation for one dollar and have it delivered to their homeroom with a message to the designated person. A white carnation was for friendship, a pink carnation meant you found the person sexy, a red one meant love. Every Valentine's morning, students would walk into homeroom and see how many carnations and messages they had on their desks, and many of the girls would carry their flowers around for the whole day. Eliza Nausbaum in Farah's homeroom always had the most, at least thirty, on her desk, in an array of white, pink, and red. During freshman year, Farah walked into homeroom to see two white carnations on her desk, one each from her friends Morgan and Stacey. She had been hoping that miraculously Jared would have sent her a pink or red one, maybe with the message saying it was from a secret admirer, and then later he would reveal that he was the sender. Every Valentine's Day she held out the same hope, but every year, she got the same two white carnations—never a pink or red. As a teen, it hadn't occurred to her what a harmful fundraiser that was. It wasn't until Farah's kids were school-age and had to give Valentines to every classmate that Farah realized her high school had basically used a popularity contest to raise money. The counselors should have known how inappropriate and unhealthy that was for teenagers.

Standing in front of Jared's driveway, she wondered if his parents still lived in the house or if they had moved as well. The basketball hoop was still there, just a rim now with a wisp of torn netting hanging from it. Farah knew that Jared himself was no longer in Cincinnati. They'd become Facebook friends a few years ago. He had initiated the request, which even as a grown-ass woman who was almost fifty gave her a little sense of satisfaction. It was almost as if she had finally gotten a carnation from him, although she wasn't sure of which color. He lived in Austin now, a lawyer, with a wife and four kids. He had settled down after all. His wife was beautiful, American.

Finally, Farah drove to her high school. It looked the same, and it still seemed just as big as it had back then. A guard stood at the front door and told her no-one was allowed into the building without permission. There hadn't been security when Farah was a student. She explained that she was an alumnus, but the guard wouldn't budge. Finally, she opened her purse and showed him the contents, then offered to leave her driver's license with him while she went inside. Reluctantly, he agreed, handing her a laminated visitor's badge. Farah stepped into the lobby. The smell was what she noticed first. All these years later, despite thousands of other teens filing in and out of the building, it had that same smell—eau de linoleum floors mixed with teen hormones and sweat. To the right in the lobby was the bench where she'd often sat, waiting for her mom to pick her up, until her driver's license in junior year had bought her the freedom to leave immediately after school. She walked to the third-floor bathroom in the far corner of the school where she would sneak on makeup every morning as soon as her mom dropped her off; then wash it off before pickup. That charade had continued for her entire freshman year. Just before the start of her sophomore year, she'd told her mom that if she was not allowed to wear makeup, then she refused to go to school.

"You can't refuse to go to school," Soraya said. "Your job is to go to school and get good grades. If you're not going to do that, you can't live in this house."

"Okay, I'll find somewhere to live. I'm sure I can move in with Morgan. Her mother won't mind." Azita, who was sitting at the kitchen table reading, had opened her mouth as if to say something and then closed it again.

"Fine," Soraya conceded. "You can wear a little blush and lipstick. But no mascara and no eyeliner until you're sixteen."

"Then I'm wearing blush and lipstick, too," Azita quickly chimed in.

Soraya just shook her head and left the room, while Farah looked at Azita and mouthed, "You're welcome." On the first day of school, Farah had also put on a hint of eyeshadow and mascara, and every week, she would add just a little more.

Standing at the sink and mirror where she'd secretly put on and taken off makeup for a full year, she studied her reflection in the mirror.

Her face was the same as the one from her teen years, except for some frown lines and some laugh lines, cheeks that were a little hollowed out from age, the beginning of jowls. Her makeup and hair were surely better now, without the three shades of eyeshadow—blue, purple, green—and the neon pink lipstick later replaced by Cherries in the Snow. Gone was the feathered hair and high bangs kept in place with half a can of Aqua Net a day. *Who are you now and what are you doing here*, she asked herself. She supposed she was here to say goodbye to whatever she had been holding on to from her past.

She walked out of the back door of the high school and down to the football field. The football team was having its practice, some parents in the stands watching. A handful of people were running around the track. Surveying the players on the field and the parents in the stands, Farah realized it was noticeably less White than when she had been in high school. It was still pretty White, maybe 70 percent or so, but not 95 percent the way it had been in her years. *Even in Cincinnati, things change*, she thought. *Progress happens.* This made her smile.

On her way back to her parents' home, Farah stopped at Skyline Chili. She got a chili cheese sandwich and had a few bites. It really was still that good. But there was no way she could have more and go out to dinner that night. A little rest at home and tea with her parents was what she was ready for now. She rarely drank tea on her own anymore, but when she was with her parents, it always felt like home.

Later that night, Farah met Parisa and her friends at Boca for dinner. They hugged and Parisa laughed. "I see Maman wasted no time shaping up your brows."

Farah had met all of Parisa's friends a few times over the last fifteen years. A couple had been Parisa's bridesmaids. The last time she had seen them had probably been at Parisa's baby shower. Initially, the conversation was dominated by all of them asking how Farah had managed to take off so much time from her life to go to Paso, saying they would love just a week away on their own. Eventually, they fell into the rhythm of their typical mom's-night-out conversations— who was reading what, which activities a child was in, if someone had tried the new spin instructor Lacey at the spin studio, the props they were voting on in their upcoming city election, and whether they wanted to form a team for the 5K fundraiser to preserve their local park.

The food was excellent, from the charred leeks with hazelnut vinaigrette to the mafaldine con Bolognese to the maple mascarpone cheesecake. The conversation and wine flowed all through dinner as Farah looked around, taking in the atmosphere of the bustling restaurant, and truly studying Parisa's friends for the first time. These were women she could be friends with. She could imagine a younger version of herself, with school-age kids and a busy career, fitting right in with them, fitting right into a Cincinnati suburb life. And as she looked around, she realized that her trip had accomplished what she'd set out to see. Here she was, back in the city that had been so difficult to grow up in, feeling like she could live here again if she needed to. It wasn't about the city anymore. It was about her. She was no longer a teenager, and she didn't have to always feel like she was caught between two cultures and two worlds. She was a grown woman who knew who she was—and she would be okay anywhere.

On her flight back to Paso, Farah sent Jared a message through the messenger app:

I visited Cincinnati and our old street after years. I passed your old house. Our street looks the same, just with more mature trees.

Within ten minutes, he messaged back:

We visited home last Thanksgiving. My parents are still there. You're still in New York, right?

Yes, kind of. I'm temporarily in Paso Robles in California, but I'll be back in New York in a few months. Just taking a little time off.

Wow, I'm intrigued, Jared wrote. **I'd love to catch up over a drink if you are ever passing through Austin. Or even better,**

maybe the next time I'm in New York. I end up there for work sometimes.

Farah paused before answering. What was she doing? Yes, it would be nice to have an adult conversation with the one guy who fantasizing about had made those years bearable, and yes, she had always wondered if away from high school, he would have an interest in her. But he was a married man, and if she was going to move forward with her life, he was not the one to do it with. She texted him back:

I'm crazy busy when in New York, but sure, maybe something will work out sometime.

She put away her phone, leaned her chair back the couple of inches allowed, and closed her eyes. It felt good to make an active decision about her life, no matter how small.

CHAPTER FORTY-TWO

JULY 1995: DURHAM, NORTH CAROLINA

"I can't believe I'm being so indecisive. How can it already be time to pick what residency we're applying to?" Farah sighed. She picked up the bottle of white zinfandel between them and emptied the remainder in her glass. The three of them were sitting on the floor in Bridget's apartment on a humid Thursday night, the wall AC unit working overtime.

"Do you ever wonder why it's called white zinfandel and not pink zinfandel?" Neesha asked.

"Seriously?" Farah turned to Neesha. "I'm in the middle of an existential crisis about my future and that's what you're wondering?"

Bridget laughed. "Have you ever thought that maybe you make decision-making too complicated? Just follow your heart and your gut. What excites you more, picturing yourself as someone's gynecologist or as someone's internist?"

"It's not that simple. I want to usher women into motherhood, help women grappling with infertility. And I enjoy operating too."

"Sounds like you have your answer," Bridget said.

"But I don't want the lifestyle of an ob-gyn. I want to have kids, to always be a mother first. I know you can be an OB and a mother, but it's not easy. Being on call for deliveries and waking up at all hours to go to the hospital. It's also much easier to work part-time as an internist for a while than as an OB. Do I want to spend my whole life in medicine?" Farah asked.

"Um. Maybe you should have asked yourself that question before medical school," Neesha said.

"Yeah. Well, it's a little too late for that. And I don't think I had a choice about medicine," Farah said.

"What? How's that possible?" Bridget asked.

"Never mind. It's too complicated to explain. I'm here now," Farah said.

"Okay, so we know what you like about OB. What excites you about being an internist?" Neesha asked.

"Nothing really excites me about it. I do like having long-term relationships with patients, but you have that in OB as well, without having to take care of everything else," Farah said.

"Sounds like we're going to need another bottle of white zin," Bridget said and stood to go to her fridge. "Weren't you supposed to have that adviser meeting yesterday? What did she say?"

"She thinks I should do an acting internship month in both internal medicine and OB early this year and then decide. But I don't want to do two acting internship months! Doing one is going to be hard enough," Farah groaned.

"If you do internal medicine, the three of us could try to match into the same program and have at least another three years together," Neesha said.

"Okay. That's super realistic," Bridget rolled her eyes at Neesha. "The way I see it, you need to forget about the internist thing. Becoming a doctor is already having to sacrifice a lot, so you may as well be sacrificing for something you're excited about. I want to have kids, too, and would love a more flexible lifestyle, but I've always pictured myself as an oncologist, so that's what I'm going to do . . . and I'll figure the rest out."

Neesha reached out her glass toward Bridget for a refill. "When you say 'always' pictured yourself as an oncologist, are we talking about when you were a little kid, or once you decided to become a doctor?"

"I guess both. I watched my mom go through her breast cancer treatment when I was eight, and I said I'd be a cancer doctor one day," Bridget replied.

"Hmm. I always knew I'd go into medicine. I guess you could say that it was an expectation that my Indian mother imposed on me fairly early on, so I understand where Farah is coming from. But I haven't really had a personal pull or reason to want to go into cardiology. I just like the physiology of it," Neesha said and then turned to Farah. "How about you? Any personal experience that's leading you more toward OB?"

"No. None at all," Farah said and took a big gulp of her wine.

CHAPTER FORTY-THREE

MARCH 2023: PASO ROBLES, CALIFORNIA

The sound of laughter came through the door. Farah stood at the front door, holding a copy of *The Lowland*, a bottle of Pinot Noir, and a veggie tray with *maste esphenage*, spinach yogurt with garlic and herbs, as the dip. Although she had read *The Lowland* before, she'd ordered herself another copy and skimmed through it to refresh her memory and allow her to participate better in her first Paso book club discussion. She noticed the doormat below her feet said, "Y'all better have wine," and the door itself was decorated with a giant floral wreath and pastel ribbons. Farah smiled, feeling like she was in a Hallmark movie on the porch of a house that changed its decorations for every holiday.

Cecily, wearing a spaghetti strap emerald-green maxi dress and glittery dangling earrings, answered the door with a big smile. She gave Farah a hug. "Come on in. I'll take these from you and introduce you to everyone." Farah stepped into the scent of vanilla and cloves.

She followed Cecily in and was relieved to see Blythe, a familiar face, among the other women. She was also happy to see that, in contrast to the potluck, she was not the only non-White person. There was also Laura, who looked Asian. It was something. Looking around, Farah was surprised to see that everyone was fairly dressed up, the way they would be if they had gone out to a nice dinner. Farah had just thrown on her Paso uniform of T-shirt, jeans, and cowboy boots. She hadn't wanted to overdress or look too New York for the occasion. Everyone already had a glass of wine in hand.

"You're more of a red gal from what I remember," Cecily said. "I have a Syrah and a GSM open, or I can open something else?"

"GSM would be great," Farah said. "I can grab it myself."

"I'll get your first. You're on your own after that."

Farah took a seat next to Blythe. She went through answering the usual questions—what had brought her to Paso, did she have children, how interesting that she had just taken six months for herself. She listened to the conversations around her. Finally, Cecily interjected, "Okay ladies, time to talk about the book. I'm just going to start by saying that I absolutely loved it. It was so sad, but sad in a good way. My heart just really broke for Subhash the entire time. He was stuck between these two worlds, and I just wanted him to be happy."

Yup, I like Cecily, Farah thought. "Stuck between two worlds" was how Farah had lived a great part of her life, and not everyone got it, but Cecily had read this story and seen it. "Farah, I know you're the newbie here, but since I know you loved this book, too, tell me some of what stood out for you," Cecily added.

"Well, I do think that Lahiri really demonstrated this being stuck between two worlds—obligation to family and culture versus obligation to self—very well. But I think what I loved about it most was that I love it when I read a book and the protagonist is a man, and I still find myself completely engrossed and invested in his plight. I think I mostly read novels about female characters, and my entire job as an ob-gyn has been centered around women. But I do think that men can have just as complex—okay maybe *almost* as complex—a range of emotional burden and they just don't express it, and we don't hear about it." Farah was surprised to hear the words coming out of her mouth as she said them.

"You're right," Laura agreed. "I really don't read nearly enough books in which the central character is male. And we've had so many male authors writing about women for years, it's nice to see a female author writing about a man. I loved the book too. I didn't want it to end yet I needed it to end so I could move on. It was heavy."

"All the parts about marriage were really interesting and foreign to me," Gina, a mother of four who taught Algebra and Geometry at Templeton High School chimed in. "This idea of arranged marriages, and then Subhash marrying his dead brother's pregnant wife. I just couldn't imagine it. And I think arranged marriages still happen all the time in India. I just don't understand it."

"My parents had kind of an arranged marriage. They were introduced to each other and married shortly after, and they've been together for fifty-five years. And happy I might add. Most of my mom's friends had arranged marriages, and at least half of them are okay. And here I am, having chosen my own husband . . . and just gotten a divorce," Farah paused. "I'm not saying I'm for arranged marriages. I would obviously not ever set one up for my kids nor would they let me. But I just don't know how different that is than meeting someone on Match.com. Marriage is a crap shoot. Or maybe I'm just in that place right now. But you have to understand the cultural context of this book and the people in it. If Subhash hadn't married Gauri, what would have become of her and her daughter?" Farah paused. Was she saying too much? Was she dominating the conversation?

"I agree, Farah," Caitlyn joined in. "And what I really liked was that then Gauri took off. It wasn't like she married her dead husband's brother and then they lived happily ever after. She was a strong woman. She was political. I had a hard time with her leaving her daughter, but there was no easy or good answer to the entire situation."

As the conversation continued, Farah realized how much she was enjoying herself. She loved reading and talking about books. In the past, sometimes she would read a book and then force one of her sisters or Julia to read it so she could discuss it with them. Why had she never made the time to join a book club in New York so she could discuss books with people who genuinely wanted to be doing that?

When it came time to pick the book for the next month, Farah learned that it was Laura's turn to host the next meeting, and the host always picked the next book so that everyone got a chance to choose a book rather than the club voting. Laura announced that their next book would be Celeste Ng's *Our Missing Hearts.* Farah loved Ng's other books and hadn't had a chance to read this one. She was looking forward to it already.

CHAPTER FORTY-FOUR

AUGUST 1986: CINCINNATI, OHIO

Azita was sprawled out on her bed, rereading the latest *Sweet Valley High* book she'd checked out from the library.

"How many times are you going to read that?" Farah asked.

Azita didn't bother to sit up or put her book down as she answered. "It's hot. I'm bored. What else is there to do?"

Farah had also read all of Elizabeth and Jessica Wakefield's high school adventures more than once. If she and Azita were going to be quintessential American blond sisters in high school, then Farah was Elizabeth, the good girl. She was the one most likely to be nice to everyone, do her homework, date the nice guy, please her parents. Azita had a little more Jessica in her, pushing the boundaries, questioning their parents, having a crush on multiple guys at once. But they were both far from being Elizabeth and Jessica, because other than their personality differences, they had nothing in common with them.

Suddenly, Azita sat up. "I know what we can do." She walked over to her dresser, opened the bottom drawer, rummaged through all the clothes, and pulled out a bottle of Sun-In.

"When did you get that? Maman will kill us if we color our hair," Farah said.

"Um, yeah. But technically, we are not coloring our hair. This is just Sun-In. And I heard that if you spray this in your hair and squeeze lemon juice on it too, it works even better."

"I don't know about this," Farah said as she grabbed the bottle from Azita, reading the directions.

"Come on. Don't be such a chicken. If we do it together and say we heard it's good for your hair, we can't get in trouble. Maman won't be home for a few hours. By the time she's home, we'll be blonds like Jessica and Elizabeth." Azita laughed.

Farah raised an eyebrow, but she agreed to it despite her skepticism. "All right, fine. We'll try it. But let me change into long sleeves and pants first. I don't need my skin getting any darker than it already is."

They both changed to cover their bodies, then lay face down on towels in the backyard, their hair fanned out around them for as much sun exposure as possible. Sweat trickled down Farah's neck and eventually her whole body was wet. She started to feel dizzy. After an hour she said, "My head hurts. I hope this isn't causing us brain damage."

"You're not getting brain damage. You're just hot," Azita said.

"Heatstroke is a real thing, you know. This better be worth it!"

Three hours and two pounds lighter from sweating later, Farah looked in the mirror. Her hair was an orange-brown dirty rust color. Who were they kidding? They could dream about being the girls in the books they read, but no amount of Sun-In and lemon juice would ever make them blonds. They would never date the popular guy. They would never try out for the cheerleading team. They would never have a group of girlfriends over for a sleepover, taking over the family room, eating fresh-baked cookies and doing each other's makeup late into the night. They would never be American. They would never be remotely like a single character in any of the books everyone their age read. And now they'd have to deal with Maman's wrath when she saw them as well. Farah could hear Soraya's voice in her head: *"Look what you've done to yourselves! You've ruined yourselves, just like American girls do."*

CHAPTER FORTY-FIVE

MARCH 2023: PASO ROBLES, CALIFORNIA

What did one wear to a first date these days? Farah stood by her open closet door, staring at the fairly minimal wardrobe she had brought to Paso. Farah was meeting Brent at the Halter Ranch tasting room for their first date. Brent was fifty-seven, a divorced father of three, a software engineer, and an avid cyclist. On paper, or rather on screen, Julia had made her a decent first match.

Farah felt a trickle of sweat making its way down her torso as she reached for a halter top. *Why am I nervous?* She shook her head and decided that simple and casual would be best, throwing on jeans, a relaxed white button-down shirt, her studded cowboy booties, a turquoise necklace, and big gold hoop earrings. She was grateful not to be young, feeling like she needed to be in a tight minidress and heels for a first date. She purposely chose mismatched underwear, telling herself there was no way she was ready to have sex with anyone. Bad underwear was a little insurance to deter her if by some miraculous turn of events she was inclined to do so.

She walked in to find Brent sitting behind one of the wine bars, waiting for her. He stood up when he saw her walking toward him and smiled. Farah was relieved that he looked like his pictures—gray hair, hazel eyes, bronze skin, about five foot ten, and clearly fit. He seemed to also have a look of relief when he saw her.

"Phew," Brent said. "You look as beautiful as your picture, and I like the shorter hair."

Farah smiled and touched her hair, which was now just past her shoulders again. "Thanks, you look like your picture too."

Making conversation with Brent was relatively easy. Having a first date over a wine flight made it easier, as the attendant poured each varietal and they could at least talk about each wine and what notes each of them smelled, the legs, how acidic or tannic it was, and ultimately, whether they liked it.

"I've been divorced for almost ten years now. My youngest is a sophomore in high school. She's mostly with my ex-wife since her house is very close to the school, but I have her at least every other weekend and whenever she needs a little mom break," Brent explained.

"So, your ex-wife lives in Paso as well," Farah said.

"No, we both live in San Luis Obispo, but I come up to Paso a lot."

"Oh," Farah said, trying to not sound disappointed. "I've been there once, and it's lovely." San Luis Obispo was about thirty miles away. Farah thought about how she was not going to drive that far to see him, and so between the weekends when he had his daughter and the distance, was this really going to go anywhere? Then she could hear Julia in her head reprimanding her for jumping ahead, so when Brent asked if they should go on to get dinner somewhere, she said yes.

"Great. I made reservations at Hatch just in case this went well and I wanted to ask you to dinner," Brent smiled.

"So, you think this is going well?" Farah raised an eyebrow. "I like a planner."

He was sweet and a complete gentleman at dinner, opening doors for her, pulling out her chair, having her pick and approve the wine, and refusing her offer to split the bill. Yet when he was driving her home, Farah had a sudden sense of not wanting to be there or ever see him again. When he walked her to her door and asked if he could call her again, she couldn't remember how she used to turn down a second date before. She said sure and gave him a quick, awkward hug, then hurriedly opened her door and went in. As she undressed and saw herself in her mismatched underwear, she laughed. She had come nowhere close to needing to worry about having sex with him. When he sent her flowers the next day, she sent him a text apologizing and saying that she'd had a lovely time but realized that she wasn't ready to date.

"I need you to deactivate my account and put a hold on this whole dating thing," she told Julia after she'd texted Brent.

"Really? Was it that bad? His profile looked so good," Julia questioned.

"No. It was fine. He was great. He was probably too good. And he is probably someone that I could date for a while, but that's just it. I don't want that. That freaked me out. I'm not ready for that."

"Okay. How about I just set you up with some younger guys that you just have fun—"

"No," Farah cut her off. "I don't want that either. If I meet someone organically, I do. And if not, I don't. I realize that's not easy to do at my age in this town. But I'm not here forever. Thank you, but . . . I don't know. Meeting Mark and dating before was just so easy. I just want easy and organic . . . and I'm not ready."

"Okay. We'll wait. Lots of time for you to be ready," Julia reassured.

"I want to ask you something, and I want you to answer honestly," Farah said.

"Have I ever not been honest with you?" Julia asked.

"No, but. Anyway, did you ever question why exactly I was divorcing Mark?"

"Uh-oh. Where is this coming from?"

"Azita mentioned no one really knows why I left my work or why I left Mark, and of all people, I probably shared the ins and outs of our relationship with you the most, so I was wondering if you feel the same way Azita claims everyone does," Farah said.

"You guys had arguments—ups and downs. Your arguments didn't seem like they were really over anything too big, but what do

I know? I wasn't in your marriage. But when you were good together, you were good," Julia admitted.

"So, you think I made a mistake?" Farah asked.

"I didn't say that. I don't know. I'm not you. I wasn't there. No one really knows what is going on in anyone's life but themselves," Julia said.

"Yeah. I've just been thinking. A lot of it probably was my fault. I wasn't necessarily always there for him, and I don't think I ever figured myself out. If you don't figure yourself out, if you don't know what you need, it's hard for someone else to give it to you, and it's easy to blame them for everything you can't figure out," Farah said.

"Wait, have you been seeing a real therapist in Paso?" Julia asked.

"No. Just having time to meditate, to think. I probably should see a real one," Farah said.

"I think you should."

When Farah hung up, she thought about one of her favorite quotes from the poet Hafez, "The words we speak become the house we live in." She hadn't spoken the words, not to Mark, not even really to herself. So how could she have expected to build a home with him without laying down the foundation?

CHAPTER FORTY-SIX

MAY 2012: BROOKLYN, NEW YORK

It was a little after midnight by the time Farah finally walked in the door, quietly closing it behind her. She turned on the entryway light and took off her surgical clogs, leaving them by the front door. She caught a glimpse of herself in the entryway mirror. Her hair, which she'd had professionally blown out earlier in the day, was now in a ponytail and matted down from being under a surgical cap. For the first time it occurred to her how ironic it was that she had chosen a profession where she had to cover her hair half the time. A line from the elastic of the surgical cap had created a crease along the middle of her forehead. Her scrubs didn't go with the dark cherry-red lipstick and glittery eyeshadow she had put on in anticipation of going out that night, knowing she may only make it home in time for a quick change. Farah walked into the office and found Mark awake.

He was still in his slacks, the top two buttons of his dress shirt undone, his tie loosened around his neck. His hair was disheveled. He was holding a glass of scotch, the bottle of Balvenie 14 on his desk, and looking out the window into the darkness. "I'm sorry," Farah said.

"Okay," Mark scoffed, still staring out the window.

"I really, really am. I wanted to be there, but I just couldn't make it," Farah said. Mark had won the Presidential Award for Outstanding Teaching at Pace. It was a big deal. "I got a call that Doug Ferguson's wife went into labor and the baby was having some decelerations, and it was just a delivery I couldn't miss."

"Right, you couldn't miss that one, because you were on call tonight. Oh, wait, no, you weren't on call. You put in the request to not be on call tonight two months ago! Your colleagues could have done it. But anyway, it doesn't matter," Mark replied, still staring out the window.

"It does matter, Mark, I just—" Farah started before Mark cut her off, finally turning to face her.

"Of course it fucking matters! I don't ask anything of you. You knew how important this night was for me, but you just don't fucking care. I'm always your last priority," Mark yelled.

"That's not true. I do care. You know that. But Doug Ferguson is the CEO of the hospital. They chose me as their OB. It wasn't a delivery I could miss," Farah said.

"He's the CEO and I'm your husband. And this is the first time in all my years of hard work at Pace that I got this award. You're more likely to miss a delivery if Delara has a basketball game or if Julia has some godforsaken fake emergency, but you wouldn't miss a delivery for one of the biggest nights in my career."

"That's not true. It wasn't just any delivery," Farah said. "But I'm sorry. I made a decision to be there, and I thought she would deliver fast and I'd make it in time. And then her labor wasn't progressing. The baby started having decels, so I couldn't just leave, and she didn't want to go to C-section and—"

Mark held up his hand. "Shut the fuck up. I don't give a *fuck* about the details of her labor. You know, afterward Joyce and Stewart and Aubrey and Malik wanted to take me out for drinks to celebrate, and their partners were there and mine wasn't. And I'm the guy in the department who got the award! How do you think that makes me look?" Mark shook his head.

Farah stayed silent. Inside, she was fuming. He didn't understand how much she had wanted to be there, or how much these choices weighed on her. She expected him to be an adult, to realize that it was more important to sacrifice her work when it involved the kids than when it involved him. And had it been any other patient, she would have missed the delivery for his event.

"Just go to bed and leave me alone. I don't want to talk to you right now, and you have to get up early anyway." Mark broke the silence.

Farah went to their bedroom, stripped off her scrubs, and crawled under the covers without bothering to wash off her makeup or even brush her teeth. She was too exhausted to do anything, but when she closed her eyes, she couldn't sleep. Was Mark right? Why did she care so much about Doug Ferguson? Why had she felt the pressure to be there for him and his wife over being there for Mark? Why had she sacrificed so much of her own well-being and her family's for her work? Her colleagues would have done a perfectly good job with that delivery. But it wasn't about the delivery or even Doug's wife, Hilary. It was about the constant pressure she felt to prove herself and stay on top. Why couldn't she let that go? But why should she let that go?

She'd thought that one advantage of marrying an American over an Iranian would be that he would be more understanding of her ambition—more supportive of her sometimes needing to put her career first. But were all men the same? She looked at her alarm clock. It was already two o'clock. She had to get up at five thirty. Mark still hadn't come to bed. She couldn't shut down her mind. He was always saying that he was her last priority—that it was the kids, work, her sisters and parents, and even Julia before him. Even tonight, he had brought up Julia again.

CHAPTER FORTY-SEVEN

MARCH 2023: PASO ROBLES, CALIFORNIA

"You got mail again," Sarah Bennet was standing there smiling when Farah answered the door.

"Thanks, Sarah. Maybe if you have another long-term tenant after me, you should ask them to get a PO box in town so you don't have to keep being bothered by their mail," Farah suggested.

"Oh, it's no bother." Sarah cocked her head to the side, examining Farah's face. "You look like you could use some company. I've got a group of ladies coming to my house in an hour for our regular Monday 'canasta and cocktails' meeting. The theme cocktail today is a pisco sour. Why don't you join us?"

"It's only noon. If I start drinking cocktails at one, I'll be asleep by four," Farah said.

"Not with these ladies, you won't."

"And I've never played canasta. I don't know how."

Sarah laughed, "Well, then I guess you are about to have the most fun you've ever had on a Monday afternoon in a long time." Sarah clapped her hands together and then leaned her head in. "What is that intoxicating smell?"

Farah laughed. "It's rosewater. I brought some back from Cincinnati and pour a little into a shot glass and leave it on the table each day. It reminds me of home."

"It's fabulous. Okay. I'm going to go finish setting up. See you soon."

Farah threw the mail on the coffee table without looking at it and jumped in the shower. An hour later, she was standing at Sarah's door in a knee-length floral dress, feeling guilty about being empty-handed. As she rang the doorbell, she heard laughing on the other side of the door as a voice she didn't recognize sang out, "The door's open. Come on in."

Farah opened the door and walked in. She was immediately greeted by Candace, a friend of Sarah's that she had met at Braxton several times before. Candace had short blond hair, blue eyes that looked like they had lost their shine due to age, big square glasses, and a wide toothy smile. She was wearing a bright multicolored caftan.

"Farah!" Candace hugged her like they were life-long friends, careful not to spill her pisco sour. "So glad Sarah asked you to join. You're in for a treat. Let's get your cocktail and introduce you to everyone."

Farah guessed that Candace was in her early seventies. *I hope that I can be that vibrant at her age,* Farah thought. As Farah was introduced to each of Sarah's canasta crew, she realized that she was at least fifteen years younger than every person there. Soon, she was sitting at one of the two round card tables set up in Sarah's living room, deck of cards and score sheets on each table, and getting a quick tutorial from Josephine, the "Queen of Canasta."

"Honey, you're going to sit by me for the first couple of rounds and watch. And then you're on your own. But you're a young one, so you'll catch on fast," Josephine reassured her.

Farah had grown up playing cards. She must have been no more than five years old when her Khaleh Nasreen had taught her and Zareen to play the card game rummy, the way Iranians play it. They'd had to learn the point value of cards and how to add to thirty in a myriad of ways before they learned how to read in order to play. But when it came to cards, Nasreen had all the patience in the world to teach. Growing up, Soraya had always had a rummy group, much like Sarah's canasta crew, that met once a week and played cards for hours. The difference was that while they played cards, Soraya's group went through multiple glasses of steaming hot tea, no matter the weather, while Sarah's friends sipped on cocktails. Farah couldn't recall any instance of seeing her mom and her friends drink alcohol in the daytime, but she did love it when she was home on rummy days. She would pretend to be playing or working on homework while she listened in to the adult conversation of her mother's friends. And sometimes, just for a little bit, she would sit on the corner of Soraya's chair, resting her head on Soraya's shoulder or chest, and watch a few rounds of the game. Even on days when Khaleh Nasreen and Zareen joined the rummy group, Farah and Zareen would stay on the periphery of the card table instead of going off on their own. When they moved to Cincinnati, it had taken Soraya less than a year to meet people through Cincinnati's Iranian Cultural Association and set up a new rummy group. But the Cincinnati group was coed and played on Sundays. Watching them play or listening to their conversation was just not the same as hanging on the periphery of the Tehran crowd. And rummy reminded Farah too much of Khaleh Nasreen and Zareen, so she would usually just retreat to her room.

Farah had a true blast at canasta and hoped she would be invited again. It made her look forward to being old, retired, and potentially having her own canasta or rummy group. She could teach her friends rummy, the Iranian way, the first and best card game she had ever learned.

The problem was that she didn't have a core group of friends anymore. Her friends were scattered and stressed. There were the undergrad friends, the medical school friends, the residency friends, all scattered across the US, and then the New York work friends. It was hard enough to get the friends from Brooklyn and Queens and Manhattan all to reunite for a ladies' night a few times a year. Everyone in New York was always so busy, so rushed, so unwilling to ride the subway back into Manhattan when it wasn't for work. Also, she couldn't imagine any of her friends being up for gathering at their apartments for a card game rather than going out to dinner or a wine bar, but maybe when they got older.

Farah grabbed the stack of mail Sarah had dropped off and sunk into her couch. There was a manila envelope of mail from her secretary. Connie would collect any personal mail she got in the office and send it to her every couple of months. As she flipped through the envelopes, she saw a card from the Hollinger-Ward family. She ripped it open and pulled out the card. On the front was a picture of a baby in a lavender onesie, smiling in its sleep. Emerson Quinn Hollinger-Ward. Born September 21, 2023. Seven pounds, five ounces, and twenty-one inches long. On the back was a picture of James and Craig, holding Emerson and beaming. It made Farah cry. There was no mention in the announcement whether Emerson was a boy or a girl. Farah remembered that they had not wanted to find out the sex of the baby, saying that it wouldn't change how they felt or how they would raise it.

"We're not going to raise a 'theyby,'" James had said. "We'll look at the genitals and use he or she pronouns. But there's no need to feed into this obsession with a baby's sex." Farah had been grateful that she knew what a "theyby" is, having just read an article in the *New York Times* about parents who were raising kids without telling anyone the sex of their child and raising them in a gender-neutral way. She was sorry to have missed that delivery, but looking at the announcement now, she realized that it didn't matter whether Rumi carried a baby or his future partner did. She just wanted him to be happy and beaming in a family picture one day, the way James was in his. Thinking about it now, it was so obvious that Farah would not have loved her own kids any less if they were not from her eggs, or if she hadn't been the one to carry them.

CHAPTER FORTY-EIGHT

MAY 2001: CHARLOTTE, NORTH CAROLINA

A giant pink banner with the words *Baby Delara* hung across Janet's living room. She'd covered her home with pink and white flowers, balloons, and streamers. At first, Farah didn't want to have a shower for Delara. She believed that baby showers should just be for the firstborn and having one for subsequent children was frivolous when you already had all the gear, especially since she was having another girl and had all the clothes as well. But the shower for Darya had been in Cincinnati at Soraya's house, organized by Azita. Farah understood that Mark's mother would want to be able to have something in her hometown and invite all her friends and family, so she'd conceded. Besides, the shower for Darya, despite Azita's best efforts, was more of a regular Iranian *mehmooni* than a traditional baby shower.

All of Soraya's friends, 90 percent of whom were Iranian, had gathered around for this tradition they didn't have in their own country. Soraya's house had been covered with pink and white flowers as well, but her dining table had been overflowing with every Persian stew, from *gheymeh* to *fesenjoon*, food her mother had spent a week preparing. Azita had tried to convince Soraya that an afternoon baby shower could just have little tea sandwiches and other finger foods, but Soraya would not hear of it. Other than a couple of traditional baby shower games like the baby food guessing game that Azita insisted on, the rest of the shower had been like any Iranian women's party. Lots of food, rounds and rounds of cardamom-scented brewed loose-leaf Darjeeling tea—Soraya had two giant samovars on the entire time—and breaking out into Iranian dancing. A living room dance party was part of every Iranian mehmooni.

Looking around Janet's living room now, Farah was glad she'd agreed to this shower. Janet had taken the time to custom order little pink napkins that had *Delara* written on them in gold foil. The party favors were little pink boots filled with Hershey kisses and almond macaroons, tied with pink ribbons that had *Delara* printed on them as well. And the centerpieces on the buffet table were all diaper tower cakes.

Janet's table was also a strong contrast to Soraya's in terms of the food. She had the event catered. Trays of little sandwiches, pasta salad, and broccoli salad covered the main table. Another table had an assortment of minicookies and minimuffins along with the cake. As Farah surveyed the room, she smiled and put her hand over her belly. Her first true American shower. Even her bridal shower had been a mehmooni at heart.

"So Farah, do you think you'll have a third? Try for that boy?" Aunt Shirley asked.

Farah was taken aback. Why did people feel it was okay to ask about a next kid when she was still pregnant? "Oh, I don't know about that. Let's see how we do with our jobs and having two kids in New York City. Anyway, I was happy to find out I'm having another girl. I want a sister for Darya. I can't imagine not having had one myself." It was true. A month earlier, when she'd had her twenty-week ultrasound, the technician had moved the wand close to the genitalia and paused. "Dr. Afshar, do you want to know the sex, or do you want to turn your head away for this part?"

"I'll look," Farah had said. The tech had squeezed a fresh glob of gel onto her abdomen and moved her wand in and deep, waiting for the baby to open its legs. Farah had been sure she was having a boy this time. The pregnancy just felt different from the last one. She didn't have nearly as much morning sickness. She was carrying differently. She was glowing rather than always looking tired the way she had with Darya. As an OB, she knew that the rumors that girl pregnancies are harder, with more vomiting and the girl "stealing the mother's beauty" were just ridiculous myths, but somehow, she'd just felt like this time was different. She was carrying a boy. She'd been certain of it. When the baby had moved, Farah and the tech had looked at each other and smiled. "I see hamburger buns," Farah had said with surprise, referring to the appearance of the labia on ultrasound.

"I do too," the tech had smiled. "It's another girl for you. Sisters that are two years apart sounds just perfect."

Just like Azita and myself, Farah had thought. And then she'd laughed at herself for believing the rumors, convincing herself that since she felt so different, she was carrying a boy. She'd started dreaming of her future daughters' relationship right then. They would be borrowing each other's clothes and stealing each other's makeup.

At the shower, Aunt Shirley smiled and squeezed Farah's hand, "Well, sisters are absolutely wonderful, but I think it would be nice to have a boy as well."

Then Mark's grandmother asked, "What does the name Delara mean, dear?"

"It means *beloved*," Farah replied. Darya means *sea*. All Persian names have a meaning and a significance. She'd explained this to Grandma Jo before.

"That's lovely," Grandma Jo replied. She seemed to mean it. "And how about the middle name for this one?"

"Delara's middle name will be Afshar as well. I know I used that for Darya, but in Iran, we don't have middle names anyway, so I think giving them all my last name as their middle name works better than a hyphenated last name," Farah said.

"Oh," Grandma Jo replied. She looked at Farah as if she was about to say something else and then held back.

"I think Delara Afshar Benedetti sounds like a fabulous name."

Mark's sister Alexis came to Farah's rescue, putting her arms protectively around her shoulders. "I love how important it is to Farah to impart her culture and values on her children."

"Yes," Janet chimed in. "My son got lucky with this one. I've just loved learning everything about Farah's culture. You'd be surprised how much they have in common with Italian culture—maybe the Irish part not as much though," she said, laughing. Farah locked eyes with Janet, using them to say a silent thank you.

"Now who's ready for a game?" Alexis clapped her hands and changed the subject.

CHAPTER FORTY-NINE

APRIL 2023: PASO ROBLES, CALIFORNIA

Sitting in lotus pose on her yoga mat, Farah focused her eyes straight ahead, staring at one of the vines until it blurred. She'd given up on traditional meditating. Ever since she'd decided to make peace with her morning meditation and allow it to be a time for free-flowing thoughts instead, memories from her past that she'd been avoiding were flooding her mind.

Just four months after moving to the US, Farah had been sitting at the kitchen table at night, working on homework. School had not gotten any better. There were some people who were friendly toward her, but she hadn't really made any friends. She missed Iran—having friends and family. She'd realized that it was worth wearing a hijab if it meant being surrounded by people who loved and understood you—who didn't see you as "other." And she didn't feel like she could tell her parents that she was having a hard time. They'd left everything and started over for them. They were having a hard enough time on their own.

The phone had rung. Her parents were in their bedroom. Farah heard Soraya answer the phone, and then realized the call was from Iran because in addition to speaking in Farsi, Soraya was speaking in a loud volume. She still didn't understand why her parents raised their voices so much when talking to family in Iran. The connection wasn't that bad. Usually, calls with family in Iran were initiated by her parents, not the other way around, but Farah didn't think anything of it. Then she heard her mother say, "Chee Shod? Chee Shod?"—What happened?

This was followed by silence.

And then a guttural wail.

Farah and her sisters ran into their parents' bedroom. Farah was terrified that the call was about Zareen.

Farah's hands trembled now as she relived the memory. She gripped the yoga mat beneath her to steady them. The call had not been about Zareen. The call had been about their home. A missile had landed in the courtyard of their quadplex in Tehran. The downstairs neighbors, Alireza and his family, were the only ones who had been home. Their quadplex had collapsed. Alireza was gone.

Farah had spent three days at home from school before going back. She knew that all she had left now was to throw herself into her education. There was no home to go back to—no potential future with her first love. She couldn't believe how immune they had become to the air raids while they were in Tehran, not being scared of them anymore. And yet, how shortly after they were gone, their home had been destroyed. Even if Alireza's parents could have someday found a way to get him and his sister out of Iran, none of that mattered now. She tried to block Alireza's face out of her mind and never longed for home again.

Remembering this scene, Farah realized that she'd never talked about these parts of her childhood with anyone. Her children had no idea that her childhood home had crumpled during the war, although they had seen pictures of that home in old albums at Soraya's house. They didn't know that her childhood playmate, her first crush Alireza, had died. Farah had blocked it all from her mind as much as she could. It had been too much to handle at that age when she was already struggling and had lost so much. Julia knew nothing about it. Mark was the only person who knew their house had crumpled. He had asked her soon after they had started dating if she had ever gone back to Iran since immigrating to the US. "No,"

Farah had answered. "My parents have, but I haven't wanted to."

"You don't want to see your extended family? Or your childhood home?" he'd sounded surprised.

"No," she answered. "It's not there anymore."

She knew that Alireza was the reason that she never dated Iranian guys. Now she wondered if she had ever properly mourned his loss or dealt with the trauma of losing him. If she had gone to therapy years ago, would she have dated Iranian guys? Ended up with a completely different life? She shook her head. It didn't matter. She had Darya and Rumi because of whatever had gotten her to Mark, and she wouldn't trade them for anything in the world.

Farah rolled up her yoga mat and went inside. She called Julia, who answered in her usual chipper voice. "Tell me something juicy. My life has become all work."

"I'm sorry but I'm going to have to disappoint you," Farah responded. Then she proceeded to tell Julia how her daily meditation had turned into her thinking time instead of her clearing her mind time. Farah told Julia that she had a past she didn't share with anyone—that there were so many things her children didn't know about her. "And then I thought, does anyone really know me? Have I allowed myself to know my full self? And how can you be my best friend and I have not told you about so much of my past? I know this is stuff from forty years ago, but it's also experiences that don't go away, no matter how much you've tried to bury them."

"Of course they don't go away. Why do you think you haven't told me any of this?" Julia asked.

"I don't know. Maybe I haven't wanted to think about it. Some of it I feel guilty about and am not ready to share, but if I'm being honest, I'm not sure if it's because I've wanted to pretend it all never happened, or if it's because I've just wanted to seem like a normal American. A fun person. I haven't wanted people to see all parts of me. I haven't wanted to be too much, to be that person, to scare people away."

"Farah *Joon*, you are normal and fun and flawed and your past and your present. You can never be too much. I want to know all parts of my friend. And your kids, they're old enough for you to start sharing some of this with them too."

Julia was right. The new Farah would return from Paso a whole person, with a tapestry of life experiences and no apologies for who she was. Her past was her terroir. How could she know what she wanted and form real relationships with anyone if she kept trying to deny it?

"You're right. I'm going to start slowly sharing this with my kids. My mom recently told me all these things about her sisters, and I told her I didn't understand why she'd kept all this from me for so long—why Iranians don't talk about these things. And I can't believe it, but here I've been doing the same with my own children. I haven't told them about foundational experiences that have made me who I am today," Farah said, surprised that she hadn't realized all this sooner.

"And what about your sisters? Especially Azita? This is your shared past. Do you talk to each other about it?" Julia asked.

"No. We never talk about Iran. But most of that is my fault."

"But you two are so close. This has probably influenced her life decisions just as it has yours, and who knows, maybe holding it all in has affected her in ways you don't know about," Julia said.

"Julia, why are you an architect? You are the best therapist in the world. But I'm making a promise to get a real one that I pay. That I tell everything to until I'm ready to tell others."

When she hung up the phone, Farah went to the music app on her phone and searched "Googoosh Do Panjereh." Since Alireza's death, every time that song came on in the background at Soraya's house, she would leave the room, unable to listen to their song. Now, she sat on the couch and pressed the play button, allowing her tears to flow as the lyrics filled the room.

CHAPTER FIFTY

OCTOBER 1987: CINCINNATI, OHIO

Farah sang the lyrics of "Lost in Emotion" by Lisa Lisa and Cult Jam as she filled out her first college application. The music blared in her headphones, and she was lost in her own world. Just as she was about to check off "other," she stopped herself. It occurred to her that for the first time, under nationality, she would be checking off "US citizen." It had been only one month since her entire family had completed their naturalization, taking an oath of allegiance to the United States.

After court, her parents had dropped off Farah and her sisters back in school for the remainder of the day. They hadn't gone to a celebratory lunch or even had a special dinner. Dinner that evening had been *khoreshte kadoo*, zucchini stew. Sitting at the dinner table that night, Farah had thought about how her family didn't look any more American or nonforeign on this night than they had the night before—although her mother had been more animated and optimistic for once. Soraya was talking about how now that they were citizens, she wasn't going to waste any time. She was going to start the process of applying for green cards for her sisters, and although it would take years for them to possibly get them, there was room for hope.

Now, staring down at the application and checking off "US Citizen," Farah felt like she was lying about who she was. Since moving to America, there had been many instances when she'd lied about her ethnicity. When they took family trips away from Cincinnati, whether to Washington DC or New York City or Virginia Beach, she would meet someone and say she was from Greece or Turkey. She could easily pass for anything Mediterranean, and that was so much easier than saying she was from Iran. It was such a nice escape to take on this new persona before having to return to school and be the Iranian girl again, associated with Khomeini and the hostage crisis and the Iran-Contra affair. Sometimes, she would feel guilty about denying who she was, when she was simultaneously proud of her relatives and the beauty of her country. At these times, she was grateful that she didn't believe in a heaven or hell, that she knew her grandmother wasn't watching her deny who she was from up above.

Would she ever pass as an American or feel like she truly was one? Ten years from now, she would have spent more of her life living in the US than in Iran—in twenty years, almost three times as much. How would she feel then? She'd already noticed that the majority of her dreams were now in English. Her thoughts had gone from always being in Farsi through a period of being in Farsi and English fairly equally to now mostly being in English. It was out of her control. And so maybe one day, she would feel like an American, unable to control it, even if the color of her skin would never allow her to pass as White.

That was the other thing, being White. Because there was the nationality box, and then the race box. And Middle Easterners all fell into the category of "White," although they were never treated that way—never privy to any of the privileges of Whiteness. And each time she checked the box for White, that seemed like a lie as well, although technically, it was true. These boxes were stupid. Hardly anyone fit into one, but everyone had to choose one. And why did it matter?

Who would she be when she started college next year, away from Cincinnati, away from everyone from junior high and high school who had placed her in their own "other" box—not one of them. She had one year to decide who she was going to be in college—to take control of a new identity before another one was decided for her.

As she completed that first college application, she felt hope for her future, just as Soraya had on the day they became citizens.

Farah took off her headphones, turned off the music, and got up and went to the kitchen to tell her mother that she'd finished her first application. When she walked into the kitchen, she saw Azita and her mother sitting on the yellow and brown linoleum floor, her mother's face buried in Azita's chest as Azita stroked Soraya's hair. "What happened?" Farah's voice quivered.

"Farah, Farah," Soraya cried as Farah kneeled down and got on her mother's level. Soraya cupped Farah's face in her hands, shaking her head. "Koshtanesh. Koshtanesh."

There had been a mass execution of some of the prisoners in Evin. Zareen was among them.

CHAPTER FIFTY-ONE

APRIL 2023: PALO ALTO, CALIFORNIA

The room had that hospital smell of bleach and stale air that Farah had been hoping to not have to face again for at least a few more months. Earlier that morning, she'd stayed in savasana for a few extra minutes at the end of her yoga class, something she would never have done in New York. She'd wiped the sweat off her mat and rolled it up, grabbed her bag, and walked to the car before noticing the three missed calls and two texts from Parisa:

Azita is in the hospital. Margi found her.

I'm at the airport with Maman and Baba. On our way.

Farah had called Parisa and her parents, none of whom answered their phone. Maybe they were already in airplane mode. She found Margi on Facebook and sent her a private message. Despite all the problems that came with social media, sometimes it was the best way to contact someone whose number you didn't know.

When Azita hadn't shown up at work without calling anyone to say she was sick or running late, Margi had known something was wrong. She'd tried calling Azita, and when there was no answer, Margi had gone to her place and used her extra key to let herself in. She'd found Azita on her bed, unresponsive, and called 911.

Now, Farah sat in Azita's room with Parisa and her parents, all of them watching the IV fluids as they trickled drop by drop down the tubing into Azita's veins. Whether this was an accidental overdose or a suicide attempt, the doctors didn't know. The full toxicology screen was pending, but so far, they'd found alcohol, and Margi had found pharmacy vials for antidepressants, Ativan, and hydroxyzine in Azita's bathroom medicine cabinet.

When the paramedics arrived, she had a pulse—although it was slow and weak, and she was breathing on her own. They were able to get her to respond to painful stimulation, so they'd placed an oxygen mask and some monitors and brought her in. She'd told the doctors that it was not a suicide attempt—that she'd just been stressed and anxious and couldn't fall asleep. Against her better judgment, after already having had a few glasses of wine, she'd taken a combination of her medications. The doctors didn't know whether to believe her. "She's only about a hundred and five pounds, so even taking a couple extra pills in combination with alcohol could cause an unresponsive state," the doctor said.

Farah was shocked to hear just how low Azita's weight had gotten, despite noticing the weight loss the last time she'd seen her. Azita had been drifting in and out of sleep since being brought to the hospital, and the doctors were strongly recommending that now that she was medically stabilized, she be transferred to a psychiatric hospital for a few days.

As Farah looked around the room, she tried to remember the last time the original Afshar nuclear family had been together—without sons-in-law and grandkids—just the five of them. She couldn't remember. It was something Soraya always asked for, but Farah imagined that this was definitely not what Soraya had in mind as the occasion to bring them together.

Azita's eyelids fluttered open again. She looked around the room and then closed her eyes, a tear trickling down her cheek. Farah and Parisa each went and grabbed one of her hands. Soraya sat on her bed, laying her head down on Azita's legs, her sobs starting again.

Azita opened her eyes. "I didn't try to kill myself. I swear. I didn't. I was just trying to fall asleep—to forget everything for one night.

Just one night."

Azita explained that after a long day at work, she'd come home to an envelope with the invoice for the storage of her eggs for the next year. She'd opened a bottle of wine on an empty stomach, and then she couldn't remember when she'd decided to take a couple of extra pills or what had happened.

"I'm so sorry I was not there for you. I was worried about you when you came to visit me, and I've been so absorbed in my own life. I should have been checking in with you more often, coming up to see you," Farah said.

"Why didn't you tell me that you were worried about her? You called Parisa and told her, but you didn't tell me. Why don't the three of you ever tell me anything?" Soraya demanded.

"What do you think that would have accomplished, Maman? Would you have visited her and told her to quit her job and find a new less stressful one? Or would you just have told her to eat more and cook her a bunch of food and leave it in her freezer? Not having time to cook and eat is not the problem. Not having time to live is," Farah said.

Soraya was silent. Farah knew that Soraya measured happiness in work and family accomplishments—all the girls knew that about her. This was true of so many immigrant parents. The type of hardship they'd experienced starting in a new country from scratch had given them a myopic vision of what mattered in life. Soraya started to cry again, while their father remained silent.

Farah sighed. "Maman, I wasn't trying to upset you. We are incredibly grateful for all the sacrifices that you and Baba had to make for us. And I know you've seen your sisters and other women be powerless and not wanted that for us. But if you want us to tell you what is going on in our lives and include you in conversations as things are happening, then you need to really listen to us. And you need to realize that we are strong and we are going to be okay and figure things out regardless of how prestigious our jobs are."

"Wait, what happened with Maman's sisters?" Parisa said.

Soraya remained silent as Parisa looked back and forth between her mom and Farah. Then Farah explained, "Maman told me that they had difficult marriages and alcoholic husbands, but felt trapped in their marriages. But I've recently been thinking about that, and they weren't just trapped because of financial concerns. They were trapped because of custody laws in Iran. The kids automatically go to the father. If they could guarantee getting custody of their kids, they may have found a way to leave as well and figured the finances out."

"Well, Maman, looks like there is a lot we're all not telling each other," Parisa said. When Soraya remained silent, Parisa turned to Azita and added, "I'm sorry too. I'm so sorry. Farah told me she was worried, and I just blew it off. I've assumed that since my kids are young, you guys should be visiting me and working around my schedule rather than really being there for you or listening and seeing that just because you don't have kids doesn't mean that you don't need me to sometimes come and take care of you. So, let's all try to really listen to each other."

"Stop apologizing," Azita said. "I don't need or want anyone to take care of me."

"You do," Farah said. "There is nothing wrong with asking for help sometimes. What is the point of having us if you can't sometimes lean on us?"

Azita said nothing. Soraya remained silent.

"Maman, you always have something to say. You don't have anything to say now? I wasn't trying to hurt your feelings." Farah tried to temper the frustration in her voice.

"What do you want me to say? I just tried to give my kids everything. I have nothing if I don't have kids who are happy. I just tried my best," Soraya said.

"We know you did. We know you tried your best. We're all trying our best, so maybe we all just get better at listening to each other," Farah said. "And Azita, since I'm not working now anyway, I can stay with you for a while and help take care of you."

"I said I don't need anyone to take care of me. Everyone needs to stop fussing and overreacting. Also, I'm not the only one who has been under stress. Maybe instead of giving us these long lectures, Farah should be sharing some of what's been on her mind," Azita said.

Parisa looked from Azita to Farah, who was now glaring back at Azita. "Okay, what is going on?"

"Nothing that would be appropriate to talk about right now, in a hospital," Farah said.

"If anyone is going to stay with Azita for a while, it will be me," Soraya sighed. "Maybe I should call Nasreen and tell her to donate some money to the mosque and sacrifice a sheep for Azita. Give the meat to the poor."

Finally, Behnam spoke up. "What nonsense are you talking about? This is the moment you're going to turn to Islam? Absolutely not." He shook his head.

CHAPTER FIFTY-TWO

SEPTEMBER 1982: TEHRAN, IRAN

"I'm going to get up early tomorrow morning so I can do namaz before going to school," Farah announced at dinner.

Behnam dropped his spoon on his plate and looked up at her. Friday nights were the only nights they ate with their father, since he got home from work too late on weeknights. "Why would you do that? Where do you get these ideas?"

"I feel guilty lying to Khanoom Nafisi about whether we pray at home. And I've been really enjoying my noon prayer at school. It's peaceful, even if I'm not sure I believe in it," Farah said.

"You're praying at school?" Behnam asked.

"Of course they are," Soraya rolled her eyes. "They all have to do namaz at school during the lunch break now."

Behnam suddenly looked angry and raised his voice. "You mean to tell me that these kids are spending half their recess time repeating the same nonsense Arabic verses every day instead of playing and running around so their minds can be fresh for the rest of the afternoon?"

Soraya bit into her radish and chewed, then put the remainder of it back on her plate and looked at him. "Yes. That's what I'm telling you. Do I have any control over these mandates? No. I do not. I keep telling you we need to figure out a way to get out of this country, and you don't listen. You say we have time, but we don't. It gets worse every day." She picked up her radish and put the rest in her mouth.

"You're not praying at home. None of you. If you have extra time on your hands or you want to get up early, you can use it to read or to practice your English. My children will not waste their time on nonsense," Behnam said and left the table.

Farah looked over at Azita, who was staring angrily at her. Farah shrugged her shoulders and looked down at her plate, blinking rapidly to hold in her tears. "I have no issue lying to Khanoom Nafisi or anyone at school," Azita said nonchalantly. "Everyone does it."

"Lying is okay?" Parisa asked Soraya.

"Only if you have to lie to bad people. Not lying to your parents or to good people," Soraya said.

"The teachers are bad people?" Parisa furrowed her eyebrows.

"Astaghforallah," Soraya threw up her hands in frustration. "The teachers are not bad, but they have to work for the government, and the government is bad."

"Why do they work for bad people if they're not bad?"

"Because they have no choice. They have to make money to have food and a place to live. That's enough questions for tonight. If you have more questions, ask your Baba. See how he answers them." Soraya got up and left the table, too, leaving the three girls staring at each other.

"I hope you're happy," Azita looked accusingly at Farah.

The next day, Farah took a walk with her cousin Nader around Maydan Vanak. Nader was seventeen, six years older than Farah. As they strolled, Farah was telling Nader about her day in school. He stopped her to reach over and pull her headscarf toward her forehead, tucking her hair inside. "Watch your hijab," he said to her. "It almost completely fell off your head."

Suddenly a jeep driven by the komiteh pulled up and stopped by the side of the curb. Two officers who only looked a few years older than Nader himself stepped out, rifles over their shoulders. "Why did you just touch her hair? That is not allowed," one of the officers asked Nader.

"Her headscarf was falling off, so I was just trying to help her adjust it," Nader replied.

"Are you married to her?" the second officer questioned.

"Married to her? She's twelve years old. She's my cousin," Nader responded in disbelief.

"Your cousin. Not your sister. You are not mahram to her. You can't touch her," the first officer said while the second one pulled out handcuffs and motioned to Nader to turn around and put his hands behind his back.

They called Soraya to come and pick up Farah, while Nader had to spend the night in jail. Behnam had to cancel all his patients and get enough money together to bail him out the next day. "What a stupid, senseless way for this regime to drive fear into people and make money off them for no reason. They're all criminals," he told Soraya when he came home.

"At least they didn't take Farah in with them. At least there were no lashings. At least we were able to solve it with money. These are the things we have to be grateful for now. Are you ready to find a way to leave yet?" Soraya asked and then left the room, not waiting for his answer.

CHAPTER FIFTY-THREE

APRIL 2023: PALO ALTO, CALIFORNIA

Soraya carried a small silver tray with three steaming glasses of tea into the living room and set it on the table. "I couldn't find anything sweet in your kitchen to have with the tea other than dried cherries, so this will have to do until I go shopping for you later this afternoon," she said to Azita.

Azita had been released from the hospital that morning, and Behnam and Parisa had flown back to Cincinnati. Farah planned to stay at least another day or two before leaving Azita alone with their mother and returning to Paso. "Dried cherries are perfect with tea. I've mostly lost my sweet tooth, although if you want to make yakh dar behesht while I'm here, I won't object," Farah said. The dessert, made of a simple combination of wheat starch, milk, sugar, and rosewater, was one that Farah had never mastered, and it truly was deserving of its name, which translated to "ice in heaven" or "ice in paradise."

"Sure. I'll make whatever you girls want," Soraya said. "What do you want me to make for dinner, Azita?"

"I want you to rest and relax. You don't have to immediately busy yourself with cooking, Maman. We can order food," Azita said.

Farah laughed. "When has Maman ever allowed ordering in food other than the occasional pizza? This is Maman's love language. Sitting around and real conversation makes her uncomfortable, so she busies herself in the kitchen. You might as well tell her what you want her to make, because you know she's going to make something."

"Fine. Just make ghormeh sabzi, I guess. I could have that every day," Azita said.

"Okay. Let me go see what you have and make a list of what I need to buy." Soraya clapped her hands together and got up, taking her tea with her.

"Well, since you brought up the topic of real conversations," Azita took a sip of her tea, pausing to make eye contact with Farah, "I think you should tell Maman about Zareen with me here. Get it off your chest."

"I don't know. I'm not sure I'm ready," Farah said.

"Now is the best time. Maman is too distracted and worried about me, and honestly, you have made this thing so much bigger than it is in your mind. And I don't think you're going to be able to fully move on and figure out the rest of your life until you move on from this," Azita said.

"Okay. You're right. I'll do it. But then you have to promise me that you're going to start taking better care of yourself. That you're going to come up with a plan for what you need and follow through with it."

Azita's lips started to quiver. "Okay," she said in a voice so soft Farah could barely hear it. She scooted over on the couch and held her sister as they both cried.

Soraya walked back in. Her head was down and she was looking at her phone and typing something in. She looked up and saw her daughters huddled together. She lifted her reading glasses and, her voice shaking, asked, "What happened?"

"Everything's fine, Maman. Everything is fine. Why don't you sit down for a little," Farah said.

Soraya looked back and forth between her daughters and then slowly sat down in the armchair across from them.

"Maman, I need to tell you about something. I've told part of it to Azita, but not all of it. I should have told you this years ago, but I didn't, and then it just seemed like too much time had passed to bring it up again and I didn't want to deal with it. But I've realized that I need to deal with it at some point," Farah said.

"Okay. What is it? Tell me." Soraya's voice started to quiver as well.

"I was there when Zareen got arrested. I told you that we said our goodbyes and we each started walking toward our homes, but I was there. I saw her get arrested and I felt like there was nothing I could do and . . . " Farah began to cry as Azita squeezed her sister's hand.

"Okay. That's okay. That was so long ago. I don't understand why you lied—" Soraya said when Farah interrupted her.

"I lied because it was my fault that she took off her hijab. I was talking to her about moving to America and then she said something about hijab, and then I dared her to take hers off. I didn't think she would do it. I didn't. But then she did and then the komiteh—"

"Basteh. Basteh."—Enough. Soraya interrupted her and went and sat beside her on the couch, holding Farah in her arms, trying to still her shaking body. Azita put her arms around both of them, all of them crying for what seemed like a long time before Soraya pulled back, wiped her face, and grabbed Farah's face, looking her right in the eyes. "I'm not crying because of Zareen. I'm crying because of you. You were a child. You should never have been in that position. You didn't do anything. It was the stupid mullahs—it was *their* fault, not yours. Do you understand?"

"But I'm the one who dared her," Farah hiccupped the words between sobs.

"NO! No. That doesn't matter. We are all victims of that regime. You remember when the komiteh arrested Nader for fixing your headscarf? What if we hadn't been able to bribe them with money and they'd done something to him? Would that have been your fault because it was your hijab that was slipping? We are all victims. Don't think for one second that if you told your Khaleh Nasreen, that she would blame you. She would never blame you. She loves you. She would love to see you again. You are like Zareen to her. She would never, ever, ever blame you," Soraya said.

Farah felt dizzy, faint. She hadn't realized until that moment that she had been waiting for those words for almost forty years. She hadn't realized how long it had been since she had truly felt mothered, and how desperately she had needed it.

CHAPTER FIFTY-FOUR

OCTOBER 1986: CINCINNATI, OHIO

As she turned the corner onto Oakhurst Drive, Farah finally relaxed. She just had to pass ten houses and then she would be home. She was always tense on the entire walk home from school, her heavy backpack weighing her down. She was one of the only juniors who didn't drive to school and back or get a ride with a friend. Walking the two miles home was a less humiliating option than being the only upperclassman on the school bus. Farah was still negotiating with her parents about getting her a used car. She was willing to get a part-time job to help pay for the expense, but Soraya insisted that they hadn't left everything behind in Iran for Farah to get a minimum-wage job at McDonald's after school and have her grades suffer. "I brought you here to become a doctor, not to make burgers. School is your job." Soraya was a broken record, and Farah didn't know why she bothered to try to make her understand.

Farah was scanning the homes on their street, most of which were decked out in Halloween decorations. They had moved from a two-bedroom apartment to this four-bedroom house in August. Farah was so happy to have her own bedroom, where she could listen to any music she wanted and storm off for privacy after arguments with her parents. When in the first week of October every house around them started to put out skeletons and gravestones and pumpkins, Parisa had begged Soraya to buy some Halloween decorations. Farah watched Parisa cry while Soraya dismissed her and thought about how, when she became a mother, she would let her kids decorate the house for every holiday. Trying to negotiate with Soraya about anything had been pointless for almost two years now. It had been almost two years since the phone call about their home and neighbors in Tehran. For the first year after that call, Soraya had seemed to just be going through the motions of life, a glazed look over her eyes, physically present but disengaged from everything. Over the second year, she'd slowly seemed to be coming back to herself again. Farah would hear Googoosh's voice coming through the cassette player in the kitchen again and see Soraya truly lost in the game when she was playing rummy with her friends. But when it came to her daughters, her vision was still singular. They were here for their education, and not to get tied up in all things American.

When Farah got to their house, she was surprised to see Roya's car in the driveway. Roya was her mom's best friend in Cincinnati, and her car was often in their driveway, but not during hours that Soraya would be at work. Before Farah was all the way up the walk at the front door, she could already hear the loud wailing of her mother on the other side. She barely managed to get the key in the lock, her hands trembling. She opened the door to find Roya next to her mother on the couch. Soraya was beating her own chest in between wails. Farah ran to her. "Maman, what happened?"

"Farah. Farah. Mord. Mord. Bee madar shodam."—She died. She died. I am motherless. Soraya clung to Farah.

Acid stung the back of Farah's throat, and she swallowed it down, gripping her mother for stability as she felt the room spinning around her.

The next few days were a blur. Farah still went to school and tried to take care of her sisters. She spent the lunch period in a corner bathroom crying, remembering all the religious stories her grandmother used to tell her despite Behnam's disapproval. She felt guilty about the excitement she'd felt when they were leaving Tehran for America, and how her grandmother had clung to her, crying and stroking Farah's face the last time she had seen her. Farah had assumed that either they would visit Iran or her grandmother would visit the US. She hadn't considered the possibility that it would be the last time she would be seeing her Maman Bozorg, but her grandmother had probably known the possibility was there. Each day, Farah would come home to her mother lying in bed or sitting on the couch, all dressed in black, staring ahead like a zombie. The only time Farah heard Soraya's voice again in those first few days was when she was on the phone with her sisters or aunts in Iran, her incoherent words swallowed between sobs. Roya came over any chance that she could, helping Farah and her sisters.

"Can I ask you something?" Farah turned to Roya.

"Of course, anything," Roya said.

"Do you believe in God?"

"Yes, of course I do," Roya said.

"So you think that there really may be a behesht? That my Maman Bozorg may be in a better place? Because my dad says that's all nonsense."

"Well, Azizam, you know I'm Jewish, right? Jewish people have a different view of the afterlife than some other religions. I don't know if she is in heaven or not. I know what matters most is how you live your life while you are on earth. And from what your Maman tells me, she was the best possible human while she was here," Roya said. Then she walked over and wrapped Farah in her arms.

One week after her grandmother's death, they had the seventh-day ceremony at their house. Roya and a few of her mom's other friends helped make all the *halva* and *sholeh zard*, the aroma of rosewater and cardamom permeating the house. Nearly every member of Cincinnati's Iranian community came over dressed in black, wearing no makeup, and took turns sitting with Soraya and paying their respects. Many had experienced having a parent die overseas while they were in the US, as they murmured condolences to Farah and reassurances that she would get through it.

On the eighth day, Soraya returned to work, still dressed in all black, with nothing but moisturizer on her face. On the fortieth day, there was a smaller ceremony, with only Soraya's closest friends coming to spend time with her. When on the forty-first day, Farah saw Soraya come downstairs, still dressed in head-to-toe black, she felt a squeezing in her chest. Who knew how long it would be before she had her mother back? Just like Soraya, Farah felt motherless.

CHAPTER FIFTY-FIVE

APRIL 2023: PASO ROBLES, CALIFORNIA

Julia sat next to Farah on her couch. It was Julia's birthday weekend, and she'd planned a four-day trip to visit Farah. Farah had made it back from Palo Alto three days earlier, and although she'd been sad to be leaving Azita, she felt lighter than she remembered feeling in years, despite likely having gained five pounds the last few days she had been there. Soraya had made every stew and rice dish Farah and Azita loved, in addition to every dessert. They had spent two days drinking tea, talking, eating, and crying together. "I'm surprised my tears aren't stained with saffron at this point," Farah had said as she cried while spooning *shole zard* into her mouth.

Now, as Julia ate some of the leftover shole zard in between sips of Grenache Blanc, she said, "This is so much better than birthday cake."

Farah laughed. "Where were you when I was a teenager? We're still going to have birthday cake tomorrow, like it or not."

It was two days into Julia's visit to Paso and the night before her birthday. Farah had packed in as much of Paso as she could in the days she had Julia there. She'd even considered taking Julia to a canasta and cocktails day at Josephine's house, but she realized she didn't want to spend too much time sharing Julia with other people in the short time they had together. Now at the end of the night, they were both in PJs on the couch, feet rolled under them. "Okay, fine. Twist my arm. I'll have some cake tomorrow." Then she paused and studied Farah's face.

"You know, despite everything you told me just happened with Azita, I haven't seen you look this relaxed and carefree in a long time," Julia said.

"Yeah. I mean, part of it is the kids. They are both doing really well right now. Those teen years took such a toll on me. But Rumi is still dating Jackie. This is the longest he's ever dated anyone. His first true girlfriend. And she obviously knows at this point, but I don't know if her parents know. I didn't ask. I really am trying to not make everything about that. And Darya has been so busy that she hasn't come down yet. But I've gone up to see her and she's doing great. And she's coming down in a week. She and her friends . . . they've been regularly volunteering at a women's shelter and involved in some environmental efforts in San Francisco. They are so political and smart, and it's just so inspiring to see them like this at their age."

"I spent my youth at fraternity parties, even for a couple of pathetic years after I graduated. I don't even think I knew what philanthropy or activism were back then," Julia laughed. "But Violet and her friends are the same. Young people today are much more impressive than we ever were."

"Yes. I spent my college years studying and wasted them worrying about getting into a good medical school. I mean, I did have some fun, but I never really thought about what I wanted from life in the same way these kids do now . . . what mark I wanted to leave in this world. I'm so glad to be doing this now. I love the physical work in the vineyards. I love all the people passing through town on vacation. I love how clean and fresh the air is and that when I'm running here, every car that passes me waves. I love learning about the wine industry and talking people through the tastings. And I've read more books these past months than I have in years."

"You can read books in New York, you know," Julia said.

"I love how everyone here knows each other. You don't have that in New York."

Julia nodded. "True, but why do I sense that there is a but in there? You love all these things about Paso, but . . . "

Farah waited a while, staring straight ahead. "But there is so much I miss about New York. At the same time as I love people knowing each other here, I miss the anonymity and possibility in New York. I miss getting swallowed up in throngs of people on the street, all of them diverse. I miss my patients and my relationships with them, but I don't miss three a.m. deliveries and getting woken up by phone calls and all the bureaucracy of that job! I love buying produce directly from the farmer who knows you here, but I also miss all the little corner markets in New York. Don't get me started on the restaurants. I miss hearing foreign languages spoken around me. And, you know what I'm realizing I can't do without? That I don't want to do without?"

"Me? You forgot to mention I miss seeing Julia in person regularly," Julia said.

"Definitely that. Definitely. I've met some lovely people here, but there's something about people you've met when you're young—before you've so-called made it. You can't make old friends," Farah said.

"No. You definitely can't. Okay, so other than me, what is it you can't do without?"

"Remember how you took that picture of the mural of Mahsa Amini in the East Village and sent it to me—there are no murals of George Floyd here, let alone of Mahsa. There are no marches in a small town. And I can't live full-time in a place like that. New York is still the first place in the US where I've felt at home."

Farah had told Julia the story of Zareen on her first night there, and Julia reached over and grabbed Farah's hand and squeezed it. "I'm glad to hear that it sounds like you'll be back in New York soon, that we'll march together again," Julia said.

"Yeah, but I don't miss the pace of my old life. I don't think I can go back to that again."

"It sounds like maybe you come back to New York, but you work less, you make more time for yourself, you vacation more."

"I wish. How do I do that?" Farah asked.

"You could start by not holding on to being the chief just

because you worked so hard to get it. You do an Elsa, and you let it go," Julia suggested.

"Believe me, I've thought about it. I just don't think that will be enough. It won't free up enough time or take away all my other frustrations with the administration. Anyway, I'll figure it out."

"Yes. You will. Just take the time to listen and follow your heart this time," Julia said. "You know, every year on the night before my birthday, I do a little journaling. I write down some goals for myself for the coming year. Why don't we do that together before we go to bed? You don't have to read me your goals—just write them."

"You know I'm not a journaling person, but for you, birthday girl, I will," Farah said. While Julia went to the room to grab her journal that traveled with her everywhere, Farah stood up to find something to write on.

Farah walked into the kitchen with her wine glass, dumping the rest down the drain and filling it with water. She found a piece of scrap paper and a pen and sat back down on the couch.

Julia came back into the room, wearing a fluffy robe. "I'm going to sit outside and do this. It's hard for me to write in front of other people. Ten minutes and I'll be back. Write something—anything."

"Okay," Farah said. She stayed on the couch once Julia was outside, staring at the candles on the table for a few minutes. Finally, she wrote, "Goals for tomorrow and beyond" on top of the paper:

Be present
Let go of resentment
Let go of regrets
Let go of What Ifs
Discover who Farah is
Make time for Farah
Don't apologize for being Farah
Be Farah

CHAPTER FIFTY-SIX

MAY 2007: BOSTON, MASSACHUSETTS

Sitting on a bench on Commonwealth Avenue drinking her morning coffee, Farah was savoring a little alone time with Neesha before the day ahead. It was only seven, but they'd agreed to meet for a quick walk and chat before all the chaos of the day started. "I'm sorry that I can't make the Vegas trip with you guys," Farah said. "I just have limited time that I can get away without the kids, especially since Mark will be in Beijing at that time. And you know that I've always hated Vegas. To spend the little vacation time I have somewhere that I really don't enjoy being—"

"Stop. You don't need to explain again. That's just where Alessandra really wanted to go for her fortieth, but it's not your thing. Don't apologize for your limited time and knowing how you want to spend it. Besides, we're all seeing each other this weekend anyway," Neesha added.

"You're right. I don't know why I feel like I need to apologize," Farah said. "You know I haven't been back to Boston since Bridget's first wedding?"

Bridget's first wedding had been in June of 1999 when Darya was just two months old. Farah had barely squeezed herself into the mint green bridesmaid dress, her engorged breasts twice their prepregnancy size, sweat collecting and dripping under her nursing bra. Bridget's first marriage was to Isaac, a researcher in the neuro-oncology lab at Massachusetts General Hospital. Isaac was a quiet, unassuming man whose world seemed to revolve around Bridget. They had twin daughters and seemed to be a perfectly happy family, until Bridget had fallen in love with Anjali.

Anjali specialized in MIGS, minimally invasive gynecologic surgery, and worked at Brigham and Women's Hospital in Boston. After she and Bridget met, her name started casually appearing more in group texts to Farah and Neesha or being dropped into a conversation. "I went to see the art exhibit with Anjali" or "I took the girls ice skating and Anjali came along." Farah assumed she had just made a new BFF. When Bridget finally told Farah that she was in love with Anjali, that she was leaving Isaac for her, Farah was glad the conversation was by telephone, so that Bridget couldn't see whatever expression was on her face. At first, she was surprised to learn about Bridget's sexuality, but then she realized that this all clicked. It was that missing part of Bridget that she hadn't quite placed a finger on.

"That wedding. Remember us standing there in our dresses dripping sweat? I'm so glad the weather is better this time," Neesha said.

"At least you weren't a cow who'd just given birth," Farah said.

"Stop. You looked beautiful. And that awful green dress just emphasized your melons," Neesha laughed.

"At least I had my prepregnancy body for your wedding. Can you imagine how I would have looked in my sari with those melons?" Farah sighed. Neesha's wedding had been a three-day Indian wedding extravaganza in Chicago with over five hundred guests, and it was followed by a second week-long celebration in Delhi that was organized by her maternal aunts. She had worn a traditional red sari, and though there were no bridesmaids at her wedding, all her close friends had worn saris as well. Neesha joked that although she was technically half-Indian, she was more Indian than most full-Indian second-generation immigrants of her age. She had become a doctor, married an Indian doctor—her husband Navin, whom she had met during her internal medicine residency—and now her three daughters were enrolled in classical Indian dance classes, not hip-hop Bollywood. Neesha had told Farah once that she always felt the need to prove that she was Indian, even if people couldn't place her ethnicity based on her looks. "An Indian mother means I'm Indian. I ate the food, I learned the dances, I had the chai, I couldn't date, I won the local spelling bee every year."

Farah had laughed, saying that she always felt like she needed to prove that she was not that different from most Americans.

"You would have looked like one of my Indian aunties with those melons. If I were ever to get married again, I'd limit it to a one-day affair. That was exhausting," Neesha said.

"You would not. You loved every second of it. If I were to get married again, maybe I would agree to that second church ceremony Mark's family had wanted."

"There you go again, still feeling guilty and apologizing for who you are. You didn't want a church wedding, so you didn't have one. The end. Let's go back to the hotel and check in with Bridget before she gets all those wedding-day jitters again." Neesha grabbed Farah's hand and pulled her off the bench.

"I don't think we're going to see the wedding-day jitters this time. I've never seen her this happy," Farah said.

Farah, Mark, Neesha, and Navin sat in the second row on Bridget's side, right behind her immediate family. They watched as Bridget was walked down the aisle by her daughters. Bridget wore a sleek white jumpsuit that had a halter top, a crystal butterfly barrette pinning back her short bangs that went with her pixie cut. Then Anjali came down the aisle flanked by her parents, wearing an elaborate white lehenga, her arms adorned in intricate henna designs. Bridget had the same henna designs on her creamy white arms, with her freckles peeking through the windows of henna. As they held matching hennaed hands, reciting their vows and looking at each other like they were the only two people in the world, Farah saw a glow in Bridget's eyes that was different from the one at her first wedding. She thought that maybe she was truly seeing who Bridget was for the first time. Her eyes filled with tears.

Mark leaned over and whispered in Farah's ear, "Don't get any ideas and leave me for Julia."

Farah whispered back, "If that were a possibility, it would have happened years ago. My life would be so much easier with a wife." *A wife would never go to Beijing and leave me to parent on my own,* she thought.

CHAPTER FIFTY-SEVEN

MAY 2007: BROOKLYN, NEW YORK

At the sound of the shower being turned on in the bathroom above her, Farah exhaled and smiled. Delara had finally gotten to the point that she could shower without Farah's assistance. For so long, she'd been scared of turning the shower on and off on her own. Farah would have to go in, turn the water on and wait for it to get to just the right temperature for Delara, and then turn it off for her when she was done. But now at eight and six, both kids could get ready for bed on their own, and then just call one of their parents when they were ready for a bedtime story. Darya always read on her own, flying through chapter books one after the other, but Delara still wanted three stories before going to sleep.

Farah leaned back on the family-room couch, turned on her laptop, and began going through her emails and electronically paying their bills. That was what she had been using this treasured gained hour for—organizing their life so she didn't have to do it after the kids went to bed. That night, Mark had volunteered to read to Delara after her shower, so Farah had grabbed a glass of Nebbiolo before sitting down to work. She was just about halfway through her emails when Mark came in and sat next to her.

"I wanted to talk to you about something important," he said.

"Okay," Farah said. She noticed Mark playing with the collar of his shirt—something he only did when nervous or stressed.

"I have the chance to teach at Columbia's Beijing campus for a year. It's an opportunity that most people never get in their entire career." Then Mark went silent.

Was he waiting for her to congratulate him? "Wait, are you actually considering going?"

"I think I should do it. I'd be crazy to pass it up."

Farah felt heat rise up her face. "You can't be fucking serious!" She looked him right in the eyes, mouth open. Mark remained silent, returning her gaze. "You'd be crazy to pass it up? You're crazy to consider it." Farah slammed her laptop shut, grabbed her now-empty glass of wine, and went to the kitchen to refill it.

Mark followed her. "Farah . . ."

She didn't answer him. She sat at the kitchen island and put her head in her hands.

"Farah, I know that this won't be easy for you. It won't be easy for me, but the kids are basically on cruise control for the moment, and I may never get an opportunity like this again."

"Cruise control?" Farah heard her voice getting louder and starting to shake. "You think the kids are on cruise control? Delara can now shower on her own, and that's it? You have no fucking clue how much I do for these kids to be on 'cruise control.'" She shook her head. "This is unfuckingbelievable. Why don't I turn the 'cruise control' button off just one fucking day and you can see how much I fucking do!" Farah was shouting at this point, but she didn't care if the kids heard. Let them hear how their father was okay with leaving for a year at the drop of a hat.

"That's not what I meant. Of course, I realize how much you do for them. And obviously, I do a lot for them too. I realize you'd probably need a second nanny to help make this easier on you. I just meant that if this is something I'm going to do, right now is a good time to do it."

"Now is a good time? NOW? As opposed to, I don't know, when they are both in fucking college?"

Mark tried to explain again. This year abroad would have a really good impact on his career. Waiting eleven more years for something that may not even be an option in the future made no sense. He had to do this. He had to. It was unusual for Columbia to send a professor from Pace to cover one of their courses abroad. Teaching at Columbia in Beijing would go on his resume forever, and even if he remained at Pace for the rest of his career, this would reinforce job security, lead to other opportunities. "And when I say the kids are on cruise control, of course I don't mean that they still don't need a ton of care, but I mean they're in that golden period of being able to do a lot on their own while still listening to us and not being defiant teenagers."

"The thing is, Mark, I can't even imagine leaving these kids for a year. I'd love to leave for a week or two and go do something for myself. I can maybe imagine leaving them for a month. But there is no way I could even imagine or consider leaving them for longer than that. But you . . ." Farah shook her head.

"That's not fair, and you know it," Mark said. He ran his hands through his hair, jaw clenched. "No one is stopping you from going away for a week or two but yourself. And you know what will probably be the hardest part for me, Farah? It will be not being with YOU for all that time, not just being apart from the kids. But you don't even mention me—you never think of me."

"Well excuse me if I'm too furious and in shock to feel like I may miss you while you're gone. I'm sorry if I always think of the kids first. Maybe I just married the wrong guy. I don't know. Anyway, if you'll excuse me, I need to finish my work." Farah grabbed her wine and went back to the family room and her laptop.

Mark shook his head, following her. "Yes, please get back to your work. I'm sorry I interrupted it. I forgot that your work is more important than mine, even though you always bring it up."

"I DO NOT!" Farah slammed her laptop shut.

"Yes, you do, Farah. It's implied in everything you say." Mark turned around and left the room.

Running through Prospect Park the next morning, Farah

processed all her thoughts. He was being so selfish, but she had to let him go. If she didn't let him go, he would never forgive her. It would always be there between them—that she'd held him back, that she thought her career was more important than his. As much as she needed him to stay, to be her coparent and partner, she knew that not sacrificing her needs would lead to a permanent rift between them.

She walked into the house, sweat still dripping down her forehead and back. Mark was sitting at the island, sipping his coffee, reading the paper. He put the paper down as she walked toward him. "You're right. You should go. Of course, your career is as important as mine and this could be huge for you, help you with your next book too. Okay."

He stood up and hugged her, burying his head in her neck, despite the sweat. "It's going to be okay. I promise. I love you."

Farah wanted to know how exactly he thought it was going to be okay, but she didn't want to start another argument. "I love you too."

CHAPTER FIFTY-EIGHT

MAY 2023: PASO ROBLES, CALIFORNIA

"Okay, just remember to ease yourself back in. And I'm here for you. We all are. And I'm glad I'll be there for your first couple of days back. Love you." Farah hung up the phone. She'd been making a point of calling Azita every day since the hospitalization. Azita had been started on a new antidepressant regimen and taken a one-month leave from work. Soraya had stayed with her, and Farah had gone back up to see her twice in the last month. Now it was time for Azita to go back to work in a few days, and Farah knew that she couldn't put off making decisions about her own future any longer.

Azita's hospitalization had Farah thinking about life more than ever, solidifying the knowledge that had been creeping up inside her—she wanted a bigger career change than simply not being chief. She sipped her coffee as she looked at the vines, now lush with leaves and ready to be pruned. She thought about the different twists and turns life takes, each event or decision leading you down a completely different path. What would have happened if she hadn't had that abortion at twenty-one?

If she'd had that baby, she would not have been able to pursue a career in medicine as a single mother. She knew it then, and she knew it now. She'd kept the secret about the abortion to herself for so many years, Mark being the only person who knew about it. Telling her mother had never been an option. Soraya would have been outraged to know she was having premarital sex, let alone gotten pregnant. But now, after the many family conversations in the hospital, she wondered if she could share this information with her mother and sisters. She still felt the weight of it after all these years. She imagined how she would feel if Darya became pregnant and decided to have an abortion. She would hold her daughter. She would go with her to the procedure. She would make her feel no guilt and no shame. Darya was still a child, after all. Farah herself at twenty-one had been a child—a child who'd had to make a very difficult decision and then take care of it on her own.

Farah rinsed out her coffee mug and set it on the drying rack. She had to go pick up Darya from the train station. Since it was Mother's Day weekend, Darya was finally visiting Farah in wine country. Farah had asked her to take a one-way train down, saying that she would drive her back up herself so she could visit Azita.

As the car turned off Highway 46 to drive through Braxton Vineyards, Darya looked at the view. "Wow, Mom. Seeing this on FaceTime does not do it justice. I should have visited you sooner."

"Yes, you should have, but you could try to squeeze in at least one more visit after this before I head back to New York," Farah said.

Once back at the guesthouse, Darya went to wash up, while Farah took out the cheese board she had prepared and a chilled bottle of Viognier. They sat on Farah's couch together, Darya catching Farah up on her life. She was dating a new guy, someone she'd met at a climate change event, and it was getting more serious. "Of course, I'm going to start applying to grad schools and who knows where I'll be in a year or two if we're still together by then, but I'm having a good time," Darya said.

"I'm glad you are, and that you're just living in the moment. When I was your age, I was always living in the future. If a guy wasn't a potential long-term partner, I thought of it as a waste of time. I guess that was your grandmother's influence and the Iranian mentality. It didn't serve me well," Farah said.

Then the conversation veered toward Azita's hospitalization.

"Azita still swears it was accidental and not any type of suicide attempt. I think I believe her, but whether accidental or not, it's still terrible. I guess the one good thing that came out of it is that we all talked a lot and had conversations with Maman Soraya that we've never really had."

"I'm so sorry, Mom. It's still so hard to believe. Every time I've seen Auntie Azita, she's been so positive, treating us and spoiling us. She's always seemed like the life of the party. All my friends think of her as this cool aunt they'd love to have. I had no idea this was all going on."

"None of us did really. I only got worried about her the very last time I saw her, but I didn't do anything about it. We'll just have to make it a point to check up on each other more often." Farah hesitated a moment before going on, "It's also made me think about the things we never tell people. When I was around your age, I had an abortion. I did it on my own at a free clinic. I never told Maman Soraya or my sisters. Years later I told your dad. He's the only person who knows."

"Wow, Mom. So, even Julia doesn't know?"

Farah shook her head. "Not even Julia. Part of me has always held on to the shame and guilt of it. Every time I wanted to tell Julia, I thought about how she struggled with secondary infertility, and then I couldn't do it. Even though I know that she would never judge me for it. I don't want you or Rumi to ever feel like you have to go through something hard alone. I don't want you to ever be so ashamed of a mistake that you feel like you can't come to me for help or just ask for help in general. I used to worry so much about Rumi having a suicide attempt. I never thought one of my sisters might have a near overdose. You just never know what's happening in people's lives."

"It's true, Mom, you don't. And I know it's many years later, but I'm still sorry you had to go through that alone."

"Yeah. I still remember what my due date would have been if I hadn't had that abortion, and every year on that day, I think about how old he or she would be now. Thirty-two. And I still remember the nurse holding my hand and the doctor at the free clinic. I remember their faces, not their names. I think that whole experience was part of why I gravitated toward becoming an ob-gyn." Farah sighed. "But I feel so much better just telling you now. I'll tell Julia, too, and Rumi, and maybe eventually Azita. Just because she did not have children doesn't mean I have to hold on to this. I know that now."

"I'm glad you feel better, Mom." Darya reached over and they held each other for a long time.

On Mother's Day morning, they met Josh Bennett early in the vineyard. Workers were pruning the zinfandel vines, and Josh was helping. He grinned at Farah and Darya when he saw them, the Braxton Vineyards baseball cap he was wearing making him look younger. "Farah, why don't you give your daughter the tutorial on how to prune the vines? You're an expert by this point," Josh said.

Farah showed Darya how they needed to break off any branches that had twinning, or any branches that were crossing over, all in an attempt to avoid overcrowding. "Wait, so we're just going to cut these vines and dump all these baby grapes on the ground? That seems so sad," Darya said.

"Yup. You'll get used to doing it. It helps improve the quality of the grapes that do remain on the vines and mature," Farah said. "And you can use pruning scissors or just use your hands. I like to use my hands."

"Your mom's pretty much an expert on viticulture," Josh said.

"And how do you know when the grapes are ready to be picked?" Darya asked.

"Ah. Harvest. It's usually in October. That's when you both really need to come back. We go out in the field every day and check the brix level of the grapes. Farah, you know what the brix level is, right?" Josh asked.

"It's the measure of the dissolved sugar in a sample of grape juice," Farah said.

"Your mom is a gold-star student. We measure it using a small handheld device called a refractometer, but I also taste the grape as well. We usually harvest the zinfandel when the brix level is between twenty-four and twenty-six. Once it gets there, we are out here from before dawn to as late as it takes harvesting all the grapes. It's an all-hands-on-deck-with-extra-help kind of event, and we'll take extra free labor anytime," Josh said.

Darya and Farah worked together side by side for three hours, talking intermittently. "I can see why you love this, Mom. It is really peaceful."

"Yeah. I used to listen to an audiobook or podcast initially, but now I don't listen to anything even when I'm by myself, not even music. It just gives me time to think, and it seems like I'm years behind on having time for that."

"What have you been thinking about most?" Darya asked.

"Returning to New York. How I'm going to figure out how to make my life different. How I ended up here. My past. Iran. My marriage. Surprisingly, not so much about you and Rumi. I guess it's because you two are the one thing I did right—that I have no regrets about," Farah said.

"Not even about Rumi, and how you handled that?" Darya said.

"That I've learned to forgive myself for. The rest, I'm working on. Let's go in to shower, then get brunch."

◆

On the car ride up to Palo Alto the next day, they spoke more about Farah's time in Paso and what she would do when she got back to New York. "I really admire all the activism you and your friends are involved in," Farah said. "I miss when my job was a lot more about the patients. We still take great care of them, but it doesn't seem to be what the insurance companies or administrators value about us. We've had to spend so much of our own uncompensated time to be able to do it. All the staying late and going in early and bringing work home at night. It took a toll on my marriage, on you guys, on me. The amount of charting and phone calls that I have to do when I get home in the last few years hasn't left any room for me to do things for myself. It wasn't as bad when you were younger. And if I'm going to be completely honest, I took more of my frustration out on your dad than I realized. I've had a lot more time to think about that while I've been here."

Darya turned to her, eyebrows raised, mouth agape. "Are you admitting that maybe you were frequently just a little too hard on Dad? Wow! Are you regretting the divorce?"

"No. I am not. I think our marriage ran its course. I'm just admitting that maybe my frustrations, my lack of honesty with myself, my not figuring out my own shit, had a bigger part in its dissolution than I realized. That's it. No regrets. Just realizations."

Darya was quiet for a little while. "Mom, you know how yesterday you were talking about still remembering the faces of the nurse and doctor from that abortion clinic? Have you ever thought about working in a free clinic? There are so many in New York."

"I thought about it when I first finished residency. But the pay wasn't great, and your father was still finishing up his thesis. And if I'm going to be completely honest, since I'm working on honesty, I wanted something more prestigious. But now, I think I may just look into it. My priorities are different now," Farah said. She looked over at Darya and squeezed her hand. "How did you get so smart? I'm one lucky mom. You've given me something to think about." Looking at Darya, Farah was filled with relief that it seemed like Darya was doing well. If nothing else, she and Mark had raised a smart, strong, beautiful, compassionate, insightful daughter. They had made something beautiful together.

CHAPTER FIFTY-NINE

AUGUST 1998: EAST VILLAGE, NEW YORK

Waiting for the five minutes to pass, Farah couldn't help but remember herself sitting in that college dorm bathroom stall, heart thumping, staring at her watch. This time, she had left the test in the bathroom and gone back to the comfort of her bed, waiting for the minutes to pass. When the time was up, she slowly walked back to the bathroom counter and craned her neck, peeking at the test. She saw two lines—one blue, one pink.

Her eyes filled with tears. Were they ready for this? Was she ready for this? How different were her emotions this time from the last time she'd had a positive pregnancy test? She felt a wave of nausea go through her body. "Mark," her voice quivered as she walked out of the single bedroom into the living room, wearing just a T-shirt and her underwear.

Mark was sitting on the couch watching TV. He looked up to see her crying, holding the test. "What's wrong?" he asked.

"It's positive. I'm pregnant. It already happened." Her voice was barely above a whisper.

Mark leaped up and went to her, picking her up and spinning her around, covering her tear-stained cheeks in kisses. "These are tears of joy, right? This is what we wanted."

Farah shook her head. "I don't know what these are. I feel . . . guilty."

Mark pulled her down on the couch. "Guilty? Why would you feel that?"

"Because. We just started trying. It happened in our first month."

"You feel guilty about getting pregnant right away? Why? Because some women have a harder time?" He brushed her hair out of her face with his hands and tucked it behind her ears.

"No. Because of the first time. Not wanting it. I always thought it would take me a long time as some sort of punishment, I guess. I know I'm a doctor and that makes no sense, but—"

"Farah! It's been over seven years. You were in college. Don't let that take away from the joy you should be feeling now. We're going to be parents!" Mark lifted her shirt and rubbed his hand over her abdomen.

"I know. Are we ready for this? I really did think it would take longer to get pregnant," she said, smiling for the first time.

"Of course we're not ready, but we'll figure it out." Mark leaned down and kissed her navel. "Hello, peanut."

A fresh stream of tears rolled down Farah's cheeks. "This peanut is at most the size of a pea right now."

"Okay, then. Hello, sweet pea." Mark grabbed a tissue from the table and handed it to Farah. "So, when do you want to tell our parents? My mother will probably start planning the baptism right away."

"Baptism! We agreed before we got married that we wouldn't raise our kids with any particular religion," Farah said.

"Yeah, but you're the one who said you'd still want to do Christmas and celebrate some holidays just for the festivity of it," Mark said.

"Christmas is festive. A baptism is not. People are not born with sin. No child of mine is getting baptized!"

"Okay, okay. Relax." Mark held up his hands in surrender. "I'll break my mom's heart with the news that there will be no baptism and her grandchild is going to hell right after I tell her she's going to be a grandmother. When do you want to tell them?"

"I don't know. I haven't thought about whether to tell our parents right away or wait until I'm past the first trimester and at less risk for miscarriage. My mom didn't have any miscarriages that I know of, so hopefully I won't either."

"Inshallah!" Mark said emphatically. Farah burst out laughing and kissed him.

CHAPTER SIXTY

MAY 2023: PASO ROBLES, CALIFORNIA

The pounding in Farah's head was something she hadn't felt in a long time, probably since she was in New York. That was the last time she had sat behind a computer screen for hours in a row. She took off her reading glasses and put her head in her hands. Maybe blue-light glasses weren't a gimmick, and she should try a pair if she was going to be behind screens for hours again. She'd spent several days updating her resume and looking through available positions in New York. All the salaried OBGYN jobs with benefits were either working for another hospital group as she was now, or small private practices looking to add someone. Farah was determined to not go back permanently to another version of what she had left.

Trying to find a full-time position in New York at a free clinic proved to be harder than she'd thought. They didn't have any openings. The only work available in clinics for the underserved was per diem, hourly work with no set schedule and no benefits. Farah called back the director of the Women's Health Free Clinic who had told her that they usually only needed one day of coverage in the downtown Manhattan branch when a physician was out. "What if I'm willing to travel throughout the five boroughs to whichever clinic needs me on a particular day? Do you think that could be a possibility?" Farah asked.

"I think we could find at least three to four days a week of work for you if you're willing to be in a different place each day, but it would still be an hourly position. We're just not able to give another person benefits right now unless someone else leaves," the director said.

Farah set up an interview for the day after she got back to New York. She might as well at least interview and then think about it. Any work she got at a free clinic, whether full-time or per diem, would be a significant step down from what she had been earning, but it would be enough to pay her rent and bills. She and Mark had put away enough money in the kids' 529 plans for them both to graduate from college and cover at least part of graduate school. She had a decent amount of money in her retirement fund. She could pay for her own health insurance. Any time off or vacation she took with a per diem job would be unpaid as well, so she would have to factor that into her living expenses. But what about malpractice coverage? She was fairly certain per diem positions covered malpractice, otherwise no one could afford to do it. She could do this temporarily and, if she liked it, hope that a more permanent position would open up. She wondered if the clinic would have medical students or residents rotating through, if she would still have the chance to teach and mentor younger physicians. She would have to ask at her interview. As a per diem, she wouldn't be having any night calls, and that in itself was probably worth the pay cut. She did not want to be on call in the hospital and pulled into deliveries of patients she didn't know anymore.

A couple of months ago, she'd decided that she would not have her malpractice attorney settle for her, and that she would go and sit in court and defend herself, even if it would be gruesome, even if she would most likely lose. That would be the advice she would give to one of the younger doctors—if you didn't do anything wrong, then don't agree to a settlement on your behalf. But now, she was fairly sure she was going to email her attorney and tell him that she had decided to settle. Why should she put herself through two weeks of court hearings to try to prove something to people who didn't matter? She didn't have to prove anything to anyone about what type of physician she was.

She didn't have the energy to fight for something that didn't hold the same value to her as before. Maybe if she'd spent her earlier years not needing to prove herself, choosing the battles that were worth fighting for, she wouldn't be where she was now.

CHAPTER SIXTY-ONE

OCTOBER 2006: BROOKLYN, NEW YORK

As the taxi passed Osteria Mama, Farah tried to savor the last few childless minutes before they were home. She'd just spent three blissful days in Napa with Mark, and she felt a renewed sense of not just loving Mark but being *in* love with him. These little trips confirmed that they could enjoy being together, just the two of them. They wouldn't be one of those couples who had nothing in common once the kids moved out. Farah's parents had come to stay with the kids, who were seven and five years old now, well past the physically exhausting baby and toddler stage, but still requiring supervision for everything and full of curiosity and questions. Her parents did have to take an earlier flight home on the last day, so Leticia had come in on a Sunday to take over for the last few hours. As the taxi pulled in front of the brownstone, Farah squeezed Mark's hand and said, "This is it. Back to reality."

Farah opened the door and announced in a sing-song voice, "We're baa-ack."

Darya and Delara rushed to the door. Farah and Mark enveloped them in a family hug. Farah buried her face in their necks to inhale them with all she had. "Tell us everything you did with Maman Soraya and Baba Joon."

The kids started recounting their time with their grandparents, which mostly revolved around all the food and particularly "crunchy rice" Soraya had made them. "Crunchy rice" was their name for *tahdig*, the layer of fried crispy rice on the bottom of the pot that only Iranians had managed to master. Iranian wives were often judged or valued by their ability to make perfectly golden tahdig without burning it. Farah's attempts always ended up in tahdig that was either undercooked and fell apart or burned to a crisp. She knew that if she covered the bottom of the pot with a generous amount of oil the way her mother did, her tahdig would at least have a chance at having the right consistency and crunch, but she just couldn't get herself to use that much oil. She'd joked with Soraya that it was a good thing she hadn't ended up marrying an Iranian man—her horrible attempts at tahdig could be enough to qualify as grounds for a divorce.

"How were your soccer games? Did Maman Soraya get you there on time?" Farah asked.

"We were only a little late," Darya said as Farah smiled at Mark and rolled her eyes. If the kids were being watched by Farah's parents, they would get homemade meals but get to their activities on Iranian Standard Time. If they were being watched by Mark's parents, they would get everywhere early but spend all weekend eating mac and cheese and cookies.

Darya was in the middle of telling Farah how Soraya had let them have sugary sweet tea with them in the mornings and afternoons when Mark ruffled her hair and said, "Sounds like you guys had a great time." Then he turned to Farah and added, "I'm going to head to the office and catch up on emails and prep for tomorrow."

The kids still needed a bath, a story, and to be tucked in. Their school lunches still had to be prepared for the next day. As Farah watched Mark head into his office, leaving her with the kids, any feeling of being in love she had regained over the weekend instantly vanished, replaced by absolute rage. In her mind, there was no worse crime Mark could commit than being thoughtless and selfish. She got up to storm into his office and throw everything off his desk, and then she stopped herself. She looked at her watch and noted the time and then proceeded to get the kids ready for bed.

Once the kids were bathed and in pajamas, she told them to go into the office and kiss their daddy goodnight. She tucked them in and went to the kitchen. She banged cabinet doors and dropped silverware to see if any of the noise would get Mark's attention. Nothing. It amazed her how Mark had the ability to tune out all his surroundings when he needed to. When she was done, she looked at her watch again. She had spent the last hour and a half on what the kids needed. She calmly walked into the office and stood in front of Mark. "The kids came in to kiss you goodnight," she said, her voice ice cold.

"I know," Mark replied, not looking up from his screen.

"Did you notice their hair was wet? Or that they were in pajamas? Do you think that happened magically? When they kissed you goodnight, did you say to yourself, 'Oh, maybe I should stop what I'm doing and read them a story and tuck them in?'"

Mark sighed, pinching the bridge of his nose. "Don't start this. Listen, I'm sorry, but when they walked in, I was in the middle of writing something and I didn't want to break my train of thought. And I have to be ready for tomorrow. Let's not do this. We just got back."

"Do you think that I don't have a full schedule tomorrow to prepare for? I spent the last hour and a half getting them ready for bed and making their lunches for tomorrow while you got to do your work."

"I would have been happy to make their lunches when I was done with my work before going to bed if you had asked me to. I would have done it on my time, not on your time," Mark said.

"What about doing their bath? That couldn't wait to be on 'your time.' You don't think about anyone but yourself. You didn't ask 'What can I help you with?' before sauntering off to your office after spending only ten minutes with them despite being away from them for three days. It's like you didn't even miss them. You are so selfish; you live in your own Mark world."

"That's enough, Farah. You've made your point. You're the better parent. You missed them more than I did. Don't ruin our last few days together by turning this into a huge fight. I had a lot of work on my mind, but I'm sorry I didn't help."

"Right, I'm the one ruining the last few days, not you. It's all me and my fault. You just had work on your mind. Not me; I never have work on my mind. I'm the one who has a way-more stressful job where people's lives and well-being are literally at stake, and I'm the one who has to think of everything."

"Don't worry. I haven't forgotten that you have the real job with the real stress. You forgot to mention that you also make more money." Mark got up and left the office, and then Farah heard him walk out the front door.

Farah knew she'd gone too far. She shouldn't have made the comment about the stress and more important job. At least she hadn't mentioned money this time, but Mark had obviously remembered and held on to that from their last fight. Stress and money were the cards Farah played over and over again in their arguments, and she knew it wasn't fair. She had purposely married a man who wasn't bothered by the woman making more money or having a more prestigious job, so why did she keep playing that card? It was just hard for her to believe that the man who had seemed so thoughtful and selfless during their dating and early marriage years was not that person once children had been added to the equation.

The next morning, Farah called Soraya and took her frustrations out on her. Why couldn't she manage to get them to their games on time? Why had she given the kids sweet tea—caffeine and sugar—both things Farah had said many times she did not want them to have?

"You grew up drinking it from when you were one. You're fine. You're a doctor," Soraya had defended herself.

Farah told her mom that she either needed to stop undermining her or she wouldn't have them stay with the kids again and would rely on Mark's parents more instead. Then she hung up the phone. She opened the freezer door to grab some ice packs for her lunch and saw twenty Ziplocs of frozen Persian stews, prepared and labeled and neatly stacked by Soraya, who had also clearly organized her freezer. Soraya had made at least a month of meals that just needed rice to be added to them in the three days she had been there. The Ziplocs she had used were not the ones Farah bought. They were probably recycled ones that she had brought with her from Cincinnati in anticipation of doing this act of love for Farah's family. Soraya didn't believe that Ziplocs were for one-time use. Her habit of reusing bags and washing yogurt and cream cheese containers to use as Tupperware was not an effort to be environmentally friendly and less wasteful but rather born of a certain frugality that came with her immigrant experience, no matter how much money she and Behnam had now. Farah shut the freezer door and sat on the kitchen floor. She laughed and then cried. Soraya was not the type of mother that left you little "I Love You" notes in your lunchbox—cooking your meals and stocking your freezer were her love language. Farah called her mom while walking from the subway to the hospital and apologized.

CHAPTER SIXTY-TWO

MAY 2023: OBERLIN, OHIO

In the Lyft on the way to Rumi's dorm, Farah thought about how much she had worried about him over the years, and yet here she was, at Oberlin for his college graduation. She had planned to get there a couple of days before everyone else arrived so she could spend some one-on-one time with him before the distraction of having to see Mark and both their extended families. When the Lyft dropped her off and she saw Rumi waiting outside the dorm building for her, she was surprised by his face. Despite having seen him in person only a few months before and on FaceTime at least once a week, he looked different. More mature. More masculine. Sometimes the facial hair made her think that it was hard to recognize the child she'd once had, but when Farah would look in his eyes or see him smile, her baby was still right there, as he'd always been.

He ran over, enveloping her in his arms. She buried her face in his neck and inhaled, feeling his beard tickle her forehead. Rumi stepped back and said, "Mom, you look great."

She smiled. "So do you. Your eyes are brighter than ever."

The plan was for Farah to meet Jackie first and then take Rumi, Jackie, and a group of their friends to dinner. Jackie was Rumi's longest relationship, and Farah had been looking forward to meeting her, seeing how they were together. They walked to the main quad, where Jackie was waiting for them.

"Dr. Afshar, so nice to meet you," she said as they hugged each other.

Farah pulled back from the hug and said, "Call me Farah, please." Dr. Afshar was still how Mark addressed Behnam, after all these years.

Jackie was petite, with curly mousy brown hair that sat just above her shoulders and amber eyes. She wore jeans and a sweatshirt and no makeup—a college girl. She was friendly and sweet and well-spoken.

At dinner, Farah observed Rumi with his circle of friends, laughing with ease as the conversation flowed. She noticed Rumi and Jackie intermittently touching each other's arms or hands. Farah had to try so hard not to get teary-eyed at the table. She loved to see how her baby was navigating the world on his own, and he was doing just fine. Maybe she could finally stop worrying about him all the time.

The next morning, or rather at noon, she met Rumi alone for breakfast. "How was your night after dinner?" Farah asked.

"Oh, you know. Went to a campus party. Had a few drinks. Went to bed at three a.m. Living that college life you wanted for me down to the last few days," Rumi smiled.

Farah nodded. "Yup. I, on the other hand, went right to bed with a book in my hand. Read less than half a page before I fell asleep. Living that fifty-three-year-old life, and I'm happy with it."

The waitress came and took their order. While they waited for their coffee and food, Farah decided that if she didn't start opening up to Rumi and sharing more with him now, then she may never do it. Although she knew she would eventually tell Rumi about her abortion, that wasn't the topic she wanted to start with. She thought that maybe it was best not to discuss an abortion with someone for whom possibly having a biological child one day would be complicated. Instead, she started with what she thought he may need to hear the most.

"You know I've had a lot of time to examine my life over these past months in Paso," she started. "And there is a lot I haven't shared with you, but I'd like to start with something today."

Just then the waitress arrived with their coffees. When she left the table, Rumi took a sip of his and then set it down on the table, crossing his arms on the table and leaning forward. "I'm all ears, Mom."

"Don't misinterpret what I'm going to say. I don't have regrets about the divorce with your dad, but I am realizing that I took out a disproportionate amount of my stress on him." Farah paused and Rumi was silent, so she continued. "I'm going to tell you something you have to keep to yourself. I've only shared this with your father and no one else, not even Darya yet. About four years ago, I was named in a lawsuit at work. The case has not gone to trial yet, but it will. The pandemic hit and it kept getting delayed. And although I know that I didn't do anything wrong, this case ate away at me daily until just recently. And having lawyers advise me to not discuss it with anyone—not my sisters, not Julia, not anyone—was really hard. I only spoke about it with your dad, and of course he was supportive. But then since he was the only person I could talk to about it, sometimes I would also lash out. That's not an excuse, obviously. But this suit hanging over my head—when I did nothing wrong and have sacrificed so much time with you guys, time with your dad, time for myself, for this career—it was the tip of the iceberg of all the other work stress, and anyway, eventually I ended up here." Farah looked at Rumi with tear-filled eyes that were begging for understanding and forgiveness.

"Wow, Mom. That's a lot. So, what happens next?" Rumi asked.

"I go back to Paso for one last month and then back to New York. I figure things out. I start the rest of my life."

"Hmmm. You start again. What else do you want to tell me about?"

"There's a lot. My years in Iran. I've hardly told you or Darya anything about those. Maybe the next time I have the two of you together, without the whole extended family, I'll start with one of those stories," Farah said and stroked his cheek. "But I want to spend the rest of our little time alone together hearing more about my son."

◆

The night before graduation, Farah sat on the bed in the hotel room her sisters were sharing, watching Azita unpack her little carry-on. Parisa was arriving in a couple of hours, along with their parents. Darya had already arrived and was in Farah's room, letting her mom have some alone time with her sister. Mark's parents were also flying in soon. Farah had always had a fairly good relationship with her in-laws, and she wasn't as nervous about seeing them as she was about seeing Mark, but she knew this was what happened when you got a divorce. Hopefully, over time, these family events celebrating their children would not feel awkward.

As Azita hung the puffy-sleeved floral dress she planned to wear for graduation, she turned to Farah and asked, "Are you nervous about seeing Mark with the girlfriend tomorrow?"

"No. Okay, I'm lying. Maybe a little, or a lot. But I've been thinking about our relationship and making peace with everything that happened. On another note, Googoosh is going on tour, and I was going to surprise Maman with concert tickets. This could end up being her last tour. Do you want to go with us?"

"Sure. Count me in," Azita said.

Then Farah reached over and grabbed Azita's hand. "Hey, I want to ask you about something else. How come we never talk about Iran? Our house crumpled. I had my first kiss from Alireza, and he died. His sister was your best friend, and she died."

Azita's lips started to quiver. She blinked back tears. She opened her mouth to say something and then shut it. Then she shook her head and said, "I can't."

Farah got up from the bed and held her, stroking her head. "I'm sorry. I just brought that up out of nowhere and I can see that it's too much. But your reaction tells me we need to talk about this. So not tonight, but a little bit at a time, okay?"

Azita just nodded as Farah continued to hold her, rocking

and shushing her like a baby. She wasn't the only one who had compartmentalized and put memories in places that were hard to reach.

◆

The next morning, Farah dragged Darya to the main lawn early so they could try to get a good row of seats for everyone. When they arrived, Darya sent their family a pin with their location. Soon Mark was walking over toward them and Darya jumped up to hug him. Farah noticed that he had a little more gray hair now. He looked a little thinner than usual. "I've missed you," Mark said to Darya, studying her face and stroking her cheek.

"I've missed you, too, Dad. It's good to see you."

Mark and Farah looked at each other for a few seconds and then both reached out for a brief awkward hug. "It's good to see you too. You look well . . . happy," Mark said, smiling at Farah.

"Yes . . . same," Farah said, although Mark didn't particularly look happy to her. "Where is Emily? Is she coming with your parents?"

"No. I'm not really sure where that's going, and I wanted this weekend to be about Rumi. It just felt like it would be too much with Emily here at the same time as your parents, so I came by myself," Mark said.

"Oh, okay," Farah tried to not let her relief show on her face. "Well, that was very considerate of you. Thank you."

When the grandparents arrived, everyone was polite and friendly to each other, focusing on the occasion. When Rumi was handed his diploma, Farah couldn't help but look over at Mark. He had his eyes on Rumi, with a big proud grin on his face, and then he turned and caught Farah watching him. They locked eyes for a few moments before Farah looked away. They had done it. Rumi was okay. After, they took a series of family pictures—Mark's family, Farah's family, all of them together, their nuclear family. Farah was so grateful Emily hadn't been there. What would they have done if she had been there? Included her in the pictures?

Dinner that night also went well. There weren't any lulls in the conversation, as everyone listened to Rumi tell them all about what each of his friends were doing next. Rumi himself would be staying on as a TA while applying for master's in education programs. He wanted to be a high school history teacher, and Farah knew he would make an excellent teacher and safe person for his future students. Mark's mom was complimenting both Rumi and Darya on their group of friends, all of whom were politically active and had plans to do their part to make the US and the world a better place.

"That's just how young people these days are, Grams. It's not a big deal. My friends and I, we're not an exception. I'm really proud of Mom. She's the one who took a leave from her job, and she's interviewing at a women's free clinic when she's back in New York. Not that many people her age are gusty enough to make a change like that," Darya commented.

Farah looked a little nervously over at Soraya, waiting to see if she was going to object to these plans she was hearing about for the first time, but Soraya didn't say anything. Farah looked over at Darya and smiled, "Thank you, honey. You and Rumi have been good role models for me." She was so happy to see that her kids had gotten over their bitterness about the divorce—about Farah needing to figure her life out.

"Really?" Mark raised his eyebrows. "What's that all about?"

"Okay, we can talk about all that later. This is Rumi's night. And I'm sure not everyone wants to hear about the latest in my life. I'm happy that both my kids are taking the time to figure out what they really want to do and pursuing their passions." Farah changed the subject and managed to keep it off herself for the rest of the night. At the end of the night, Rumi asked Farah if she would mind if he spent some alone time with Mark at a local bar he liked to go to with his friends.

"No, I don't mind, honey. He's your dad and you guys should get alone time together too," Farah said. She hid her disappointment.

Rumi had always gravitated toward Mark. When he was a child, this would frustrate Farah, who was the one most actively involved in the day-to-day of raising kids. Once Rumi came out and Mark handled it much better than Farah, she felt them grow even closer, but now, it was time to move on from all that. Her relationship with Rumi was much better now that she had accepted it all and he could be himself, and she was no longer competing with Mark or anyone.

CHAPTER SIXTY-THREE

SEPTEMBER 2018: BROOKLYN, NEW YORK

"Is this really necessary, Mom? I'm going to be late if I don't leave now," Rumi said.

"Yes, it's necessary. It will take five seconds and it's your last first day of school," Farah replied, grabbing her phone off the kitchen island and following him to the front door.

Rumi slung his backpack over his left shoulder and paused with the front door half open, turning to face Farah.

"No. We're doing this outside like every year," Farah said and went out ahead of him, going down the steps of their brownstone. "Okay, ready. Say senior year!"

Rumi shook his head. "Don't be so cheesy, Mom." But then he gave her a big smile. Once Farah had taken a few pictures, he ran down the stairs, gave her a hug, and headed toward the subway. Then he turned around, "Oh and Mom, I won't be home for dinner. I already told Dad. I'm grabbing something with Kyle and Holden tonight."

Farah paused at the base of the half flight of stairs to their brownstone before heading back inside. She surveyed their block, taking in the sounds and smells of the street. The songs of birds chirping mixed in with the noise of car engines and honks. Soon, the magnolia trees would start to change color. She loved fall in New York. She saw a father trailing his toddler pedaling a tricycle, a little purple helmet with pink flowers on her head. She remembered when they had first seen this home with the realtor. Darya was learning to pedal while Rumi was still a baby, not even crawling yet. How was it his senior year already?

Farah climbed the stairs and went inside. She grabbed a second cup of coffee and sat at the kitchen island. She had blocked her schedule until ten o'clock that morning. She scrolled through the pictures she'd just taken. She hadn't seen Rumi smile ear to ear like that in a first day of school picture in years, but she still felt a heaviness in her chest.

She texted Mark:

I don't know if I can do this.

Her phone pinged immediately.

Do what?

I don't know. Rumi just left for school. Nothing. Never mind. Let's talk tonight. Okay?

I'm on call tonight and expecting some late deliveries. Rumi's not going to be home for dinner anyway, so I'll just stay at the hospital. Don't know when or if I'll get home. It's fine.

Farah wrote and clicked off her phone.

Riding the subway into Manhattan, Farah tried to identify what the root of the heaviness she was feeling was. Maybe it was because it was the last year of having a child at home. Just when her relationship with Rumi had gotten better after years—just when he was finally happy and she could see that and enjoy his happiness—it was almost time for him to go. Was that it, or was it something else? What would she do once he was in college too? Who would she be? She looked at her phone. Mark hadn't replied to her last text. She felt disappointed, but what did she want him to say?

"This is Ninety-Sixth Street," a Barry White–smooth, deep voice announced through the speakers as the subway came to a halt, jolting Farah out of her thoughts. She was momentarily confused as she saw people rushing in and out of the subway doors. She had to get up or she'd miss her stop. The moment she stood up, a teen boy listening to music so loudly that it could be heard despite his headphones took her seat as Farah squeezed through all the standing passengers and just made it out the sliding doors before they shut. She had to get herself out of this head fog.

Once she stepped into Mount Sinai, there was no time to think or feel sorry for herself. She already had a full schedule, in addition to being on call. Before she knew it, it was after 10 p.m. She had a patient in labor who she expected to deliver soon. When she had last checked on her, she was seven centimeters dilated, but it had been at least an hour since then, so she walked back into her room. "How are you doing, Jessica?"

"Pretty okay. This epidural is magic," Jessica said.

"They are magic. Glad you decided to go for it. Let's see—" Farah was interrupted by a nurse who came into the room.

"Dr. Afshar, we need you in L-D-R-Five right away!"

When Farah finally crawled into bed after three that night, she could not fall asleep despite her complete exhaustion. Every time she tried to close her eyes, she saw Hannah Raye's face as she'd awakened from the anesthesia and asked for her baby. When her alarm rang at five thirty, she realized that she must have finally fallen asleep. There was no way she could get up to go for a run. She pulled the covers back over her head and drifted in and out of sleep until seven.

Mark was sitting at the kitchen island, reading the *New York Times*. He looked at Farah still in a bathrobe and said, "You must have gotten in really late if you skipped your run. I didn't hear you come in. When did you get home?"

"Around three," Farah said as she poured herself a mug of coffee. She sat at the island and stared ahead.

"Everything okay?" Mark asked.

"Sure," Farah said, continuing to look ahead and not make eye contact. Mark resumed reading the paper and Farah said, "Actually, everything is not fine. I texted you yesterday morning saying I couldn't do this, and you never followed up to check in on me the rest of the day."

"I asked what's wrong. I said let's talk tonight, and then you said you couldn't and never mind," Mark said.

"Yes, but you knew I wasn't feeling right. It was Rumi's last first day of school. It was a hard day for me. And you didn't check in with me one time through the rest of the day."

Mark rolled his eyes. "Farah, why are you trying to pick a fight?" He scrolled through his text messages with her and held up his phone. "I asked what was wrong. You said nothing, never mind. I said let's talk tonight. You said I'm on call and it's fine. It's all right here. I'm supposed to keep texting you when I know your phone is already blowing up on a call day?" His voice sounded progressively more irritated to Farah.

"Yup. You're right. Never mind," she said.

Mark sighed, looked like he was going to say something, and then shook his head and dumped his coffee down the sink before turning to leave the kitchen.

"I had to deliver a dead baby last night." A tear rolled down her cheek as she continued to stare straight ahead.

Mark paused. "See, I knew it. You take out all your frustrations on me. This isn't about me. It almost never is." Then he continued to walk out of the kitchen toward the front door.

CHAPTER SIXTY-FOUR

JUNE 2023: PASO ROBLES, CALIFORNIA

"We've been seeing more and more of you in the tasting room these days," Miguel said.

"Yeah. I can't believe it's my last month here. I love being in here, so I'm trying to get my fill before moving on," Farah said.

Miguel grabbed a bottle of the Reserve 2018 Cabernet Sauvignon. "Since you don't have too much time left here, let's open this and try it. You can use it as your bonus pour today for people who seem like they may want to join the club."

"That sounds great." Farah grinned and watched Miguel smell the cork and pour them each a small taste in warm glasses that he'd just removed from the dishwasher. They held up their glasses to the light, swirled, sniffed, clicked glasses, and then tasted. All Farah could say was "Wow" as she savored the complexity of the wine.

Miguel put his glass down and clasped his hands together, leaning toward Farah over the bar. "So, have you come up with your grand plan for when you get back?"

The way he looked directly into her eyes was so intense that it was hard for Farah to maintain eye contact. She reminded herself that this was how Miguel was with everyone. She looked down at her glass and looked back up. "That's the million-dollar question," Farah said. "I'll go back to my prior position, but only until I find something else. I have an interview set up with a free women's health clinic. I'm hoping to work less, or at least definitely work differently. And to figure out how to incorporate some of what I love about Paso into a New York life. How about you, Miguel? You're at Braxton for the long haul?"

Miguel broke his gaze and laughed. "You're trying to get me in trouble."

"I am not. I'm genuinely interested in knowing where Miguel sees himself five years from now. And I promise, whatever you tell me, it stays between us," Farah said.

"Every winemaker makes their own wine on the side. I've been doing that in small batches, sharing with friends. But eventually, I'd like to have my own label," he said.

"And will that be happening in Paso, or do you have your eyes set on Sonoma or Napa or somewhere else?"

"No. I fell in love with Paso the first time I came here, just like you did. If I wanted to be in Napa, I could be there now—just like you could be."

"Well, I look forward to visiting you in your tasting room one day." Farah clinked glasses with him again and took the last sip of her wine. "I need to get back to work now."

◆

Sitting on her couch with her feet up on the table, Farah drank a glass of water as she reflected on her day. The one thing she noticed about working in the tasting room was that on those days, by the end of it, she had no desire to drink wine. Even though she would have less than half a glass of wine all day between the bottles she opened, most of which she would swish and spit into the spittoon, she would be wined out by four o'clock. Being a tasting room attendant was definitely a job she could not do full-time. Making small talk with new patrons every day was fun, but how many times could she describe all the tasting notes of the same five wines in the flight or tell the story of Braxton Vineyards? If she did somehow incorporate walking people through tastings into her future life, she would want it to be different wines from different regions, not the same thing every time. She was glad to have the next day off from the tasting room and be able to truly enjoy her dinner with Cecily that night.

Cecily was the person Farah had become closest to during her stay, someone she could imagine being good lifelong friends with. She reminded Farah of Julia. She was fun, boisterous, smart, big-hearted, hilarious. People gravitated toward Cecily, wanting to be in her inner circle, just like Farah had. For their last solo dinner together, they chose to go to Fish Gaucho. While New York City had all the best restaurants with cuisine from every part of the world, the Mexican food in California far surpassed anything Farah had eaten in New York. Over gaucho margaritas and Oaxaca Flocka nachos, Farah thanked Cecily for inviting her not just to join her book club but for extending an invitation to her for so many other social events. "I feel so grateful that you were sitting next to me at that first potluck. I had been worried about finding like-minded people in Paso."

"Paso is not so bad. I find that in smaller places, liberals always manage to find each other and take each other in—create their own community," Cecily said.

"I think you're right. It reminds me of all the Iranians in Cincinnati knowing each other. There are only a few hundred, so when a new family comes, everyone takes them in. But in New York, you hear Farsi on the streets all the time. Despite there being so many more Iranians, most people have their established friend group and it can be harder for someone new to infiltrate. I'm going to miss everyone I met here. I'm promising myself to be back in Paso hopefully at least once a year, but you have to visit me in New York so I can show you all my favorite spots in the city."

"Be careful, I'm going to take you up on it. What will you miss most about Paso? Besides me, of course," Cecily winked.

"The mornings. The peace and quiet in the mornings. The smell and feel of the fresh clean air when I open my front door and step outside and just look at the views. It makes me feel so small, so filled with hope and gratitude." And then Farah decided to do something a little uncharacteristic. "You know, I started trying to meditate while I was here. And then when that wasn't going so well, I decided that rather than meditate, I'd just sit and let memories from my past fill my head. A lot of scenes from my teen years have come back to me, both from Iran and from when we moved to Cincinnati. Scenes, or I guess experiences, that I've either suppressed or tried to forget ever happened. But there are some things you carry with you forever."

Cecily sat back with a look of intrigue, waiting for Farah to say more. When Farah was silent, Cecily leaned in and grabbed her hand. "Farah, I would love to hear about your experiences and stories, if you feel comfortable sharing them."

Farah found herself telling Cecily about the revolution, the air raids, the war—about leaving everything. "And it seems like every time I recount a memory or share it, a new memory resurfaces." She didn't care if she was being too much. This was who she was. After all, "Be Farah" was what she had written last as her goal on the eve of Julia's birthday.

CHAPTER SIXTY-FIVE

JULY 2023: WEST VILLAGE, NEW YORK

Walking to her apartment from the subway, Farah couldn't help grinning. She'd missed the sensory experience of the city—the cabs, the crowds, the honking, the smells of street food and roasted nuts. The humidity she had not missed, she realized as sweat trickled down her neck and pooled into her bra. She lugged her baggage up the steps and opened her door. Her apartment looked the same as when she left it. Her tenants had taken meticulous care of it. Julia had arranged for it to be professionally cleaned before her arrival. On the coffee table, there was a vase with fresh peonies in water. Farah read the card by the vase:

Welcome home. Looking forward to hearing about more Farah past stories in person. Cheers. XX, J.

Farah leaned down and took a whiff of the peonies. They smelled wonderful, but she thought that once they died, she would continue the little tradition she had started in Paso—she would put a shot glass of rosewater on the table each day. Farah walked to the window and opened it, letting the street noise come in. A family picture from two years prior that she kept on the kitchen shelf caught her eye. She held it and looked at Mark. She would never regret the years they'd had together or the life they'd built, even if the two of them hadn't lasted. She put the picture down and hopped in the shower. She was meeting Julia for an early dinner and then preparing for her interview the next day. Farah couldn't wait to see Julia. As lovely as people in Paso were, she wouldn't trade Julia for all of them. There was something about a girlfriend you had known for over twenty years who often seemed to know you better than you knew yourself.

After dinner, Farah came back to her apartment and brewed herself some mint tea. She mentally rehearsed potential interview questions for the next day. As she was getting ready for bed, Farah debated about what to wear for her interview at the Women's Health Free Clinic. She could wear her simple navy pantsuit and her nude pumps, but that seemed so boring, so devoid of personality. She would love to wear a flowy dress and some cowboy boots. She had lived in cowboy boots in Paso, but this was a job interview, after all. She decided to stick with her navy pantsuit but wear a paisley-printed blouse underneath instead of a basic shell. In the morning, she took one last look at herself in the mirror. She took off her small diamond stud earrings and replaced them with miniature turquoise and gold chandelier earrings that belonged to her maternal grandmother and stepped out her door.

At the clinic, the site manager gave her a tour, introducing her to staff along the way while they were waiting for Dr. Gottlieb to finish up with a patient. The waiting room was simple but clean, with posters about contraception, STI prevention, and domestic violence on the walls. Then Farah saw a poster that made her pause. The picture was of a trans woman about to get a mammogram. The caption said, "At the Women's Health Free Clinic, we take care of all women."

I love you, New York, she thought to herself. The exam rooms were small but functional, with updated equipment. The doctors' room was not an office but a shared space with multiple cubicles where physicians, nurses, physician assistants, and medical assistants sat side by side and finished their charting. There would be no big fancy office at any point, and that made Farah smile. She was ready for it.

Farah met with Dr. Leah Gottlieb, who went over the demographics of the patients the clinic serves, the patient volume, and the type of services they provide. "In the last couple of years, we've been providing more gender-affirming care, which includes hormone therapy in line with what organizations like Planned Parenthood have been doing. We have internists who can provide that care for patients, but if you're seeing a patient and they need a refill or adjustments, it would be good if you could check their labs and do that. We don't know when the patient will be able to come back, and we want to help minimize a lapse in their care. Is that something you are able to do?"

"I haven't done it before," Farah replied, "but I have attended some conferences on transgender health care. I have the CME certificates. I would just need to review the protocols and make sure that I'm staying current on gender-affirming care, which I'm happy to do." Farah hesitated a moment, and then added, "I have a close family member who is transgender. This is an area of medicine that is close to my heart."

Dr. Gottlieb nodded and continued. "Of course, the bulk of what we do is still providing free contraception and performing abortions. Since Roe vs. Wade got overturned, we worry about our hands getting tied someday, even in New York. And we're thinking about if we're able to allocate some funds to help women who are in states where abortion is illegal get to clinics in adjacent states where they can have an abortion."

"It's really unbelievable," Farah said.

Dr. Gottlieb shrugged her shoulders and shook her head. Finally, she asked Farah why she wanted to leave her position to work there.

"Because I went into OBGYN to see patients and not to fight insurance companies." Farah paused before adding, "Because my own most memorable experience as a patient took place in a free clinic in my early twenties."

"I understand that." Dr. Gottlieb nodded. She pinched the top of her nose between her eyebrows, then continued. "But this is still very different from what you've been doing for the last twenty-plus years. And of course, it will come with its own set of frustrations. You're certainly more than qualified, but I'm not sure if it will end up being the right fit."

"Well," Farah said, "this is a per diem position. You need help, and I want to be here. And the beauty of it is that you could decide to let me go at any moment, and I could decide to leave at any moment. But I don't think that's going to happen. What I do know is that I can't continue where I am now, and I think I'll be surprising us both. I can see myself staying here until I'm ready to retire from medicine altogether."

Farah left the clinic and reached into her purse for her phone. There were three texts from Julia:

Hope you are kicking ass. Call me as soon as it's done.

What's taking so long? Hopefully, a long interview is good news.

Hello . . . waiting . . . are we celebrating tonight or not? Call me!

Farah clicked on Julia's name and was about to hit the call button when she changed her mind. There was someone else she wanted to talk to first. The phone rang three times before Darya picked up. "Hi honey. I had my interview at the women's free clinic. I'm taking the job. Thank you for suggesting it, for taking care of your mom."

Darya squealed, "I'm so proud of you, Mom! RBG would have been so proud of you, too!"

Farah laughed, "Right, RBG. If only she had retired when Obama asked her to."

"Yeah, Mom. But who could have predicted this." It was more of a statement than a question.

"I don't know. Ever since Trump's term, I always find myself predicting or anticipating the worst. But I've been working on getting out of this mindset. It hasn't served me well."

CHAPTER SIXTY-SIX

NOVEMBER 2016: BROOKLYN, NEW YORK

Once again, Mark wanted to have an election party, and Farah was hesitant. But when he'd reminded her that she had vetoed an election party for Obama and only invited Julia's family, she had promised him she'd consider it. If America had voted for Obama over McCain, surely they would vote for Hillary over Trump. How could they not? Mark had convinced her, as he'd added almost everyone they knew to the guestlist.

"If Trump won the primary, then it means he can also win the election. I'm nervous," Farah said. But Mark kept pointing out what all the polls and predictions were saying, and Farah wanted to believe so badly that there was no way Trump would win. His run had literally been a laughing matter at first, the greatest of all reality shows, sad and funny, until he won the primary. Suddenly it wasn't a joke anymore, and Farah's heart was broken. It had felt personal, like once again, all of America was telling her that she didn't belong in this country—that this was a country where bullies won.

In the end, she'd agreed to the party, because it wasn't just about Mark. Darya and Rumi were also excited about the first female president, and Farah had to show them that she believed, that she had faith in Americans. And although Farah herself wasn't exactly all in for Hillary, she realized that Hillary was being scrutinized way beyond any degree any male candidate is ever scrutinized.

They decided to go all out for the party, decorating their house in red, white, and blue, and ordering multiple life-size Hillary cardboard cutouts to display around the house. Helium balloons with Hillary's face floated throughout the house. Streamers hung from the ceiling surrounding a Trump piñata in the center of the living room. Farah ordered plates and napkins with the words *I'm With Her* and *Nasty Woman* printed on them. And for the signature cocktail, Julia arrived early and prepared one she'd found online called the "Shattered Glass."

Guests filed in, many of the women in white pantsuits. As the night went on, the mood of the party regressed from excited to somber, everyone going quiet and staring at the TV in disbelief. One by one, guests quietly left without saying goodbye to anyone. When only Julia, Ethan, and Violet were left, Farah started crying.

"Oh honey," Julia said. "We're going to get through this. Just like we get through everything. What's that old two-steps-forward-one-step-back thing? Obama was our two steps forward, Hillary is our one step back, but we'll take two steps forward again."

"Okay, Mom. Let's go home. No one is in the mood for your optimism tonight," Violet said.

As everyone went to bed, Farah stayed down in the living room. She wept for her daughter, who'd had to witness a man who said "Grab them by the pussy" become president. She wept for her trans son whose rights were in even greater danger now. She wept for herself, the Brown girl who had been caught between two worlds and was once again being told that she didn't belong. She picked up the stick and started smashing the last bits of the Trump piñata into pieces. Mark came back down.

"What are you doing, Farah? It's going to be fine. Come up to bed," he said.

"It's not going to be fine. Everyone thought it would be fine when Khomeini came into power. Everyone celebrated, believing that he was going to be better than the puppet put in place by the US."

"I don't know that you can compare this to the Islamic Revolution," Mark said.

"Can't I? Leave me alone. Please, just leave me alone," Farah said and lay on the couch.

CHAPTER SIXTY-SEVEN

JULY 2023: GREENWICH VILLAGE, NEW YORK

Aniyah walked in the door at Olio e Più and spotted Farah at a corner table. Aniyah was still in her scrubs and surgical clogs, her dark hair pulled back into a big box braid bun, the way she usually had her hair on operating days. She walked toward Farah with a huge smile and Farah got up from her chair, squeezing Aniyah tight. "Thank you for meeting me out here. I just didn't want to have this talk close to work," Farah said.

"Sure. I've missed you. We all have. And I don't mind not rushing home after work every once in a while, getting to stay in Manhattan," Aniyah said. Aniyah and her wife had moved from the East Village to Williamsburg once they'd had their twins. After a bit of catch-up, Aniyah said, "I'm guessing you've brought me here to tell me you're not coming back at all."

Farah sighed. "Yes and no. I'm coming back for just one last month, but that's not why I wanted to talk. Before I announce that my position is now permanently open, I think you should be the next chief, and I wanted to see if you'd be interested in having me talk to Ferguson and Oppenheim about it."

"You want me to take the position that led you to leave this job altogether?" Aniyah smirked.

Farah tried to explain to Aniyah how their circumstances were different. Aniyah had just turned forty. She had many more years of practice ahead of her. Aniyah's wife worked in IT and was very involved with their twins, having the flexibility of being able to work remotely most of the time. "Being chief at forty can open more doors for you. Maybe you could replace Oppenheim one day. Not to mention that you're just the best person for this job. You are an excellent physician. You care about every patient. You watch out for the younger OBs. It would kill me to have this go to Brian permanently."

Aniyah shook her head. "I don't think so, Farah. Don't think I haven't known that you may not come back. I've thought about this a lot while you were gone. Why do I have to keep pushing? Why should I keep trying to do more? When I was growing up, I never thought that this little Black girl from Queens was going to go to medical school one day, to be able to marry a woman, an Asian one at that! To have children and our own little home. I've already broken the glass ceiling. I don't feel the need to break the next one. Having a family with a wife is the dream I didn't even know I could have as a child. I want to save those extra hours a week enjoying them, not dealing with administration. No offense, but I don't want to run off when I'm fifty to figure out my life. I'm trying to figure it out now."

Farah nodded her understanding. "I had to at least try, right?"

"Sure, you had to try. But what are you going to be doing? Moving back to wine country forever?" Aniyah asked.

"No. New York is home. I'm going to do some per diem work at the Women's Health Free Clinic, and hopefully it will turn into a more permanent position over time."

Aniyah's eyebrows were raised. "Are you serious right now?"

"I'm serious," Farah nodded.

"Wow, Farah. Just wow! I was not expecting that. You are definitely done with the rat race." Aniyah sat back and crossed her arms, smiling ear to ear.

"What were you expecting?" Farah asked.

"I don't know. Maybe some sort of part-time concierge cash practice. Becoming a 'menopause specialist' or 'women over forty weight-loss specialist' or a 'physician life coach' or something like that," Aniyah said, laughing.

"And then I write a book and get a bunch of TikTok followers and sit back and make passive income? Honestly, there is nothing wrong with doing that. Insurance companies have made practicing medicine so difficult and unenjoyable that I understand people who are choosing to do that. But it's just not me, and fortunately, I'm privileged enough to be in a financial state in which I don't need to consider those options," Farah said.

Aniyah nodded, "Yup. It's not me either. But who knows what will happen over time. Never say never, right?"

◆

One week later, Farah looked at all her colleagues seated around the conference table. Two of the younger OBs were pregnant, each sitting with their hand over their abdomen. For the first time, Brian looked a little fatigued. Being a new father was probably responsible for that. Farah could imagine his wife Charlotte being the type to insist that he do some of the night feedings. *Good for her*, Farah thought. When her own kids had been babies, Farah had been a martyr, insisting that she nurse during the night rather than having Mark give them a bottle or two while she slept. Now she could see that she'd done all that for herself, to ease her guilt over the time she wasn't spending with them during the day. Mark never felt guilty about the hours he spent at work. Farah hoped that Darya and the younger pregnant OBs sitting around the table would not impose that sense of guilt on themselves.

Farah was going to miss this job and all these people, even Brian. After all, Brian was smart, hardworking, reliable, and funny. He did care about the department, and she would miss their banter. She would miss being a mentor to the younger OBs just starting their families, but she could still be available to them, even if she would no longer be in a position to advocate for them. "I want to thank you all for taking such incredible care of my patients during my absence. And thank you, Brian, for stepping up as acting chief while I was gone. Seeing how well all of you took care of my patients makes this easier for me. I am leaving this job permanently in one month." Farah paused and took a sip of her coffee, looking around the room to gauge people's reactions. No one looked surprised. Aniyah hadn't been the only one to think she may not be coming back permanently.

"I'm guessing most of you knew this may be coming. I will take the next month to reach out to any patients that want to see me one last time and make sure that everything is taken care of so their transition of care to you is as smooth as possible. I'm incredibly grateful that I've had the opportunity to do this work for over twenty years, but it's time for me to move on and leave it in your more-than-capable hands. I'm going to miss all of you. But I'll always just be a phone call away, so hopefully we can see each other outside of work sometimes."

"Are you moving to private practice?" Mei asked.

"No. I'm taking a perdiem position at the Women's Health Free Clinic that I hope will eventually turn into something more permanent." Farah saw several raised eyebrows around the conference table. It seemed like this was the only surprising news she had delivered.

Everyone thanked her for the years and work she had put in, telling her the department wouldn't be the same without her. And then, her colleagues stood up to move on with their day and get back to patient care.

◆

Walking from the subway back to her apartment that night, Farah walked into her local wine shop. The owner, Roberto, recognized her. "You haven't been here in a long time."

"I left New York for a little while. Interestingly, I was in Paso Robles working in a family-owned vineyard, Braxton, for six months. But I'm back permanently now. I'll bring you a couple of bottles of their wine next time I stop by. Their GSM is one of the best I've ever had."

"Sounds terrific. I would love to try it. Welcome back. Can I help you find anything in particular today?" Roberto smiled.

"Hmm. Maybe a Pinot. That's one varietal I didn't have much of in Paso. I guess they don't have the soil and climate for it," Farah said. "And oh, let's keep it under thirty dollars," she added, remembering that she needed to be a little more careful with her spending habits.

"I just got a new Willamette Valley Pinot I love, and it's twenty-eight dollars a bottle. Let me grab you one," Roberto said.

Farah stepped out of the store with her Pinot in hand and started walking when she noticed there was a bookstore right next to the wine shop. They were advertising an author event for Ann Napolitano's new novel, *Hello Beautiful*. Had the bookstore been there all along and she'd never noticed it? She walked in and was greeted by the store owner, Anita.

"Is *the* Ann Napolitano really doing a reading here?" Farah asked, surprised that an author of her caliber would visit a small local bookshop in Brooklyn when every bookstore would love to host her.

"Yes," Anita smiled. "I have some personal connections to her, so that's how that happened. You should come." Farah bought a copy of the book and put the date of the author reading in her phone calendar.

◆

Farah was surrounded by boxes, packing up her office. She couldn't believe how fast the last month had gone by. Most things she threw away, but there were so many letters and birth announcements and holiday cards from patients over the years that she just couldn't part with. She packed them all in two big boxes and thought maybe she would ship them to her mom to store for her. There was no room for anything extra in her West Village apartment.

She looked at all the patient satisfaction survey awards that she'd received over the years. These she didn't need. She was glad to be moving to a position in which your job isn't sending surveys to patients asking them to rate you after their visit, as if they'd just bought something from Macy's. She didn't need these surveys and awards to know when she was impacting people. She wouldn't need them where she was going. She knew that when she truly focused on listening to what a patient was saying, they felt seen and heard. Farah took down her framed degrees from her office wall. There would be no new personal office to display them in at the Women's Health Free Clinic, but maybe she would send these to her mother as well. Soraya could very well end up hanging her daughter's degrees up in her living room.

Lastly, she packed the old family pictures and the pictures of the kids when they were younger that sat on her office shelves. These were the hardest to take down, since many were of Rumi pretransition. He had made her take down all the old photos from their home a few years ago, and Farah had allowed herself to leave some in her office, knowing he would probably never see them. Now all the old evidence of her baby was packed away, and anytime she wanted a reminder, she would have to take them out of the boxes in her closet. Farah said goodbye to her office and left.

◆

On a perfect New York Sunday, Farah sat across from Julia at Buvette, her first time back there since her return. She'd missed it, and as she took the first bite of her *pain perdue*, she was reminded that it was absolutely worth going to a place so packed that your legs were basically touching the legs of the person at the table next to you. "You'll be very proud of me," Farah said to Julia.

"I'm intrigued." Julia raised her eyebrow and her mimosa glass simultaneously.

"I didn't run by myself this morning. I finally joined one of those

Central Park running groups, and it was fun."

"Run with anyone cute?" Julia always got to the point.

"There were some cute people, but I'm not sure that any were single and age-appropriate for me. But there is always next week," Farah said.

"There is, but I'd like to remind you that you are single and any adult is age-appropriate," Julia winked.

"Okay." Farah rolled her eyes. "Anyway, there is more. I arranged with the wine and bookstore that are right next door to each other in my neighborhood to host a monthly wine tasting at the bookstore's book club events."

"Shut up! Who are you? I am so proud of you I could cry." Julia's mouth was wide open.

"Well, let's see how it goes. I'm a little nervous. Can you come to my first event?" Farah asked, knowing the answer.

"Yes, I just may need the CliffsNotes version of the book, though. Do they still make those?"

"Not sure, but I think there are similar summaries online and in podcasts now. You don't need to read the book. Just be there for me like you always are."

"Nothing could keep me away. Plus, you had me at wine tasting. Of course I will be there. I can't wait," Julia said. "How are you feeling about the new job?"

"I'm excited, but for some reason, a little nervous. It's just different from what I've done before," Farah said.

"You're going to be okay. Look at everything you've done in the last year. Your life has completely changed. You're a new person. You can do this," Julia reached over and squeezed her arm.

CHAPTER SIXTY-EIGHT

JUNE 1996: CINCINNATI, OHIO

Lying on the twin bed she'd had since her teen years, Farah looked up at the canopy overhead and felt caged in. Why was she feeling this way? The rehearsal dinner had gone as perfectly as possible, although there had been no actual rehearsal since there was no church ceremony the next day. But still, it had been nice for Mark's parents to be able to host this dinner before their wedding day, and Janet had made sure that every last detail was perfect. Now as she lay in bed, she couldn't believe that this was her last night of being single—of not being a wife. She loved Mark with every cell in her body, but why was she having an aversion to the word *wife* right now? It had to be wedding jitters—she had finally gotten them.

Soraya knocked on her door and simultaneously opened it without waiting for Farah to say she could come in. She sat on the edge of Farah's bed and Farah scooted to the other edge to make room for her. "I wanted to talk to you about something," Soraya started. "I know that you just graduated medical school and you're a doctor, but still, tomorrow is your wedding night, so I wanted to see if you had any questions."

"Astaghfirullah, Maman!" Farah laughed with disbelief. She would have to tell her sisters about this. "I don't have any questions." Did her mom really think there was any possibility that she was still a virgin? The one and only time she had ever tried to talk to Farah about sex, Farah had been in tenth grade. Soraya had asked her if she knew what sex was and if she needed her to explain it to her. Farah had laughed then, too, telling her she already knew. Soraya had said that although they were living in America, they were still Iranians, and that Iranians don't have sex before marriage. Farah had told her not to worry, that she didn't plan to, which she hadn't at the time. But then she had gone away for college—reinvented herself, started dating, had sex, and an eventual abortion.

"Okay, fine. I'm just making sure," Soraya said. "Your Maman Bozorg never talked to me about these things. I was only twenty years old. I hadn't even kissed anyone yet."

"Were you scared on your wedding night?" Farah asked.

"Not really. I knew your father would be a good, gentle man," Soraya said, and then they were both quiet. "Anything else you want to talk about? Are you excited for tomorrow?" Soraya waited and when Farah didn't say anything, she asked, "Farah, what's going on in your head right now?"

"I don't know. I'm excited and I love Mark, but starting tomorrow, I'm going to be someone's wife. I just suddenly feel like I haven't had enough time to be myself or figure out who I am, and now I'll be a wife."

"And what is wrong with being a wife?"

"Nothing. Except you're not your own person anymore," Farah said. "Haven't you ever wanted more?"

"Sure I have. If I could go back, I would have become a doctor. I thought being a teacher was the best option for having kids, being home in the summers with them. But now you are a doctor, and no one can take that away from you. And you are your own person even when you're a wife. It's once you become a mother that you're not your own person anymore. Don't make the mistake I did and get pregnant right away. I don't think I ever told you that I almost got an abortion when I found out I was pregnant with you. I was still in college. It was so hard to finish school and get my degree with a baby. I regret that I didn't push myself to go to graduate school, too, but

I'm so glad I didn't have that abortion, because then I wouldn't have had you. And you are getting to do everything I didn't do." Soraya leaned over and kissed Farah's forehead.

Farah knew that Soraya only had good intentions in what she was saying. She would never think that her daughter may have gotten pregnant in college, too, when she hadn't been married, and then had an abortion—that her daughter's first pregnancy hadn't resulted in the birth of a child she could watch blossom as an adult. "Maman, I think you have also gotten to do things that I didn't get to do," Farah said.

"What do you mean? What have I done that you didn't get to do?"

"Never mind. I think I'm just having prewedding crazy brain right now. I love Mark. I'm excited for tomorrow." And she believed what she said. Mark was the only person who knew about her abortion. She had shared things with Mark that she hadn't shared with anyone else. He was her best friend. She wanted to be his wife.

"Okay. I know you love Mark. I can see it. And I can see how much he loves you. I'm sure you're just having this prewedding crazy brain thing you're talking about. But if in the morning you wake up and you are not one hundred percent excited for the day, you tell me. I won't be upset. We'll cancel everything. Baba won't be upset. We brought you girls here so you would have choices. You understand?" Soraya cupped Farah's face in her hands.

Farah turned her head and kissed her mother's hand. "I understand. Thank you."

CHAPTER SIXTY-NINE

SEPTEMBER 2023: MANHATTAN, NEW YORK

Farah opened her front door and saw Julia dressed from head to toe in kelly green and holding a poster board with Mahsa Amini's picture. Her eyes filled with tears for what seemed like the one-hundredth time in the last few days. It was the one-year anniversary of Mahsa Amini's death, and the organization Woman Life Freedom NYC was leading a march across the Brooklyn Bridge and opening an art exhibition reflecting on Iran's past and future. Julia had been the one to call Farah a week prior, saying, "Farah Joon, I'm going on this march with you, no matter what you say." As Farah had started to share stories with Julia about her past, Julia had been taking the initiative to learn more about Iran's history, sharing links to places all over Iran that she said she hoped to be able to visit with Farah one day.

Three days prior, on the one-year anniversary of Mahsa's arrest, Farah had done a group FaceTime call with Darya and Rumi. She had finally told them about Zareen—that she had been there—that she had blamed herself for so many years. Every time she told the story and heard the words coming out of her mouth, it became more apparent to her how crazy it was that she had held on to this secret for so long, feeling responsible when she was just a child herself. "I think—no, I know—that Zareen's arrest and execution have impacted me in more ways than I ever realized. It impacted my dating choices, my career decisions, my friendships, my marriage. Obviously, it hasn't just been

Zareen but a multitude of factors that have affected who I am and where I am today, but what happened to her has had a larger role in my life than I should have allowed. I don't want the two of you to ever feel like you have to hold something big in. There is always someone you can talk to," Farah told her children, as all three of them cried over FaceTime together. The only person left that she knew she had to tell was her Khaleh Nasreen, and whether she would do it in a letter, over the phone, or possibly see her one day in Tehran in person and do it, she didn't know. She had avoided traveling to Iran for so long, and with the current political situation, she didn't know when she would be able to go. But in a way, she also knew that it didn't matter whether she told Nasreen or not. Farah was the one who had given this secret so much weight. No one else had. All she really had to do was to reach out to Nasreen and tell her how much she loved and missed her.

As Farah and Julia marched across the Brooklyn Bridge, Farah heard the words *Zan, Zendeghi, Azadi* coming out of her friend's mouth repeatedly. Farah squeezed Julia's hand tightly, so grateful to have her by her side. "You know, I think this is the most time I've spent with you without you cracking a joke," Farah said.

Julia stopped and looked at Farah. "Which Julia do you like better?"

"I like every version of Julia there is."

◆

Farah hurriedly wrapped up her charting at work so she could get back to the West Village in time for a quick shower before her first wine and book event. That day, she had been sent to a clinic in Queens, so she had a longer subway ride home than usual. During her eight hours there, she'd seen fifteen patients total, performed two abortions, and felt a breast mass she was sure was a later-stage cancer in an uninsured twenty-seven-year-old who had kept putting off getting checked, thinking that she was too young to not have something benign. Farah shook her head, trying to force work out of her mind so she could look forward to her first event that night. She was simultaneously feeling nervous and excited. The book club pick was *The Covenant of Water* by Abraham Verghese, and Farah had chosen four bottles of Syrah from different regions in California—Napa, Paso Robles, Los Olivos, and Santa Barbara—for the tasting. She was excited to guide people through tasting the same varietal of grape from the same vintage but from these different California regions and show them how different the wines were—what a difference terroir makes.

While Farah was getting ready, her cell phone kept pinging with new messages. Darya, Rumi, her sisters—all wishing her good luck and telling her to have fun. Even Soraya called and left her a voicemail to say she hoped the event went well. This wasn't the type of thing Soraya would usually remember or comment on, but Farah had noticed small and steady changes in her mother since their conversation after Azita's hospitalization. Julia had offered to meet Farah at her place and walk over together, but Farah said that she would just see her there. She wanted to do this alone.

Farah arrived at the wine shop half an hour early, and Roberto helped her set up. They opened each bottle to allow the wine to breathe. She took a swish-and-spit taste of each wine, making sure none were corked. She set up little note cards about each one and some pens so people could take notes. She brought out a charcuterie and cheese platter donated by the local specialty boulangerie close by in exchange for setting out some of their cards. Julia arrived first with a vase of sunflowers that she set on Farah's table. Farah introduced Julia to Roberto and Julia looked at Farah quizzically. Farah rolled her eyes and mouthed, "Married . . . to a man."

People started piling in. Most of the attendees were women, but there were a fair number of men, as well. As Farah started pouring wine and talking to each of the attendees, she felt her shoulders relax. She was in her element. Farah was surprised by the turnout, but Darya had helped her create Instagram posts for both the bookstore and wine shop to share, and her efforts seemed to have paid off.

People were buying wine, asking her questions, some of which she had to defer to Roberto, and making suggestions on other varietal theme nights they would want to attend. An attendee named Paul, who looked to be around her age, went up for a repeat tasting of a wine a couple of times, asking Farah questions each time. Julia watched him like a hawk, shooting knowing glances and smirks at Farah. At the end of the event, he bought several bottles of wine from Roberto. Then he walked over to Farah and handed her his card.

"Thank you for a really enjoyable evening. It was interesting to see how the terroir made these Syrahs each so unique. I'd love to do a wine tasting together sometime when you don't have to play host and can be more of an active participant," Paul said.

Farah took his card. "Well, I just moved back to New York and am busy settling in, but I will consider it. I'm glad you enjoyed the night." She smiled and then turned to the next person to thank them for coming.

The night was an overall success, with both Roberto and Anita, the bookshop owner, happy with the turnout and the sales. "Events like this can really help create a sense of community here. I'm so glad you're doing this, Farah. Thank you," Anita said.

"That was fantastic. I'm so proud of you. I saw that guy give you his card and I want to hear no lame excuses about why you're not going to call him. I'll help you clean up and then we'll go get a celebratory drink and bite," Julia said, squeezing Farah in a hug.

"Okay. I'm not going to argue with you. And thank you," Farah replied.

Sitting across from Julia at Sevilla, Farah felt truly happy. She was proud of herself for all that she'd been through over the last few years, and for finally making the leap of leaving her old job and figuring out how she could continue practicing medicine in a way that was both more fulfilling and allowed her to pursue her personal interests more. She didn't know what would come of this per diem position at the free clinics, but she wasn't afraid. She knew that no matter what happened, she had learned to listen to herself and that she could always figure things out.

Julia excused herself to use the restroom and got up. Farah felt her phone vibrate in her purse. She looked at her phone and saw a text from Mark:

I hope your first event went well. I asked the kids the date but then decided not to come and distract you on your first night. Maybe next time. I've always believed in you and been proud of you.

Farah was smiling looking at the text as Julia walked back to the table. "What's got you smiling?" Julia questioned, raising an eyebrow.

"Oh, nothing. Just a silly meme," Farah responded, putting her phone back in her purse.

ACKNOWLEDGMENTS

If you've made it here, you've given me the gift of reading my words. Thank you.

My heartfelt thanks to the entire team at Köehler Books for helping me share this story. My editor, Becky Hilliker, clearly saw and supported my vision from our first meeting. Lauren Sheldon created the cover of my dreams.

Jill Marsal read part of an earlier version of this novel. Her valuable feedback inspired Zareen's entire storyline, which helps shine light on the Women, Life, Freedom Movement—thank you.

I am grateful for my talented writer friends, Juliet Burton and Wendy Burg, who read a couple of versions of my first few chapters and pointed me in the right direction—your steady support and cheerleading have been invaluable.

I've had the privilege of taking some creative writing classes at UCLA Extension. Both the instructors and fellow student writers I've met have helped me become a memoirist first and then foray into fiction.

Amy Alderfer, thank you for encouraging me to take that first UCLA class. I wish you were still here to read this book. I know how proud you would be, unobjectively singing its praises to everyone.

The sisters in this novel are not my sisters Parastou and Parimah, but the relationship between the sisters was inspired by my own. I could not imagine a life without the two of you.

The parents in this novel are not my parents, Parvin and Hassan Hassouri, but like many immigrant parents, mine sacrificed everything to provide their children a bright, secure, and independent future.

My husband Babak, in our thirty years together, has always been unwavering in his support, encouraging me to follow my heart and pivot, knowing he'll always be home.

To my beautiful, now adult children, Armon, Ava, and Shayda—you are among the most incredible humans I know. Nothing fulfills me more than watching you listening to yourselves and pursuing your passions. My heart sings because of the three of you.

www.ingramcontent.com/pod-product-compliance
Lightning Source LLC
LaVergne TN
LVHW041747060526
838201LV00046B/940